Kirin Rise

The Shadows Within

Ed Cruz

Illustrated by Ron Langtiw

PREFACE

How does one recover from a near-death experience? For many, the fighting spirit crumbles as the weight of reality smothers the desire to reach a goal, testing one's resolve. Young Kirin Rise's journey has been a roller coaster of emotions. Within a year, she has lived more than most people have in a lifetime. She has gone from the elation of victory in the UFMF Dome Championship to narrowly escaping death at the hands of Justice—and yet, Kirin is poised to face her greatest challenge.

Her teacher, Sifu, is still locked away in prison. Her love life is once again riddled with confusion, and her last match left many unanswered questions. The nation wonders if she will endure and still be their voice. It is not within Kirin to simply accept that she has done her best and to leave matters unresolved, but doubt and fear loom heavily within her conscience, reminding her that failure is always near. Even with the future unknown, it is she who must rise and find new focus.

However, life is always a battle between two sides who believe that their actions are for the better. One cannot exist without the other. As Kirin positions herself as the nation's voice, the head of the UFMF Youshiro Watanabe decides he has waited long enough. His determination has grown into an obsession, and his goal is far greater than world order. In fact, he has revealed his true place as one piece of a larger entity—a shadow government consisting of a handful of ultra-wealthy individuals playing games with lives of people.

A single thought sparked adventure for young Kirin Rise, yet we still question how powerful one thought—one person—can truly be. A single thought blossoms into a decision that forges the very path we walk along. Fear lays the blame on outside forces beyond our control, but the search within reveals the inner truth: that we truly are the creators of our own destinies. For Kirin, the culmination of her efforts is about to come full circle as her day of reckoning is at hand.

Are her skills and will enough to bring the balance she desires?

For information regarding permissions, write to Kirin Rise Studios, LLC.
email info@kirinrise.com
http://kirinrise.com
https://www.facebook.com/kirinrisethecastofshadows
https://twitter.com/kirinrise#
https://www.instagram.com/kirinrise/

ISBN: 1946003034
ISBN 13: 978-1946003034
Kirin Rise Studios, LLC, Chicago, IL

This book is dedicated to my wife: When you're young and all along, you wonder if you'll ever find love. I think that emptiness is something that everyone has shared. But for me I made love my priority above all other things. Filled with doubt, you came into my life and quickly dismissed those fears. It was silly not to realize it sooner, when you were always so close, just a breath away. I love you, if I could say it more I would. You are my everything. I look to you as my light, from the first thing I see in the morning to your soft touch at the end of the day. You inspire me to be better, to push beyond satisfied. The look you give me is mine alone, which I cherish every time. I wish everyone in their lifetime could experience the love we have. Thank you for allowing me the freedom to dream and share it with the rest of the world.

CONTENTS

Character Information

Name: Megumi Kwan, nicknamed Simo
Family: Wife of Sifu; mother of three kids: Hana, Hideo, and Akira
Profession: Homemaker
Interests: Cooking, gardening bonsai
Tidbits: She introduced Sifu to ramen. When she was young, she took Aikido for several years. She is a talented artist and loves drawing anime.

Name: Hana Kwan
Family: Oldest child of Sifu and Simo
Profession: 4th grade student
Interests: Wing Chun Gung Fu
Tidbits: At an early age, Hana took an interest in watching her dad practice Wing Chun. She would watch and listen to every class. For a child, her knowledge about the art is impressive, as is her skill.

Name: Hideo and Akira Kwan
Family: Twins of Sifu and Simo
Profession: Kindergarten students
Interests: Video games and tennis
Tidbits: The twins have many things in common, but Hideo is more outgoing than Akira. Also, Akira is left-handed while Hideo is right-handed. Hideo starts most fights. Both the boys look up to Hana as much as they do Sifu.

	**Name:** Lance Anderson **Family:** Single **Profession:** Retired Special Forces; works with Sifu making ramen **Interests:** Painting **Tidbits:** His right leg is fake below his knee; he lost it during a mission. He paints to relax, and he reads tons of books. Kirin and Gwen normally invite Lance to watch Korean dramas with them.
	**Name:** April Welch **Profession:** Owns a chicken and waffle shop in Japan **Interests:** Traveling and listening to Prince music **Tidbits:** She does things on the fly and never has a plan. She became a lifelong friend of Sifu upon his visit to Japan. She has unusually good luck in most cases. She was raised in the South Side of Chicago.
	**Name:** Sigung **Family:** Widower with two boys **Profession:** Retired Gung Fu Master**Interests:** Wing Chun Gung Fu **Tidbits:** He has been working on a Wing Chun book his entire life. He closed his school after the passing of his wife. He is the teacher of Sifu.

CHAPTER 1
Four Walls

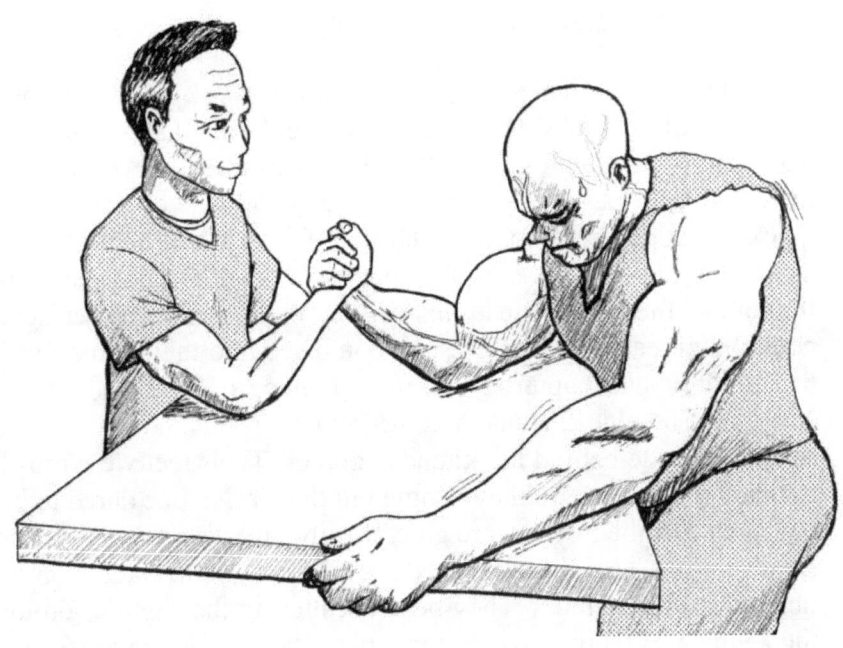

Mid-December 2033

The group was finally gathered in their official meeting room. They all felt the tension. One by one the seats were filled in an orderly manner, and folded hands rested upon the cold granite counter-top as they waited to see what would happen next. Even though time was of the essence, the individuals resisted the temptation to look at the clock. All eyes were focused on only one thing: Sifu.

He had summoned those at hand for a task so important that everyone knew what was at stake. Sifu's look said it all; his demeanor was serious as thoughts raced through his head. However, turning to the counter, he saw three faces that clung to his every move, which quickly changed his emotional state. He felt a rush of humility as well as a sense of pride. Even with the troubles and burdens that existed throughout the world, life at this very moment seemed as perfect as it could be. In each of their eyes, he could see into their souls. Each of his children had captured a different piece of him and his wife, Megumi. The eldest, Hana, and the younger twins, Hideo and Akira, sat side by side behind the kitchen counter. Their feet were too short to touch the ground, so they dangled in the air. No one dared to break the silence as their eyes were glued firmly on Sifu. He finally made a small gesture as they reached below for their bags, snuggled underneath their chairs. They began scattering the supplies on top of the counter. Wrapping paper, tape, pens, bows, and crayons—all the things that Sifu had requested were now in plain sight. He waited until they were done before he spun away and began pacing back and forth parallel to their table, all the while remaining silent.

When the shuffling noise dissipated and he felt all eyes upon him again, he stopped dead in his tracks and finally broke the silence. Sifu's face was serious, but it was the tone of his voice that captured everyone's attention. It was deeper than usual with purpose behind it. Sifu said, "We've got approximately one hour before Mommy gets home." He held his index finger up to emphasize his point. "So we need to move fast, keep the place neat, and not quibble amongst each other."

Hideo's face tightened as one of Sifu's words left him unsure. He was always quick to want answers, more aggressive than his twin brother. "Dad, what's 'quibble' mean?"

Hana, who was never shy when it came to dealing with her twin brothers, beat Sifu to the punch. "It means no arguing. At all," she emphasized the last words with her eyes, making sure her comments were directed to both of them. Hideo's eyes locked onto Sifu, whose mouth was still open. He nodded to confirm that she was, in fact, correct.

Akira looked at her strangely as he leaned forward and made an impassioned but whiny response. "But, we never argue!"

Hideo did not like his response and slapped his brother's arm. "That's not true!"

"Yes, it is."

"No, it's not."

"Yes, it is! You...." Akira's voice raised, elevating the tension.

Seconds later, shoves followed the words as both Sifu and Hana watched the twins ... quibble. Sifu cleared his throat, doing his best to control his temper. "That's enough, and that's exactly what Hana meant. Congratulations on perfectly demonstrating what it means to quibble."

Hideo snuck in a last push, earning him a serious stare from Sifu. He feared any kind of eye contact, as he realized that he had gone too far. He knew that look was more damning than any words that could come out of his father's mouth.

Sifu took a deep breath and slowly exhaled. Wing Chun was of no use to him here, as their actions defied any form of logic or common sense. "Alright, in front of you is all the wrapping material you need for Mom's Christmas present. I'll help you when needed in wrapping the gifts, but I want you to at least attempt to wrap them yourself. After you're done, to your right is a piece of paper and several colored pens and crayons. What you need to do is make a list of what you want for Christmas." He paused before adding, "Now, just because you wrote it down doesn't mean Santa Claus is going to get it for you. So, are we all clear on this?"

Hana nodded her head immediately, and the twins followed suit.

Roughly ten minutes passed as Hana finished wrapping her mother's gift and immediately shifted her focus. Always the responsible one, she began writing on the paper, determined to meet her father's deadline. The twins, on the other hand, were covered in tape and wrapping paper. They tried their best not to argue, but they fell quite short of the goal. It was difficult for Sifu not to jump in between the two, but he figured that, as long as they were not fighting and no one lost an eye, he would chalk that up as a positive.

Sifu's phone rang, drawing his attention away. He grabbed it and realized it was Megumi. He moved into the next room in order not to distract the children. He spoke briefly, sounding coy and inquiring when she would return. As he hurried back from the kitchen, he found that the twins were exactly as he had left them, in a state of civilized chaos. Hana, however, was simply watching them, not saying a word. She wore a look of regret, as if wondering why she had to be the oldest one, cursed with the task of always being responsible.

Sifu came behind her and placed both his hands gently on her shoulders. She looked up as he leaned over and whispered into her ear, "Sweetie, you can begin writing your wish list for Santa."

"I'm already done, Daddy." Her voice warmed Sifu's heart every time she spoke.

Sifu looked somewhat surprised. He gazed over her shoulder and saw, lying on the table, a colorful card along with a perfectly wrapped present. Hana was the spitting image of Megumi, not only in her looks but also in her personality and skill. He played along and asked, "You've finished already?"

She nodded and said, "Is it okay if I go watch some TV? Uh … I think the twins will be awhile before they finish. So, you're stuck with the responsibility."

Sifu sighed. He did not even bother looking at them as he said, "Sure, sweetie. Go ahead."

Hana leaped off her seat and raced to the family room, leaving her card lying on top of the dining table. It was well decorated, as colors blended smoothly together along with lines neatly etched onto the paper. Sifu shook his head, realizing that her artwork was far from the typical ten-year-old's. Curiosity got the better of him, and he wanted a peek at what Hana had written. Sifu turned to see if the twins would snitch on him, but they were still too occupied quibbling with one another.

Then he opened the card. His eyes began to water, and his hand twitched as he read it.

Dear Santa, All I want for Xmas is for my family to always be together.

The toughest guy on the planet crumbled in seconds, brought down by his daughter's words. Even his structure was no match as his heart melted. Hana had a kindness similar to that of Megumi, but she was strong and independent, much like himself. He admired it briefly before his moment of pride was quickly wiped out as the twins began shouting at one another. Their cause for distraction was an argument

5

over a crayon. Neither boy could apply patience or logic. He put Hana's card down as each twin was trying to get his attention.

Hideo sounded off as he clung onto half of the crayon. "Dad!"

Akira raised his voice, trying to outdo his twin brother. "Daddy!" He began to shake in his chair, clinging onto the other side of the crayon.

"Dad … Dad … Daddy … Dad!" Their words clashed as Sifu stood there, trying to figure out a way to resolve the situation.

Suddenly, the sound of his name began to be distorted. "Dad. Daddy. Dad … Si … Sifu … Sifuuu…."

"Sifu? Uh, Sifu," a voice whispered. It bore a slight Spanish accent, and the speaker seemed to be hoping for response.

Sifu remained motionless, aware of the request but hoping his nonresponse would be enough to suffice. He sighed as he awoke from his dream, knowing sadly that was the closest he could be to seeing his family again.

"Sifu, are you sleeping? Sifu…?" The voice continued pressing and nearing Sifu.

Sifu took in a deep breath and cleared his throat, though he kept his eyes closed as he finally answered, "Usually when a man has both eyes closed, that means exactly that."

His cellmate leaned over him just to confirm. He was dressed in a drab orange outfit, which no one could make look better. His crinkly hair flowed in all directions, always interfering with his glasses. His tall stature combined with his outfit formed a silhouette of a carrot. Raf, short for Rafael, knew he was disturbing Sifu, but his questions took precedence over his manners. "Oh, sorry to bother you, Sifu … but I was wondering if you could check out my punch motion."

Sifu kept his eyes shut in protest. "Raf, considering that you and I are both in prison with our busy schedules," he emphasized it in a sarcastic tone, "don't you think you might ask me that at some time other than bright and early in the morning?"

"Yeah, I know, but I've been practicing for the last thirty minutes, you see, and this question has really been bothering me." Raf continued to invade Sifu's space, hovering above him and waiting to see if he had opened his eyes yet.

Sifu replied, "You know what bothers me, Raf?"

Raf leaned back slightly from Sifu as he answered tentatively, "Uh, me asking you a question early in the morning?"

"Normally, I'd say questions never bother me." Sifu lifted his arms up and spread them far apart, stretching to get more blood flow. His body ached just a pinch as his mattress was no retreat for comfort. "But, being in prison seems to have tested my patience."

Raf snickered at Sifu's comment. "I know you're gonna hate me saying this, but I kinda like that you're in prison with me, Sifu. You know, you're my *carnal*."

Sifu understood what Raf was getting at and said, "I'd prefer to enjoy your company in a less-confined environment, preferably a coffee shop. But, then again, any place is better than here." Sifu looked at Raf oddly and asked, "Remind me again what *carnal* means? You sure it's not 'boyfriend' in Spanish?" Raf chuckled and continued practicing his punches.

With that, Sifu shifted his gaze to the dull white ceiling above. It was in need of a paint job, much like the entire room. This nine-by-twelve-foot cell had been his home for the last several months, and it did not matter where he looked because every inch was exactly the same. He tilted his head to the side as he watched Raf practicing his punch. His trained eye quickly caught the problem, but he remained silent till he was ready to speak. Sifu scuttled to the side of his bed as he placed both feet on the cold cement floor. He quickly snapped them back, missing the comforts of his own room.

Another glance at Raf revealed he was still making the same mistake. Sifu finally pointed out a correction, hoping that words would be enough to remedy his situation. "Both fists need to occupy the centerline. You're not covering your center when you pull back your punch—it's a pinch off to the side. That's why you're feeling the imbalance."

Raf considered what Sifu said and punched several more times. At first, the words were simply that, but he took a moment to digest the information. Finally, a moment of awareness kicked in. "*Menso* ... Dang, you're right. That's what I was screwing up. I could feel something was off, but I just couldn't put my finger on it." He muttered something in Spanish, smacking the top of his head.

Sifu nodded and began to stretch. He thought, *Would it kill them to give me a better bed?* He decided to try again as he dropped his foot over the edge of the bed, but as his flesh touched the cold morning floor, he shivered in disgust. He hung his head as he tried to talk himself into a better mood.

Raf continued to punch as Sifu occasionally checked on him. Noticing something different about Sifu this morning, he broke the silence. "Sifu, usually you're impossible to read, but I sense something today. Maybe my Wing Chun is getting better ... or I could totally be wrong. But, I gotta ask, is something bothering you? You're not your cheerful self ... I think? No ... maybe?" Raf, now filled with doubt, waited. He hoped this was one of those rare occasions when he was right.

Sifu did not answer right away. Always one to be truthful, but in this case not direct, he answered, "I have some work to do, Raf."

Raf replied, "Wait, did you get stuck doing cafeteria duty this week? 'Cause I thought you were set for that next week."

"No ... no, it's far more important than that.... In fact, I need some help from my *carnal*."

"Yo man ... I mean, Sifu, sorry. Anything, you name it. I'm your man."

Sifu looked at Raf oddly and cracked a smile. "Not literally, of course? Not even for the stay?"

Raf chuckled and said, "You crack me up, Sifu. I don't swing that way and not even for the stay." They shared a moment of laughter.

Sifu said, "Sadly, this could be the highlight of our day."

Sifu walked to the main door and peered through the little glass to see if anyone was around. Satisfied that it was just the two of them, he spun around to face Raf. The look on Sifu's face changed, and Raf realized this was something that required all his attention. He finally stopped practicing his punches and approached Sifu.

"What is it, Sifu?" A concerned look combined with a hint of curiosity engulfed him.

"Well, it took a while before I finally got transferred to this section of the prison." Sifu shook his head and muttered, "Thanks, Gwen." He recalled her assurance that it would not be a problem.

"What'd you say?"

"Oh, nothing. Anyway, I kinda need the 411 on how this area works. I've observed quite a bit the last several weeks, but you've been here way longer."

Raf smiled. "No problem, we've got our regular schedule of chores and duties...."

Sifu raised his hand, stopping Raf mid-speech. "Sorry, Raf, I didn't make myself clear enough. I need to go a bit deeper than what's on the surface. I need to know who's in charge." Sifu's eyes locked onto Raf, carrying more weight than any word spoken. Raf leaned back as he felt his energy overcome him.

This time, it was Raf that approached the front of their cell door and peered through the glass window. He paused for a second and checked twice. With his back still turned to Sifu, he said, "Uh, would you mind me asking why?"

Sifu put his hand on Raf's shoulder, which startled him. "Raf, the less you know, the safer it is for you."

Raf nodded in agreement and then began pacing back and forth inside the cell. "That's cool.... That's cool, Sifu." He began muttering to himself in Spanish, almost as if he were carrying on a conversation without Sifu.

Sifu could see that Raf was agitated. He said in a passive voice, "Rafael ... just breathe."

Raf looked at Sifu as he motioned to him to control his breathing. He raised his shaking hand and clenched his fist to control it.

"Focus on one thing: the breath going in and out, that's all ... and don't worry about anything with the outside world."

Raf did as Sifu had instructed and took a moment to control his breathing. "Okay ... I feel much better now. Still worried as shit, but better. So, here's how it is...." Raf lowered his voice and moved to sit on Sifu's bed, waving the older man closer to listen. Sifu sat next to Raf and leaned in.

Raf whispered into Sifu's ear, "So you see, you came from the east side of the prison. The way things are run here is totally different. The rest of this prison, you could say, is run by...." He hesitated and checked his surroundings again as a bead of sweat formed on top of his brow, gathering weight. "My people call him ... *El Profeta.*"

"Prophet?" Sifu took a guess at the meaning.

Raf waved his hands down in a sporadic manner and quickly shushed Sifu. "Dang, Sifu. Not too loud, man ... these walls have ears, you know?"

"Obviously, I don't. That's why I'm asking you."

Raf said, "This is no laughing matter, Sifu."

"Sorry, Raf, Go on."

"And it's not *a* prophet, it's The Prophet."

"So, he needs the 'the' before 'Prophet.'"

"Well, that's his name, Sifu. A name is a name. Who am I to question why they call him that?"

"Okay, okay. Whatever. Go on with ... The Prophet." Sifu used his hand to emphasize the quote.

"Well, The Prophet runs three-fourths of this prison. He's been in a long dragged-out war with the east side for some time. His word is like God in these parts. So, if you want anything done, you have to go through him. You dig?"

"I dig."

"Sifu, he's not one to mess with. Most of the guards working here will look the other way, know what I'm saying?" He paused and leaned closer to Sifu. "He's a lifer, with nothing to lose, so they say.... I always thought he was *el diablo*, the devil, but from what I heard, he made a deal with someone beyond that. Who that is, even I don't know, or do I care to. But, for now, all I know is The Prophet won't rest till he has total control of this place."

Sifu looked Raf straight in the eye. "So, how do I go about arranging a meeting with The Prophet?"

"Say, what? You want a meeting with The Prophet? *Estas demente*, Sifu!" Raf screamed it out and jumped up. He then realized he had broken his own rule as he covered his mouth and darted back to the glass door to see if anyone was around. Sweat dripped from his head as the look of panic could not be erased from his face. He shivered in fear for a second and tried to regain his composure before he slowly lowered himself next to Sifu again.

Raf began whispering, "Sifu, you can't just request a meeting with The Prophet. He's protected 24/7 by his own bodyguards. And let me tell you: These are big muther f'ing *pendejos* who are quick to react and have little patience. If he nods and wishes it to be, you die. *Entiendo?*"

"There's always an opening, Raf. There must be a point during the day when I can say a quick *hola*."

"Dammit, Sifu. Are you not hearing what I'm saying? This guy is bad news. He won't hesitate to have you killed." Raf stood up. "Now I get it: you're also a bad muther, but seriously he's got the numbers, and I don't think you can just punch your way through this."

"Who said anything about punching?" Sifu chuckled, but Raf could not fathom another alternative. "Besides, violence only leads to more violence. I'm sure I can negotiate something that he'd like." Raf shook his head as his imagination failed him. Sifu said, "Now think, Raf. Humor me for a second, and just think…."

Raf got up, still agitated by the thought. He began to pace back and forth. He said, "Think, Raf. Think. There's gotta be an opening." Suddenly, he stopped in his tracks and smirked. "Okay, okay … listen now. I'm not 100% sure about this, and I could be sending you to your death."

"Well, I'm sure it'll be more exciting than grabbing that bar of soap that fell in the shower room," said Sifu.

"No guarantees, Sifu. None." Raf gestured, his hand cutting through the air. "But, there's a slight chance during lunch."

"Go on."

"While the rest of us chumps are herded together to eat, The Prophet is in an isolated area with his own lunch room. There, he eats by himself while his bodyguards stand watch. For us, that's considered fancy dining. No outsider dare step into that room, otherwise…." Raf used his hand and slowly slashed across his neck.

Sifu smiled, "That is exactly what I'm looking for."

Raf kneeled next to Sifu and said, "Sifu, you can't just walk in there and eat your meal next to him."

"Why not?"

Raf just stared at Sifu befuddled. If nothing else in the art confused him, Sifu's unpredictability always did. Like most people, he had found that his short stint with Sifu had shown the man unreadable.

"Do the unexpected, Raf…. Besides, I just want to talk to him."

Raf shook his head, concerned for his teacher's well-being. "You are one crazy, m'fer, Sifu."

Sifu said, "Tell me more about The Prophet, Raf. I need to know everything that you know."

Raf let out a sigh. Fearfully, he said, "Everything?"

Sifu replied, "*Todo.*"

The Next Day

The alarm sounded, echoing throughout the entire prison. It was not an escape but a reminder that meal time was for the next hour. Many ignored the dull sound, as all those who were there had grown accustomed to their daily routines. Over a hundred orange-clad inmates of every shape, size, and color could be found within these halls. Each one had his own story. Incoherent chatter blanketed the cafeteria and a distinct odor, either from the food or those eating it, wafted. Each inmate protected his meal as if it was his last. There were grouped cliques, which at their lowest level were determined usually by race. Guards were positioned throughout the cafeteria keeping a watchful eye for suspicious activity. Their primary concern was for their own safety. Tension could be felt throughout, as the chance for a brawl could be set off by the slightest of misunderstandings.

Sifu had grabbed his sorry excuse for a lunch and noticed the area that Raf had mentioned in the far corner. Within a few seconds, Raf crossed paths with Sifu and muttered, "Good luck," staring at his shoes as he continued on his way.

Sifu headed into the room into which no inmate had ever dared venture. He had no plan other than to get to The Prophet and strike up a conversation. *Go with the flow* was his motto, which held true not only in his teachings but in his everyday life. He continued his pace and was fully ignored. Just like he'd said: no one would suspect anyone to simply walk through the doors.

From a distance, Sifu observed a bald black man with battle scars etched on his weathered face. He was seated by himself and appeared to be enjoying his meal. Although he was dressed like everyone else, he stood out from the rest. His air of confidence clearly identified him as The Prophet without further need for Raf's description. He was perched at the end of a long cafeteria table perpendicular to where Sifu stood. The arrangement resulted in a strong barrier between him and Sifu, who had already calculated the distance to be a good twenty-five feet away. Four of The Prophet's bodyguards were standing behind him talking amongst themselves.

Sifu casually approached from the opposite end of the table and set his tray down. He made no eye contact and began to eat as if he had done this many times before. His focus was simply on enjoying the meal, which was a more difficult task then he would have imagined. Sifu remained calm, not giving a hint of any negative intent that might instigate The Prophet into a defensive mode. Just as Sifu had said, the unexpected action caught everyone off-guard as The Prophet's guards exchanged confused looks.

The Prophet stopped mid-bite to examine Sifu from afar.

One of his guards finally took the initiative and broke rank. The Prophet raised his hand, and the man stopped dead in his tracks. The Prophet motioned for him to return, and the bodyguard fell back into position. He chuckled and then grabbed a napkin, wiping his face as he crossed his legs and leaned back in his chair. He seemed almost amused at this turn of events that deviated from the monotony of prison life.

The Prophet shouted, "You must be the bravest or the dumbest mother fucker I've ever met! I guess in the next couple of minutes we'll figure out which one you are."

15

Sifu kept his cool and continued to eat. He had a much more difficult time convincing himself he was enjoying the meal. He thought, *What part of this meatloaf actually has meat?* He had heard The Prophet but wanted to see how he reacted to silence. Sifu closed his eyes and pretended to savor his meal.

The Prophet waited for a response, wondering whether the older man had heard him. He looked at his guards on both sides and shook his head, taken again by surprise with Sifu's behavior.

The Prophet raised his voice. "I said, you must be—"

His focus still on his food, Sifu replied, "I heard what you said, but I was taught it's rude to speak with food in your mouth." He calmly took another bite.

The Prophet scratched his head, as his eyes shifted from side to side. He took a second to ponder what to say next and then blurted, "Sifu … it's Sifu, right?"

This time, Sifu stopped mid-chew and then swallowed. He kept his poker face on, though he was surprised that The Prophet was aware of his nickname.

"You see, I'm not sure if you haven't heard, but everything in these parts of the prison…." He gestured, waving his hand in a circle. "I see all. I know all…. I am all," he said with a sound of arrogance.

Sifu replied, "So, the east side is unfamiliar to you?" Sifu grabbed his utensil, poked at the piece of what passed as a meat, and then downed it. He let his comment and his food digest at the same time.

The dig caught The Prophet's attention, as his guards stared at each other in shock. The Prophet looked at his guards, but no one dared make eye contact with him. He took a deep breath and managed to keep his cool. "You know it was only a matter of time before we met. Last year, your student cost me a ton of credits by beating Diesel in the Dome Championship."

Sifu replied, "Don't feel special; you weren't alone."

The Prophet chucked and said, "Do you have a death wish, or are you hoping you caught me in a good mood?"

Sifu snidely replied, "Let's hope it's the latter."

The Prophet said, "With a snap of my finger, I could have all my men beat the living shit out of you, and not a single guard would come to your aid when they hear you scream."

"Where's the fun in that?"

The Prophet was intrigued by his response as he scratched his head. "What do you mean?"

"I mean, for someone who'll be spending his entire life here, seeing the same thing day in and day out has got to be boring. Don't you think?" Sifu turned away and grabbed more of his food.

The Prophet leaned back in his chair, played with his cross-shaped ring, and mulled over Sifu's statement. "You know what? I think I like you...."

Sifu responded. "I have no opinion about you at this time," as he dangled the little insult as bait.

"Now, there you go. I was beginning to enjoy our little conversation, and you have to doggone insult me like that? Disrespect me in front of my men?"

"I don't see how being neutral is an insult." Sifu realized that he would have to force The Prophet into action. Words would not be enough to get what he wanted.

The Prophet looked back at all his men, signaling them to get ready. "You see, that right there is the problem. You assume that seeing a man beg and plead for his life gets boring, that everyone sounds the same when they get beaten or killed. But, the fact is it never gets old. It never gets boring. In fact, for me, it's like a new show every single time. You know why? Because you're never quite sure how a man will react when they stare directly into death's eyes."

For the first time, Sifu stared the Prophet directly in the eyes. He then turned back to his meal and took another bite. He continued to pretend that soothing his empty stomach was his focus, but he was watching everything with his peripheral vision. The Prophet had enough, as he turned to his guards and gave a hand signal.

The Prophet's guards had similar features: broad shoulders, thick necks, and huge muscles. Their only distinguishing marks: their unique tattoos. Moving on The Prophet's command, all four approached Sifu. The group looked like a bunch of starved rabid dogs, and they cast a dark shadow across Sifu. The Prophet's lead man paused for a moment, turning toward his boss for confirmation.

The Prophet sat back and played with his ring. In a dark, chilling voice, he said, "Remember, Sifu … you wanted this."

A slight flinch of his two fingers was the signal to proceed as he did not hesitate to play God. Not an ounce of regret existed in his soul. The Prophet needed entertainment, and this appeared to be today's main feature.

Three of The Prophet's guards lingered back, forming a half circle several feet from Sifu, while the biggest and baddest of the group took initiative and approached the older man. It appeared to be somewhat overkill for four of them to take on one little man, but it had been a while for all of them, and they were looking to get their hands dirty. The lead guard flexed his tattoo covered, tree trunk right arm, and reached for Sifu's shoulder. Sifu continued to chew his food and appeared to be oblivious to the movement. Just as the guard's hand was about to touch Sifu's shoulder, Sifu leaned slightly to the left, evading his grasp. The guard stumbled, off balance, as his hand closed around air.

Still seated, Sifu grabbed the bodyguard's hand and locked his wrist in place, drawing his center closer to the table. His lean was all Sifu needed as momentum built up. He used his right hand to elevate the guard's body as he flung two-hundred-fifty pounds of solid muscle over the table with ease. He flew several feet and rolled to the ground, dealing the first blow, which appeared to have stunned everyone in the room. Sifu had kept to his promise as the first threat was swiftly handled without a single punch being thrown.

Sifu felt movement from his left rear side as a footstep rustled forward. He flung his tray of food onto the ground, happy to finally get rid of it. The Prophet's guard took a step toward Sifu and planted his foot firmly onto the tray. He lost his balance and flew into the air. His feet were above him, so his impact on the ground would have been solid; however, Sifu dashed off his seat and caught him, softening the landing. The guard lay there, disoriented from the sudden motion. He was not sure what had happened as Sifu looked up to see the two remaining guards springing into action.

Sifu thought, *All that size but no stance. What a waste.*

The Prophet stood up from his seat and slammed the table with his fist. "Will someone get this piece of shit!" He extended his arm toward Sifu.

As the two remaining guards closed the gap, Sifu stayed on one knee, waiting for them to get into range and letting them commit to the first motion. The guard on his right was eager to dish out some punishment as he launched the attack with a left front kick well out of range. Sifu moved right for it, not concerned about the attack as he went for his opponent's center, always. The man sacrificed his structure for an attack as he stood on a single leg, so Sifu caught the kick and directed it toward the other guard, who was just a split-second behind. He ran into his partner's foot and stumbled back, falling to the ground.

The bodyguards stared at each other, stunned, as the one on the ground nursed his face from the kick. Flustered, the last standing guard let out a yell and came swinging at Sifu. The old man stood his ground. He saw the attack coming but was more concerned with the individual's center. He went with the flow as the first hit came close but only touched air. Then the guard chained together several attacks one after another, but Sifu met each attack, dissolving the force and allowing no power to connect. Even with the aggressive nature of the attacks, Sifu did not take a step back, showcasing his skill.

Across the table, the other guard had finally recovered and leaped from behind, lunging at Sifu's back. Sifu heard the footsteps and could feel his intent as the guard in front launched a head-on football charge right at Sifu. Sifu shifted to the side, and the bodyguards collided. The one jumping from the table went flailing backward. He ended up right where he started, which was on the side of the table. "Shit!" he screamed as his second hit resulted in another friendly fire.

The bodyguard who slipped on the tray was finally back up. He was at Sifu's side, who appeared to be distracted with his other opponent. Thinking he had a gap of opportunity; the man went for a heavy hook. Sifu saw this and lured the other guard in. Instead of ducking or trying to block the hook attack from the side, he simply stepped right inside the circular attack's path and was now literally body to body with the side guard. He clocked his companion right in the jaw, and his consciousness disappeared on the spot as he crumpled to the floor.

To the untrained eye, the events appeared almost comedic. Four large guards were mostly hitting one another, stumbling around like a bunch of buffoons. All the while a little old man danced in between them, avoiding any harm or contact. However, this was precision and skill to a high degree that even The Prophet could not deny.

Sifu was still pressed upon the guard who continued his spinning momentum. He grabbed him by the chest and didn't allow him to stop, but instead used it. The size differential was great, but Sifu had complete control of his opponent's center, puppeteering him around. The last remaining guard was now back on his feet and quickly approaching Sifu, who used his new best friend as a shield and whipped him to the last guard, bowling him down. The two hugged each other in the crash, toppling over one another.

Sifu thought, *So much for a peaceful negotiation, but technically I didn't throw a punch.*

The Prophet was watching in disbelief. He realized his protection was down, and he was vulnerable. The only thing separating him from Sifu was twenty-five feet of table. By the time he began to react, Sifu had sprinted on top of the cafeteria table, charging at full speed to close the gap. The Prophet had never seen anyone move at that speed before. He got up and was prepared to run, but the next thing he knew, his face was pressed upon the table and his arm locked behind his back.

Sifu leaned forward and whispered into his ear, "Your men are alive because I chose not to kill them. You are alive for the very same reason. I do not intend to hurt you, so please do not struggle. Do you understand the current situation you are in?"

The Prophet began to grumble, "I'm going to—"

Sifu snapped the lock even tighter, hitting his core as The Prophet's pain was too excruciating for him to finish his word.

"Now I'm going to finish what I was saying to you, and you're going to listen. Nod your head if you understand."

The Prophet did just that and stopped resisting to ease the pain.

"You look like a good businessman; am I correct in assuming that?"

The Prophet nodded again as he looked at his downed guards. He wondered when backup would be arriving.

"Now I want you to tell your men to stand down … uh, once they get back up, of course."

No sooner had Sifu spoken, ten more inmates came rushing into the cafeteria from the main entrance. Sifu angled his lock on The Prophet slightly, which caused him to squirm reminding him who was in charge.

The Prophet shouted, "Listen! Everyone, stand down!" Two of the men were out cold, while the remaining two grumbled and were collecting themselves. "That goes for all of you."

Sifu scanned the area and saw that everyone was listening. "That's good. I'm here to propose a deal—one that would benefit you significantly. Are you interested?"

The Prophet acknowledged him with a jerk of his head, and Sifu slowly released his lock on him, allowing him to sit back up. The Prophet took a moment to massage his arm as he looked around to see where everyone was. He finally had numbers, but after seeing Sifu's skill, he decided to listen to what the older man had to offer.

Sifu grabbed a seat next to The Prophet but placed his back toward everyone. He was well aware of his surroundings and took a more vulnerable position so as not to escalate the situation any further.

With a calm voice, Sifu began to speak. "This is what I'm proposing. I know you want control of the entire prison, but you've got a little problem that you can't seem to resolve out on the east side. I'll help you get full control of it, but in exchange, there's something that I want."

The Prophet stared Sifu straight in the eye. "What could you possibly want in here?"

Sifu leaned forward and said in a soft voice, "You are in charge of making sure that someone—someone very important—is safe. Am I correct in assuming this?"

The Prophet looked around instead of answering Sifu right away. He kept his head still and answered with only his eyes. Sifu slowly nodded, reciprocating the response as they both understood the significance of the situation.

Inching nearer, Sifu murmured, "All I want to do is talk to him. I need some answers."

The Prophet shortened the distance between the two and said, "You know he's not quite right in the head. Only on rare occasions he's there, but most of the time, he's in la-la land."

Sifu nodded. "I need full access to him then, until he's cognitive of his surroundings. Once I get the answers I'm looking for, I'll be done with him…. So, do we have a deal?"

The Prophet said, "If anyone finds out that you've been talking to him, they'll have my head."

Sifu asked, "Who's gonna have your head?" even though he was well aware of the answer.

The Prophet shook his head. "The man with no name, no identity, and quite possibly no soul. However, I've figured out one thing … he's the real guy calling the shots for the UFMF."

Sifu's eyes widened slightly as the thought intrigued him. He turned as more of The Prophet's men came running into the room. They were prepared to take care of business, but The Prophet held his hand up, and they all stopped where they stood. The numbers were daunting; even for Sifu, this would be a challenge. He glanced back and waved at them with a smile as he had gathered an audience.

The Prophet made a gesture to the men to ease down as he took a moment to think. His greed was consuming, as the possibility for total control, no matter how obscure, was tempting. "You get to talk to him once I have full control. Agreed?"

"You'll get what you want." Sifu's response matched The Prophet's desire for control. He knew his offer was not enough, that his ego had been bruised. So, Sifu extended his hand to seal the deal, knowing that a counter offer was coming. He had done his homework and knew The Prophet needed to feel in charge.

Sifu looked at him, knowing well enough the answer to his question. "This deal isn't to your liking?"

The Prophet snickered. "It's not the deal…. It's the circumstances. You see, the way I see it, we aren't on even ground at this time. If I were to agree to this deal, I'd lose face."

"Fair enough … but then again, four on one wasn't that fair."

"My house, my rules." The Prophet smirked. "Besides, what you're promising will require … great skill. I'm not fully convinced that you can pull off your end of the bargain."

Sifu smiled, "Perhaps a demonstration, or better yet, a wager could change your mind."

"What are you proposing?"

Sifu looked around, noting that over thirty men were standing in the room. Everyone was carrying significant beef, even the ones who were still lying on the floor. However, one in particular stood apart from all the rest. His right arm was twice the size of his left arm, which happened to be bigger still than any other arm in the room.

24

"Your man over there." Sifu pointed to him.

The Prophet glanced over, wondering why he picked him. "You mean, Bicep?"

"Uh, yeah, Bicep," replied Sifu.

"Well, look at him from head to toe ... what other name is fitting for him, other than Bicep?" said The Prophet.

Sifu gave him another glance and could find no argument against it.

"What about him?"

"My little proposal to you."

"And that is?"

"Say I challenge your man in arm wrestling. This way, only one's ego gets hurt. Would that be enough proof for you that I can accomplish what I said?"

The Prophet immediately broke out in laughter as everyone followed his lead. It took several minutes for him to regain his composure. "That's gotta be the funniest or dumbest thing I've heard all day." He stopped in mid-chuckle to look at Sifu's arm, which was still extended as he waited for an answer.

"Do we have a deal?"

Upon looking at Sifu's stoic expression, The Prophet realized that Sifu was being serious. He said, "Let me get this straight. If you win...." He barked a laugh and shook his head as though that possibility was beyond the stretch of his imagination. "If you win, the deal's on, but what happens—and I use a *big* but—"

Sifu interrupted by saying, "And I cannot lie."

The Prophet said, "What?"

"Uh, nothing … Sorry. Please continue."

"When you lose … I'd like to know what I get in return."

Sifu conceded, "If I lose, then you'll get to do what you originally planned on doing: beat an Asian man to a pulp."

The Prophet had an evil grin. "Oh, it's not gonna be a beat down. It's gonna cost you your life."

Sifu did not hesitate as his arm was still out, waiting to seal the deal. "Fair enough."

The Prophet was slightly taken aback by Sifu's confidence. He gripped Sifu's hand and firmly clenched it, sealing the deal. He ordered the other men to prepare the area. A table was laid out with two seats across from one another. Sifu walked toward the table as his opponent Bicep began flexing his muscles. The rest of The Prophet's men began shouting and throwing out betting odds. The opportunity to barter for cigarettes and other prison commodities was always exciting. At the very least, they could exploit this situation and benefit from it. Several minutes went by before all bets were made, and the entertainment was about to begin.

Bicep swung his seat around and then approached the table. He raised his right forearm above his head and slammed it hard on the edge, screaming, "SMASH!" His fist left a dent at the edge of the table. The booming sound caused further uproar from the inmate crowd. It further solidified their resolve that this was going to be a one-sided match. He stared Sifu down and pointed at his tattoo that was etched on his right arm, which read, 'No ragrets.'

Sifu did not say a word about the spelling and did a good job of silently laughing inside. He leaned over the table and looked at the dent with curiosity. He nodded his head in a sign of approval. He gently placed his fist on top of the metallic table. With a quick jerk, he snapped his wrist and pounded a groove twice the depth of the one left by Bicep. The room fell into a stunned silence. Still, this demonstration was not enough to sway those in betting against Sifu. They could not resist the possibility of a sure thing.

The Prophet stood to see what Sifu had done. Shocked but unwilling to admit it, he broke the spell of Sifu's action and gathered everyone's attention. "The rules are simple: winner take all. As soon as I let go of their fists, the first one to pin his opponent's hand down is the winner."

Bicep laid his humongous arm on the table and opened his hand, ready to clench. It looked like a croc out of water ready to snap. Sifu reached forward but hesitated as he stared closely at Bicep's hand.

"You afraid, little man?" Bicep tried his best to intimidate Sifu.

Sifu nodded and said, "I am. I'm afraid no one will have any hand sanitizer after this match."

The insult rubbed Bicep the wrong way as he raised his fist and smashed it again onto the table. He leaned forward and growled at Sifu with drool hanging from the side of his mouth.

"Mental note, win or lose, I'm giving this man mouth wash as well."

Another dig from Sifu led to the crowd bursting out in laughter at the expense of Bicep. He was about to act, but from a distance he heard his named called from the only person he'd listen to. He looked to the side and acknowledged he had heard the word of The Prophet. He trembled in anger, allowing it to fester insider ready to explode.

Sifu was dwarfed in size, especially when comparing his arm to that of Bicep. He finally reached out and grabbed Bicep's hand as the group of inmates erupted in cheer. Deep down, he knew he was right to have hesitated: it felt like it had been a while since soap and water had been used on Bicep's grimy hand. He cringed upon the touch. If there was one thing Sifu never let anyone know, it was his pet peeve of sticky fingers.

The Prophet looked at both of them. "Are you ready?" Bicep nodded and grunted like a bull. He fidgeted for a better position till he was satisfied. Bicep leaned deep toward Sifu and said, "I'm gonna rip your arm off, little man."

Sifu, unfazed, yawned and stared blankly at Bicep. Most people would bite on that comment and become emotional; to Sifu, they were just words which he gave no meaning to at all.

The Prophet looked at Sifu. "Are you ready?"

Sifu bowed slightly, nodding his head once.

The Prophet held both of their hands in the center, gave each contestant one last look, and finally released, screaming, "Gooo!"

The crowd erupted, and the sound of their entertainment echoed into the other room. All eyes were centered on the two as everyone thought this would be a fast and easy win for Bicep. The enormous man clenched Sifu's hand tightly and flexed his muscles to the max as veins popped and sweat dripped down his arm. The bets were based off how quickly he would pin Sifu's arm. Not a single soul thought Sifu would come close to challenging Bicep. The only one who knew better was Sifu.

After a brief moment of excitement, the crowd's noise began to dwindle down as they witnessed something extremely odd, if not unbelievable. Voices began to murmur; shock and confusion followed suit as the sounds of cheers suddenly became silent.

"What the f...?"

"Dammnnn…."

"Yo, man, that guy's gotta be cheating."

"Bicep, are you trying?"

Even The Prophet was taken aback as he watched Bicep continue to flex his muscles, grunting and exerting all of his energy. However, it was Sifu that threw everyone off balance. No one could understand what exactly was happening.

There he was, somewhat smug but trying to keep it all in check. Knowing he was in foreign territory surrounded by hostiles, Sifu watched Bicep trying to move his arm into position. But, Sifu held his arm in place, not even flexing a single muscle. He had not budged an inch. In fact, every time Bicep tried to put power and push Sifu's hand, Sifu would neutralize the force and lock his arm in place. It was a brilliant demonstration of structure versus muscle, but he was the only one who knew what was going on.

Bicep was probably the most in shock as he grunted and yelled, "How the hell am I not pinning your bitch ass?" Sifu's arm felt like a wall each time he pressed upon it.

Sifu smiled and shrugged his shoulders, faking a yawn just to emphasize his dominance. "Uh, is that a question or more of a statement?"

Bicep roared, trying to summon more power to win the match.

The Prophet waved his hands up, gathering the energy from the crowd. He got right next to Bicep's ear and tried to find the right words to motivate him. "Bicep, you beat this piece of shit, right now! Do it … dammit … do it. Or else!" The crowd followed his orders and cheered him on. They began chanting Bicep's name over and over again. However, nothing changed. The energy of the crowd could not remedy the situation. The Prophet spun around, grabbed what little hair he had, and pulled on it violently out of frustration. Sifu was static and fully relaxed, though Bicep had built up a sweat. Exhausted from his efforts, he had nothing to show from it as Sifu's arm remained exactly in place.

"What the hell is going on?" Bicep screamed.

Someone from the crowd uttered, "It's like magic."

Sifu began to lecture the crowd. "It's not magic. It's structure. More powerful than all the muscle in the world." He turned his attention to The Prophet, whose back was turned, and said, "You have no idea what it's capable of doing. This is only a glimpse of its power…." The bait could no longer be resisted as The Prophet turned to face Sifu.

Sifu waited till their eyes locked. The Prophet stood just a few feet away as Bicep continued his struggle almost independently from the two. Sifu ignored him, as he finally decided and said to The Prophet, "It's time to end this."

Bicep said, "You ain't gonna win shit!"

Those were the last words that left his mouth. Sifu slowly began going the other way. Bicep clenched hard and continued to fight against Sifu. In one continuous flow, Sifu kept moving Bicep's arm closer to the table top. He looked Bicep in the eyes as he was explaining to him what was happening. In a way, Sifu was kindly trash talking. "The more you push, the easier it is for me to control. All the muscle you use is locked up in that big arm of yours, and there's no chance I'll let you ever release it upon mine. It's a wall, an unbreakable wall that's draining your energy with each passing second."

Bicep was screaming, "Shiiiitttt! Why can't I stop this?"

Sifu stopped just an inch away from pinning Bicep as he said, "Use two hands."

At first, Bicep did not do as Sifu had asked. His stubbornness was clear, and his ego was already hurt.

In a raised voice, Sifu demanded, "Two hands!" This was the first time Sifu had showed any emotion, but it was calculated.

In frustration, Bicep shook his head and then grabbed Sifu's one arm with both of his hands.

"What the fucckkk! This … is … not … possible!"

Sifu smiled at Bicep and then looked at The Prophet. He had but one inch left to pin Bicep. "Do we have a deal?"

The Prophet's eyes already answered the question, and a mutual understanding passed between the two. But, he could tell Sifu wanted verbal confirmation. He finalized it with his own words. "We have a deal."

Despite the confirmation, Sifu wanted to leave a lasting impression upon everyone there. Even with a short distance left, he slammed Bicep's hand into the table and created a huge dent. Bicep's body contorted by the force as he found himself tumbling to the ground and lying on his back. The loud sound was followed by dead silence as everyone stood in shock with mouths open in disbelief. Bicep was exhausted and beaten as he grabbed his strained arm. He looked in pain as he felt something was off. Sifu got up from his chair and didn't bask in the win; instead, he began casually walking away. Shock and awe filled the air, and Sifu's steps were all that could be heard.

Bicep moaned in agony, which made Sifu pause and turn around. He retraced his steps and approached Bicep, who could not raise his prized arm.

Sifu said, "If you will, let me fix it."

Bicep looked at The Prophet for permission. When he nodded and complied, Sifu massaged part of his arm and then cracked it back into place. A surge of energy shot through him, as if lightning had just struck. He asked, "Does that feel better?"

Bicep nodded but did not say thanks; again, Sifu's action had him confused. Sifu held his structure in place as Bicep used him to hoist himself back up to his feet. Sifu turned away and began walking toward the crowd, heading for the exit. The crowd formed a circle, blocking his path and preventing him from leaving. Sifu held his ground and didn't even turn back to look at The Prophet. No words were spoken as he waited, but he was prepared to unleash hell if needed. A moment passed before a signal was given. With that, an opening presented itself as everyone backed off, taking several steps away. The room was still quiet, and no one knew exactly what to say or do.

As Sifu walked by, one of The Prophet's guards could not help but whisper, "You are one bad mutha…."

"There is no set path other than the one you create." — Sifu

Section 1 Short Stories #1—Kirin's P.O.V.

One Year, Six Months Prior to Chum Night: June 1, 2030

<u>Graduation Day—Day 1</u>

Two weeks had passed, and my thoughts were still haunted by what had happened at the amusement park. Not a night went by that I didn't awake from another nightmare. Every time I thought I had gotten some form of peace, another wrench was tossed into my life.

We had lost Sifu's school, our place to train. Our home was closed forever, and there wasn't anything that I—or anyone else—could do about it. I looked down at my foot, which was still wrapped with a brace to remind me of my failure. The doctor said it would be another two weeks before I could walk on it without crutches. The lie was good enough that my parents believed me, but the truth was in the end results.

You would think this would be a time for celebration as I was in my standard blue cap and gown. A gold tassel hung by my face, and I was ready to receive a diploma. For many, this moment symbolized an accomplishment and served as a reflection of the last four years in high school. But, for me, it was simply a piece of paper—nothing more, nothing less. My thoughts were elsewhere that day.

My entire family was in the stands, and even my older brother Jim had gotten leave from the military just to see me graduate. So, I flashed an occasional smile and pretended to feel like everyone else. Deep down, I really appreciated the support of my family, but I couldn't help but feel empty.

I was sitting toward the back row of our graduating class, and I saw her in the middle section. She acted like nothing had ever happened. In fact, Ripley was all smiles. It sickened me when she passed by me in the hallways with her smug look. She even had the audacity to ask what had happened to my leg. But for me the memory was imprinted forever, replaying in my mind like an animated gif. Our encounter at the amusement park remained incomplete. Every time I saw her or heard her name, I wanted to smash her face in with my fist. From a distance, I could see her chatting up a storm, giggling along with her two sycophant groupies Jessica and Trina. I'm not even sure how she managed to do that, since seating assignments were based on last names. She always craved being the center of attention. I didn't care. She could have it all, but she had stolen the most important thing to me, and our business was far from done. Somehow, I hoped fate would lead us to one another in the future so that we could finally settle the score.

For the next ten minutes, Principal Murray went through the motions as his monotonous voice led to a less than exciting introduction of teachers and faculty before finally reaching the only moment that really mattered to me. He called forth the student who would be doing the commencement speech, and that was none other than Sage.

He stood from within the crowd as he gathered the attention of all that were present. While he was never openly social, he was brilliant and had finished first in the class, of course. He never told us, but I was willing to bet he could have graduated earlier if he'd wanted. I, for one, was glad that my two closest friends were at least with me. Sage walked toward the podium, passing Gwen, who was seated all the way in the front. There was a surprisingly confident aura about him. When he reached the podium, he adjusted the microphone, taking his time to make sure he was positioned comfortably before speaking. And then he finally began his speech in the spotlight of a sun ray.

Sage cleared his throat, made eye contact with those in the crowd, and spoke, "Good afternoon, everybody, and congratulations to the 2030 class of Forest Sky High. I thought I'd begin by doing away with the formalities first." Sage paused and smiled at the crowd. Strangely, someone from the class shouted his name, cheering him on as the crowd chuckled. He gave it a moment for them to settle down and said, "I see before me a mixture of emotions amongst my fellow students, from happiness to sadness, from pride to eager anticipation for tomorrow ... all of which culminates today as new beginnings and eventual endings come clashing together. This journey with you, all of you, is something so special to each and every one as well as those who share this moment with us. I wanted to do something different for today's speech, something worthy for future generations, in hopes that, as I search for the perfect words to lead us to a new tomorrow, it can resonate beyond just this day and carry on with you forever.

"We look to the future with hope that the possibility of a better tomorrow exists, and we know that the burden of responsibility falls upon us, the next generation. But, times are difficult as political unrest and unemployment are skyrocketing and social injustice continues. The truth is the unknown can be a scary thing, and to have that weight fall upon us is not something that is easily accepted. As I stand here in the very spot where individuals in years past gave this same speech or watched from the crowd, I can't help but wonder if they are looking back and wondering if their lives turned out exactly as they had imagined. Did they make a difference or change the world for the better?

"Change is a slow and often painful process. Whether we realize it or not ... we fear it ... all of us. Mankind has shown that, even if we were put in the worst of circumstances and given the opportunity for a better life, change—the unknown—represents a taller obstacle for us to overcome. We as humans, to a fault, will endure great suffering before change can occur.

"But, my fellow graduates, I call upon you today to be different, to be unique, to stand above the rest where no one has gone before, and to reach deep down for your inner strength. It is too easy for each and every one of us to go the traditional route, the comfortable path. Sure, who wouldn't want the American dream, the house, the great job, the incredible family, and the occasional trips? Who wouldn't want to have a storyboard picture-perfect life? However, the world is asking for a sacrifice from someone who could very well be sitting in the crowd before us, to go beyond who they are right now, to stand head and shoulders above the crowd, to do better than great … and forever change the course of history. I throw before you that challenge, and I say that that opportunity exists right here, right now. Search deep down inside you and seize it."

Sage paused, letting his words sink into the crowd. His silence commanded that everyone look at each other and at themselves. For the first time, Sage shined in front of his classmates unlike never before.

He continued, "It is not through your accomplishments and accolades that you will go beyond greatness. Instead, it is your actions, that will eventually lead to a better tomorrow. It is within you to push beyond the limits and forge the world you believe we all deserve."

For the next several minutes, Sage's speech was not only touching, but I could see the reactions on people's faces. They were moved, if not inspired. With all that had happened to me, it made me think. His speech made me question the route I was planning to take. This was going to require more reflection on my part. I couldn't help but repeat what he said, "Do better than great and forever change the course of history."

"Define yourself not by your possessions, but by the number of people you've inspired." — Kirin

A New Home—Day 7

I looked at Ryan, who was sucking on an ice cream cone while the others were watching him eat. The sun provided some shade, but Chicago's humidity was inescapable in midsummer and made for a miserable day of hanging out. His hands were covered with the drippings as the heat proved too much for Ryan's ice cream. We were all sitting around waiting for our meeting with Tobias. Ryan gulped the last bite of his cone and looked up to notice the entire gang watching him.

"What's up?"

Robert lowered his shades and gave Ryan *that* look. He was always dressed fashionably regardless of the occasion. "You could have at least offered to get us some ice cream?"

Ryan replied, "With what credits? I only had enough for one. Besides, I only have two hands."

Danny looked at his watch nervously, his quirk for being on time was being tested by Tobias. He was pacing back and forth as he said, "Whose idea was it to meet here at this park? Why couldn't we just meet at a coffee shop or inside a mall? Somewhere that at least has air conditioning." Fortunately for us, we used him as the barometer to measure how dire a situation was.

Big T looked around, assessing the situation. His laid-back personality was the polar opposite of Danny, which is why I think they complemented one another so well. He eventually faced Danny and said, "Twenty credits Tobias shows up in five minutes."

Danny and Big T both looked around the park, but Tobias was still nowhere in sight. Danny gave him a fist bump that connected with Big T's paw, and that was a sign. The bet was on.

I was getting a little flustered as well, and the heat seemed to be getting on everyone's nerves. Hiding under the tree, seeking comfort in the shade, I said, "Someone want to call Tobias and see what's taking so long?"

Doc was lying on the grass. He seemed to be the least bothered by the heat; in fact, he appeared to be enjoying it. He dangled a blade of grass from the side of his mouth and said, "Ken, give him a buzz.

My phone's low on battery."

Ken obliged. Ever the nice guy, he whipped out his phone as sweat poured down his face. He had the same hot and sweaty look he had after he finished eating spicy food. He held the phone by the side of his face, but from the looks of it, no one was answering. Ken turned to Doc, who looked like he was asleep, and shook his head.

"No answer."

I finally stood up and took charge. "Okay, let's text Tobias and tell him to meet up somewhere else that's not hot as hell." I felt a hand on my shoulder, and a voice from behind me spoke.

Tobias muttered, "You in charge now?"

I brushed off his hand and said, "You're thirty minutes late, and you weren't responding to anyone's calls or texts.... Besides, you had us waiting in some park with the bugs and the heat."

Tobias stepped in front of me, "Well, I was busy, and there's a rhyme to the reason." He slowly pulled out a bag from behind him and said, "I got drinks and some ice cream for everyone."

Ryan jumped up from his place and charged in to be first in line. "Thank god, I'm starving."

Everyone looked at him with judging eyes. That was the quickest we had seen him move in a long time. I wondered how he could possibly be starving. When I glanced at Tobias, I saw he seemed as cocky and as arrogant as ever. "And, how come you're not sweating like the rest of us?"

Tobias didn't answer, brushing me off like always. He continued handing out the refreshments to the gang. "Unlike you guys, I was doing some work."

Doc finally got off the grass and brushed himself off. He was the only one who seemed okay with the current situation. "So, there's gotta be a reason you made us sweat for this long."

Robert was quick to answer with his sharp tongue. "I bet one of them is so Ryan could burn some calories."

With ice cream all over his face, Ryan said, "Not after having two of these."

Tobias said, "Two?"

Danny handed over some credits to Big T, but all eyes, including theirs, were on Tobias's response. The gang began moving toward him as I stood from behind, waiting to see what he had in store for us.

Tobias said, "The reason I asked you to this park, in this particular location at this time … it's all because I found us a new home."

My eyes flew wide at his unexpected answer. "What do you mean?"

Tobias glanced over and gave me a wink. "Exactly what I said. I found us a new home, a place to train. Besides, hanging out in the alleys and working out in secluded parks just wasn't going to cut it."

Robert said, "But, it was interesting training there and seeing Danny's future exes."

Danny shouted, "Shut up, Robert!"

I moved toward Tobias and pressed further. "How is this possible?"

"Hey, it's me." Tobias began to walk away and waved everyone to follow him. "I'll explain on the way. It's about ten minutes from this location. That's why I asked you all to meet me here."

At that very moment, I wasn't sure if I was impressed or annoyed. There was something about Tobias that always kept me off-center. Deep down, I wasn't sure if that was a good thing or not.

Danny complained, "Why not meet there?"

Tobias said, "Ten minutes. Walk. I'm too lazy to explain this all again." We stood there for a second as Tobias started to create some distance.

"Let's move," I said and began leading the group behind Tobias.

We all followed Tobias as he made a concerted effort not to be spotted by anyone. Soon, we found our way to the corner of the lake. Several abandoned buildings stood within arm's reach of one another. The trees and the bushes provided ample coverage, as much of this area was left unkept and allowed to grow wild.

Ryan said, "Is this one of those fixer-upper projects?"

Big T smiled and said, "Time for my moment to shine."

Danny mumbled and said, "I don't know if you can work your magic on this, buddy."

Tobias held up his fist as we stood at the edge of the park. He said, "Everyone follow me and run to the middle of the that building." He pointed to the north.

Ryan pouted, "Run? But, I just ate! Isn't that bad for you?"

Robert said, "You've had two ice creams. You could use the cardio."

Tobias turned around again, "Seriously, Ryan ... two?" He

looked at us for confirmation as we gave the uniformed nod.

Ryan touted, "That's Wing Chun balance. A ying with a yang … seems like I learned that lesson before the rest of you guys."

I rolled my eyes and kept quiet while the rest of the group waved his comments off.

We all followed Tobias and sprinted toward the middle building. At first glance, it was an eyesore, and we all worried it might not be stable enough to even stand by itself. We reached a door that was covered in dust, and Tobias wiped away some cobwebs. He opened the door and gestured for all of us to enter. We weren't quite sure what to expect as we followed him inside, but all of us were soon pleasantly surprised.

Tobias said, "I know from the outside the place looks like a dump, but that's actually a good thing. As you can tell, no one's been in this area, so that means no unwanted visitors. Now, as you can see, this large room has been kept intact. Yeah, it's going to need some cleaning up, but I've tested it out. Somehow there's still power being sent to this area, so we still have light, and we can power it up for the winter with heat."

Ken agreed, "Yeah, we can get some electrical heaters…. That should work."

Ryan pointed to the corner. "Hey, that spot would be perfect. I got an extra mini fridge to store drinks and stuff."

I pointed to the ceiling, where a crossed metal grating hung above. "What's that?"

Tobias said, "Not really sure … but seems like some railing running along the top. I told you this place is pretty big, don't you think?"

Big T cut in, "Rafters."

"Rafters?"

Big T added, "Probably just for maintenance to access things above. From the looks of it, this is a really old building. Love the high ceilings."

Ryan said, "We could actually hang some Christmas lights up there and string it all across."

Big T nodded, "We could, but that's gonna require some work."

Ryan groaned, "Forget it then. It looks fine as is."

Doc looked around and added, "The insulation of this room looks pretty decent, and we've got a ton of space as well. What about Sifu's stuff? Should we move it in here?"

I stepped in right away. "No … I mean, that's Sifu's stuff. When he comes back … I just don't want anyone to touch his things." No one said a word, but from the looks of it, I was the only clinging to the hope.

Danny said, "What's with our ninja maneuvers to get in?"

Tobias stated, "Obviously we're trespassing, and we don't want anyone to know that we're training here … so that's a bad thing."

Robert quipped, "And I'm assuming the best part is that rent is zero."

Tobias nodded vigorously, "Bingo." He approached Big T and put his arm around his shoulder. He said, "Do you think you can do some of your handiwork around here to make it look like a gym?"

Big T looked at Danny, "You want to bet?"

Danny said, "I ain't no sucker. I know you've got the skills for this."

Big T turned to Tobias and asked, "What do you have in mind?"

"I've got some ideas."

Ken was walking around and examining the place like the rest of us when he asked, "This is a pretty big building. Technically, this is just one room.... Have you checked out the other rooms?"

Tobias answered. "Nah, this was a love-at-first-sight moment for me. We can explore them later, but for now this room should be our focus." Tobias turned to me with a look that was yearning for confirmation. There was confidence in his question, almost as if he knew my answer. "What do you think, Kirin?"

I took a moment and spun around, making sure this was real, as a warmth surrounded me. Then I looked at him and said, "We're home."

"Home isn't about the location, but the people you make memories with." — Kirin

Lollipop Chicken Wings—Day 20

It was three weeks into my summer break, and for the first time in a long time, things seemed back to normal. After Tobias solidified a training facility for us, the gang felt like a celebration was necessary. It had been a while since we ate out together, and it was Danny's turn to pick a spot. Surprisingly, it wasn't vegetarian, though we all wondered about his choice.

We had gathered at lunchtime as he suggested, but we were still waiting for Danny to arrive. Fortunately, the waitress seated us anyway since our party was fairly larger than normal.

Robert said, "Typical of Danny to be late, and it's his turn. I say we bypass his choice and go to my place."

Tobias responded, "You know, Robert, I'd usually agree with you, but the fact that this restaurant is called Cock in Hand ... we're staying here to eat." Everyone giggled as Tobias looked at the entire group. "All in favor?"

I watched as all the guys quickly raised their hands, and then they looked at me. "Sure, whatever ... but, uh ... what's the big deal?" I held up the menu and stared at all the chicken choices. Then I noticed several of the guys snickering. "What?!"

My train of thought was interrupted as Danny finally came running in and grabbed the only empty seat. "My bad, I know I'm late, but it's not my fault. My grandma needed tech support. How could I say no to her?"

Big T coughed and extended his big hand out toward Danny. He looked at it, confused, for a second. Danny said, "What?"

Big T said, "We made a bet that, the next time you were late, you'd end up using the grandma tech support excuse."

Danny thought about it for a second and then swore silently, realizing it was true. He reached into his pocket and then tossed some credits at Big T. He shook his head in frustration, "I should've gone with my ovaries were bothering me."

Doc chuckled and said, "Danny, food!"

Danny looked at everyone, "Okay, did you guys look at the menu already?"

Ken said, "Yeah, but there're so many choices.... I thought you'd be recommending something."

I asked, "Why'd you pick this place? Aren't you a vegetarian or vegan or something?"

Danny answered. "Long ago, I used to eat meat, and back in the day, this was my favorite place for...."

Robert shouted, "Cock!"

The gang erupted in laughter, as I joined along with the amusement.

Danny cleared his throat, snapped Robert the middle finger, and continued, "As I was saying, before being rudely interrupted, I chose this place because I was thinking of a place you guys would like to try." Danny spread his arms open, "Thus ... here we are."

Ryan tossed his menu at Danny, "Hurry, pick the food already. I've been waiting forever."

Danny said, "Let me guess ... you're starving."

Ryan simply rubbed his belly and gave a sad look.

Robert was about to make a comment, but then shook his head, muttering, "That's too easy."

Doc followed Ryan's lead and tossed his menu at Danny, and then everyone else followed suit. All the menus lay in disarray in front of him. Danny got the hint and waved to the waitress. He pointed to several times on the menu as she quickly wrote down his order. She spun around and left for the kitchen in haste.

I asked, "Wait, what are you going to eat?"

Danny replied with a smirk, "I'm eating chicken with you."

Jaws dropped, Robert spilled his glass in shock, and Big T turned pale as a ghost, as a hush fell over the entire table.

Ryan took a moment to grasping the situation and asked, "So ... uh, you're not vegetarian or vegan or whatever anymore?"

Robert said, "You mean Mr. Killjoy at all our eating events."

Ignoring Robert, Danny replied, "First of all, it's vegan. Second, I still am vegan, but like Christmas and Easter, I'll find times to enjoy meals with you guys."

I asked, "Why the change?"

Danny said, "I recall Sifu saying something. So, he said, if you were at a party and everyone is drinking, it's your ego that prevents you from blending in to match the flow.... I wasn't quite clear at the time what he meant, so I asked him if that meant I should drink. He said, 'Just have a glass and carry it with you. It's not necessary to drink but you bring about a harmony.'"

I had to ask, "That kind of goes against being who you are, doesn't it?"

"No, because just like the art, I need to be flexible, and I realized my own attitude was too rigid in thinking."

Tobias commented, "That's probably the smartest thing you've said."

Robert snuck in, "Ever."

Danny added, "So, yes, I'm still mainly vegan 99% of the time. But, on occasion to match the universal harmony, I can eat a piece of meat, chicken, or fish with you guys and still be me."

We all agreed with Danny's comments—a rarity, so we allowed

him to bask in it for a moment.

Afterward, for the next several minutes, the conversation was dominated by food, video games, Wing Chun, and of course, being surrounded by all guys … women.

Tobias gaze wandered, "Twelve o'clock."

I checked the time and frowned. It was way past twelve, but I didn't say a word. Instead, I began to observe the guys as they socialized with one another, leaving me out of the loop. They continued to whisper different times, leaving me more confused. "Uh, I know that's not the time. What gives?" They exchanged looks before turning to Tobias for permission.

Tobias tried to brush it off, "Kirin, it's just guy talk."

"Tell me … I'm curious."

Tobias replied, "Don't you have four brothers?"

"I do … but besides their typical guy behavior such as foul bodily sounds and questionable language, they've been overly protective about any guy talk in front of me."

Tobias hesitated, but I stood my ground and gave him a look that demanded an answer. "I've been with you guys more than anyone else for years. You might as well let me in on all your side jokes and stories."

He raised his hands in a rare and quick surrender. "Okay, okay. If you must know, it's just how guys point out if there's someone eye-worthy to pay attention to."

"Explain!"

Tobias looked around, though I wasn't sure why, as if this were

47

a secret guy code that couldn't be revealed. He lowered his voice slightly, "Okay, so you heard him say three o'clock, right? So, you look from the perspective of whoever gives the time and see the girl that we should focus our attention on."

I looked at him and then calculated what he was saying. Then I glanced to his right and saw a pretty girl talking to her boyfriend. "Seriously?"

"You asked; I explained."

Ryan said, "Everyone, check your phone."

I looked at my phone, but there was nothing on it. "I got nothing on mine."

Tobias just looked at me, "Of course not, you're not on group guy chat."

I shouted at Ryan, "What is it?"

He held up his phone, and I saw a picture of the girl already on it. I asked, "How'd you get that pic? I didn't even see you photograph her."

Robert high-fived Ryan, "Ryan's got skills besides eating. At least it's not from Ken's phone. His are always blurry."

Ken said in defense, "It's not me! My phone is old." Robert rolled his eyes in response.

"You guys don't think this is really immature or possibly a bit creepy?"

Tobias shrugged, "This is what guys do. We're visual creatures…. Would you rather I lie?"

I wasn't sure my feelings were typical of a girl, or maybe it was because of my training, but their pictures didn't bother me after he mentioned it.

Suddenly, our conversation was interrupted by our waitress as she started bringing out the food. Several plates of chicken were laid out before us in a fashion I was unfamiliar with. The smell was incredible as the dark brown, deep fried flavor with the smoke rising made me lunge at it before anyone else.

I began devouring the chicken and eating it to the bone, leaving not a morsel of meat. Before I realized it, I had already eaten ten pieces, but I was unaware that the rest of the guys were watching me. I still had a piece in my mouth when I looked around. In a muffled voice, I asked, "What?"

Ryan scurried around the table and dropped to one knee by me. In Japanese, he said, "*Kekkon Shitte kudasai.*"

"Huh?"

The rest of the guys threw napkins at him and ushered him back to his seat.

I finally licked my fingers clean and then finished my bite. "Let me guess … another stupid guy thing."

All of them looked away, and none seemed to be in a rush to answer me.

I looked at Tobias who, for the first time, seemed hesitant as well. "Tobias…? Tobias!"

He slowly turned back to me and said, "Chicken's good…. Isn't it?" He pretended to lunge for the plate.

I pulled it away from him. "Yes, but tell me what guy thing I just did that has you all looking like a bunch of dorks."

He paused for several seconds before finally answering me. "Well, if you must know … this was from Sifu, not me. I want to clarify that … Sifu. But, he told us that, when you go on a first date, take her out to a place where you can see how she eats chicken or, at the very least, a place where she can use her hands to eat."

I looked at him with some doubt and said, "Sifu?"

"Yes … now this isn't exactly how he phrased it, but you can tell how good a girl is in…."

"In … soccer?" I was trying to finish his sentence oddly, just to make him squirm.

"Uh, no … in umm … in bed."

"Yeah, I figured that. I was kidding."

"Yeah, I knew that … how good she is … in bed by how she eats. Thus, you take her somewhere where she has to use her hands. So, like this place, for example, with chicken. If a girl was, say, to eat a piece of chicken with a fork or with a single hand, then she'd be labeled kind of a sleeper."

Robert said, "Yeah, but the way you devoured your chicken—"

Tobias waved his hand across his throat, telling Robert to cut it.

I shook my head and began to laugh. "You guys can't be serious about this and the fact that you're pinning this on Sifu…? Now I know you both are pulling my leg." I continued to eat and enjoy the meal as the rest of the lunch seemed particularly awkward.

The waitress came by and looked at our table. "Do you guys want to order more chicken?"

All the guys shouted in unison, "Yes, yes … more chicken!"

"It's the difference between men and women that actually bring us closer to equality." —Kirin

Section 2 Sifu's Journey Entry #1—First Customer

January 20, 2031

The day's focus was on soup. It was a routine they had been performing to perfection for months, but today was no ordinary day. Lance and Sifu stood close together as they prepared to finally reveal their creation to the public. Sifu was chopping and prepping, almost machine-like from the months of practice. Not much conversation existed between the two. Lance would occasionally make small talk, breaking the silence, while Sifu was steadfast. Like a blank book, he was impossible to read. Lance had a look of concern written all over his face. He continued to do his job but kept glancing at the front door, which remained open. Only a casual breeze greeted them.

Sifu took a final sip of the broth, smacking his lips together as the taste brought that warm feeling inside. Lance waited for the verdict. Sifu turned to his friend and said, "The soup looks good. We've been consistent with the process, don't you think?"

Lance did not respond, as his mind was elsewhere.

Sifu put down the ladle and walked over to his friend, who looked frozen in thought. He rested his hand on Lance's shoulder allowing him to bear his weight.

Startled, Lance jumped, breaking his train of thought. He apologized to Sifu, "You really think this is gonna work? I mean…."

Sifu said, "What I think and what will happen are two different things. Besides, my focus is on the process, not the goal."

Lance shook his head; the statement was profound yet too much for him to digest. "I doubt I'll ever master your level of detachment from things, Sifu."

Sifu pulled away, the comment tugging at him, "Levels, yes, but mastery … far from it."

Evening was approaching. For two hours, Sifu remained as cold as ice, not concerned with the result. He perfectly offset his partner, who was the polar opposite. Lance felt the time drag as his frequency of checking the door increased. He hoped that someone would peek in to give life to this faint dream. In his mind, he couldn't see how any of this could possibly work. Suddenly, the monotony of the moment finally got a breath of fresh air.

A stranger stepped into foreign territory, somehow drawn through the door by fate or the universe. He said, "Well, hello there."

The one time Lance hadn't been expecting anyone, someone had finally appeared. *Figures*, Lance thought as he looked at Sifu, who gave him a nudge forward, making an obvious hint. Lance protested, whispering, "You're the social butterfly. Go ahead and work your charm."

Sifu took his time. In no rush to impress, he wiped his hands on a towel longer than one would think and began making his way toward the stranger.

Sifu waved with his hand and greeted him with a warm smile. "Hello, how can I help you?" he said sincerely.

The stranger, still with a confused look on his face, scanned the establishment. It took a moment for him to respond, but he eventually came about and introduced himself. He grimaced, causing his eyes to squint behind his glasses as he said, "Uh, I was just walking by and noticed this place." He continued to circle around, lightly touching the fixtures, looking under the tables, which was a bit of a struggle because of his tall stature, and eventually peeking over to the kitchen area. There was a counter table, with napkins, chopsticks, and spoons neatly laid out, and yet oddly the place gave the feeling that he was in someone's home. He stared at the kanji writing on the wall. "Is this, uh … a restaurant? Or something? I didn't really see a sign."

Sifu thought about the question, "Well, not really, but we do have food here."

The stranger said, "Food? I'm starving." Without hesitation, he hopped onto the nearest chair and looked at Sifu. He began fidgeting for a brief moment, noticing a menu was nowhere to be found. "Am I missing something?"

Sifu kept the conversation short. "Nope ... fortunately, you've come at the right time.... Give me a few." With that, he turned away and headed back to the kitchen.

The stranger waited patiently and occupied his time with his phone. For the next fifteen minutes, not a word was spoken, nor did an awkward silence exist. Sifu finally reappeared from the kitchen while Lance remained in the background and watched with great anticipation. Sifu approached the man with a bowl of ramen, and a simple glass of water. He placed it in front of the stranger, just like a waiter would do, and said, "Enjoy."

For the first time, the stranger had a sudden burst of mixed emotions. Questions that were unasked were finally answered. "Wow, this raaamen looks incredible." Oddly, he extended the pronunciation of the word. He began fanning the heat toward his face and then stopped suddenly, "Umm ... I don't see any prices anywhere."

Sifu said in a nonchalant voice, "There's no cost."

"No cost?" The man's brow raised, followed by a bewildered look.

"None ... however, I leave it optional to you if you want to donate anything," replied Sifu.

The stranger thought about it, "So, you're telling me I could eat this raaamen and, if I wanted to, just walk out of here afterward at no cost at all?"

Sifu nodded and replied, "Well, that's what I said."

The stranger struggled with the thought for a moment, but the sight and the smell of the ramen dominated all of his senses, dispelling the need for justification. He reached for his phone and took several snaps of his meal from different angles and then asked, "Oh, can I have a Coke?"

Sifu pointed to Lance, who remained half-hidden in the kitchen. He half-waved toward the stranger and then continued with his work. "My fellow chef Lance over there can get you more water if needed, but that's the only liquid that we carry."

He thought about it and replied, "That's right. It's not a restaurant." The steam hit his face and captured his attention once again. The stranger decided that he had waited long enough before diving into the soup. He stirred it several times before, holding the broth in his spoon, he cautiously tasted it. Sifu did not wait for a reaction and decided to go back to the kitchen. He didn't need confirmation; he already knew how good his soup was.

Several minutes passed as the sound of slurping could be heard from the other room. Neither Sifu nor Lance checked up on their customer, making Lance feel uneasy, his doubt seeping through.

The stranger took it upon himself and finally burst into the kitchen. "Holy shit ... that was without a doubt the greatest raaamen that I have ever had. Period!" He frantically searched the kitchen from top to bottom and said, "Am I being videotaped or punked here?"

Sifu looked at him, "No," and continued with his work.

Lance was about to make a comment but decided to hold his tongue and follow Sifu's next move.

The stranger, still unsure, asked, "So, you're telling me that incredible raaamen is absolutely free, if I choose not to pay for it?"

Sifu nodded his head and didn't make eye contact, feeling that repeating himself was unnecessary.

Lance was still uptight, and the stranger's quirky pronunciation forced him to blurt out, "It's pronounced 'ramen,' not 'raaamen.'"

The stranger ignored Lance's correction and added, "So, there's no catch or anything?"

Sifu said, "Well, there is a catch."

The stranger snapped his fingers and said, "Aha … I knew it!"

Before he could muster up another word, Sifu explained, "I make only seventy-five bowls of ramen a day and only one kind of ramen. It's always the same kind of ramen—no exceptions, no changes at all to the recipe. Any allergies are your karma, not mine, and you get only one bowl."

The stranger's mouth dropped open as he said, "So, I only get one bowl for today?"

Sifu nodded. "Only one."

The stranger looked behind him even though he knew it was an empty room on the other side. "Even if I'm the only one here?"

"Only one," Sifu repeated.

The stranger asked, "What time do you guys normally open?"

Sifu replied, "There's really no set time, but basically when and if I feel like it."

"When and if…?" The stranger paused. "And just to clarify again … you are not a restaurant?" Everything he learned added further to the mystery.

"Do you think a restaurant could survive with this business model?" Sifu was snide in his remark.

"So, let me get this straight. You're not a restaurant, you only serve one kind of raaamen—excuse me, I mean ramen—and you don't charge anything?"

"Yes, yes, yes." Sifu confirmed each question with a pointed hand gesture.

Lance watched and waited, wondering what this stranger's next step would be.

The stranger said, "By the way, my name is Eric." He extended his hand as Lance shook it and introduced himself before introducing Sifu as Sifu.

Eric said, "Well, I gotta tell you guys, I'm still not quite sure what you have going here ... but, damn, that was absolutely one of the most incredible meals I have ever had. I'm a bit of a foodie," he said as he held his flat belly, not really proving his point. "Well...." He bobbed his head several times and slowly spun around before he began to stride out. Lance watched as he walked past the donation jar, but within a blink he dashed out of the restaurant.

Lance was curious to see Sifu's reaction. He turned to find that Sifu remained the same, not biting on a moment that would elicit a reaction from just about anyone else. Lance ran to the window to see where Eric had scurried off to.

"Well, look at that son of a bitch! He didn't even donate a single credit and took off like that." He turned only to realize he was speaking to himself. Sifu had disappeared from his spot and was already busy washing the bowl, though he remained stoic.

Lance's face pressed against the glass as he said, "That cheap peace of crap! He drives a Benz, and he couldn't even toss us a single credit … bastard." Lance flicked him the finger as his temper began to boil, but then he glanced at Sifu, whose reaction caused him to pull back. He had begun to understand his friend and teacher from time to time, but this left him completely puzzled.

That night, Eric remained the only individual to come to Sifu's restaurant. They decided to close up shop and call it quits for the day. Lance never brought up the subject of whether Sifu's plan would be a success or not. The two enjoyed a quiet meal eating their ramen and discussing Wing Chun.

The Next Day

Lance and Sifu were walking toward their shop when they noticed a huge crowd that rounded a corner. It was unusual for this neck of the woods, so immediately Lance thought the worst and looked at Sifu. He took off without giving it a second thought. "Something must be wrong!"

Within seconds, Lance was a blur—not bad for a guy with a fake leg. He hustled to the corner to get answers. However, Sifu didn't feel an urgent need to run and casually maintained the same pace.

A few minutes later, he caught up with Lance, who was hunched over, catching his breath. Lance pointed to the front of the line as he struggled for several breaths. There, just a few feet away, Sifu spotted a familiar face. Standing in the very front was Eric, eagerly awaiting what appeared to be their arrival. It seemed like he had been there for some time, as a small chair and several empty cups were parked at the entrance.

Eric ran up to Sifu and clamored, "It's 9:30 pm! Finally, you guys decided to show up."

Lance approached Sifu from the side, still gasping for air as he sought an answer. He turned to Sifu first and said, "Remind me to start some kind of cardio training tomorrow." Sifu chuckled, helping his friend stand straight as all eyes were on them.

Lance eyed Eric, "Sifu did say we come when we feel like it, and that goes for cooking as well."

Eric nodded, "Yes, yes. I recall that, but…."

Lance inquired, "How long have you been waiting here?"

"I'd say about two-and-a-half hours."

Lance was shocked at the amount of time invested and his level of commitment. He pointed to the crowd behind him. "What's all that?"

"Well, yesterday after having your phenomenal ramen, I decided to tell some friends about it, and lo and behold," he paused, gesturing to the crowd, "here we are."

The crowd on the sidewalk cheered as they all began chanting, "Ramen!"

Lance warned, "It's gonna be a good hour before we'll have our first meal ready." Subconsciously, he was wondering if any of them would actually pay.

Eric said, "Not a problem." He looked to Sifu for confirmation. He held both hands out in a prayer position and asked, "Ramen?"

Sifu stayed stone-faced, making Eric squirm just a pinch longer, even though he got no satisfaction from the tease. He approached his shop door and grabbed the handle. Then he stopped and, without looking at Eric, Lance, or the crowd, said, "Let's have ramen tonight."

Even though they were relying solely on Eric's word about the quality of the soup, the crowd began to cheer.

Sifu did not reciprocate the enthusiasm and focused on the task at hand. It was time to share Megumi's soup with the world.

That night, after the last bowl was served, talk continued outside the restaurant about the delicious taste of Sifu's soup. Sifu showed the last customer out the door as he was about to close shop. Eric, who was the first in line, was also the last to leave as his core group of friends could not stop talking about the ramen.

Before Sifu closed the door, Eric ran back up and stopped him. "Sifu, thanks again for making the soup. My friends and I were wondering if you have a name for it?"

"Actually, it's a *tonkotsu* soup, but I have no name for it."

Eric's female friend, with short hair and a ring in her nose, approached from behind. "By the way, my name is Tina.... You know, I just wanted to thank you again for making your soup. This may sound weird to say, but I've always thought food isn't just food.... You know what I mean? I've always looked at it as a memory, you know. Like my mom—my grandma taught her a recipe, and then she eventually shared it with me. So, anytime I make my dish, *menudo*, that my friends love so much, it makes me think—" Tina paused as she reminisced. "It makes me think of my mom as well as my *abuela*, and it's like they're sharing that moment with me."

Sifu stared at Tina before slowly approaching her and giving her a hug. "Thank you for the kind words."

Lance was taken back, surprised that Sifu displayed an emotion so visibly. It didn't matter if he was training or not, his teacher's actions continued to keep him off center.

Tina praised, "This is absolutely the best ramen I've ever tasted."

Sifu chuckled and paused as he recalled a memory. He added, "I guess … I guess you could say this is the most bestest soup."

The awkward phrasing caused everyone to laugh, and Eric found the need to join the group hug. He said, "There's a good chance I might be here again tomorrow. By the way, 'most bestest' is very catchy."

Sifu nodded and acknowledged his goal as the trio finally separated. He waved good night, even though dawn was about to break, and then entered the shop, closing the door behind him. Inside, the donation box was overflowing with credits, but Sifu was too busy to deal with it. An hour passed as Sifu spent time washing the dishes and tasked Lance with counting the credits. Lance looked at his teacher, who remained the same throughout their venture.

After calculating the total credits, he shouted from afar, "Sifu, you're not going to believe this! We made a shit load today." Even though the evidence was right in front of him, he still couldn't believe that this was actually happening.

Sifu muttered, "That's nice," as he continued to wash the remaining bowls in the sink. Lance was ecstatic but amazed by Sifu's detachment from the entire moment.

> *"When you do something for the love of it, everything else will take care of itself." — Sifu*

CHAPTER 2 *New Blood*

Lying comfortably on her bed, Gwen was enjoying her Saturday morning away from the daily grind of work and school. Sunlight had just broken into her condo, while the cold winter snow remained outside. Gwen made little effort to roll out of bed; instead, she hugged her pillow tightly as she cracked a smile. She knew today required no brain effort at all, so she stretched her arms and decided to bury herself further into her blankets.

She thought, *No responsibility day.*

Her minute of pure enjoyment was suddenly interrupted by a foul odor. She took a second sniff, just to make sure, as she looked for the source of this unpleasantness.

She muttered, "Oh my god! Why does it smell so bad? What the heck just died in here?" She pinched her nose and buried herself underneath the bed sheets, hoping to avoid this foul demon.

The sheets failed to protect her from the odor, so she popped out from her covers, finally sitting upright as she scanned the area. Several feet away at the edge of her bed, she saw two stubby hind legs propped next to her. There was the source: Partially rolled in her blankets on top of her bed was Bacon. He remained in deep sleep, his snore rumbling throughout her room.

"How many times have I told you not to come on my bed, Bacon!"

Bacon did not react to her question as he continued his nap.

She buried herself within her blankets and tried to regain a comfortable position. She struggled for the next several minutes, flipping and flopping before she finally found the right comfortable position. She closed her eyes and took a slight breath, aware she had achieved the rare second chance.

Her moment of peace and tranquility was fleeting. A loud snore rumbled throughout her room, reminding her that Bacon was still there. Gwen shook her head, realizing her moment of serenity had passed. There was no going back. She screamed in annoyance. She waited for a second but didn't get the response she was waiting for. *Strange*, she thought as she peeked from behind her blanket and at her door.

Gwen raised herself halfway up from the bed and called out, "Kirin?"

The door was cracked slightly open, enough to still be heard. "Kirin?" she repeated, just loud enough for her to hear, but not enough to disturb her neighbors. This time, it was Bacon who turned around and stared at Gwen. He looked almost annoyed that Gwen had disturbed his sleep. She pointed at him and said, "Don't you even dare."

She called out one last time for Kirin but with the same result. Looking concerned, Gwen shared a glance with Bacon. "Are you thinking what I'm thinking?"

Bacon yawned and then tucked his head into the sheets and went back to sleep.

"I guess that's a no." Flustered, Gwen realized her Saturday morning was going to start earlier and far differently than she had hoped.

By the side of Gwen's bed sat her wheelchair. She positioned herself to scoot on top of it and paused for a moment, struggling with her daily reminder. Like always, she found the will to get back on it.

Oh my god ... why's it so cold this morning? she wondered.

Gwen grabbed her phone from her bedside table and checked for messages. The first thing she saw was a good morning text from

Sage. That brought her some warmth as she quickly mashed on her phone to write him back. They exchanged pleasantries for a moment before she told Sage she'd call him in a bit. For now, she had something more pressing on her mind: Kirin's whereabouts.

Gwen swung open her bedroom door and began rolling down her hallway. She peeked into her guest room where Kirin should have been sleeping, but Gwen found the bed empty and the sheets unruffled. Gwen thought, *She either didn't sleep last night or folded up her stuff....*

Gwen knew her best friend all too well, and her sloppy manners answered the question immediately. She turned her head slightly in response to the faint sound of music she heard in the distance. As she continued down the hallway, the sound grew louder. Eventually, she got to her dining room and found the answer to her question.

With her back turned to Gwen, Kirin was drenched in sweat. She had been practicing relentlessly for the last two hours. This morning was dedicated to footwork and hand coordination.

Gwen stayed back and continued to watch her friend. She moved her arms in a smooth and graceful manner, almost as if she were figure skating on her hardwood floor. Much of what Kirin spoke about always went over Gwen's head, but Gwen knew skill when she saw it. She took a moment to appreciate what she was watching, but a slight breeze caught the back of her neck, reminding her of why her morning was ruined.

"I should've known," muttered Gwen. With a look of disdain, Gwen shouted, "Kirin Rise!" This time, it didn't matter who she bothered; she wanted Kirin's attention.

Those words remained unheard, as Kirin was focused on her training and the sound of her music, which blocked out Gwen's rant. Gwen reached back and grabbed some treats she kept for Bacon from the back of her wheelchair. A small bone the size of her thumb hurled through the air and was about to land on the target.

Kirin snapped around and caught the piece in the air. She smiled and looked at Gwen from afar. She popped the small item she held into her mouth. When the taste of dog food hit her tongue, she spit it right back out.

"Blah ... why are you giving me dog food for breakfast?" She wiped her mouth, tossed the dog treat to the side, and rolled her shoulders back to loosen her muscles. She stood for a moment, facing Gwen but completely ignoring her, and then blasted several punches into the air.

"Strange way to say good morning," said Kirin. The momentary pause didn't last long as Kirin immediately went back to what she was doing.

Gwen shook her head in disbelief and finally erupted, "Kirin Rise!!" She gripped her hair, striking a pose in frustration.

Kirin finally froze in her tracks and pressed her earrings, shutting down the music that was connected to the speaker. Gwen's condo finally was quiet. She turned around and smiled at Gwen, hoping that would be enough to appease her. "I'm sensing something is troubling you this morning."

Gwen approached her friend and said sternly, "What are you doing?"

Kirin raised an eyebrow, knowing exactly what Gwen was asking, though she continued to play dumb. "We've been friends long enough, Gwen. By now, you should know what I study and practice ... and it ain't, Karate."

"That's not what I'm asking you." Gwen's face showed a combination of frustration and aggravation, along with a slew of other emotions which were close to exploding.

"Uh, what are you asking?" She played coy and continued to stretch her arms and body.

"You want me to do this…? Fine, let's do this, Kirin. You know you're not supposed to be practicing, and you also know you're not supposed to do anything but rest. It's been a month since you got back from the hospital and I was 'kind enough' to let you stay with me at my place. I was thinking this would be all fun and cool like old times, but you've been … what's the word I'm looking for? Oh yeah, horrible. You've been on some crazy Rocky workout routine since you got here, and that's all you've been doing."

Kirin gave a confused look, "Who's Rocky?"

Gwen rolled her eyes. "You've heard Sage's quote…."

Kirin shrugged and stared at Gwen, hoping she'd answer.

"Adrian, yo, Adrian," Gwen mustered out a bad imitation.

Kirin's face remained blank.

Gwen was flustered and replied, "Oh, it doesn't matter. My point is, Kirin, you're my best friend, and you're also staying with me at *my* place. It's like … you know … you're not even here. I didn't say anything to you in the beginning, figuring you'd snap out of it. But, one month later, here we are. So, I'm finally telling you how it is."

Kirin grabbed a towel lying on the floor and began drying herself. She remained aloof from Gwen and still didn't say a word. The room was quiet until Kirin cracked her neck, which broke the silence between the two. She was searching for the words to say to her best friend, but she was so fixated on her training.

"I don't know what to say," she answered honestly.

Gwen sighed, "Just talk to me. We've always talked to each other, no matter what." She rolled her wheelchair closer to Kirin.

"I know. But, this time, it's different. This time, my focus has turned to … it's turned into an obsession," Kirin admitted.

Gwen looked away in disgust. She whispered, "You can't be serious. Not after last time. You really want to go back … you want to go back to the Dome?"

"Last season, I didn't even know if I wanted to return, but after my last fight…."

Gwen shouted, "Your last fight? You mean the last fight where I watched my best friend nearly get killed?"

"Gwen, I've made up my mind. There's nothing anyone can say or do that will change it. I want to go back … in fact, I *need* to." Kirin's voice lowered at the end, but it held no hint of doubt.

"Kirin, I'm begging you. It's not just me. It's your family … your mom. You can't keep dodging these bullets and expecting that everyone who loves you will just sit back and hope for the best."

"I know I'm being selfish." Kirin looked at Gwen as tears started forming in her eyes. "But, what do you want me to tell you? Every inch of my body is telling me to do this. It's like I'm destined for this route."

"No, Kirin. That can't be true. You always have choices. It's up to you to choose. For all you know, you've made your own illusion of choice."

"I don't see it that way, Gwen."

"You don't see it, or you don't want to see it? There's big difference, Kirin."

"Gwen, maybe I need to get you up to speed. Sifu's still in jail, the entire world is a crap hole, for some reason you've been moved out of the list for your surgery, and I end up freezing in a fight as a punch flies at me full speed, intent on ending my life." Kirin moved forward and stared out of Gwen's window. All the images kept racing through her head, and nothing she could do would silence the noise. She closed her eyes in frustration, but the thoughts continued to haunt her.

"How can you tell me not to continue?" She hung her head down, lost and hoping for answers. She whispered to herself, "What else can I do?"

"Don't you see…? At this point, it's no longer about bringing balance. Right … I see it in your eyes. It's all about revenge." Gwen approached her friend from behind.

"Well, if you have a better plan, I'd sure love to hear it."

"All I'm saying, Kirin … is there's gotta be more than one way—another way that doesn't involve you risking your life."

"Gwen, the change I want may require that sacrifice."

"Fine, Kirin. You may be prepared to sacrifice yourself for your cause, but are you willing to sacrifice those around you?" She threw her hands up in frustration and then grabbed her hair firmly. She was about to explode, but one deep breath helped contain her frustration.

"What do you mean?"

Gwen took a moment to gather herself before answering Kirin. "You can't be that naive to think that, if you go down, it's only you that'll be in harm's way. You've already seen what you're up against and what they've been willing to do. These are powerful people … more powerful than either you or I can imagine. In the end, your sacrifice means nothing to them."

Those words finally hit Kirin like a brick. She collapsed on her knees and began to cry. Gwen watched for a moment before edging closer in her wheelchair. Even with all her frustration, Kirin was her dearest friend, and she put her ego aside to comfort her.

Gwen spoke softly, "Kirin, you know me. I would never say anything to hurt you. I've been your BFF since grade school, and I love you like the sister I never had … and I get it. Always be you." She put her hand on Kirin's shoulder. "You always say, 'center target, own it,' right?"

Kirin nodded.

"Well, isn't it possible that, to get to your target, you need to find another route? One that doesn't fight the force, but flows with it?"

Kirin pulled back and cracked a smile. "Wow, you sound like Sifu."

Gwen replied, "It's not like I don't listen to what you say. Besides, all the merchandise I have of you contains all these stupid quotes." Gwen pointed to her shirt, which was Kirin Rise gear. "By the way, thank god this is free. Did you know they charge forty-five credits for this shirt?"

Kirin looked surprised, her tears stopping for a moment. She was never involved in any of the business aspect with the UFMF. "That much?"

"I know, right?"

Kirin added, "I had no idea. The UFMF does all the marketing and merchandising."

The useless talk helped snap Kirin out of her slight depression. For a moment she felt normal, almost as if all her problems were behind her. The silence kept her warm, soothing her briefly. However, her past quickly snapped back, never straying far from her thoughts. It was in escapable. She paused briefly and tried to think of a way to appease Gwen. She whimpered. "You know, you're right ... and here I am, bottled up, keeping secrets from you. I've never done that before, and I know you never have."

Gwen looked away briefly as she hoped Kirin didn't sense anything awkward about that moment. She shifted out of her wheelchair and sat next to Kirin. She hugged her tightly, hoping to ease her friend's pain as they shared a moment of silence and comfort.

Knock. Knock.

Both of them released each other from the hug and stared at the door. Neither knew who that could be.

Gwen asked, "It's too early for you to order something out, but just in case ... did you?"

"No, I've been training all morning."

Knock. Knock.

"Help me up," Gwen requested. "Who could it be then?" Once she was back in her wheelchair, Gwen rolled toward the door. "Who is it?"

This time, the knock played out a particular rhythm.

After that knock, Kirin knew instantly. She said, "Oh my god," as she placed her hand over her face in annoyance.

71

Gwen glanced backward and asked, "What?"

Kirin replied, "It's—"

From behind the door came a high-pitched voice. "It's me … Angelo."

They exchanged a glance and sighed in relief as Gwen approached the door, unlocked it, and pulled it open. She greeted Angelo, "How'd you get by my doorman below?"

Angelo pranced in and spun in a circle and then twitched his behind. "Is that a good enough answer?" Dressed in an outfit that would sparkle for miles, he was pristine from head to toe.

Gwen replied, "I always wondered about my doorman. I guess that pretty much confirms it."

Kirin stood up and asked, "Why are you here, Angelo? I gave you clear instructions that I needed to be left alone."

Angelo came running to Kirin and dropped to his knees, where he bowed and began to grovel by her feet. "I know! I know what you told me, but it's been close to a month—maybe even longer! And I've been handling everything for you, Kirin. I need you back. I'm so lost without you." Angelo continued sycophanting as he took a quick peek up to see Kirin's reaction.

Kirin rolled her eyes and tried walking away. "Can you quit with the drama, Angelo? You're perfectly fine without me." Angelo continued to cling onto her leg as he was dragged on the floor.

"No, no … I swear on Gwen's doorman's phone number that I got. I need you. You complete me."

Kirin finally surrendered a chuckle and said, "I do miss your melodramatics."

Angelo jumped to his feet and hugged Kirin tightly. "You do miss me! I knew it."

"You know I do," Kirin gasped as Angelo's hug smothered her.

"Take me back. Please take me back. I'm begging you."

"Will you quit it, Angelo? I didn't fire you."

"I know, but I need to see you daily."

"Why? Is there something pressing?"

Angelo snapped his fingers and pointed at Kirin's nose. "Is there something pressing? The most popular fighter in the world—actually, the most popular *person* in the world—and she's asking if there's something pressing. I didn't know you did comedy, Kirin."

Gwen rolled by the two and said, "Looks like we're going to have company for breakfast."

"Gwen, let me make it," Angelo offered sweetly. Then he ruined the gesture by adding, "Besides, you can't cook."

"Hey!" Gwen gave Angelo a look.

"Just saying," Angelo answered, looking to Kirin for confirmation. "Please, Kirin, just for one day? Let me be at your beck and call once again. Just like old times. Please, please, pretty please...."

Kirin shouted, "I have nothing for you to do!"

"Doesn't matter."

The three were still arguing when suddenly the TV turned on. They froze for a second and then turned to it. It was oddly placed in Gwen's dining room, and they watched as it flashed an alert on the screen, capturing everyone's attention. It read, 'UFMF breaking news.' All of them stared at the screen as Kirin ordered, "Show TV alert."

The screen flashed on to show several channels already covering the news. Kirin cringed as she laid eyes on Thorne, who stood in front of reporters, preparing to hold a press conference.

Kirin thought, *This ... should be interesting*, as she cautiously approached the TV.

Thorne waited until all eyes were upon him and the room was fully silent. He was sporting a new suit unlike any he'd worn in the past. It didn't matter whether he was loved or hated, he always commanded full attention. He stared into the camera, gave a quick grin to all, and began to speak.

"Thank you, everyone, for coming here today. As you know, the UFMF has continued to shatter all records and record double-digit growth each year, and I say this with the utmost of confidence, I believe we are going to exceed the experts' predictions ... once again." He paused and gave a small chuckle.

"But, I'm not here today to boast of my accomplishments. Our stock prices are a daily reminder of just how well our company is doing. In addition, I also have no plans to go into detail about this year's further expansion of the UFMF in other countries. Today's focus is something I believe is even bigger."

Kirin and Gwen looked at each other, both wondering what this could all be about. Angelo came from behind and squeezed himself in between them.

Thorne was about to speak, when a voice a shouted from the crowd. "Rumors have been circulating that Justice will not be returning for this season, is this true?"

He kept his composure even with the interruption and gave no hint of annoyance. He smiled and said, "Let me deal with this right away. That rumor is a fact. I've spoken with him directly and his wishes are simple … to enjoy the riches of his winning and take the 2034 season off."

The crowd of reporters gasped, holding the tension for a mere second before erupting. Pushing followed as they jockeyed for position, and soon yelling ensued wanting for more answers. Thorne never wavered from command, as he raised both hands slightly up, allowing his presence to take over the crowd. He waited for it to be completely silent and then spoke. "Let me first request that you please hold all your questions till after I'm done. I'll be more than happy to answer as many as time permits. Also, this press conference is not about Justice, so what I've said is all that will be said." He gave a stern look to all those there. "Today, the UFMF is going to do something that is unprecedented. This historic event required alignment of the stars combined with the hard work and perseverance of many. It's not unusual for the UFMF to promote its stars. We have many who, through the years, have been admired and loved by the fans. However, this will be the first fighter who has risen from the amateur leagues, and we strongly believe she will capture the hearts and minds of all our UFMF fans."

"She?" Kirin muttered in confusion. Both Gwen and Angelo looked at Kirin, unsure what that could mean.

"As an amateur, she is undefeated and has obliterated every single record held by all our previous fighters. Her beauty is unquestionable, and her skill in the ring is unmatched. It was not difficult to make this decision to bring her up to our pro ranks, but the time has come to reveal the future of the UFMF. I'm proud to present to you our newest fighter, who will be joining our family this year in the 2034 season. Here is the incredibly beautiful and talented, but extremely deadly … Ripley Hawkins, aka Whiskey." Thorne waved his hand to the corner, directing all eyes to the main entrance.

Two men pulled the doors open as the UFMF logo split in half, revealing Ripley. She was immediately bathed in camera flashes. All the men in the room gaped, their jaws dropping, while a handful of women began to question their sexual orientation. Ripley looked absolutely stunning, better yet, breathtaking. From head to toe, she was perfection—blonde, with glistening white teeth perfectly aligned, a unique combination of one green eye and one blue, and a body that had all the right curves in every spot imaginable. She was in fact genetic perfection. Ripley Hawkins had finally been introduced to the world, and immediately she was a star.

In Gwen's dining room, the three individuals stared at one another. Together, Gwen and Angelo said, "Holy shit!" while Kirin silently mouthed it. They continued to watch the TV as things began to unfold.

At the press conference, Ripley was taking questions, posing for the cameras like she was a natural. She knew right away when to smile, which camera to focus on, and she was simply stunning at every angle. This was the big time—everything she did mattered. Within the public eye, an image of perfection always had to be maintained. The reporters began feeding her more questions as everyone seemed starved for another hero. From the start, she fielded several questions like a pro, picking and choosing from the crowd of reporters. She was commanding and dictated the pace of the interview.

A reporter overzealously raised his hand and garnered Ripley's attention. He asked, "Over here, Ripley. Quick question?"

Ripley focused her attention solely on him. She replied, "Sure, what is it?" As she waited for the question, she flashed a smile that quickly melted his heart, causing him to pause awkwardly.

"Uh ... oh, uh ... uh, Josh Thompson with TNC News ... Ripley, I was wondering if you could give us a little insight into the nickname, Whiskey?"

"Thanks, Josh. You're so cute for asking. By the way, I love your tie. It totally coordinates with the rest of your suit. First, let me tell you, it has nothing to do with alcohol." She waved at the camera and put on a sad, apologetic face. "Sorry, sponsors, but I believe children should come first, always. So, stay in school, boys and girls, and no drinking till you're twenty-one…. Oh, where was I? Right, the nickname Whiskey was given to me after I had a little accident in my teen years, tripping over a bottle of whiskey that someone left on the street…. Yeah, I wish it was more interesting than that, oh well, clumsy me. But, remember: this wouldn't have happened had someone done their duty for our planet and recycled that bottle."

Kirin looked at Gwen and said, "That's a total lie. She told me she got it from cracking a whiskey bottle over her opponent's head in one of her back-alley fights."

Gwen replied, "What's with this save-the-planet B.S.? In high school, her gas-guzzling car tore a hole through our ozone layer."

Kirin nodded. "She is unbelievable!"

Gwen said, "Get ready for the snow storm! It's coming in thick."

"Over here, Ripley." She pointed to the newsman and waited. "Rumor has it that both you and Kirin Rise went to the same high school. Is that correct?"

Ripley flashed a big smile, blinding everyone with her pearly whites. She then flicked her golden blonde hair as a hush fell on the room. "Kirin Rise," she began to tear up. "Sorry, I hope my makeup doesn't run. Kirin and I were, like, best friends back in high school. We were inseparable…. Did I mention that we even went to the same church together? Anyways, we kinda lost touch with one another … you know, after she became the biggest star on the planet. But, I totally understand with her crazy schedule and all the fans around. I mean, it's just me … a nobody." She made a heart sign and blew a kiss. "Wherever you are, Kirin, I miss and love yah." She followed her display up with a 'call me' hand gesture.

Kirin said, "I think I'm going to throw up."

Gwen added. "I already did."

Angelo snuck up behind Kirin and began rubbing her back. "Do you want me to get a bag?"

"Figuratively speaking."

"Ripley, I have another question!" shouted Dan from *VRAI* magazine. "Kirin Rise hasn't confirmed she's going to join the 2034 season yet. But, in the likelihood she does come back, what are your feelings about fighting her?"

Ripley brushed her hair, and the light bounced off it, giving her a perfect glow. It appeared to snap back to the exact same spot. She replied, "I'm new to all this. And, yes, I would love to win the Dome Championship. I mean, like, who wouldn't, right? But, at the same time, I would be torn if I did have to fight Kirin. She's like a sister to me, and I'd find it extremely difficult to lay a hand on her pretty little head. Let's hope that, if by chance we do end up against each other someday, the fight ends quickly and with minimal damage to either one of us." She turned away as the question seemed to bother her.

Kirin shook her head and laughed. "Now this … this is fake news." For the next five minutes Ripley continued to answer questions and mesmerize the masses. Kirin, Gwen, and Angelo stayed glued to the TV, wondering when this would all end.

#

Thorne stepped in and interrupted the press conference. "Thank you, everyone, for listening to our big announcement. I'm sure you have more questions, but time is limited, and Ripley has an extremely

78

busy schedule. You can go on the UFMF website and find out more information about Ripley Hawkins there. And, in the upcoming weeks, you'll be seeing a lot more of her … I promise."

Thorne extended his hand and guided Ripley off the podium and away from the crowd and reporters. Behind them, the news reporters continued to press for more answers. The two of them walked side by side, wearing glass smiles as they passed through the doors and finally out of sight.

Once behind the doors, they found Linda waiting patiently. Dressed in a rather short business suit, she caught Thorne's attention immediately, but he managed to maintain his focus.

Thorne said, "Well, I think that went rather well."

Linda smiled and said, "We're gathering data already to find out how well she's trending."

Thorne kissed Ripley on the cheek and said, "I've got business to attend to, but I'm leaving you in good hands with Linda."

Ripley whined, "Are you really leaving me?"

Thorne didn't repeat himself and walked away while Ripley sulked and stomped her foot.

Linda addressed Ripley, "Follow me. We have further promotional events scheduled for you today."

Ripley, craving attention, asked, "Did you like the little spin I put on my nickname?"

Linda smiled. "Yes, that was quite clever. Several of the biggest brands of whiskey have now upped their offer so you can be their spokesperson."

"Which one should I pick?"

"No need to worry about that. It'll all be selected for you. Your only concern is where to spend those endorsement credits."

Ripley muttered in frustration, "I can't believe how stupid those questions were— and why the fuck were they all asking me about Kirin Rise?"

Linda rolled her eyes, "As of today, she's still the biggest thing since sliced bread. Your job before the start of the season is to win the hearts of all those fans and dethrone her. By the way, watch your mouth. Even behind closed doors, eyes and ears are always present."

Ripley looked at Linda. "God ... I hate that bitch!" as a vein could be seen bulging form her forehead.

Linda raised her voice. "Language!" She gave a silent glance at Ripley and added. "Remember the truth is nothing more than perception. That's all that matters."

Suddenly both of them stopped in their tracks as a well-dressed young man with glasses, a chiseled chin, and a very stylish suit appeared before them.

Linda said, "This is…."

Ripley blurted, "His name doesn't really matter, he's cu…."

Linda interrupted and said, "As I was saying. His name is Gunther. He will be your personal assistant from now on."

Ripley hungrily asked, "Only one?"

Linda lowered her glasses and looked down her nose at Ripley. "Once you're on top, you can have as many as you want. But, until then, get to work."

Ripley checked him out seductively pressing her body to his suit. She could smell his cologne from a distance but wanted to get closer to the source. She leaned up into him and whispered in his ear, "You'll do."

Gunther pulled away slightly as Ripley held a firm grip on his arm. He cleared his throat and straightened his glasses. "I'm here to serve you, Ms. Hawkins."

Ripley smiled devilishly and said, "That's your job."

They made their way to Ripley's dressing room, where Linda stopped before the door, "You have forty-five minutes till our next promotion. I'll be waiting for you in the limo. Gunther, make sure she's on time and ready." Linda spun on her heels, leaving Ripley with her assistant.

Gunther opened the door for Ripley, who said, "Thank you," and walked in.

He smiled at her and said, "Is there anything you need right now?"

Ripley grabbed him by the tie and pulled him in. "Come in. I'm in need of your assistance." Gunther did as she said as the door slammed shut.

#

That night, Kirin was in her room as everything finally settled down. The UFMF news had been blasting on every screen all day, and there was no escaping it. Hundreds of sites had already popped up with fans worshipping Ripley and asking her to marry them. The UFMF showed the power of marketing, demonstrating how, when done right, one could turn into an instant celebrity. All this didn't matter to Kirin, who was still focused on her own comeback. Kirin had always felt that her stardom was forced upon her, and she had never cared about the perks that so many people desired. She knew everything came with a cost—and that was one thing she could do without.

At midnight, Kirin lay down on her bed. She was alone; once again, Bacon chose to stay with Gwen. Her eyes began to grow heavy as it had been a while since she had gotten a good night's sleep. Suddenly, her phone vibrated from a distance. Normally, she would ignore it, but something pressed inside her to check. As she held the phone in her hands and looked at the words, Kirin lost control. Overcome with emotion as she read the text, Kirin dropped her phone and began to cry.

Since she had gone against the wishes of her tormentors several months ago, the harassment had stopped. It had been difficult, knowing that her decision to fight last year had jeopardized her biological parents' lives. Kirin never followed up if it was true or not. Now, out of the blue, her torment returned, with a picture of them and another warning about the upcoming season. Kirin began to sob and felt lost.

She thought, *Sifu, I need you.*

"It is impossible to escape an unresolved past." — *Watanabe*

Section 1 Short Stories #2—Kirin's P.O.V.

<u>Fork in the Road—Day 28</u>

The weather outside matched my mood. It was an unusual heavy rain day smack dab in the middle of summer. I stared outside my window for a bit, watching the raindrops and listening to them pelting our roof. The rain showed no sign of stopping, but the sound was monotonous, which quieted my mind for the time being. I was too lazy to check the weather report, only a swipe away on my phone. Instead, I chucked my phone onto my bed and headed back to my desk.

On top of my desk was a list of all the things I had to do to get ready for college. It seemed like the right thing to do, or possibly the safest bet, but Sage's words from graduation continued to haunt me. I asked myself over and over again if that was what I really wanted. And instead of hearing a resounding 'yes' from my inner voice, I only heard crickets chirping. I kept my uncertainty to myself.

I sat by my desk, twirling my pen as I continued to stare at my list until it eventually faded out into nothingness. That feeling of doubt and uncertainty seemed to be following me, and I really wished Sifu were around, now more than ever. I was searching for something, an answer, a sign. Honestly, divine intervention would have been welcomed. I was about to grab my phone and call my friends, but I knew that was just a distraction and the easiest path to escape reality. So, I jumped on my bed and asked for the TV to be turned on.

The TV flashed on as I began scanning through different channels. Thousands to pick from, but none captured my attention—a case of too much being a bad thing.

"Find me something interesting," I commanded, as the TV began to search for specific news channels.

After several quick scans and the usual results of weather,

politics, and Korean dramas, I saw something that caught my eye.

"TV stop," my stare intensified.

There was a group of people protesting, which I found unusual. Since I could recall, protesting had been illegal in the States. It was punishable with jail time, yet here these people were, doing something they knew held strict consequences.

At first, I wondered why. With so little to gain and so much to lose, these twenty individuals were risking everything. Even with the cameras rolling, capturing everything that was happening, the Strategic Tactical Defense—otherwise known as the STDs—and the police were manhandling these protestors. Still, they stood their ground, strong and fast in their own conviction. They were our everyday neighbors, men and women of varying ages, convinced that what they believed in was stronger than any law. I saw that the protestors were bound together to make hauling them away a more difficult task. But, they were the few versus the many, and the officers took their time spraying them with pepper spray and dragging them off.

The camera zoomed in on one of the protestors, who had tears flowing down her cheeks. As she was being dragged into the squad car, a reporter ran up and asked her, "Why are you doing this?"

With one eye cracked open, she tried to speak into the camera, but she struggled to get her breath, and her voice was haggard. "When good people do nothing, they allow evil to create laws to justify their means. This is something that cannot be changed by votes. It requires the greatest sacrifice. Action must be taken, regardless of the cos—" her speech fell short, as one of the officers grabbed a stunner and zapped her on the leg, leaving her unconscious.

I covered my mouth in shock. Her words rang in my head, but even worse was the image of her face, which was now ingrained in my memory. But, this seemed raw, too familiar. My history had somehow found its way back to me. I stood up and tried to figure out exactly what had happened.

I asked myself, *Where are we living? How can people watch this and justify what's happening?*

Now flashes of injustices from my past entered my head. I closed my eyes, hoping to block out any of my nightmares. But, no matter what I did, I couldn't unsee the horror. Suddenly, the screen changed as a commercial came up. I turned away, distraught by what I saw, and shook my head. Then I heard the ad. The timing of the UFMF commercial was too perfect. As much as I hated them, I had to see what they were trying to sell, so I turned back and increased the volume.

"Do you want to be the next UFMF superstar? It's possible! Start young, and train early. Learn to fight like Dryden Rodriguez, the three-time UFMF champion. Find your local UFMF training facilities that are just around the corner. And, if there isn't one next to you, don't worry: more facilities will be opening up soon." I began clenching my fist and gritting my teeth as the perfect storm was brewing inside me. My blood was boiling. Since the TV knew my location, they flashed a sign of the latest UFMF school opening up. When my eyes locked on the location, pain shot through my body. It was where Sifu's school used to be, but now redesigned with a UFMF logo.

Angered and frustrated, I launched a punch right at the TV but stopped just an inch away. I was breathing heavily, and my fist shook in frustration. I turned and ran to my table, where I threw all my college stuff on the ground.

"Screw this!" I said. "Screw it all. What's this going to do? Absolutely nothing."

I stared at my college information that was now scattered everywhere. On top was a pamphlet that proclaimed, 'Be the Future.'

It spoke to me, as those three words continued to echo. I thought, *There is no future if I go this route.* My path wasn't quite clear yet, but I knew for sure what I didn't want to do.

I repeated the protestor's words aloud, "Action must be taken regardless of the cost."

Jaw Drop—Day 36

Across the dining table where we were having lunch, I looked at my two best friends. They both looked stunned. Sage, who was sitting to my left, looked as if he had seen a ghost. His eyes were bulging behind his slightly tilted glasses. Gwen's mouth was open, grossly dribbling food, as she gaped at me in disbelief. Had I moved quicker, this would've been a perfect picture to snap.

I had said my peace and was waiting for some feedback, but their facial reactions spoke volumes, more than words ever could.

If this is the reaction from my friends, then this is not good. I thought to myself.

Sage finally snapped out of his trance and broke the silence. He straightened his glasses and looked more stressed about my decision than I was. He blurted out, "Are you fricking crazy!" He extended both hands, shaking them at me with disdain.

Gwen swallowed the rest of her meal and followed up with, "You've gone off the deep end, Kirin. If the earth was flat, you just walked off it."

"The earth is flat?" I asked.

"Of course not, but that's exactly what it sounded like when you told us you're not going to school." Her voice raised at the tail end.

I sat quietly, pondering my decision. It wasn't about not going

86

to school, but how I told my friends. Both of them were muttering so quickly at me that I had no idea what exactly they were saying. The only thing I was confident about was that they were not happy with my decision.

I finally waved them down and tried to control the situation. "Okay, everyone, calm down. Let's all calm down. One at a time. It does no good when I can't understand a word either of you are saying ... 'cause neither one of you are making any sense." I paused and realized that, in the history of the world, at no point had saying 'calm down' to anyone ever worked.

Sage looked to Gwen and said, "Is it okay if I go first?" She gestured that it was fine, and he immediately began to speak. "We're not making any sense? Mmm, let me repeat ... are you fricking crazy? You've got a full scholarship at one of the finest universities in the country, and you're going to throw it all away? Full! Need I remind you? Not partial, but full!"

"May I?" Gwen asked Sage before cutting in. He nodded, and she spoke. "Not only do I agree with Sage, but there's no way your parents are going to be okay with this. I mean, without me doing the numbers, isn't a full scholarship to Stanford about 200K a year?" Gwen paused before leaning forward, narrowing her eyes at me. I pulled back slightly before realizing she had no telepathic power.

"Wait a minute, Kirin Rise. I know you too well. Oh my god ... I know why you told us! It's because you haven't told them yet ... have you?" She attempted to stand up and realized it was impossible. She hit the side of Sage's arm and said, "Stand up for me and point at her." Sage looked confused and then pieced it together and stood.

"Sit down, Sage," I said, and he obeyed.

"Wait, is this a two-part question?" I turned my attention back to Gwen, who was peering at me with judging eyes. Her silence forced me to spill the beans. "Yes, you are correct. I haven't told my parents.

I figured I'd use you guys first as a barometer and see how you reacted."

"Let me simplify this for you," Gwen cut in. "Imagine our reaction and multiply that by a million, but with more shouting and the parent phrase 'what are you thinking' being repeated."

I couldn't argue with Gwen because I was just postponing the inevitable. No matter what fancy words I used, there was no way I could sugarcoat my decision not to attend college. I faced Sage, who looked like he was still waiting for my response. I said, "First, I don't think I'm necessarily throwing it away. But, at the same time, this is partially your fault. Your speech at graduation inspired me. You said to go beyond great and not take the easy path."

Sage was taken aback by my comment and leaned away. "Wait … what?"

"You heard me. You said, 'Don't be comfortable…. Don't go the safe route.' So, I took that to heart, and I'm gonna follow your advice."

Sage shook his head. "I wasn't referring to you. I was talking about the other schmucks with no future. You've got a full scholarship worth thousands, and you're going to do … uh … what exactly are you planning on doing?"

Both Sage and Gwen leaned in, waiting for some answer that might justify my action. I thought about it and replied, "Well, to be honest … I'm not quite sure. I know deep down I don't want to go the traditional route. All through senior year, something was bothering me, but I couldn't quite put my finger on it. Then the universe, in its own strange way, found a way to talk to me. All I had to do was listen. On a side note, I've been making good credits with my photography, and that might be something I want to pursue further."

Gwen scoffed at my comment and said, "As brilliant as you are, my BFF, you honestly think this argument you're giving us"—she pointed to her and Sage— "has any chance at all of flying with your parents?" She rolled her eyes. "There's a better chance they find a way for me to walk again or seeing pigs fly."

Confused, I asked, "Pigs fly?"

Sage took his glasses off and began to wipe them. "Honestly, Kirin, I don't think you fully thought this through. Petty credits from photography isn't a sustainable business plan, especially in this economy. Besides, I'm not quite sure how exactly that's supposed to change the world to be a better place."

I took a bite out of my meal and didn't say a word, keeping them waiting. "I don't have all the answers, like I said, but I do have to disagree." I reached into my pocket and got my phone. I then forwarded several pictures to both of them. "Take a look at these pictures I sent you."

Sage and Gwen began scanning through the pictures on their phones. I could see from their reaction that they had an impact on them.

"You see, throughout history, these are famous photographs that were taken. I can't disregard these images as simply that. It was something I saw on TV that started this landslide. You see, you were right, Sage. Whether through actions, words, or even an image, one single thing can inspire someone to take action." I closed my eyes for a second and cringed as I saw that protestor's face again.

For the first time, I had Gwen and Sage thinking instead of judging me.

"So, right now, I'm pretty much going with the flow of things. But, if there's one thing I'm positive about, I'm not going to college just like everyone else."

Sage parroted me, "So, you're gonna go with the flow?" The sound of his voice lacked conviction.

"I figure I'm moving in a direction, and eventually, I'll figure things out. But, I know I'm not going to make the world a better place just by hitting the books."

Gwen sighed, "I've known you long enough to know that, once a thought enters that itty-bitty skull of yours, there's nothing anyone can say or do to change your mind."

Sage glanced at Gwen, and paused, "I agree with Gwen. Besides, there's nothing else you can possibly say that'll shock us after this."

I looked at both of them as they took a breather from judging me and began drinking their water. The timing was too perfect, "By the way … I'm also moving out."

Firing Squad—Day 38

It was early Sunday evening. Two days after telling Sage and Gwen about my plans, I was about to tell my parents. The initial goal was to tell them right after church, figuring God's good grace would protect me. But, I found reasons to stall and chickened out. Another opportunity presented itself right after lunch, but it's funny how easily we can find excuses to justify not doing something. So, here I was at the tail end of the day, sitting at the dinner table with the entire family. In my head, I had pictured over and over again exactly how everything was going to unfold, including my clever, witty responses to make my argument for not going to college as well as moving out.

I figured I'd let the conversation come out naturally, and when the time was right, I'd know exactly when to close the gap and lay it on them.

My mom had prepared an incredible meal with no help from me because of my own distractions. I always admired how she balanced

90

things. Even with her crazy work schedule, she still managed to be mom and always appeared to do everything so perfectly. She was a rare gem. I admired her; achieving that balance must be more difficult than decoding Wing Chun.

"Kirin … Kirin, can you pass me the *tteok-bokki*?"

Dad broke my focus as he asked me to pass some food. It was a Korean dish that my mom had learned, and she made it as good as it gets. The color was vibrant, and the heat could be felt from a distance.

He was at the other end of the table, so I handed it first to Kyle, who began to pass it along to my dad. I wasn't sure what got into me or why I justified that as the perfect time, but I blurted out. "I'm not going to college … and I plan on moving out."

Kyle froze and suddenly dropped the bowl from his hands. My words played second to my dad, who reacted to the spill that was about to happen. For me, everything moved in slow motion, and I caught the bowl of *tteok-bokki* before it spilled.

I held it in my hand and said, "Ta-da!" as I let out a small giggle.

Now all eyes were focused entirely on me. I smiled, hoping my charm would neutralize some of the tension, and began walking over to my dad to make sure he got what he originally had asked for. I looked at Butterscotch and Bacon, who were oddly quiet. Strangely, both of them moved under the table and out of sight. I thought, *Cowards*.

I looked at Kyle, whose mouth was hanging open, and whispered, "Close your mouth."

Still not a word was spoken, so I began scooping some of the *tteok-bokki* and placing it on Dad's dish. He whispered thanks, but otherwise the silence became deafening. I returned to my seat but decided to stand up and at least state my case. I placed the food down and began to speak. "Uh, not sure if you heard, but I've decided not to go to college, and I'm also planning to move out." I slowly turned to my mom to see her reaction.

Steven and Mark were somewhat ducked in a position to avoid any flying objects. Kyle finally recovered from the shock and put more food on his plate. He stopped when Mom gave him a stare. Dad was stone-faced with sweat forming on his forehead.

Mom grabbed her glass of water and drank it. She made us wait, making me suffer a little inside, before she finally spoke. "Hmm, I had a feeling something like this would happen. You were acting strange the last several weeks. So, I've had some time to prepare for this and not be totally in shock."

"Mom, you knew?" I asked, surprised.

Mom said, "I'm not mad. I'm sure you've given this a lot of thought, but I want to make it clear. Your decision is your decision. You stand by it and are prepared to live with it. Are we clear on that?"

Mark threw his napkin on the side, almost like a penalty flag. He said, "What gives? You give her the hall pass and the benefit of the doubt?"

My mom looked at Mark without uttering a word. He reached for his napkin, folded it back to its original shape and cowered in his seat. Next to Mark, Steven was locked in place, staring straight ahead and avoiding all eye contact. He was, for that very moment, a chair.

I was stunned, but I needed to contain my excitement and not press my luck. No scenario I had played out in my head had included this as a possible outcome. I stood there silent, not sure what to say. I turned to my dad, who was always my support, and asked, "Dad?"

Dad said, "You heard your mom. We've talked about it, and we're in agreement. You've always had a wandering soul, something we don't believe we should limit or contain. Part of being an adult is owning up to your decision. But, I speak for your mom as well as myself. The beginning of every month, the first Sunday, we as a family will always gather together and have dinner. Are we clear on that?" He stared at me first and then got confirmation from my mom.

I smiled and said, "I promise I will never miss it."

Kyle looked at everyone and then said, "So, can we eat now? I'm starving."

"We fail to understand the power of our mind. It is the creator of our reality for either good or bad." — Sifu

Section 2 Sifu's Journey Entry #2—Empty Bowl

Middle of February

Several weeks had passed, and word about Sifu's ramen had spread like wildfire. The lines formed earlier, and the numbers became greater with each passing day. From a single customer who had ventured into the store by apparent random luck, the restaurant quickly amassed a slew of regulars who worshiped the ramen along with the chefs who created it.

Regulars began to become familiar faces to both Sifu and Lance as well as to each other. As the crowd grew, they began bragging about the number of times they had been there. Somehow, even during these difficult economic times, Sifu had created the ultimate business model: a no-name non-restaurant, with no form of payment required, and a limited amount of soup creating a huge demand. It had become the biggest thing. No one could have predicted that such a formula could even exist, let alone work, but somehow the Gung Fu master had found a way to do what no one thought was possible. Since it was not a restaurant, there were no reviews about Sifu's place. Old-fashioned word of mouth demonstrated its power against the might of technology and social media.

The mystery behind Sifu continued to grow as customers came for the food but stayed for Sifu. Rumor also began to spread that the soup was created out of Sifu's love for his wife. As people continued to dig to find out, Sifu remained tight-lipped about the truth. Even so, Sifu was more social than he had ever been in the past, which was somewhat strange since his goal was never about promoting the soup. To Sifu, it was so much more than a token of a warm belly. He treasured the happiness everyone got from enjoying the meal. However, that sensation soon became stagnant, and the unrest he thought he had cured resurfaced.

It was early in the morning when the last customer finished his soup and said his goodbye. Lance closed the doors, stretched, and took a moment to enjoy another successful but busy night. From the counter, he glanced at the donation box, which was overflowing. Lance decided that would be dealt with last. He turned and found, to his surprise, that Sifu was not cleaning up, but was removing his apron and making his way toward him. He was about to ask a question, but Sifu beat him to the punch.

Sifu said, "Lance, why don't we call it a night and just show up a bit earlier to clean up and prep?"

Lance replied, "What about the donations? You sure you don't want me to count it and put it away?"

Sifu said, "It'll be here when we get back…."

Lance could feel the change in Sifu but had said nothing during the last several weeks. Something about Sifu was off, and the fact that he could sense it meant things were really off. Their relationship—friends but also student and teacher—made asking Sifu personal questions somewhat difficult. Lance wanted to help him but decided to do it passively.

Lance offered, "Why don't I stay for a pinch and just finish the dishes? It'll only take a few minutes."

Sifu didn't even bother looking at the sink. "It's not important. Besides, we could both use a break…. We've been working straight ever since the opening."

Lance knew something was up because Sifu, of all people, never needed a break from anything. He decided to dig a bit more. "Okay, let's cut out early. You want to grab something to eat or hang at my place?"

"Not tonight, Lance." Sifu began leading them both to the door. Sifu was not going to budge. Whatever it was that he intended to do, there was no changing it.

As Lance opened the door, he made a last desperate attempt. "Last chance, Sifu. You'll close up?" A simple wave was all that Sifu mustered up, as Lance followed up with a good night. Looking dejected, he walked out with unanswered questions.

Sifu stood there looking around. This was his world that he had created. He took a breath and grabbed one of the bowls that lay next to the table. There was definitely a ton of cleaning that needed to be done, but that was the least of his concerns. He grabbed the bowl and looked inside. Not a hint of broth remained. He stared directly into the center and got lost in his own thoughts.

#

"Bing…? Bing!" said Megumi as she waved her hands in front of Sifu's face, trying to garner his attention.

Sifu looked up, still dazed, as he held an empty bowl in his hand. He shuffled back and forth, trying to clear the vision in his head. Suddenly, as his name was called again, he recognized the voice along with the face that went with it. His eyes took several seconds to focus, and he immediately smiled once his vision was clear. His wife's soft features warmed him as her hair lay on one side. She continued to speak, but the words coming out of her mouth fell on deaf ears.

"Bing … Hana asked you a question," said Megumi.

"So, Daddy, can you take me to the zoo and chaperone me and my classmates? It was really easy to convince everyone because my class knows you're a Gung Fu teacher. So, I said you would do it already, but you still need to confirm with my teacher."

Again, Sifu didn't respond as he looked at his daughter's tender eyes and smiled. The moment, as trivial as it seemed, was precious to Sifu. She had the same eyes as her mother, but Hana wasn't her cheerful self. She looked to be impatiently waiting for a response, but Sifu was not quite sure what she needed. To his right, both the boys were busy eating and arguing. Even their bickering didn't bother him, but the words escaped him as their argument was lost in the air.

Megumi said, "Bing, will you please get the boys to eat?" She pointed in their direction.

Sifu simply nodded as the words came with no sound and thus had no meaning. It was his family, and the warm feeling surrounded him even if it wasn't peaceful. Hana began to reach out to Sifu to get his attention, but as she extended her arm, she was pulled further away. He got up from his table and extended his arm for hers, but she was too far. Her image began to fade away as he panicked, wondering how he could stop it. He switched his attention to the twins, and they began to blur and drift further away from his touch. He watched in horror but could do nothing as his feet felt locked in place.

Finally, his last hold was for Megumi, who no longer spoke a word but sat silently in the chair as she began to slowly disappear. There was a hint of sadness on her face that made Sifu clench his entire body. He tried lifting his foot, but it was planted firmly to the ground. His one hand continued to stretch toward her, but still she was out of his reach. He looked to his other hand, and the same bowl was glued to it. He tried to move, but he was held hostage by his own stance. All he had was a bowl, which he tried to shake from his hand, but it was locked firmly onto his skin. He wondered why he couldn't get rid of it. As he stared into the center of the bowl, his eyes blurred, his mouth clenched, and his entire body was petrified.

Sifu closed his eyes and blinked himself back to reality. He was staring at the empty bowl in his hand. He looked around and realized he had only been dreaming. He squeezed the bowl in his hand with all his might. Frustration built up, anger won out, and Sifu flung the bowl to the wall, where it shattered into pieces.

He fell to his knees and hung his head in disgust. Reality once again echoed the truth. He kneeled on the ground, the silence was a reminder that he was forever alone. There was no bringing them back, no matter what he did. The peace he had hoped to bring from his wife's recipe did not return.

CHAPTER 3
A Better World

February 1, 2034

Through the glass panel of the high-rise office building, New York Harbor casted a reflection that was worthy of a picture. Watanabe gazed outside as the elements of both the sun and the winter cold blended in harmony. He admired the view and allowed the silence to dominate the moment. The UFMF building was a beacon, the symbol of New York, if not the entire United States. It stood the tallest and most dominant amongst all those in the city. He turned just before the morning sun hit his face and then took several steps back toward a desk. There on top was a weathered old map of the entire world laid flat with colored pieces scattered in an organized manner. He smiled as he looked down and noticed that the yellow color was covering the majority of the map. His plan was coming to fruition. For the first time, he could feel the possibility of achieving something that had never been done before. It felt tangible, within his grasp.

So close, he thought as he clenched his fist tightly, his joints cracking. "Is it possible? I could be the first to win this," he muttered quietly.

He took a breath to make sure he didn't get ahead of himself. Next to the board, lying dead in the center, was a thin computerized screen. Watanabe's focus was on it as it flashed 12:00 pm, right on the dime. A few seconds later, the screen turned black as a series of instructions began to scroll down. He did as the screen had instructed and covered another territory with his yellow pieces. This was an odd combination of new age technology blended with old school props. Seconds later, an instruction gave out a warning to no longer touch the board. A light beam scanned the entire map as a picture was taken and sent to those participating. Watanabe took one last look and began walking to his main desk, which stood at the far end of the office.

He thought for a moment and felt he had given ample time for his request. "Kristen, will you please come here?"

Within seconds, Kristen responded, "I'm just finishing up something, sir. I'll be there in five minutes. Is that okay?"

Watanabe cleared his throat and didn't answer. His silence gave a definitive, "no" to her question as Kristen was always attuned to his demands. "My apologies, sir. I'm headed there right now."

Watanabe sat on the fine leather chair that engulfed his body. It creaked slightly as his weight settled fully on it. He touched the edge of his desk with his index finger and felt a slight imperfection in the wood. Over to his right lay the clear container with all the years that he had invested. He stared at the clear crystal balls housed inside, as the background behind it began to lose focus. He waited patiently, and a knock soon echoed from behind the doors.

"Come in, please." His polite voice echoed through the room. Even as the boss, Watanabe paid attention to manners. Ingrained from both birth and culture, he always believed manners were key to much of his success.

The doors slid open from opposite sides, and Kristen scurried through them while maintaining a ladylike manner. One foot stepped in front of the other, perfectly in line, as she rushed toward Watanabe. Her glasses were slightly askew, and her hair was not perfect, probably due to the distance she had to cover to keep her word to Watanabe. Even from afar, Watanabe noticed everything. However, he realized it was not easy for anyone to run with heels that high off the ground and chose to say nothing.

"Thank you for coming, Kristen."

"Sorry for keeping you waiting, sir." Kristen fidgeted as she dealt with her slight imperfections. She was well aware of them as Watanabe's judging eye saw all.

"No need to apologize. In fact, it's my fault for losing my patience. You did say you need twenty-four hours to gather all the info, and here I am not giving you the allotted time. I am sorry for taking you away from your work, but I wondered about the result of Thorne's press conference and the rest of Whiskey's engagement for that day."

"My apologies once again, sir. That was what I was working on. I have about 95% of the information you need completed."

"That's fine; just give me what you have. I'm quite curious."

Kristen began keying entries on her pad, and information started popping up on Watanabe's screen.

"Don't worry about all of the nuts and bolts, sir. I'll give you a rundown of everything that we've gathered."

"That's fine." Watanabe sat back and listened as Kristen briefly explained the details.

_"Sir?'

Watanabe looked at her and waited.

"You're close, sir."

Kristen caught a hint of a smirk from Watanabe. He commented, "You have such a good eye. I'm not quite sure how you were able to capture the sight of the board as you crossed the room, given the angle."

"I couldn't help it, sir."

"No, no. It's quite impressive. You've always been most impressive, Kristen."

Kristen smiled and took the compliment well. She repeated, "You're really close."

"I know." Watanabe stood up and pushed himself away from the desk. He continued to speak with his back turned toward Kristen. "It's times like this, that moment when you have to recognize that it's up to you to take … what's that expression, Kristen?" He turned slightly, looking for some help.

"The bull by the horn, sir?"

He chuckled and said, "Ah, yes, the burr … burl by the horn." Watanabe turned toward Kristen and then held his tongue. The double LLs were always a struggle for him to pronounce, even with years of practice. He took a deep breath and focused before finally saying, "The *bull* by the horn."

"Sir?"

"Do you think I'm being selfish?" as the tone of his voice had a hint of humility. However, he didn't give Kristen any time to respond as he spoke in Japanese, "*Ippai-me wa hito sake o nomi, nihai-me wa sake sake o nomi, sanbai-me wa sake hito o nomu.*" He looked at Kristen and asked her to translate it.

"I believe the translation is 'with the first glass a man drinks wine, with the second glass the wine drinks the wine, with the third glass the wine drinks the man.' My apologies, sir, I've always found the literal translation from Japanese to English somewhat difficult."

"No, it's correct. Do you know what that means?"

"I've always felt that proverbs could be interpreted in many different ways, all depending on the individual's point of view. However, for me, I take it to mean that, at some point, you'll be consumed by what you desire."

"Well, you and I are in agreement. My concern is exactly that, and once again you do not fail to impress me."

Kristen found the opening to give her thoughts and said, "I can honestly tell you, sir. I don't believe you are."

"What?"

"You asked me earlier if I thought you were being selfish."

"That's right," Watanabe murmured as he found himself lost in thought. A few seconds passed before he finally spoke again. "The inch of self-doubt that most people find within themselves when making a decision … it doesn't exist in me at all. So, I'm asking you, just in case I am too blind to see it from any other perspective. Could I be consumed by my own intoxication?"

"Sir, we're in an age of technological advancement, where every day new ground is broken in things that we imagined sixty years ago in books and stories. TV revolutionized the world, and then eventually the internet leap-frogged us to the next level, and now robots and AI. Yet, look around…." Kristen turned, "TV on."

Several projections popped up before their eyes, surrounding them as the windows converged to form a fully immersive view. The screens were filled with the struggles of man. Scenes of poverty, war, and riots dominated the news.

"You see that, sir? That is the same problem we've been facing since the beginning of time." Kristen's voice changed as she got emotional. "What you're planning on doing … with every bone in my soul, I believe in what you are doing. We can't begin to make the changes necessary for a better future when we continue to deal with the same societal woes that have existed throughout time."

"So, you can picture it as well, a world finally rid of the bickering and fighting, where control and order finally reign over the masses—all for the greater good."

"Yes. Yes, indeed. And you'll be remembered as the man who revolutionized the way people think and act."

"That's the thing, Kristen. I don't want the notoriety. No matter what I achieve, it all came at a cost." He paused and thought, *A debt I will live with forever.*

Kristen looked down and couldn't bear to look Watanabe in the eyes. She dared not mention his son's name at this moment.

"But, that's the price. The price I was willing to sacrifice, losing my son."

"You never know. You can't think like that, sir. We're making breakthroughs all the time. Maybe there's hope … or a way we can restore him to what he used to be."

"That time has long come and gone. I've had to let him go in order to proceed further. Otherwise, we would never have progressed to this stage."

Kristen knew not to push Watanabe any further as she decided to bring something up to change his focus.

"Sir, we have one issue that's still unresolved."

On the screen, a replay of the Dome fight last year popped up. Watanabe walked up to it and said, "Perfect timing." He cleared his throat and asked, "So, what has our little star Kirin Rise been up to?"

Kristen began to pace, "She's been in hiding. We know that she's been staying at her friend's house, but unfortunately that's all we've gathered."

"Have we attempted to contact her?"

"Yes, but you know how she is … and she's been a total recluse since the fight."

"I'm assuming that we'll figure a way around this?"

"We will, sir, but I'm wondering if our plans have changed since she defied our last attempts."

Watanabe's voice carried a sinister tone. "The plan is still the same, but we have to burn her and her followers once and for all. That means, in order for our plan to work, she can't be part of the UFMF once this season starts. In fact, we can use her to our advantage and let her followers attach to their new queen."

"You believe strongly in Ripley?"

"I believe in the power of suggestion. If we craft this story perfectly, this will give Kirin Rise a beautiful finale."

"How should we do it, sir?"

"It's all about the timing. We need to use her demise, along with the opening of the UFMF season. It appears, in the end, her loss is really our gain." Watanabe looked at Kristen with a fire in his eyes, "I'll leave you in charge of her fate."

Kristen's body tightened as excitement filled her. She struggled to keep her cool as she looked on her pad, which had one last note. "Last thing, sir … it's Thorne."

"What about him?"

"He's been pressing me, more and more, about what's happening."

"Thorne need not know about these plans. For now, continue to keep him out of the loop. I'll give him other projects to keep him occupied."

"May I ask why, sir?"

"The fewer people who know about our overall plan, the better. Thorne has always been loyal to me, but his ambition for more makes him dangerous."

Kristen toed the floor, watching her pointed shoe twist back and forth. She forced it out, "Sir, I apologize for stepping out of line, but I think it's dangerous that we keep him out of the loop … I, uh."

"I'm aware, Kristen…. Thank you for sharing your concerns."

Kristen pulled back, "I understand."

Having seen enough, Watanabe pulled away from his pad and glanced around the office. When he felt a presence nearby, he said, "Why don't you finish up your work for now, Kristen? We can speak later." Taking the subtle hint, Kristen gathered her things and walked out of his office.

Watanabe waited until the doors slid closed. "Lock the doors." After he heard the automated locks sealing, he once again, walked toward the table with the map and barked out another command, "Light setting, number twenty." The room began to darken, and the windows tinted, not allowing a single beam of light to enter as silence creeped over the room.

Watanabe said, "Authorization code, *ni, ichi, nana, yon, san, san, hachi, ni, hachi, ichi*." He waited for a second and got confirmation from the computer. He added, "Security check alpha fourteen." The computers began a security scan of his office, as a solid green laser encompassing the entire room moved from one end to the other.

107

After a minute, the computer stated, "Security check confirmed."

Except for the monitor that shed light onto the map, Watanabe's office was bathed in darkness. He stood with his eyes closed, focusing on his breathing and allowing his thoughts to go empty. Suddenly, in the silence a shadow materialized several feet away. Its outline was of a man dressed in dark clothes, with only a hint of his eyes shining, revealing him.

Aware of his presence, Watanabe opened his eyes. "Do you have news?"

The shadow spoke in a low and toneless voice. "Yes, master."

Watanabe continued to admire his board. "The time has come. Our wait has been long and difficult. Our silence will finally be over. From the depths of the shadows, we shall rise once again. For seventy-five years since the death of our creator, we were sworn by blood to stay in the shadows. By coincidence or possibly fate, on the same day that the UFMF will begin its season, our vow of secrecy will finally end."

The shadow approached Watanabe and kneeled. Watanabe turned around to the barely visible image. The shadow reached from behind his dark uniform and gently placed a clear bag on the floor. The bag was streaked with blood from a severed hand, and a ring decorated with a cross and still attached to the finger reflected dully. Next to it still intact was a piece of flesh with a misspelled tattoo.

Watanabe asked, "I gather everything went as planned?"

"It did, my master. The message was sent and the information we needed was extracted."

Watanabe nodded, "Well done. I expect nothing less." He turned around again, "Tell the men to continue their training and that our time is near."

"Yes, my master." The shadow paused briefly, "What of the girl, Kristen?"

"She is unaware of our real plans. For now, we continue with the ploy to try to win control of the council through our regular play, but I'm well aware the others have their own plan to prevent me from winning."

"Master, when the time presents itself, we are well prepared to eliminate future competition."

"I know you are, but for now, remain in the shadows and keep eyes on all."

"Yes, my master." Slowly, the shadow figured disappeared into the background. No sound could be heard; no figure could be seen as the lights began to brighten and the windows turned clear. The room was empty except for Watanabe.

"One's self-interest is best handled by the individual himself because the rarest commodity is finding someone who puts yours above theirs." — Watanabe

Section 1 Short Stories #3—Kirin's P.O.V.

Adulting—Day 77

I was doing my best to guide my brothers, who were kind enough to help. In this rare instance, muscle was needed over structure. Jim was home for the weekend, but instead of hanging with his friends, he was lifting a futon with Dad.

Kyle, my youngest brother, seemed like he was helping the least. I saw him hold a single bag while everyone else was struggling with my move, I yelled at him, "How come you aren't helping Dad?"

He looked back at me. "How come you aren't helping Dad?"

I showed off the amount of stuff in both my hands as well as my backpack. It was quite obvious why, and even Bacon who stood next to me was carrying a bag in his mouth. I gave Kyle a look, and he had the nerve to return the same look.

Steven and Mark slid the sofa to the far end of my loft. Then both of them picked a side and plopped down on it.

Mark let out a sigh of exhaustion, "Honestly, Kirin, how exactly did you accumulate all this shit?"

I looked at Mark as I dropped all my stuff with a resounding thud. "It's not that much, considering I've only been in the States for, uh, ten years…. Has it been ten years?"

Steven wiped the sweat from his forehead. "I'm with Mark. Where did all this crap come from?"

Dad gently set down one end of the futon, "Will you guys stop bitching at your sister? I'm sure you have more crap than she does." He stood up, struggling to straighten himself. "This time, your mom lucked out. I should've been on call today."

110

"Dad!"

He smiled, "Sorry, sweetie. I'm blaming your mom. It was her idea to take the couch."

"I was fine keeping things to a minimum, but Mom insisted on giving it to me. I didn't *ask* for it."

Jim chuckled. "I know what that means. Mom's gonna upgrade the entire living room at home, Dad."

"Live and learn, boys. What Mom wants, she gets. You have to pick and choose your battles."

"Dad?!" I exclaimed, laughing. He winked at me.

Jim added, "But, in the end, doesn't Mom win the war?"

Dad looked at Jim and pondered that statement. "Jim, you're grounded."

Jim chuckled and rolled his eyes, giving me a little shove, but to his surprise my stance held, and he bounced off.

Jim frowned in confusion. "You working out more, Kirin?"

"Nah, you're working out less." I gave him a light shove and pretend to lose my balance.

Ignoring us, Kyle began walking around my loft. He always found a way to avoid doing any kind of work.

I called out, "We have some more stuff to move downstairs."

He asked, "How are you paying for all this, Kirin? I mean, Steven and Mark are older than you, and they don't have five credits to their name."

Both of them shouted at Kyle, cussing.

Dad shouted over them, "Language."

Kyle played innocent and raised his arms. "Am I lying?"

They glanced at each other but remained silent.

Dad and Mom never bothered going into the details of the move, so I had never made an active attempt to explain. Dad's curiosity arose from Kyle's inquisition as he said, "Uh, I never really asked, Kirin. How exactly are you paying for this and other living necessities? You know, like food and water."

I was about to answer when Mark cut in, "It's drugs. She's peddling drugs. I know it."

I chuckled and retorted, "It's not drugs … you jerk."

Everyone looked at me and waited for an answer. I pointed to the far corner as to how I was able to pay for everything.

Steven replied, "Uh, are you doing a casting couch?"

I looked at him awkwardly, "A what?!"

Dad stepped in and gave a look we all recognized to Steven. Steven tried to back pedal, "Oh, photography? Uh, yeah … I get it. Wow, never knew photography was such a good business to pay for everything. Makes sense, makes sense."

I asked, "What's a casting—"

Dad interrupted me. "Now that we've got that answered, we still have a ton of stuff to move." He got up from his seat and pointed at Steven, who didn't make eye contact. In fact, he sprang up from where he was seated and appeared to have a second wind.

He said, "I'm ready to move some more stuff," as he clapped his hands and left quickly.

For the next hour, we unloaded the truck until everything was finally set up in my loft. I was exhausted, as were my father and brothers—except for Jim, who seemed like he could lift more if needed.

I asked, "Jim, what gives?"

"Kirin, I usually lug about one-hundred-and-fifty pounds-plus of extra equipment when I'm training. All this moving is light as a feather."

Mark complained, "Explain to me again why we didn't hire movers?"

"To be clear, you," Dad replied as he pointed to Mark, "didn't hire movers because you have no money. I didn't hire them because I have four strong boys who are in their prime and should be able to lift this stuff for free."

Kyle whined, "Dad, let's eat something…. I'm starving."

Dad looked at me, "Kirin, why don't we grab a bite to eat around here?"

"I'd love to, Dad … and thanks for all the help, but I actually have some work to do for tomorrow, and I'm pretty beat."

Dad asked, "You sure?"

"Sorry, I have to adult tomorrow."

Dad waved my brothers together and said, "All right, sweetie. Why don't you get some rest? I'm sure you can figure out where everything else is going. Now remember, if you ever need anything, don't hesitate to ask. Anyway, I have to feed the starving child in the corner." He pointed to Kyle, who was holding his stomach and wincing in pain.

"Thanks again, Dad." I gave him a kiss on the cheek and then hugged each of my brothers and thanked them as well.

As they were exiting my door, Kyle whispered into my ear, "I still think it's drugs."

I chuckled at his comment and punched him in the arm.

"Ow!" He winced in pain.

Thirty minutes passed, and I found myself alone in my own place lying on the couch. Bacon had already found a spot that he deemed his. The sound of his snores was all that kept me company. It all finally sank in: I was by myself. For the first time, all decisions came from me. I basked in the moment briefly, realizing how quickly things had changed for me. Suddenly, I heard the buzz of my doorbell, which interrupted my moment of reflection.

"Who's there?" I called. I got no response and waved it off as a mistake from below. Besides, everything was still new for me here. Instead of being a responsible adult, I found myself back on the couch vegging. I closed my eyes and enjoyed the peace and quiet of my solitude—and then heard a knock on the door.

Knock. Knock. Knock.

I thought, *Well, that was short.* I didn't buzz anyone in but approached the door and asked, "Who is it?"

No one responded as I looked through the peephole and saw no one. I grabbed the handle and cautiously opened the door. As I stuck my head out, the entire gang shouted from the sides, scaring the hell out of me. I found myself falling back as they all came walking into my loft.

"You jerks!"

Doc extended his hand and helped me up. He apologized for everyone as they filed in. "It was their idea to scare you. I was totally against it."

Ken stepped around us and began walking further into my house as I yelled at him. "Hey, Blanco! Asian house … shoes off." He jumped up as if he had seen a mouse and landed in Big T's arms.

Big T laughed, "Can I put you down now?"

Ken nodded but directed Big T to put him by the entrance.

Ryan looked at him, "Damn, Ken. That's a really white thing to do. How barbaric."

Ken scoffed back, "I know. I know. I'm well aware of oriental cultures."

I chuckled at Ken's response and rolled my eyes, "You are so white."

Big T took up the doorway, "Dang … this is nice! How are you paying for this place?"

Danny echoed my brothers, "She's selling drugs."

Ken was busy taking of his shoes, "I second that."

Robert added, "Raise your hand if you think it's drugs." One by one, everyone began raising their hands, except Tobias, who still hadn't entered.

"I repeat … jerks. What are you guys doing here?"

Tobias entered last, "I told the guys I thought it would be cool to check out your new place and surprise you. So ... here we are."

"Well, you could've called or texted first."

Danny replied, "Then it wouldn't be a surprise."

Big T looked around in awe, "When I grow up, I want a place like this on my own."

"You're, like, several years older than me, T."

Big T smiled, "That doesn't mean I'm grown up."

Robert said, "Dang ... this is a nice place." He paused and circled around before muttering, "Definitely drugs."

"You know it would've been nice if you were here about two hours ago when I was lifting stuff with my family."

Tobias shrugged, "Hey, we offered! You're the one who said you didn't want to explain all of us to your family."

I was about to say something, but Tobias was right.

Danny opened up the fridge and said, "Hey, you got nothing to eat."

"Duh," I said. "I literally just moved in ... and why are you opening my fridge without asking me?"

Danny replied, "We're family."

Doc frowned, "Not much of a housewarming. Maybe we should order something for Kirin."

Robert pointed to Danny, "He's treating."

"Why am I treating?"

Robert winked, "We're family."

As we began to chatter about what to do for dinner, I heard my doorbell ring. I thought, *Who could that be?*

This time, I asked, "Who's there?"

"It's Jim. We brought you back some dinner."

My eyes widened as I stuttered, "Uh, sure thing … uh, give me a second. I'll buzz you up." I turned around in a panic and said, "Guys, everyone get the heck out of here. My brother's back, and he brought me dinner."

Danny's eyes lit up, "Awesome, I'm starving…."

"You idiot, he can't know all of you are here."

Danny's glow faded, "Oh yeah," as the realization set in and panic struck his face. "Shit, what are we going to do?"

"That's more like it. That's the Danny I know."

Robert was lacking urgency, "Let's just head downstairs. What's the big deal?"

"I can't drop another bombshell on my family. I'm fortunate that I got this far with school and moving out … I'm not about to explain my side hobby of kicking butt."

Robert replied, "I'll buy what you're selling," as he threw in the white flag.

Tobias argued, "Honestly, I don't see the problem. So, what if they find out about you fighting?"

I smacked my head, "The problem ... here, let me spell it out so even you can understand. Mom ... Dad, I've been studying martial arts under your nose for years. My foot injury was because I almost died at an amusement park in a hundred-man gang fight. Oh, and I've been illegally fighting in the past against other gangsters, etc., etc."

"Point taken," Tobias said. "Yeah ... I got nothing. Let's hide."

I began pacing back and forth. "Hide? Oh yeah, everyone in the crate elevator, and don't make a sound." I began to escort the gang and then pointed back to them to grab their shoes. I yanked on the metal grate door and began directing everyone into it.

Ryan patted Ryan's shoulder, "Does this have a weight limit?"

Robert looked at Ryan and said, "Bet you wish you started that diet yesterday."

"Shut up, Robert."

I stroked my invisible beard, "Hmm, weight limit. I guess we'll find out."

Just as everyone had entered, I closed the door to hide the guys. I heard a knock on the front door. "I'm coming!" I called as I went running back to the front entrance.

As I opened the door, an arm reached in with a bag of food that smelled delicious. Eventually, Jim came in and handed it to me. "Jim, you didn't have to!"

"Don't thank me. It was Dad."

"Where's everyone else?"

"Where else? They're all downstairs in the car. You know the other guys are complete slackers, and I didn't want Dad to bother with finding a parking spot."

"So, you're not staying?"

"Nah … we got some food in the car. Mom called Dad and told him she has some free time on her call. So, we're all headed back to have dinner with her…. You want to come?"

"Oh, I wish I could, but I got stuff to do still."

"Okay, enjoy the food," said Jim, as he reached over and adjusted my glasses.

"I almost forgot I was wearing them."

"Sorry, sis … still not used to seeing you with those on a regular basis."

I thanked Jim for the food and closed the door. With my back against the door, I let out a sigh of relief that everything worked out okay. My heart was pounding. This was more excitement than I needed.

I shook my head and said, "Is it too much to ask for just one normal day?"

Paying the Bills—Day 88

As I said goodbye to my last client of the day, I realized that it was already evening. It had been a long day and so different from high school. Back then, my only worries had been to make sure I had good grades and did my chores. Everything else was taken care of for me— the food, the rent, the power … and the thing I missed the most: the laundry. I never thought something could have been more painful than

Mr. Lassy's AP Physics class, but there you had it: doing your own laundry. Now I was on my own. The long shadows melted into one as the sun set in a less than spectacular display. The days were definitely shorter as fall was around the corner.

I closed my eyes, hoping for a quick rest, but then my phone beeped. I glanced at it, frowning at the reminder that it might be something grownup and important. Begrudgingly, I looked at the message and read the reminder that my rent was due in less than a week. I quickly checked online to see how much was left in my bank account, leading to another realization.

"Crap," I said as my voice and facial reaction were in sync.

I began doing the math, but it soon became clear that I was going to be short for rent. I asked myself, "Ugh, how's this possible?" I thought about it for a moment and then remembered. "Oh yeah, when the guys came over and we ate dinner." I clenched my fist and said, "Dammit, Danny."

Glancing over my schedule, I saw I only had one more client set up for pictures this month. The bulk of my new appointments weren't until after the beginning of the month. *Sigh.* Now I was faced with my first big grownup decision about how to handle this.

What to do ... what to do?

"Options, Kirin." I looked at Bacon, but he was no help. "All right, first, I could ask my parents for some help, but that would be the cowardly thing to do. Second, Danny still owes me money for dinner, but the chances he's going to pay me back on time are slim, which leads me to my third option." I stood up and began pacing back and forth. "I need credits fast ... hmm, I could sell some stuff."

I walked around, looking at my empty loft, and realized that the most valuable stuff, my camera equipment, I needed. Then I thought, *Well, how did I pay for that in the first place?*

The extra cash I pocketed from the illegal fights helped pay for it.

I had been pretty good. Since the incident at Greatest America Park, I hadn't gone to any of the underground areas for fighting. Actually, there had been no reason to go that route, since we no longer had Sifu's rent to pay. Temptation got the better of me as I searched online to see if anything was happening tonight. Several clicks later, I found some activity. I decided to text the main host and see what the payout was. The number of zeroes along with the conditions seemed favorable. Not only would it cover several months' rent if I won, but I desperately needed some more camera gear.

In the back of my mind, I could hear Tobias nagging me. He specifically told the entire group that there would be no more underground fighting for anyone. I knew he was always looking out for the group's best interests. Regardless, this was my first adult decision to make. As I wrestled with the consequences, I paused and tried to ask myself what Sifu would do. Considering all the time I spent with him, I dug deep and tried to picture what he would do.

Seriously ... what would *Sifu do?*

I thought long and hard as I tried to squeeze out an answer. And then it dawned on me. I had no idea *what* Sifu would do—but I knew what I wanted to do.

Thirty Minutes Later

With my standard red hoodie, black Cons, and cropped blue jeans, I remained concealed in the crowds. This was unlike any of the underground fights I had ever gone to before. In fact, it was at a night club that apparently had some secret dwellings that only the regulars knew about. This was definitely a step up from the back alleys and abandoned warehouses where we had fought in the past.

I found my main contact Chun and told him I was here. Dressed like a Chinese car salesman with a bald head, he greeted me. "Hey, Blink what's up? It's been awhile...."

I replied, "Yeah, been busy with stuff. You look the same."

"You know me, I still train when I can. You know beauty has a price." He winked at me. Chun used to fight on the streets back in the day, but he realized he was a better bookie than a fighter. He began small talk, which I mostly ignored as I checked out the venue. It wasn't the typical scrubs wagering on fights, but more of a high-end group looking to exchange big credits to cure their boredom.

Chun asked, "You up for this? 'Cause if you win, the payout is awesome."

I said, "If....?"

"Uh, by the way, there's something I kinda failed to mention. The reason the payout is awesome is because it's a two-on-one match."

I stopped in my tracks right next to him and said, "Two-on-one?"

"Well, that's the reason the payout is huge, but I can renegotiate it and make it one-on-one, but it won't be as large."

"Do you know who I'm going to fight at least?"

"That, I know for sure ... two brothers from the hood with a ton of experience in street fighting."

I looked straight ahead and saw two identical Korean guys clearing through the crowd before finally getting to their end of the ring. I pinched the bridge of my nose and said, "Uh, Chun, are you sure about that? From the looks of it, these two 'brothers from the hood' look fairly lighter and are sporting some massively fugly bowl haircuts."

122

Chun looked at them and then went searching through his phone. "I swear, it's not me. Look for yourself." He raised his phone to my face.

"Just make sure the payout is as great as you say it is."

Chun fidgeted for several seconds, and I heard a ding on his phone. He looked at me and then showed me the proof. The need for credits was my reminder, and the greed took over me. There was no hesitation on my part, "I'll do it."

Prior to the introduction, I kept telling myself, *Just this one fight.* Aloud, I muttered, "I go in and out and collect the credits just this one time. I swear."

The bets were placed as my opponents began warming up and stretching. The twin brothers were dressed identically as they began flashing out some impressive kicks. I stood there watching and did nothing, since I did not want to give them a hint of anything at all. Fortunately, for all their flash, their movements fell flat.

Hmm ... twins think the same and act the same. I was at a disadvantage since it was two on one, and they had some unique, unspoken bond between them.

I cut through the crowd and stood across from them. I unzipped my hoodie but kept it on. The crowd's cheer was rowdier than usual; one guy with a whiney voice began razzing me from the start. I saw him from the corner of my eye—some preppy-looking jerk with his collar popped, sporting a tie that hung lower than it should.

He shouted, "Look, a girl! I want to fight like a girl!"

His taunts didn't matter to me, nor did my opponents. My goal was my rent, and I knew what had to be done. I cracked my neck and clenched my fist just to shake the last of any nerves. While I had been training continuously, it had been awhile since my last fight.

Chun cupped his mouth and shouted one last thing. "If you can beat them in under two minutes, there's an extra bonus!"

I only caught a pinch of what he shouted as the rest was drowned by the crowd's cheer. The main ref for the evening finally took center stage, prepping us for the battle. There weren't really any rules to go over, as his role was more about keeping the fights moving along. He signaled to both sides and waited for a nod.

The referee screamed out, "Fight!"

"Center, target, own it."

The twins looked at me like I was fresh meat.

Come and get me.

They shouted as a high-pitched shriek overtook the crowd. No hesitation on their part as they charged in like gang busters. Without words being spoken, they came zigzagging one another in a set formation and charged toward me.

Once they moved, I charged in—two people, three, it didn't matter to me. I had bills to pay. I took the left side and watched how they reacted. I hoped to draw them unevenly from one another and give myself an advantage. However, they somehow stayed even to me, launching kicks from different angles and heights. I blocked a series of them, but it was just too many for me to deal with. I finally ate a low kick from one brother while blocking the other, and I landed hard on my back.

The crowd cheered as I rolled back onto my knee and prepared for another onslaught. The preppy guy's nasally voice pierced through the crowd. He shouted, "I told you she can't fight!" He chuckled.

Let's try this again.

I took a second to recoup from my hit and then went straight back in. *It's not the number of times you get hit, but the number of times you're willing to go back*, I reminded myself.

Thirsty for blood, I tried to draw them off-center by darting in again. They reacted by crossing each other like before. This time, I picked the right side to see if I could throw them off. Once again, they didn't bite, and I had to deal with both of their attacks at the same time. They mainly stuck to kicks, delivering a knee to the face on one side while simultaneously attacking from a different angle. Dealing with the barrage of attacks proved to be difficult as I found myself on the defensive. Block after block, I flowed with the force, which was saving my ass. But, a person can dodge only so much before her luck runs out. I successfully blocked a single-sided double roundhouse kick going from low to high, but a split-second celebration resulted in me eating a side kick to the stomach that sent me flying several feet back.

I grunted as I held my stomach and lay on my back. I muttered, "This isn't working!"

As I re-examined my game plan, I heard Chun yell from a distance, "You gotta win! Thirty-five seconds left, Kirin!" As I staggered to my feet, I wasn't quite sure what he meant, but that wasn't my main concern.

The stranger continued to taunt me. "Hey, I want to fight like a girl! Teach me."

My opponents took a moment to enjoy the crowd's cheers, high-fiving one another with their kicks. But then, I saw it: while they may have been identical twins, they finally revealed their weakness. I couldn't believe I hadn't noticed it right away. One brother favored the right side while the other favored the left. I watched just to make sure, checking their center of gravity. That confirmed it as each one leaned toward the side he favored.

Bingo!

They took the initiative and repeated their attack formation. They zigzagged toward me at full speed, looking like blurs. This time, I didn't pick a side and rushed straight down the center. I timed my move perfectly, causing them to split up with me dead in the middle.

Perfect.

They both threw opposite roundhouse kicks, each one favoring his strong side as I stood there. At the last second, I ducked out of the way, and they kicked each other in the shin. The first twin, who favored his right, stood half erect, grabbing his leg in pain. He was wide open as I rushed in. The look of panic overtook him as his main weapon was now damaged. He threw out a punch but was weak as he leaned on a gimped leg, no different from when he kicked. Grabbing his pitiful attack, I wanted to showcase the difference in our kicks.

Thanks for the help, I thought as I used him to stabilize myself while delivering my kick. With his arm outstretched and both my hands controlling him, I made sure his right leg was rendered totally useless and kicked his knee out. I spun around, getting underneath his center and tossing him with a full sweep as I caught sight of my target.

The right-legged Korean flew into the air and was knocked unconscious as he crash-landed onto the loud mouth stranger. I snapped back and saw that his brother was hovering around, rubbing his left shin. I shook my head and rushed toward him. Looking scared and lost without his brother, he quickly retreated. In a defensive state, his center shifted as he did a last-minute turning reverse crescent kick. I ducked underneath as he missed, leaving himself fully exposed. I grabbed him by the chest and landed an instep kick to his groin. His face contorted like he was giving birth as he slowly he crumpled. I rolled on my back and looked for my favorite target.

The stranger was pissed and finally stood up, dusting the dirt off himself. He whined, "What kind of bull—"

I pelted him again with my limp Korean object. "Bullseye!"

All three lay on the floor next to one another as I stood up to see my work. The crowd was caught off-guard as many had believed that I was going to lose. Only a handful cheered, probably the ones who had taken the long shot and bet on me. While this payday was more difficult, everyone had underestimated my size, gender, and most importantly my skill. It was perfect. But, what really caught me by surprise was how I could see things that I hadn't seen before in a fight, albeit a little late.

"Blink … Blink, here are credits," said Chun.

I stared and took them from him, "I didn't catch what you said before the match."

Chun replied, "I said you would earn even more if you could end this fight in under two minutes."

I hurried and counted my winnings. I could not believe how much I had made as I tried my best to contain my emotions. This would set me for rent for a good three months, and I had more than enough for some added camera equipment. I began walking away but turned back and called, "Chun!"

He turned around and looked at me. I tossed him a credit, which he snatched from the air.

"You know my number…?"

He smiled, admiring my generous credit tip, and said, "I most certainly do."

Blindfold—Day 95

Our training facility was really starting to feel like home. Big T had been working on it for some time as everyone added their own personal touch to the place. I thought I had arrived early, but when I entered, I saw that Doc and Robert had beaten me to the punch. They were already working out with each other, practicing chi sao. Ken was in the far corner practicing the first form, Siu Lim Tao by himself. I said a quick hi to everyone, but they seemed focused on what they were doing.

Robert was still working with Doc, but finally gave me the time of day. Noticing what I was carrying, he said, "What's with the plant?"

I replied, "Since this is our place, we should make it look more like a school. Don't you think?"

Robert, as always, had an attitude, "We never had a plant before."

Doc eyed the plant, "I like it."

"You're such a kiss ass, Doc."

"Shut up, Robert … and you're not square," said Doc as he used the opening and landed a punch an inch away from Robert's center.

"Dammit, Kirin. Stop distracting me." Robert pouted as he shifted his focus entirely on Doc.

"What, you blaming me or the plant?" I waited for a brief moment, but Robert didn't respond.

I took my plant and did a little Feng Shui, even though I had no clue how that worked. The corner at the far end where Ken was training looked like it could use some color, so I placed it there.

"There, that looks better.... Don't you think, Ken?" I adjusted the angle of the plant to its prominent side.

Ken replied, "I think you just racially profiled me, Kirin."

"What?"

"I'm the whitest thing in this room. Let me guess: you put the plant by me 'cause you think it could use some color?"

Glancing away, I replied, "No."

Jeez, I have to be less obvious next time.

I stood for a moment and admired the work everyone had done to the place so far. Hopefully, we were prepared for the fall and winter season, and this place was up to par for training. I grabbed a broom and began sweeping a bit; there were food wrappers and just general mess everywhere. I couldn't really say anything because I was no better than the guys.

A few minutes later, the rest of the gang came in with Tobias trailing at the end. He quickly took charge of the class, clapping his hands and drawing everyone's attention. He said, "Everyone, warm up and get a partner. We're going to do something different today."

I looked at him curiously.

For the next fifteen minutes, we partnered up and did our standard exercise. Since Sifu's absence, Tobias had begun developing a more distinctive style in his teaching. He was becoming his own. He began straying away from Sifu's set routine and was being more creative in his approach. While I noticed the difference, I didn't bother mentioning it to him or anyone else. Besides, I was sure the guys had noticed the difference as well.

Tobias gave us enough time to roll with at least several different partners, and then he gathered us in the center of the room as we circled around him and listened. He was holding a bag in his hand, but the contents of it were not visible. He remained silent, creating suspense as he teased us and waved the bag in front of everyone.

"Who brought the plant?" When I raised my hand, he said, "I like it, makes this place feel like home. Much better than Big T's bikini babe calendar that he has in that corner."

I smiled at Tobias and then quickly looked away. It was easier when we bickered with each other. The compliments, which came rarely made me feel uncomfortable at times. Sometimes he made comments that touched me, and I wasn't quite sure how that made me feel or how to react.

Big T shouted, "Hey, you told everyone to put a touch of themselves in the school! This was my choice."

Robert said, "Just make sure you don't touch yourself in the school, Big T."

All the guys were chuckling as I looked at the calendar with the scantily dressed women. After our chicken incident at the restaurant, I started getting a deeper understanding of the guys.

Big T tried to explain, "Told you guys we need a calendar to know the days. Kirin, what day is today?"

I replied, "Thursday."

Big T continued, "Uh, well, Doc, what's the date?"

Doc said, "The seventh."

Big T focused harder and asked, "Ken, what year is it?"

Ken responded, "2030."

Big T looked annoyed with the quick response from everyone and said, "It's a necessary evil, okay!"

Danny waved his phone in the air, "Yeah, 'cause the one on our phones doesn't do the job, right?"

Everyone busted out in laughter, but from the looks of it, Big T was trying to really make a case for himself.

Tobias took over our useless talk, "Okay, enough with the calendar." He took a quick snapshot with his phone, which caused me to roll my eyes and shake my head. "Anyway, I brought something, and we're going to do something I don't think any of you have done yet."

Robert pointed at Ryan and said, "Get laid."

Ryan thrusted his chest forward, "Some things in life are choices."

Robert replied, "Like weight gain."

Ryan started charging toward Robert, but Danny and Big T held him back. Ken, always the good guy, stood in front of Robert just to make sure things didn't escalate. The guys were being guys, and I couldn't help but chuckle a little bit at Robert's jokes. At least, I thought he was joking.

Tobias cleared his throat and got everyone to focus on him again. He reached into his bag and began pulling something out. "Like I was saying before I got interrupted … I've got something in store for you guys and gal that I don't believe any of you have done before." I watched as he handed a blindfold to Danny.

Danny held it in his hand, "Hey, I'm not playing hide the zucchini … again."

Tobias looked at him curiously, "Again?"

"Uh, never mind."

"Anyway, I got each of you a blindfold, and what we're going to work on is chi saoing with one another and focusing entirely on the touch."

Everyone was somewhat caught off-guard, but the idea sounded pretty cool.

Tobias said, "Sifu stopped doing this because he didn't think it was anything special being able to see through touch. He thought it was pretty easy, but I think there's some cool aspects of doing this drill that can benefit all of us in our training. Back in the day, he would do demonstrations blindfolded, for you younglings who didn't know."

Ken thought aloud, "Blindfold fighting … seriously, do you think one day we're going to be fighting in the dark against ninjas?"

Everyone laughed until Tobias cut us off. "Sometimes the eyes can lie, but the touch is real. Through touch, you can feel an individual's center of gravity as soon as he begins a motion. So, every motion that he initiates, you'll know right away. Thus, his attack isn't important to us, his center of gravity is the key."

I really thought the idea behind it was cool, but to take it to this level was something I'd never experienced before.

Doc made a request, "Perhaps a demonstration is called for."

Tobias looked at Doc. "You really need one?"

I watched as the rest of the guys nodded and asked for Tobias to show his skills.

Tobias always loved the attention and didn't want to miss this opportunity. He pointed at Big T and said, "T, let me demo on you." Then he grabbed the blindfold from Danny.

"Hey!" Danny gave a sad face at being the odd man out.

The two men stood arm's length apart and placed their blindfolds on themselves. They then got into sticky hands position as we all watched.

Tobias began, "Like I said, you go fully by the touch and don't have any use of the eyes to rely on. Now, for example, just by touching Big T, I can tell you he's black."

I laughed so hard along with the rest of the gang.

Ken joked, "Can you also tell how long he is?"

Tobias shouted, "Okay, people, Kirin's here. Let's keep this PG-13."

I looked at Ken and said, "This joke … I don't get it."

Ken looked around at everyone, "See? She doesn't get it. All is good."

Robert clung behind him and was bawling in tears. "Every so often, a white guy has his moments."

I punched him in the arm as Tobias and Big T began to roll.

Ignoring us, Tobias explained, "So, as you can see, nothing is different, other than the fact that I'm wearing a blindfold. Through the touch, I can feel for everything. Now remember, I feel for myself...." He turned toward Robert's direction, "Shut up, Robert. Don't make your comment."

Robert shrugged his shoulders and gave an innocent look.

Tobias continued, "Like I was saying, I feel for myself, my center of gravity, and through that, I can feel exactly what my opponent is doing. Never forget that. You are still the main focus. You are not reacting to the individual. Oh, also, I remember Sifu hated this. When you chi sao blindfolded, don't turn your head, as if you are listening to the force. He always thought it looked so stupid for Wing Chun practitioners to turn their head. It makes no sense at all. You're not listening to music, and by turning your head, you also kill your own structure."

I liked when people would reference Sifu now and then. Warmth and longing for our old teacher flooded through me as they continued to do the basic roll back and forth, and then Tobias said, "Big T, whenever you are ready, anything you want, just attack."

With that green light, Big T attacked, and Tobias not only held his ground, but simply went with the flow. Big T was really trying his best to get an attack through as well as offset Tobias's center, but this was more than a demonstration of being blindfolded. It was a reminder to the class of just how bad ass Tobias really was.

Several minutes went by where nothing got through Tobias's defense. Big T appeared to have the advantage with sight, but like Tobias said, he could feel everything through the touch.

Tobias said, "Okay, Big T. Time for me to attack. Do your best."

Big T nodded, and Tobias just unleashed the attacks. Just as he blocked all the incoming attacks from Big T, he dominated as he went on the offensive. No matter what Big T did, he could not block anything that Tobias threw at him. Hit after hit would've landed, as Tobias also demonstrated his mastery of control. It looked totally effortless. He did a final move against Big T that led to a shin na. Before we knew it, Big T was on the ground in a joint lock that he couldn't counter out of.

Everyone began to clap at this demonstration of skill. Tobias removed his blindfold and hoisted Big T off the ground. "See? Like Sifu said, simple, easy. Now, go grab a partner, and let's work on this."

Big T groaned, "Did you have to make me look so bad?"

Tobias patted him on the back. "No, seriously, you did well."

Big T shook his head, his ego bruised, "More practice, I guess."

I broke up this moment of male bonding, "Should just one of us be blindfolded?"

Tobias answered, "It's up to you. Both of you can be blindfolded at the same time or just one. You can experiment with it. I'll be going around the room to see if you have any questions."

I put the blindfold on and immediately the loss of my most dominate sense felt awkward. It took me a minute to settle in before finally touching hands with my partner. Now all I could rely on was simply the touch. From the point of contact upon my wrist, I began to breathe, trusting what I felt and allowing the force to take over my body. First, it was odd. I didn't feel my partner, but I slowly felt the flow of the force run from my arm past my shoulder and into my body, then eventually all the way to the ground. I could literally feel my own center of gravity, the slightest of motions, every nuance of my structure. It was amazing, something I wasn't fully aware of until I cut off my sight. Then as I stayed static for a pinch longer, my sense of feeling began to extend outside my own body. Now from the point of contact, I could feel everything my opponent was doing. For the first time in my training, I had finally connected with my opponent. His move was now my move, and our structures merged to become one.

Holy crap.

"We have a skill beyond the five senses that very few train to develop. Ignore this, and you miss seeing what the world and those in it truly are." —Sifu

Section 2 Sifu's Journey Entry #3—Strange Encounter

First Week of March

It was early March, which meant the weather in Chicago was pretty much a roll of the dice. Some years, spring came early, but today winter decided to lag behind and show its miserable self. Sifu had just stopped by the local grocery store and was making his way back to his shop. Everything was typical about this day—same time, same route and, for the last several weeks, same routine. That emptiness Sifu had been feeling lingered, much like the cold, snowy days, and the answers he sought were nowhere to be found. He mused that the snow had a warmth about it, which was ironic, as each breath he took had a puff of cold air. Sometimes a distraction is its own reward, and Sifu welcomed anything that kept his mind off his melancholy.

It was early Sunday morning, a little past eight, and Armitage Avenue was still quite empty, absent of the typical bumper-to-bumper traffic. The weather was taking credit for the lack of activity. With two grocery bags in each hand, Sifu was trudging through the snow that had remained uncleaned on the sidewalk. Several more blocks to go, and then he'd catch a train and eventually make it back to his shop. Sifu hated to drive and did his best to avoid it. Walking and public transportation provided him with time to reflect on life.

The snow continued to fall as Sifu quickened his pace. Out of nowhere, he was suddenly bumped from behind. His stance stood solid as he turned around. There, on the ground, was a person, covered as if prepared for a blizzard. The only visible feature was the individual's eyes; Sifu noticed something distinct about them. Sifu extended his hand to help the person up.

Sifu asked, "You okay?"

"Thanks, mister," said the voice in a panic.

Sifu realized it was a girl as he helped hoist her from the ground. He asked, "What's the rush?" He smiled, hoping to lighten her mood.

The girl snapped backward, looked behind her, and then took off without saying another word.

Sifu watched her dash away and disappear. She left only her footprints behind. The breeze hit him as he wrapped his scarf securely upon his lower face and neck. Soon afterward, several drones buzzed above him, and he heard shouting from behind. He didn't react to either and was more concerned about the snow and the cold. Several STDs were in pursuit, and Sifu deducted they were after the girl as he watched them charge past him.

Sifu kept his regular pace, not detouring from his path. The snow had left a track of footprints that eventually turned left into the alley. He thought, *Bad choice. That's a dead end.* He could hear the drones buzzing from above as four STDs surrounded the same girl, who was now lying on the ground. From a distance, Sifu could hear them chuckle as they spoke. As he began walking past them, he peeked to see what was happening.

The girl on the ground screamed, "Help me ... please!"

Sifu ignored her cries as one of the STDs kicked her in the stomach to silence her. He walked by the alley, aware of the STDs who were checking to see if he was paying attention to their actions. He was stone cold and progressed ahead without giving any attention to the matter.

He heard her scream again, her voice echoing through the alley. Laughter grew from a distance as Sifu walked away. He stopped in his tracks just out of view and leaned against the wall. Something was drawing him to the moment, just a feeling that Sifu could not shake. He closed his eyes and pictured the girl he had just met a moment ago. Her eyes, which he had seen for only a brief second, made him take a deep breath.

In the Alley

Several drones hovered above the STDs, recording the event. One STD grabbed the girl's hat and stripped it from her head. He said, "Finally caught you, bitch!"

She looked up and spat at his mask, but her breath was weak as she was still trying to recover from the prior kick to the stomach.

The spit dripped from his mask as he gave a hidden smile. The STD turned to his partner and said, "Turn off the cameras on the drones." His fellow STD did as he was told. He reached for his controller on his sleeve, and all the drones stopped recording, though they remained above hovering over them.

The first STD yanked the girl by the hair pulling her back on her feet. He slapped her hard on the face sending her back to ground. She cried out, and her vision went blurry. The impact left a mark across her face. She moaned and tried to get up and shake the hit off.

The STD said, "We've been looking for you for some time. We're not going to bring you in … but there's a nice, hefty reward on your head that we're all going to collect. Right, boys?" Two of his comrades high-fived one another.

They were celebrating their catch as the lead STD grinded his knee further into her back. There was no reason for it, other than to inflict more pain upon her. She grunted at the weight, but she was helpless and outnumbered as her faith rested in those who supposedly serve and protect.

"Shut up!" he shouted and leaned his weight into her.

Smash. Crash. Wham. Thud.

All the drones that had been hovering above came crashing down to the ground. Caught by surprise, the four STDs looked at the downed drones and then began scanning the area. As one began to shout out, a figure appeared out of nowhere in a flash. Violent and swift, they were dealt with one by one, as no time was given to react. Even with their armored gear and weapons, each fell within seconds. The last, and lead STD was flung to the wall like a ragdoll. He kissed the pavement hard as karma was swift to balance the universe. The girl was still recovering as the last STD fell several feet from her. The impact of his fall jolted her, and she feared what was to come.

The stranger approached the girl, who curled in fear and backed against the wall. He extended his hand slowly toward her without saying a word. She hesitated for a second, looking up as things were still a blur. Behind him were the drones that crashed on the ground along with the STDs. The sun caught an angle in between the cracks of the alley to silhouette her savior. His hands were rough but familiar as he easily helped her up from the ground.

He said, "Shhh, it's okay. It's okay. I won't hurt you," as he tried to calm her down.

She took a moment to gather herself, dusting the dirt off her. Her vision finally returned to normal. She looked at the STDs lying scattered through the alley. "Oh my gosh ... did a blizzard hit these guys?" She took a couple steps forward to see the main STD who had hit her. She wound up and kicked him in the ribs ... twice.

"Bastard," she said as she landed one last kick and spat at him.

After releasing her anger, she wiped her mouth and looked around, only to realize that her protector was nowhere in sight. She staggered forward searching, but he was gone, leaving no trail behind. Within seconds, she made a dash away from her surroundings, leaving the downed men on the ground.

CHAPTER 4
Intervention

Mid-April 2034

Kirin sat in the passenger seat of Sage's car, enjoying the fresh spring air that passed through the small crack left open in the window. As much as she loved her hometown Chicago, the winter months gave her the blues. Today was the first sign that spring was here, and people were taking full advantage of it outside.

Matters weighed heavily on Kirin, who had kept her secret bottled up for so long. A burden of that nature festers until it finds a way to release itself at the most unpredictable of times. Today, she was taking a breather to get away and celebrate her best friend's birthday. Kirin was staring outside, enjoying the moment, when her happy place was suddenly disrupted.

"Will you close the window? It's still cold outside." Sage shivered to emphasize his point.

"Don't be such a wuss. It's the first sunlight in months, and you don't want to enjoy it."

"Oh, it's not that," Sage said, fumbling for words. "Uh, it's fine … uh, you can leave it open for now."

Kirin thought he was acting strange, but she blew it off as just Sage being Sage.

For the next several minutes it was unusually quiet inside the car. Kirin couldn't recall either of them ever being at a loss for words, yet they were struggling now. She decided to break the silence and start a conversation. "It's pretty cool that Lance said we can have Gwen's party at the shop today."

"Yeah," agreed Sage, who continued to be somewhat distant.

"What's up with you, Sage?" asked Kirin. "Is it Gwen's surprise birthday party?"

Sage fidgeted and squirmed in his seat. He said, "Uh, I'm just hoping she likes the gift I got her; that's all. You know Gwen—she can be picky about presents. And, this is something I've never done before, throw a birthday party for my girlfriend."

"Yeah, but I'm sure she'll like whatever you got her." Kirin hid her grin and finished with, "You know, she does love you." Kirin peeked at Sage, who blushed.

"Yeah ... I know."

Kirin rolled her eyes and shook her head. "Thanks for ruining the moment."

Sage said, "If anything ... I consider that perfect timing."

"I can't believe that I feed you that line, and you don't run with it."

"It's not my fault. My game is off today until after she opens her gift." Sage checked the time on the car again.

Kirin bought the excuse and decided to switch gears, "Sage, turn on the radio. Let's see what's on."

Sage pressed a button as his car scanned for something worthy of their ears. Several stations paused, previewing their choices as they listened.

"With the 2034 season just two and a half months away," said a voice on one station, "where is Kirin Rise? One of the hottest topics still in discussion is last year's contender, who has been a total recluse. Fortunately for us, Ripley Hawkins has stolen some of her thunder."

The radio switched to the next channel and said, "Much of Vegas appears to be betting heavily on Ripley Hawkins. Can the unproven rookie do what Kirin did? Vegas is also betting on whether or not the young phenom returns to the Dome this year...."

Kirin rubbed her eyes in frustration and turned off the radio with a sigh. "Sage, how's school going?"

"Nothing special ... but, with a double major in computer science and biochemistry, it does keep me pretty busy."

"What are you talking about?" Kirin chuckled. "I see you spend more time streaming your games online and being in your VR world."

"Hey, I need my relaxation time. Besides, it's extra cash on the side with all the donations I get."

"Please, I'm sure these classes are easy for my genius friend."

"Well, yeah, they are, but I have to make it look like it's a challenge. Otherwise, everyone thinks I'm a dick."

"Don't they think that already?" said Angelo from the back of the car.

"Oh my gosh, Angelo! You scared the crap out of me. You've been so quiet, I forgot you were back there." Kirin put her hand on her chest.

Angelo rolled his eyes, "Oh, great. I guess that shows my worth."

"You know what I mean," Kirin half-apologized.

Sage chimed in, "Well, maybe Kirin just didn't want to appear like a dick."

"Touché," said Angelo. "For someone whose disappeared from the public eye for the last several months, I swear you've gotten more popular than ever. The golden blonde hussy Ripley has nothing on you."

Kirin leaned her head against the window, "I was really hoping all of the attention would go to Ripley since the announcement."

Angelo leaned forward between the two front seats, "What's with that? The UFMF must have some big bucks invested into her 'cause they're really promoting her hard."

Kirin asked, "Is it working?"

Angelo turned to look at her, "To some degree, but you're still trending above her."

Now, Kirin rolled her eyes. "Great. I'm sure that must be eating Ripley inside." Kirin closed her eyes and thought about the past. The last time she had encountered Ripley had been their showdown in the park. Feelings quickly returned as anger overwhelmed her. She took a deep breath to keep herself in check. Over the next several minutes, Kirin's mind wandered, and she started to drift off to sleep. Suddenly, the car screeched to a halt, jolting her back to reality.

"What the—?"

"We're here," said Sage.

Kirin took a quick peek to the side and saw Sage was right. A little drool tried to escape her mouth, but she quickly wiped it, looking to make sure no one had seen.

Kirin was revved up, "Pop the trunk," which Sage immediately did. She sprang out of the car and ran to the back, grabbing her gift. She didn't bother waiting for Sage or Angelo, who were taking their time. Excited to set up for Gwen's party, she strode to the door and grabbed the handle, ready to open it. She turned to ask, "How much time before Gwen gets here?"

Angelo and Sage looked at each other and didn't answer right away. They exchanged a look of concern that Kirin didn't seem to notice as Sage bumped Angelo in the arm. Angelo rushed to say, "We've got an hour."

"Cool! That's more than enough time to get ready." She pulled open the door and jumped through the entrance.

Sage sighed, "This is not going to go well."

Angelo nodded. "After you."

Sage gave Angelo a concerned look, "It scares me when you're behind me."

Angelo whispered into Sage's ear, "It should." Sage's eyes opened wide as his butt muscles clenched, and he gulped some spit and turned around.

"Not funny, Angelo."

Angelo chuckled, "I'm just trying to lighten the mood."

Sage shook his, "Nothing's going to save us today."

Kirin leaped into the restaurant, exaggerating her landing, and shouted, "This is gonna be…." With a stunned look on her face, she trailed off as she scanned the room, dropping her gift on the ground. Just before her were her closest friends: Gwen, Hunter, and the gang were all seated in a circle along with Lance. They had rearranged the room to accommodate the setting. In the middle of this was a stranger Kirin had never seen before. Wearing glasses with her hair in a bun, she gave a smile. Kirin felt it was fake. Kirin was caught off-guard as she was still trying to grasp what was about to happen.

Angelo and Sage followed behind her, and Sage closed the door once they got in.

Kirin just stood there, "Uh, what's going on here?" An ill feeling set in, and she knew that, regardless of the answer, she was not going to like it.

Tobias stood up from his seat and said, "Kirin, this is what we in America call an intervention. Everyone here is concerned about you, and we'd like you to hear what we have to say."

Kirin spun around and glared daggers at both Angelo and Sage.

Angelo quickly pointed to Sage, "It was his idea."

Kirin's eyes pierced through both of them, but neither dared to look back at her. She hung her head.

I should've gone with my gut. I knew something was off.

Tobias stepped in, "It was a group decision and not just one. So, if you want to blame someone, you're going to have to blame all of us. Please, just grab a seat and listen for a bit. I promise you it's not as bad as you think." His hand directed her to join the group. At first, she hesitated, weighing her options before giving her friends the benefit of the doubt. Piecing together that the empty chair was for her, she walked toward it.

Kirin walked by the stranger, whose hand was left unshaken, and simply said, "I'm assuming you're the shrink."

The stranger took no offense from Kirin's rude gesture, simply retracting her hand as she said, "My name is Kathy, and I'm not a shrink. But, my job for today is to make sure everything moves smoothly. I believe the best way to describe today is a kind of group discussion."

Kirin didn't care for the sugar coat description as she sat on her chair and seemed less than open to anything.

Kathy watched Tobias as he took his seat. "Thank you, everyone," she said, "for being here today, and especially thank you, Kirin, for deciding to stay. All I ask is that you allow everyone to speak their minds. We're not here to force you to do anything against your will. We're just here to share our thoughts with you. Does that sound fair?"

Kirin gave a slight nod, which Kathy accepted as a confirmation.

Kathy continued, "Let's get this moving right along. Previously, we discussed a set order in which to speak. So, if you will, Gwen, you may begin."

Kirin still refused to make eye contact with anyone in the room. Her face was emotionless, like a Korean pop star who just had one too many plastic surgery procedures.

Gwen hesitated as she sat on her wheelchair and stared at her best friend. Her voice cracked as she said, "I...."

The sound of her friend's voice struggling to speak began to break the wall that Kirin had formed.

A sniffle shortly followed as this appeared to be more difficult for Gwen than it was for Kirin. "I'm here today, Kirin ... because I love you. You're more than my friend. You're my sister, even if it isn't by blood. You will always be my sister, that's how important you are to me. We have always been there for one another, since the first day we met. I'm here today, just like everyone else, because I'm concerned about you. I'll get right to the point and say ... I don't want you to fight. I know you feel you need to. But, you once told me Wing Chun is about more than fighting, that to use your fist was the lowest level of the art, and that it was possible to achieve what you want without putting your life in danger or throwing a single punch. You are the most powerful voice in the world right now, so why not use it to make the change that you desire? Stop hiding from what you can really be because I know you are so much more." Tears ran down

Gwen's face as Sage hugged her. It was difficult to watch as Kirin held back her own tears and felt her heart get squeezed. Gwen motioned to Kathy that that was all she had to say.

Kathy nodded briefly as she consulted her notes before pointing in the opposite direction. "The next person ... Hunter, please begin."

Hunter stood up from the crowd. He combed his hair and took a deep breath as Kirin watched him with gentle eyes. She glanced away, scanning the entire room. It seemed as though this was more difficult for her friends than it was for her.

Hunter started, "You know, you've always meant the world to me. You're the most bad-ass girl I've ever met.... I remember the first day I laid eyes on you, I knew right there ... that something was so special about you."

Danny mumbled, "Her ass?"

Everyone stared at Danny, whose timing was off as usual. He shrank in his seat and muttered, "I thought it was a question."

Hunter made a face, trying to recover from that comment. "Uh, as I was trying to say, you've done things that no one could imagine, and you've inspired me along with millions to become better. But, there comes a point that every time you step into that ring, every one of your friends and family suffers more than you can imagine. It's hard to think about your last match because I honestly thought I was going to lose you. So, you see, you have to stop. In fact, I'm willing to beg for you to stop. I know you think that's the only way right now, but there's gotta be another way ... because I can't lose you; none of us can." Hunter turned away, unable to look at Kirin directly.

For the next hour, everyone shared their thoughts with Kirin. Sage, Lance, Big T, Danny, Ken, Doc, Robert, Ryan, and even Angelo all gave convincing arguments to stop what she was planning on doing.

149

"Thank you for being so patient, Kirin," Kathy said. Then she glanced over at the one person who still had not spoken. "Tobias, if you will ... he's going to be the last one sharing his thoughts."

Tobias stood up. He pulled out his phone, which had some notes jotted down on it. He was about to read and shook his head, placing it back in his pocket. "I'm not good with speeches. That's why I thought I'd write things in advance. But, I have to admit, I'm torn. I don't know if I can say anything that hasn't already been said. In some demented way, I understand where you are coming from, but I also get why everyone else is struggling with your decision. I'm like you. I guess that's why we've always gotten along so well.... No one wants to be told what to do, but for you it's different. It's not about that. It stems from your past—a pain none of us can ever begin to understand that remains unresolved in your life. You've always been so strong-willed.... In the end, you're going to have to decide what's best for you." He turned away and sat down.

Kathy started to wrap up, "Thank you, everyone, for sharing your feelings with Kirin. And also, I'd—"

Kirin stood up, interrupting her in mid-sentence. "Sorry ... I'm sorry for putting everyone through this and being so ... selfish. Thank you so much for taking the time today, but even before all of this, I'd already decided not to enter the 2034 season. Sometimes it's difficult for me to express my feelings with you guys, but I love each and every one of you from the bottom of my heart." She stood there with her head hanging down as everyone was taken aback by her response. No one had believed it would be this easy, knowing how stubborn Kirin could be. Kathy nudged the group to move forward as everyone began to surround her and gave her a hug. The moment was touching and complete as they all breathed a sigh of relief.

Lance pulled away from the group hug, initiating a domino effect. One by one, they peeled away until Kirin remained standing alone in the center. All eyes were still upon her as she took a moment to wipe her tears and gather herself.

Lance decided to take away the pressure and clapped. Heads turned toward him as he said, "Well, this turned out to be a happy ending."

Danny slipped in, "Uh, what?"

Lance furrowed his brow and gave Danny a meaningful look. While his skill in Wing Chun superseded Lance's, he knew not to push his humor on this occasion. Lance said, "Fortunately for everyone, I can have lunch ready in thirty."

For the next hour, the mood shifted, and festivities were much lighter. Smiles returned, bellies were full, and the task at hand was considered successfully completed. Eventually, the gang began to dwindle. By early evening, Kirin said her last goodbyes to Gwen and Sage, and only she and Lance remained in the restaurant.

Small chitchat between Lance and Kirin felt like old times. Even though Lance wasn't much for words, his speech always had a purpose. Both of them could feel the emptiness caused by Sifu's absence. If there was one thing that Kirin admired about Lance, it was his loyalty. Once a person earned Lance's trust like Sifu had, Lance would be there for them till the very end, without question.

There were still several hours before Lance would open the place up for business, but he headed back to the kitchen to see if everything was ready for the evening.

Kirin followed behind, watching him as they entered the kitchen.

Lance went to the back of the kitchen and looked at the dishes that needed to be cleaned. He didn't say a word, but for a brief moment he pictured Sifu hovering around him. He closed his eyes and shook the image from his head.

Kirin ran her hand on the counter, "His presence is so strong. He's, like, here … around us?"

"Nah." Lance brushed it off as the subject would've made him emotional.

Kirin spoke softly. "Lance?"

He turned toward Kirin and waited.

"You know, everyone was right that the Dome is not the answer."

He stayed neutral and replied, "Go on."

"But, Sifu always said, there's gotta be a better way. There always is…." It was eating Kirin up that all her training had not prepared her. She felt inadequate to deal with her current situation as questions remained unanswered. She looked at her hands and said, "What good has Wing Chun been for me, when I can't punch my way out of this mess?"

Lance smiled and then belted out a laugh. For a moment, all the lessons Sifu had taught him seemed to sync in perfect harmony, as if he finally understood what Sifu had been trying to teach.

Kirin asked, "What's so funny?"

"You sounded just like me now. Don't get me wrong. Your level of Wing Chun is beyond mine, Kirin, but I remember saying something kinda similar to Sifu, and he laughed at me."

Kirin frowned, but Lance responded, "No need to sulk." He came around the counter and patted her on the back. "I remember saying to him that I thought the entire purpose of Wing Chun or martial arts in general was for self-defense, and he kinda scoffed at me."

Kirin smiled as everyone had experienced that sensation with Sifu before.

"Sifu always stressed to use it as the very last resort, when all other options have been exhausted. But most people end up making it their first choice. It's a common mistake made by people who don't realize that every action has a tax that comes with it. However, if you use your last resort, it'll take you awhile to recover and get back to zero. And sometimes, it's even possible you may never return."

Kirin looked confused, "What do you mean?"

"I mean that you're gonna have to repay that debt, if not in this lifetime, then maybe in the next."

Kirin shook her head, "God, I hate that he's always right."

"Kirin, do you remember the story he told? It was awhile back … the one about him not being a hero?"

"Yeah, I remember that one." Kirin wondered why Lance would bring that up.

"I'm pretty sure he gave you kids the PG version of that story."

"What do you mean? I thought the story was pretty straightforward. His friend got harassed, and he ended up saving him using his Wing Chun. The bad guys were beaten … the end."

Lance gave a wry look as he let out a breath. "Okay, just as I suspected, he did give you the Disney version of the story. But, since I've hung out with Sifu on such a regular basis, that story isn't exactly as he painted it." Lance wrestled with the decision, causing him to pause before speaking further. "Now you didn't hear this from me, but ya see, he kinda believes that his actions on that day are what led him to pay the ultimate price in karma."

Kirin's face said it all, a look of confusion followed by sadness as she realized that Lance was referring to Sifu's family. "How so, Lance?" She leaned forward, Lance's words now carried more weight.

"Now, I'm not heavy into the details of spirituality, but everything is cause and effect. And, remember this is from Sifu, not me, but he believes his actions on that day put him where he is today."

"I don't get it. He saved his friend and knocked out several bad guys."

"Well, there's truth to everything, isn't there? What Sifu said was true, to a certain degree. That day, Sifu and his friend decided to put themselves in a bad situation. They had no business hanging out in the neighborhood they were in, but Sifu felt invincible at the time and decided to go there regardless. So, right there is one of the things he regrets. A good Gung Fu man doesn't put himself in a bad situation. His ego took over, and he failed to follow one of the first rules of self-defense."

Kirin nodded, "Okay, I get that, wrong place at the wrong time. But … he still ended up saving his friend."

Lance grimaced at the thought. "He saved his friend from harm because they decided to place themselves in a bad situation … because of that choice, he also put away four guys permanently."

"What do you mean?" Kirin drew closer to Lance. As they stood side by side, both their shape as well as their personalities clashed with one another. The odd couple shared a common bond, united together because of Sifu. Kirin pulled up her sleeves, while the military veteran prepared to share his story.

"I know the version he told you guys is that he sent those thugs to the hospital. Technically he did…. The problem is they went to the hospital but never came out. In the end, Sifu was cleared of all charges, but he took four lives in self-defense, and then he believes karma took four lives from him as well."

Kirin covered her mouth in shock. "Do you really think the universe works that way, Lance?"

Lance shrugged his shoulders, "I don't know. Maybe … perhaps. But, I do know Sifu believes that's what happened."

Kirin remained silent, still trying to digest the possibility.

"You see … when he told you that story about not being a hero, he felt that all of it was avoidable, had he used Wing Chun in the right way."

"I've always had a tough time tackling all three aspects of the art. The physical always came so easy, but the mental … and … don't even start talking about the spiritual because that constantly goes way over my head," said Kirin.

"As Sifu would say, you always need all three. Otherwise, you'll never have balance. And, if you resolve things with violence, the circle will continue to happen, over and over again."

Kirin had a wistful look on her face. It had been too long since she had last seen her teacher. "Lance…."

Lance already knew what she was going to do. He walked over and hugged her. In his raspy voice, he said, "Say hello to Sifu for me."

"How'd you …?"

Lance ignored her question. "I'm sure Sifu will be glad to see you."

Kirin gave one last squeeze, pressing her face against Lance's chest. She needed that hug more than she let on, thankful Lance was there to give some guidance. She made her way to the back of the shop, but before exiting she covered up, pulling her red hoodie over her head. She glanced back toward Lance as she said her final goodbye. Always cautious of media or fans, she slowly opened the back door to the alley. A quick peek was needed to make sure she was in the clear before she finally stepped out. After taking several steps, a voice caught her attention, startling her.

"So, you're off to see Sifu?"

She froze before switching into action mode. Within seconds, her footsteps closed the gap with the source of the sound.

Both hands raised up, and a voice she recognized spoke. "It's me. Chill. It's me, Quinn." He dropped his cane in fear.

"Quinn, what are you doing here?"

Dressed in a blue spring jacket, he blended well with the background of the alley brick. Quinn approached her by following the sound of her voice. "Kirin, it's been months. I've texted. I've called you, and you continue to blow me off." He drew close to her, cautious not to overstep her boundaries.

Kirin lowered her voice, "I'm sorry, Quinn. I know I should have handled that better, but my plate's been kinda full, and I hate to say this … my love life hasn't been my top priority."

"No. You don't need to apologize at all. I, uh … I have something to tell you, something that needed to be said face to face, and not by text, email, or phone."

Kirin could hear the change in his voice. "What is it?"

"First of all, let me say this. The time we spent meant everything to me, and the night we shared was beyond special. I think about that night all the time. In fact, it made me realize how much you mean to me."

"Quinn…?" Her fear was exposed in the light from the streetlamps.

"I know you might not want to hear this, and the timing is probably all wrong, but I need to tell you that ... I love you. I love you, Kirin." His voice trembled except for the most three important words.

Strangely, Kirin wasn't caught off-guard; in fact, she expected it. She'd heard the three words people wait their entire lives to hear, yet she felt empty—not exactly the sensation she would've expected. She reached out to touch his face as the feeling was definitely stronger for him. "Quinn?" she asked in confusion as a tear began to trickle down his cheek. "What is it?"

A gentle touch caressed her hand as Quinn took a deep breath. "I have more to say. I know it's going to be difficult for you to understand this, but please just listen to me. Promise me you'll give me a chance and listen to everything I have to say. I know that nothing I say can justify what I've done, no matter how bad my financial situation was. What I did was absolutely wrong, and I can understand why you never want to talk to me ever again."

"What are you trying to say?"

"I'm trying to say ... you were right. I was working for the UFMF in the beginning."

She pulled her hand away immediately as Quinn's head lowered in shame. Even without being able to look at her, he could feel the distance between them.

"I can't believe what I'm hearing." Kirin turned away, realizing it was the second time she had been caught by surprise today.

"Please, Kirin, they asked me to gather information from you at the start, and I agreed. But, what I didn't expect was to fall in love with you," he pleaded as he inched forward.

"You fricking jerk!" She spun around and slapped him on the face, knocking his sun glasses to the ground. "I asked you to tell me the truth, and you said to my face that you had no idea what I was talking about!"

"I didn't know what to do. I was confused, Kirin. You have to believe me." He was clinging to any chance that she might understand.

"Believe you? You liar!"

"I swear, I didn't mean to hurt you." He tried to reach out, but Kirin jerked away.

"You were my first. I gave myself to you … and…."

"Please don't be mad. I know what I did was wrong. I can't undo it. I didn't even take the money they gave me, and I quit the UFMF."

"Liar!" cried Kirin. "I can't believe a word you say."

"Look, I'm here to help you. I swear it. I found out something. It's not only m—"

"Shut up. Just shut up! I don't want to hear any more of your lies." Kirin's voice trembled as tears flowed down her face and confusion and anger engulfed her. She couldn't take any more and sprinted away from Quinn.

"Kirin!" he shouted, but his voice faded through the alley along with his hopes. He took several steps before falling to his knees. He knew right then that there was no getting her back.

"A lie leads to more lies. Only the truth can break the cycle." — Sifu

<u>Game of Risk—Day 110</u>

Since I'd gotten my own place, the gang seemed to venture to my loft quite often. I wasn't sure if it was because my place offered the most space, or if I was in a centralized location that made it convenient for everyone. Either way, I didn't mind their company. As for Bacon, the guys would shower him with tons of dog treats, so he especially liked it when they came.

It was a Thursday night but no ordinary Thursday. Once every blue moon, we would gather to play a board game. We restricted the frequency since friendships would be tested, and the game always turned heated.

We were all gathered around my kitchen table, ready for several hours of excitement. The trash talking had already started when Tobias said, "We can have up to six players, so who's sitting out this round?"

Danny was already positioned on my couch, and he leaned over to look at us. "Big T and I are out. We've got a big football game and a ton of bets to settle."

Tobias said, "That's fine. So, let's see … we got Ken, Robert, Ryan, Doc, Kirin, and me. Perfect, let's choose our colors, and begin."

"Wait, I thought we always rolled for color?" Doc interjected.

I replied, "We have to roll for our colored pieces? Really?"

Doc stared Robert down, "I'm just saying, last time, Robert complained that he got the yellow pieces."

Tobias said, "You don't see me complain when I get the black one."

159

Robert replied, "That's because you're black."

"Blasian, bitch!"

Just as expected, they were already beginning to argue. I had to step in. It was just the game setup, and we were already having, uh, debates. "Okay, guys, this always gets so heated. Just remember it's a game. The color doesn't matter."

"Damn straight, just the size," said Tobias.

"Uh, what?"

"Nothing, Kirin." Tobias looked away and began shuffling a deck of cards.

Ken chimed in, "It's all good. We're all friends. Whatever happens during the game never lingers ... that long."

"For now," Robert gave me an evil smirk and jostled his fingers together.

Doc continued to ruffle feathers, "It's all cool, as long as Ryan doesn't cheat again."

Ryan looked around incredulously, "I told you I didn't cheat. I just counted wrong.... What? An Asian guy can't make a mistake in math?"

"Questionable," said Doc. "Questionable," he repeated as his eyes seared through Ryan.

Ryan then pointed to Ken, "Oh, and another thing ... no white pauses, Ken?"

Upon hearing that, Ken frantically searched for something as he first patted himself down and then looked all around. "Where is it?"

Ryan pulled out a small hourglass, "Looking for this?"

Ken tried to swipe for it from his hand. "Give that back to me!"

Tobias jumped in, "I'm with, Ryan. None of this bullshit white pause during the game."

I eyed them all with confusion, "I must've missed this last time, but what's a white pause?"

Ryan explained, "This hourglass I hold is Ken's white privilege tool. For some reason, during a game, he whipped it out and just paused a speed round we were having. Seriously, who thinks like that?"

Tobias coughed out, "White people."

Doc chuckled. "I remember that."

Ryan added, "Then after that, he tried to modify the rules of the game during the actual game ... which I'd like to say only white people would have the nerve to do."

Doc nodded in agreement, "Yeah, had Tobias tried to do that, he'd be shot."

Tobias shouted, "Hey!"

Robert said, "Can't be mad when it's the truth."

I raised my hand up slowly, "I'd like a white pause button."

"Kirin, it's not real," Ryan said with a sigh. "It's some stupid white thing he came up with."

"Oh," I began to chuckle.

Tobias then pointed his fingers at each and every one of us. "Just remember, no allies."

"What do you mean no allies? You jerks do your little hand signals and then automatically ally with one another and then end up back stabbing each other," I said.

Ken said, "It's an unwritten rule, Kirin."

I demanded, "Show me!"

Ken had a dumbfounded look on his face—well, more so than usual. I laughed at him, and he finally realized my joke as he chuckled back.

For the next hour, we played Risk, otherwise known as the game that destroys friendships. Surprisingly, everyone was still in the game, but some had stronger positions than others. For the moment, Tobias and Robert had the two strongest armies. I was hanging on by a thread, as my last stand was fortified in Australia. They always said the least skilled players bunker down there—but, heck, I was still alive.

It was just a matter of time before a big battle would ensue between the two of them. Both Tobias and Robert had been talking smack throughout the entire game, and they were ready to determine the outcome. While everyone one had a Wing Chun mindset, due to our training, our personalities came out during the game. Tobias was straightforward, always looking for the kill, willing to risk it all if it ensured victory. The used car salesman of our group, Robert was stealthy in his approach, waiting for a sign of weakness before he would strike.

Tobias stood and pointed at Robert. "Time for you to go down, Robert."

Robert replied, "You think you have enough guys to beat me and fortify afterward? 'Cause my turn is right after yours." I watched and listened to their psychological game.

If it's even possible, Tobias's face got even more serious. "Oh, I'm gonna make sure I wipe you out totally."

"I'm telling you now, you should think twice. If you don't finish me completely, you're finished."

Tobias's face change from serious to confident, "I've been watching the cards … your luck can't be that good."

"Bring it," Robert dared.

I couldn't tell if Robert was bluffing or not. At the same time, I didn't think Tobias cared. He always seemed so sure of himself.

Tobias grabbed the dice and acquired his army, ready to do battle with Robert. The first roll led to cheers, as sides were picked and pieces quickly began disappearing from the board. Everyone was watching as allies were ready to see if they had chosen the right side. For ten minutes, it felt like a seesaw battle, as pieces began to fall by the wayside. However, at the very end, Robert was able to hold on with a single guy left.

"Frick!" screamed Tobias. "I can't believe how lucky your roll was. There was no way you should've held. No fricking way!" He stormed away from the table and turned his back to Robert.

"What can I say? Korean army." A cocky Robert grinned at Tobias.

Tobias snapped around and said, "Well, there's no way you can advance with such a depleted army."

"Are you sure about that?" Robert grabbed several cards and slowly raised them and then lowered them onto the table.

"No, way … no way!" cried Tobias. "You can't possibly have a set of three."

Tobias waited along with everyone else as Robert placed three cards down. He shook his head, knowing that Robert would have a slew of new army members to attack. "Reinforcement." Tobias's facial expression changed to defeat. The game was over. Robert raised his fist in exhilaration as he pounded his chest several times.

"It's interesting, isn't it?" I mused as I stared at the board.

Robert replied, "That I'm gonna overrun Tobias and kick his ass?"

I looked at the board and then thought about the actions of Tobias and Robert. For some weird reason, it had me thinking in a way I had never thought before. I continued my train of thought, "You know, if you think about it, there's, like, no hesitation to move groups of armies to attack or defend. They're just pieces of the game with no consequence if you lose them or not."

Tobias countered, "Well, I wouldn't say that. Robert's one guy is why he's going to win."

"That's not the point. I know this is a game, but hear me out here … how different is that from real life?" I asked.

Robert said, "What do you mean?"

"I mean, it's all about the value we place on things. So, if you saw a single credit on the floor, would you even bother to pick it up?"

Ryan called out, "I would. In a heartbeat."

Robert joked, "She said 'credit,' not 'cupcake.'"

Ryan made a fist at Robert, "Cupcakes are delicious."

I interrupted their little squabble, "That's my point. If you take someone with a ton of money … I mean more money than you and I can ever imagine … that single credit would be worthless to them. They'd probably walk past it."

Doc joined in. "I see what you are saying, but how is this related to the game … and to life?"

"I mean … all this, the world we live in, isn't it possible we're pieces in a game? That we're being manipulated as easily as you move these armies to do their own bidding? Human nature in theory is somewhat fixed, behavior-wise, I think. So say, for example, you had all the money in the world. What then…? What makes you look forward to the next day? I mean, if you can buy everything, have anything, what else is there left to conquer? No matter what … you still need that drive."

Tobias dismissed me, "You're talking crazy talk."

"No, I'm not. I've lived it. Back in Korea, we were simply pawns. Whether we lived or died made no difference to those who were running things."

"I'm sorry, Kirin," Tobias murmured, "I didn't mean anything by it."

"I know you didn't. But, as far-fetched as it may sound, there just might be some truth to what I'm saying."

Ken put in his two-cents, "I'm kind of digging this conspiracy theory of yours, Kirin. Imagine a handful of individuals using everyday people in a real game of Risk."

Robert chided, "That's great, guys, but that's all fantasy, and this is reality. At least let me savor this victory."

While the discussion may have ended, the thought continued to linger. To me, the idea wasn't too far-fetched. None of the guys could ever imagine where I came from.

"Kirin ... Kirin?" Danny broke my train of thought. He was waving his hand in front of my face. "Is your game over?"

"Uh ... what are you asking?" It took me a moment to figure out what was going on.

"I said, is your game over?"

"It's over. How about you? Who won the football game?" I asked.

Big T pulled out his credits and was showcasing it to the group. "I told you their defense sucked."

"Whatever," sulked Danny. "Wait, you never answered my question ... who won the board game?"

Robert pointed at himself as Danny's frown turned into a smile. "Oh yeah, baby!"

Big T frowned and then gave the credits right back to Danny. He looked at Tobias, "Come on, man! You always come through for me on this game."

Tobias held a single digit up, "One piece, man. It was just one piece."

Ryan chimed in, "Speaking of piece, I could use a piece of pizza."

Ken corrected him, "It's referred to as a slice."

Ryan waved him off, "Piece, slice … bottom line, I'm starving."

Doc came over and put his arm around my shoulder. "See, Kirin? You were all worried that everyone would be upset with one another. Now that Robert won, you can see we all have common ground 'cause we all hate him."

"Hey!" Robert exclaimed.

Origin of Sigung—Day 119

The entire gang was gathered on a Saturday night at Tobias's apartment. We had no plans, but we had already ordered some Chinese food as the main meal for the evening.

Robert complained, "Uh, why couldn't we do this at Kirin's place?"

"What's wrong with my place?" Tobias shouted.

Ken added, "It's about a third of the size of Kirin's loft."

Tobias looked at Ken and gave him the middle finger.

"What gives? I'm just telling the truth," said Ken.

"I'm also being honest," Tobias bantered.

Ken shrugged, offering no argument.

My stomach growled, "Everyone, chill. Tobias's place is just fine. Besides, when's the Chinese arriving?"

Ryan looked at his phone and said, "Not for another forty-five minutes. You guys want to watch a movie in the meantime?"

Danny suggested, "There's nothing good to watch. How about some sports or some UFMF fights?"

Doc seemed frustrated, "I can't watch those. It's boring. Everyone just muscles themselves to death. Besides, you only watch it to gamble with Big T."

Danny replied, "Hey, you're making me sound like a one-dimensional character."

I stepped in, "You know what? Let's do something different. How about story time? I've heard the story of Ipman and how Sifu and Tobias first met, but I've never really heard anything about Sigung."

Robert spoke up, a hint of jealousy in his voice, "Well, it's going to have to come from Tobias because he's the only one who's had a chance to see Sigung before."

I asked, "Really? So, what do you think, Tobias? You up for storytelling time?"

Tobias took one last bite from his cereal bowl and put it to the side. He took his time to swallow but still didn't answer.

I glanced at the bowl and then back at Tobias, "Dinners coming soon. Why are you eating that crap?"

Tobias thought about it and then stood up. "We got some time to kill. So, yes, I'll talk a bit about the origin of Sigung. Also, this isn't crap."

Ryan was scanning through Tobias's cupboard and it appeared he had literally every cereal one could imagine. "Do you mind if I help myself to some of this crap?"

"Knock yourself out."

I didn't want to encourage anyone else further, but his cereal collection was quite impressive. But then again, I was comparing it to my empty shelves. We all gathered around, and I picked a spot on the floor since the couches were maxed out. The rest of the guys were nestled in place, with Big T and Danny sitting side by side on the loveseat. Doc sat uncomfortably on Tobias's computer chair, while Robert, Ken, and Ryan stretched along the couch.

Tobias started, "So, where do I begin...? Ah, yeah. Now I remember. So, the one and only time I ever met Sigung ... it was definitely a long time ago. Kinda as long as it's been since Ryan had a date."

"Hey!" Ryan protested and some cereal fell from his mouth.

"Well, whatever, exact date isn't so important, but I had been in the art for just over a year and a half. Back in the day, from what Sifu told me, he would host seminars for Sigung, who would venture out to Chicago. But, fortunately for me, I caught him on his farewell seminar. I later found out from Sifu that Sigung hated to fly, and as he got older, didn't want to travel as much."

I was sitting at full attention, "I'm already jealous that you were the last one to meet Sigung."

Tobias added, "Yeah, it was pretty cool, but what was even cooler was what happened when we met. So, a bit of description about Sigung and his personality. He's probably about one or two inches shorter than Sifu. His hair was pretty thin on top, and I would've never guessed he was a Wing Chun master just from looking at him."

Robert made his usual snide remark, "So, that's the only thing Ryan has in common with him."

"Shut up," Ryan muttered.

Tobias continued, "Anyway, his back was kinda hurting him that day, so he was sitting doing single sticky hands with everyone. So, I grabbed a seat opposite him and touched his hands."

Ken said, "Dang, that is *so* cool."

Tobias replied, "Well, I guess you could say that, but what happened next was even cooler. I was touching hands with Sigung, and Sifu was standing behind me, watching and translating anything that Sigung said. So, there I was with my tan sau and Sigung had his fok sau over mine. I was about to begin the motion to roll, and the next thing you know … I couldn't move my arm."

Doc guessed, "He froze you right away?"

Big T couldn't contain his excitement, "Dang! So, what it'd feel like?"

I shook my head, unable to imagine that.

Tobias went on, "Well, everyone here has felt it when Sifu's frozen you. I'd say it feels exactly the same, but you have to remember that was the first time I'd ever felt it … so I had no idea what was happening other than the fact I couldn't move my arm. At the time, I was just in shock. I thought he literally had some kind of superpower or at the very least was hypnotizing me."

Ken asked, "Did he freeze only you?"

Tobias tried to remember, "I think so…."

I questioned, "Why?"

"'Cause he's black?" Robert winked.

Tobias immediately gave Robert a look, but his comment got a chuckle from the entire group.

After we finally settled down, Tobias tried to answer our questions, "Well, I later asked Sifu, and he said that it was because he didn't know me, so he wanted to make sure that I didn't try to do something cheap."

"I can't believe he thought you'd do something cheap," Ryan rolled his eyes.

Robert started, "Maybe it really is because he's—"

At Tobias's warning look, Robert cut off abruptly. "What's there to believe?" Tobias said before turning back to his story. "That was the first time I ever experienced something like that, and that very moment … that sold me on the art."

Big T added, "So, if you really think about it, both Sifu and Sigung totally bitched your ass."

The doorbell rang, and Tobias went to answer it instead of responding. "Time to eat. Chinese is here, bitches."

Working Day—Day 132

Twenty minutes had passed, and I was still waiting for the model to come. We had agreed on a specific time so I could capture the perfect picture. I whipped out my phone and sent a third text to her, regretting my choice not to hire a professional. I had already spent the entire day preparing for this, and the only thing missing was the main ingredient. Unfortunately, that was the most important part.

There was no point getting upset. At least the view by the planetarium was beautiful. Time was running out, and things were definitely not looking good. I checked my phone again and, still, nothing. No text, no reply to the several voicemails I'd left her. It looked like I had gotten stuck with a no-show. *Mental note: There's a reason she said she would do it for free.*

I watched as several boats passed by, the wind blowing just enough to catch their sail. The lake had a tranquility about it that drew me to this spot to take pictures. A slight gust sent a chill down my spine. The fall weather was a reminder that winter was around the corner. I brushed my hair back as the sun hit my face. I closed my eyes and began to absorb the remaining heat before the sun faded.

"Hey, it doesn't look like you are working?"

I quickly turned around, surprised by a familiar voice.

"I'm 99.9% working. It's the .1% that's preventing me from actually doing the work." My gaze fell on Tobias, who was standing right behind me.

There's a sight for sore eyes.

He let out a chuckle and moved next to me. "You went cheap and didn't pay the model again—am I right?"

"Quiet, you ... but, yes, you're right. I got stood up for my shoot." I spun around and faced the lake again, not wanting to give him the satisfaction. He stood behind me to my right, wearing his biker jacket with only a t-shirt underneath, even though it was starting to get chilly. I asked, "Aren't you cold?"

I heard no response and turned around.

He answered by removing his jacket and flexing his muscles. I rolled my eyes, but was impressed; he does work out.

"That's not an answer."

"By your reaction, I believe it is."

"Don't flatter yourself." I blushed and looked away, knowing he'd see right through any smart comeback. "So, what brings you up here? I didn't think you'd hang around this area." I took a final glimpse at the sun before it set.

"Well, usually I don't, but I was—"

"Holy smoke!" I said as I looked at the sunset and then at Tobias. "Tobias, I can use you…."

"Uh…?"

"For the shoot, silly." I rushed to grab my camera.

"What do you want me to do?" He watched me scrambling around. "Do you want me with or without my shirt?"

"No time to explain. Just do what I say, and I can still get my job done for the day." I tried to ignore his last comment, which of course had me imagining him without a shirt.

Tobias nodded and stood still while I moved in a frenzy.

I positioned him against the backdrop of the lake and gave him quick instructions on how I wanted him to pose. The image of what I wanted was already in my head. I wasn't taking pictures; I was creating them. Then it was a race against the sun. After several minutes of shooting, I still wasn't able to get the shot I wanted.

Tobias asked, "What's wrong?"

I put my camera to the side and approached him. "Okay, the look you're giving me is … I'm going to kick your ass. For this picture, I need the model to look like you're in love. You know what I mean?"

"In love…?"

"Can you do that?" I didn't bother to confirm, but I just was hoping he could pull it off. Time was running out.

I began to take more shots, and Tobias changed his demeanor. A few more minutes passed before I said, "Break." I was frustrated, but I knew it wasn't his fault. Searching for a solution I asked, "What's wrong?"

His aura of confidence wasn't about him, "Uh, look. It's not so easy for me to play ... uh, being in ... love."

"Why's that?"

"I don't know how to say this, but I've never really been in ... you know, in love."

It was a touchy subject, something I wasn't an expert in either. "I've seen you with different girlfriends ... *many* different girlfriends." A weird feeling of annoyance, possibly jealousy, kinda overtook me. "Look, it's just like Wing Chun. What I'm asking you is to show a feeling."

"Yeah, that's great, but it's a feeling ... I've never felt before," as he shied away from eye contact.

Tobias had a point, but the sunset inched across the sky, hinting at my limited time. Then I asked, "Okay, how about this? Picture the girl you think you'd be in love with or care about. What she'd look like, act like, and be like, I guess. What would you say to her? I'm not sure what else to say. Try it, please.... There isn't much time."

I got back into position and waited. He stood still and looked like he was really taking my advice to heart. I had to bite my lip and not say a word, hoping that he would somehow find a way.

Tobias looked at me, "Come here for a second."

I approached him wondering what he wanted. He grabbed me by the waist and pulled me next to him, as he stared at me closely.

"What are you doing?" I whispered.

"Do you trust me?"

It was difficult for me to look away, but I mustered the courage, "Yes … I, uh … I trust you."

"If you want this shot, then I need your help. You asked me to visualize, but it's difficult for me to use my imagination. The truth is, none of those girls … none of them, I've ever cared about. And, the closest thing, like you said, that I do care about are you guys in my Wing Chun school."

I stood quiet, staring into his eyes. I could tell by his expression that his words were genuine.

"But, it's kinda weird picturing one of the guys, so I figured it'd be easier just picturing you."

I blushed at the thought, embarrassed, but I was locked into his stare. I'm not sure what made me do it, but I asked, "You care about me?"

He didn't hesitate, "Of course, I do." He held my gaze, and added, "I mean … all of you guys mean the world to me."

I whispered, "Okay, can you picture things now?"

He drew me in closer until I could feel his breath upon me. "I can picture her now." His grip was comforting, and his face said it all. "Kirin?"

I stood there and trembled. "What?"

"Take your picture now," he encouraged.

I shook my head and stared at the sun. "Oh, crap…." I scrambled to get into position.

Shot after shot, my finger was clicking away as my camera sounded like a gun. He finally had the look and was taking orders fairly well from me. He turned out to be a pretty decent model, considering he had never done this stuff before. But, I had no intention of telling him that; his ego did not need any more padding.

For the last ten minutes, I worked frantically. I could not believe my luck as desperation turned to elation. I had gotten the shots I wanted—and, more importantly, I was going to get paid.

I put my camera down and gave a thumbs up. "I really owe you. You saved my butt for these shots."

"Don't I always do that?"

I had to think about it, but he was right. "Yeah, you do."

"How about we grab something to eat? I am kinda hungry," He put his jacket back on and added, "You can treat me."

"Sounds like a plan." I began packing up my equipment in the dwindling sunlight. "I'm assuming you brought your bike here."

"Obviously. What do you feel like eating?"

Then I realized something, "Hey, one last pic." I retrieved my camera and added, "Turn around for a sec."

Tobias looked at me strangely as I repeated my request. He finally submitted and spun around.

I said, "Don't drop me."

"Don't drop—?"

I jumped on his back, and he was quick to react as he was able to easily hold me from behind. I faced my camera and held it in front of us.

"Uh, if you wanted to do a selfie, I have my phone."

As I struggled to position my camera, I said, "You really want to compare specs against my camera?"

Tobias begrudgingly agreed, "Okay, fine. Hurry up. You're not light, you know."

"Quiet, you … what's the point of having all these muscles if you don't use them. Just hold still and move a pinch to our right … uh, I mean, your left. Yeah, your left."

"You sure?"

"Hurry, Tobias!" I held my camera and took several shots, hoping that it would come out perfect. "You can put me down now." Even though we studied the same art where using muscle was frowned upon, I could feel how strong he was as he lowered me to the ground.

"I wasn't heavy at all."

"I know…. I just wanted to make you think that. Let me see the pic."

I looked through several shots until there it was. It was perfect, a picture of me and him with the beautiful city background.

How quickly things can go from bad to good.

Tobias looked at the picture, "You know what…? We look good together."

I smiled and wasn't sure what to say to him as I looked deep into his eyes.

We do look good together.

Section 2 Sifu's Journey Entry #4—Watchful Eyes

Three Weeks Later

It was just late afternoon as Lance looked outside the shop and saw a line had already formed. He was waiting on Sifu to decide whether they would be opening or not. They had been working for two weeks straight without a break, straying from the formula that they dictated how things would be run. Normally, by now, Sifu would make the call to inform the crowd if they were opening, but Sifu had not been himself lately. Lance did not press and instead continued to make himself look busy.

Sifu called out, "Hey, Lance…?"

Lance turned, eagerly waiting for a decision. He took a moment to try to read his teacher and mentally bet that he would say yes.

Sifu stared at him decisively, "Tell the crowd … no ramen tonight. We're gonna take a break."

He waited for Sifu to turn around before he shook his head. Even with his experience and elite military training, he thought, *He's the only guy I just can't read.* Lance began heading toward the entrance, ready to inform the crowd about the bad news. He heard footsteps headed the other way, and Sifu shouted from a distance, "Close up for me, will you, Lance? I have somewhere to go."

Lance waited until he heard Sifu exit the rear door into the alley. The door slammed as Lance muttered, "I hope you find what you're looking for, Sifu…."

Thirty Minutes Later

Sifu hopped off the bus and stood opposite from where it all began. His thoughts had been occupied since the incident several weeks ago with the STDs. The girl he had helped continued to haunt him, but so far, no ill repercussions had resulted. Sifu knew nothing was ever random. There was a reason for that encounter and the universe stirring his pot into action.

He stood at a distance and looked at the ramen shop where he had met Megumi. He took a deep breath and began walking toward it. Everything looked the same from the outside; nothing had changed, but for him everything had. He grabbed the handle, hesitating for moment before he found the courage and let himself in.

Inside, it was fairly empty, almost exactly like the night fate had brought the two of them together. Deep down, Sifu knew there was no going back. Fate had also taken away his love and everything they had created together. He decided to seat himself at the very same spot. Just like before, he ordered the same ramen and went through the motions.

Sifu placed his order with the waiter and decided to sit back. He didn't grab his phone to kill the time, instead he looked around to reminisce. On top of his table were a pair of chopsticks, which he grabbed and separated. Habit almost forced him to roll them together until he remembered how rude that was to do. Sifu chuckled at his own ignorance, and then the waiter came over to set down the bowl of ramen.

He looked at it and smelled it. Now, with a trained eye from his cooking, he could tell why Megumi knew right away how bad it was. He grabbed his sticks and placed them in between his hands as he said, "*Itadakimasu*," and performed a little bow. He was about to dig in to taste the broth when he stopped and turned around. He noticed one individual like himself eating his meal in the far corner. He was heavyset, as if he had been here many times before. He then turned in the opposite direction and saw another fellow wearing a baseball cap. Sifu didn't make eye contact, but the man jerked away from his meal, grabbing his phone as he pretended to have a quick conversation.

Sifu returned his attention to his meal, making sure that those watching saw what he was doing. He closed his eyes, quieting his surroundings, and then allowed his thoughts to empty out. Something was off. Something about these two individuals did not flow with the moment. He knew eyes were upon him, and he wanted answers. He decided to eat his meal hastily and left enough credits to take care of the bill along with the tip. Instead of taking the bus, he planned to walk for a while.

It was evening by the time he left the ramen shop, and the neighborhood wasn't the safest to be strolling alone. But, Sifu decided to pick a place that was even more isolated than the rest. He could feel them trailing him but decided to continue his normal pace down the long strip by himself. Several feet away, he saw an alley and decided to turn into it once he got there.

When the two men who had been trailing Sifu reached the alley, they looked at each other and decided to go inside. The heavyset one, Nolan, took a moment to catch his breath. He said, "Are you sure he went in here?"

Rick replied, "I'm positive…. Come on, suck it up before we lose him."

The smell and the darkness made it unwelcoming. Only a single light cast a glow that stretched the distance. The two men scanned the area and noticed nothing but a large garbage bin along the brick wall.

Nolan took a swipe at his friend, "I thought you said he went this way."

Rick took several steps forward and continued to look everywhere that he could. "I don't get it. I saw him go this way … I swear!" He raised both hands up in frustration.

Using their distraction, Sifu struck. In a blink, he appeared out of nowhere, first tripping Nolan as he quickly rolled on the dirty

180

ground. Rick was the next target, and he found himself kissing the brick wall as he was placed in a painful joint lock that he could not escape.

Sifu spoke into his ear sternly, "I know that someone's been following me for the last week. I would like to know why and who it is that finds me so interesting."

Rick groaned. "We're not here to hurt you. I swear. I swear!"

Sifu cranked on his shoulder a pinch harder as he turned slightly to see the status of his partner on the ground.

Nolan got to his knees and moaned. "What hit me?" He looked up to see his partner in a compromised position.

Rick grunted in pain as Sifu looked at Nolan.

Nolan reached out and shouted, "He's telling the truth! We just wanted to get in touch with you. That's all."

Sifu said, "And why should I believe you?"

Rick cried, "I'm in an arm bar that hurts like heck, and my fat friend on the ground is in no shape to hurt you at all. Please let us explain…."

Sifu eased his grip on Rick and cautiously took several steps back. "Explain yourself."

Rick began to massage his arm as he walked toward his friend Nolan. He offered his other arm to help him up. Nolan staggered to his feet, grabbing his back as he winced in pain. Then Rick turned his focus back to Sifu and put both his hands up, trying to keep Sifu calm.

Rick tried to de-escalate, "Ease down. Like I said, no one's here to hurt you, but then again, who can, right?"

Sifu was still at full alert, but the man's comment tugged at his heart slightly.

Rick continued to talk. "This is my associate Nolan, and I'm Rick. This isn't the best place to talk 'cause the walls have ears." He raised his right hand and slowly began to reach into his pocket. He said, "I'm just reaching for my card; that's all." He reached into his pocket and handed a thin object to Sifu.

Sifu grabbed it and glanced at the card while keeping another eye on both of them. There was not much on it, other than some numbers. "What is this?"

Nolan said, "Look, we have to play it safe and not just broadcast our location. Those are coordinates for a pickup. From there, you will be escorted to our main location…. I know it seems very cloak-and-dagger, but I assure you that, if you come, we will answer all your questions."

Sifu stared at the card and at both of them. "Why would I even care about this?"

Rick took a slight step forward. "That girl you helped several weeks ago, she was not just any girl being picked on by the STDs."

Nolan said, "Look, our job was to give you the info. It's up to you to decide if you want to find out what we know or not. If you decide not to come tomorrow, then we will never bother you again … I swear."

Rick was getting restless, "It's not safe for any of us to continue talking here. Is it cool if we all leave and you decide for yourself one way or another?"

Sifu looked at the card one last time and nodded. "It is."

Rick turned to Nolan, "Can you walk?"

Nolan replied, "I'm not that out of shape; besides, I just lost my balance."

"You lost your balance, or this guy over here just whopped your butt?" Rick pointed to Sifu.

Nolan looked forward and stared at nothing. "Uh, what guy?"

Rick looked in the same direction as Nolan, and then they both began to scan the alley. Sifu was nowhere to be found.

CHAPTER 5

Never Second

Even though it was a weekend when most people would sleep in, Thorne's eyes opened at exactly six am. He took a deep breath and slowly exhaled. By the numbers, he did all the necessary things one does in the morning. The only difference was that he did them better than anyone else. He grabbed his morning coffee, which was done exactly when he needed it, and put on a robe. He took a quick peek at his bed, where Linda was draped with only a blanket covering her and another female companion.

Thorne's mind had been racing for the last several months. He was deep in thought, calculating how to make sure his move would end him on top. He stood by the glass window looking outside his penthouse, unable to enjoy the magnificent view.

He took a sip as the warmth of coffee did not bring him pleasure either. He heard a rustling from behind but ignored it, allowing his thoughts to remain his priority.

From behind, Linda stood naked and hugged Thorne. She leaned her head on his shoulder, but neither said a word. Her toned body pressed upon his back—the soft texture of his robe felt good to the touch.

Linda whispered softly, "I always admired that about you … your focus."

Thorne took another sip and closed his eyes, allowing himself to finally enjoy the brief moment.

"You know, sometimes if you focus too much, you lose sight of the big picture."

Thorne put his coffee on the ledge, grabbed Linda's hand firmly, and spun around. He planted a deep kiss on her lips but still did not speak a word.

She smiled devilishly, "That's the other thing I like about you. Unlike others who go by the book, you make your own. That unpredictability is what makes you so sexy."

Thorne smirked and then let go of Linda as he grabbed his coffee. This time, he downed it, but something caught his eye when he glanced outside. He asked, "Do you see that over there, Linda?" He continued to gaze at the sight that had garnered his attention.

She peered over his shoulder to see two men washing windows on a tall building opposite theirs.

Thorne thought out loud, "Of all the lessons I've ever learned in life, there's nothing more valuable than trust. Those men out there hanging by a scaffold. They've laid their trust on some rope and metal, believing that it will keep them alive."

Linda encouraged, "Go on…."

Thorne continued, "It's not just the objects, but the individuals or machines that created that scaffold. The depth that human beings are willing to lay their lives on, hoping that everyone involved in the process did their jobs correctly. I find it quite fascinating."

Linda gave him a yearning look, "And you trust me?" She already knew his answer to the question but wanted to hear confirmation.

"Trust is earned, not given." He turned toward her again and said, "When I became the president of the UFMF, you and Fawn earned that trust. I had positioned myself to test out who I could or could not trust. At the end of the day, it was the two of you who stood by my side."

Linda shook her head as memories of that day felt fresh. "I remember that day so vividly. You created that disaster to weed out people. One by one, everyone's true colors showed."

Thorne let out a deep sigh. He felt frustrated from his lack of control. He was not comfortable being in a position that was not of strength.

Linda saw his brow furrow, "What is it?"

"Little did I realize that my promotion was a farce." He felt disgust at himself for not seeing it clearer.

"Why would you say that? As you stand and speak, right now, you are the most powerful man running the largest corporation in the world."

"My actions that you see before you came about after I discovered that Justice actually knew Watanabe. That's when I started to dig, and I realized that Watanabe had bigger plans, the scope of which went further than I could imagine, beyond the simplicity of corporate profitability and pleasing shareholders."

Linda looked behind her as the other girl in the room was still sleeping. "Is it safe to speak here?"

Thorne didn't even bother to look. "Don't worry. She'll do whatever I say." Throne looked to an antique grandfather clock that stood in the corner. "Fawn will be here within the hour."

Linda tried to comfort Thorne. "Everything will be all right."

Thorne looked at Linda, "Deep down, I always knew that I could never settle for being second, even if it was to Watanabe. I thought it was only a matter of time before an opportunity would present itself. At the time, I believed it was going to be difficult since I hold Watanabe in such high regard, but after I realized he was planning things without me, this has made it so much easier."

Linda planted another kiss on Thorne's lips. "What are we going to do about her today?"

"From what you told me, she's got a busy schedule for today."

Linda said, "You have no concerns about her at all?"

"I've done this long enough to see someone who'd sell their soul to be a star. She's yearning for that. It runs deep in her blood, and she's willing to do anything to get to the top. I can't quite put my finger on it yet, but there's something that's driving her as well." He paused for a moment and added, "When Fawn gets here, I'll instruct him further on what to do with Bryce. I figure we can use this to our advantage and tie up all our loose ends in one swoop." Thorne looked at Linda wanting confirmation. "There's no issue with him ... is there?"

Linda replied, "The debt of his sick daughter gives us total control. What are you going to tell him?"

"We know the play that Watanabe is gunning for, so let Bryce play the hero. Besides, the last thing we want Kirin to do is back out of this arranged meeting."

"I believe that it will go according to plan; however, our backup has literally backed out."

Thorne took the bad news in stride. In fact, Linda could hear a slight chuckle. "When it comes to money or women, there are times that the value to a man becomes skewed. Guess this time, the dollar value lost out to love."

With an evil smirk, Linda said, "Thorne, regarding all our loose ends, we can kill two birds with one stone. He was seen visiting Kirin's Sifu's shop not so long ago. Our informant also told us that their meeting was less than cordial."

"Make it happen," Thorne admired the plan that was unfolding. He added, "Linda ... all loose ends."

#

Just on the outskirts of the Chicago border lay a little mom-and-pop grocery store, oddly named Oinkers. It had been there for over ninety-three years, a landmark establishment for the neighborhood nestled in a corner. It was struggling to stay afloat, much like the other businesses in the surrounding areas. Fixed high above the roof towered a large statue of a pig, which drew the attention of many from afar. However, it was in much need of repair along with the grocery's rundown parking lot.

In the middle of the cereal aisle, stood Bryce. He looked over the slim selections and wasn't quite sure how ten choices of cereal constituted the naming of the entire aisle. He was wearing a raincoat and shades, which were fortunately fitting due to the bad weather outside. His cart was filled with food, many items he had never purchased before, as he stood continuing to look at the array of selections. He pulled his sleeve and tilted his hand to see the time, finding that it was already 12:35 pm.

She's late, he thought, which led to a surge of tension throughout his body. He continued to pretend to search through the cereals when someone appeared in the corner of his eye. Bryce did a double take as the disguise caught him by surprise. The two eventually met with their backs turned to one another.

Bryce grabbed the nearest cereal box and pretended to read it. He spoke while facing away from the stranger. "I didn't expect your disguise to look like that. Although, I do like the blonde hair."

Kirin wasn't in her usual red hoodie, jeans, and Cons. She was dressed far out of her comfort zone, and she looked like a provocative K-pop star who got lost and walked into a grocery store. Kirin grabbed a can of pork and beans and said, "Who eats this?" She continued to read the label, "Isn't there, like, only one piece of pork and all beans?"

Bryce said, "Is that a question or statement?"

"I'm just talking to myself, and this is just a wig, since you're wondering."

"I kind of like that look…. Maybe you should think about a real color change. The blonde suits you."

Kirin didn't respond but gave Bryce's suggestion some consideration.

Bryce asked, "Are you sure you weren't followed?" He scanned both sides of the aisle.

Kirin assured him, "I've got no tech on me at all, and lately I've hired Gavin to keep fans and paparazzi from stalking me."

"Gavin?"

"I met him last year at the Comic Con. He's a huge fan who literally looks like me when he dresses up. I decided to hire him— actually, it was Angelo's suggestion—when I need to get around."

"Hmm, that's brilliant. Wait, did you say 'he'?"

"Long story, never mind. Besides, we're not here to talk about that."

"Yeah, I thought you wanted to talk about the pork and beans," replied Bryce.

"Bryce, get to the point. This outfit is really uncomfortable." Kirin fidgeted in discomfort; her leather pants felt like it was painted on.

Bryce decided to move his cart next to Kirin as he scanned the other side of the aisle. He grabbed a box of Uncle Ben's and stared at it. He said, "I know this is off topic, but I used to think they made fried rice using Uncle Ben's."

Kirin could not resist staring at him with a dumbfounded look. She quickly turned around after realizing her actions were too obvious.

He added, "You know … I do love fried rice."

Kirin rolled her eyes and shook her head. "Bryce, you asked me to meet you here. The point … please!"

He decided to toss the box into his cart and did one final check of his surroundings. "I know it's been a while since we've talked, and there's no reason for you to explain why you haven't returned any of my calls, text, or emails … but, I know something that can help you."

Kirin walked closer to him, standing at his side as she looked at other food products aligned on the shelf. She grabbed a glass jar and pretended to read the label.

Bryce whispered, "I know about your parents, and I know that someone is blackmailing you."

Kirin was in shock, so much so that she dropped what she was holding. As the jar began to fall, Bryce reacted quickly and grabbed it before it made a mess. She responded in an agitated fashion, "Hah … how do you know? You shouldn't at all." She moved slightly away, trying to regain her composure after the hearing the news.

Bryce returned the item to the shelf and looked around once again. "Kirin, I have connections, and when you weren't responding to me … I figured something was wrong. You know I'm your friend. You know I'm here to help you."

"They said if I told anyone—*anyone*—they would have my biological parents killed." Her inner conflict continued to eat her up as a traitorous voice said, *At least I* think *it's them….*

"I know," soothed Bryce. "Is that the reason you aren't entering the 2034 season?"

"Yes. And they want assurance that I won't."

"You're not alone, Kirin. You have a friend in me. You'll have to trust me."

Kirin saw someone at the end of the aisle, which caused her to walk away from Bryce. He also waited until the stranger was out of their view before he said, "I think I may know who's behind this."

Kirin raised her voice slightly. "Is it the UFMF?"

Bryce shook his head. "I don't believe so."

Kirin couldn't restrain herself as she looked at Bryce directly. He motioned to her to calm down. She asked, "You sure…? You're 100% positive?"

"My source is pretty rock solid."

"What about my biological parents?" She cringed from the sound of desperation echoing in her voice.

"That, I can't confirm either. It might or might not be them."

Kirin's voice was hollow, "In my mind, I remember seeing my father get shot. It's haunted me forever. I dreamed the same thing happening in an endless loop. But, at the same time … I don't know. Maybe … is it possible? Or, I could be hoping for the impossible."

Bryce looked at her trying to hide his pity, "What if we can negotiate a way for you to get your parents back…? Are you willing to do that?"

"Of course … do whatever it takes so we can arrange a meeting to see my parents." All form of logic and reason left Kirin at even the possibility—no matter how remote—of seeing her parents again.

He walked past Kirin and grabbed another item that he placed in his cart. He took a moment to digest her words. "Then I'll be in touch with you, but you need to be prepared to move when I say." He faded down the aisle along with his words.

She nodded and began walking away, clinging to her last shred of hope.

Section 1 Short Stories #5—Kirin's P.O.V.

Bad Boyfriend—Day 146

It was a Friday night, and I was alone at my place with Bacon by my side, watching some TV. This was my first day off from photography in a week. With the holiday season nearing, I was busier than ever, which was a good thing, but tiring. Bacon kept a relaxing snore, which was quickly hypnotizing me to an early bedtime. One might think a nineteen-year-old with her own place would be venturing off to the night life, but my occasional nighttime brawls were more exciting than loud music, alcohol, and useless small talk in a club.

My eyes were slowly feeling the weight when I heard a text pop up. I decided to ignore it, since it couldn't have been work-related. A few seconds later, when I heard several more pops from my phone, I glanced to the side of my couch, but I decided that it was just too far a reach for me.

The next thing I knew, the phone rang, breaking me from my daze. "What the heck…?" I reached for the phone, but not in time as the call was forwarded to my voicemail. I looked at the time and realized it was only 8:30 pm. Then I noticed all the text messages that were on the screen.

I began to read them, my eyes widening, and then quickly checked my voicemail. "Guys, this is an emergency. Please meet me at the corner of Rush and Division. I, uh…. I gotta go." It was Danny's voice, and it seemed like he was in major trouble. I turned toward Bacon, who didn't seem to care what was happening in the world around him. However, that was the norm for Bacon, who somehow put life into perspective for me.

I texted the group as I locked the door. I had made my decision. I was off to help Danny, as I wasn't sure who else was on their way.

195

Twenty Minutes Later

I was dropped off at my location and saw the guys were already waiting at the corner. It appeared the entire gang was there in the chilly fall night. Danny was the center of attention as all eyes were focused on him.

I announced my arrival, "I'm here. What's the emergency?"

Danny stepped forward with a look of concern on his face. "Sorry, everyone. I need your help…. I didn't know who else to turn to. I'm looking for Tess. We got into a spat, and she just took off."

Ryan said, "Who's Tess?"

"What do you mean 'who's Tess?' She's been my girlfriend for the last year!" shouted Danny.

Big T slid forward, "Oh yeah, that cute blonde with the buck teeth."

"No, she's the redhead with the glasses and curly hair." Danny pulled out his phone and showed a picture of her.

Ken took a look, "Oh, yeah. She's pretty hot."

Robert asked, "Hey, can you send us her picture? You know, so we know what she looks like?"

Danny did what Robert asked and sent it out. Then he looked up and said, "Wait a second…."

Doc blew into his hands as he shivered in the night air. "So, what do you want us to do?"

Danny was about to answer, but Tobias cut him off. "Something's not adding up. How'd you lose her? I mean, she stormed off and … what? You sat down for a couple of minutes and then decided to look for her?"

Ryan added, "What was the spat about? Inquiring minds want to know."

"Seriously, guys, is all this detail really necessary?"

I finally chimed in, "We ain't looking until you tell us what really happened."

Danny hesitated for a moment, checked his phone for the millionth time, and sighed. "Okay, so the truth is, I think she might have broken up with me … but that's to be determined. As for losing her, when she took off, I was going to chase her down, but my stomach hurt really bad … so I had to hit the can first, then look for her."

Robert said, "Whoa, one second there, Romeo. What do you mean you *think* she broke up with you?"

"Like I said … she wasn't clear and—"

Tobias gave Danny *the* look, "What were the exact words that came out of her mouth?"

Danny looked downward, almost ashamed to say it as he mumbled words that no one was able to hear.

Tobias leaned forward, "I can't hear you?"

"She said, 'I think we should break up,'" Danny admitted.

Everyone made the same face and turned away. Robert was the first to say, "I can't believe you called us out here for that." I stood there as the rest of the guys were beginning to walk away. It appeared all help was about to fade, and Danny would be on his own.

"Please, help me this one time," Danny said. "I'm begging you." When no one responded, he shouted out at the top of his lungs, "I love her!"

The guys froze, and heads seemed to simultaneously hang at that those three words. One by one, Danny's friends turned around as the call for help seemed genuine.

"You owe us." Tobias pointed at Danny just for emphasis. "You owe us!"

Danny remained silent as a pact was made.

Tobias added, "Let's split into groups, and we'll see if we can find her. Okay, so Danny, Kirin, and I will search together and be team one. Ken, Doc, and Big T are the second search party. Robert and Ryan, you will be the dynamic duo and form the last group. Everyone, keep your phones handy, and text if you find anything. If there's no luck, let's meet back here exactly in one hour."

Team One

Twenty minutes into our search, we'd had no luck at all. It was like looking for a needle in a haystack because we were in downtown Chicago, and she could literally be anywhere.

Tobias finally broke the silence, "So, what gives? Why'd she break up with you?"

"Honestly, I have no idea. Things were great, and just out of the blue, we're having dinner, and she drops this bomb out of nowhere."

I asked, "I'm kinda wondering if your idea of great isn't on the same page as hers."

Tobias nodded, "Yeah, point of view makes all the difference, you know."

"I know it does, especially in por—" Danny coughed and said, "Uh, never mind."

Tobias looked at him funny, but I frowned, unsure what he was going to say. "All right, as best as you can, describe a typical day—and be honest."

Danny looked to be giving it some serious thought. "Well, she would text me several times a day, and you know women, sometimes it's useless stuff.... Anyway, we're usually both busy with work. I'd come home to my place, and she would make dinner. She has her things to do afterward, and I have mine, which is usually play video games ... and then pretty much head off to bed." He stopped in his tracks and thought about it some more before adding, "Yeah, that's a pretty typical day."

Tobias looked at him funny and then stared at me.

"What?" I asked.

Tobias said, "That's your typical day?"

"Yeah."

"How often did you text her back or call her?"

"Well, she usually initiated the conversations, but I always text back or call later ... uh, usually ... I think."

"And, did she do the majority of the cooking?"

"Of course, she loves to cook."

"And at night, you'd be playing video games most of the time?"

"Duh, of course, she was busy watching TV."

"So, how long would you say you've kept this kind of living pattern?"

"I'd say, the last four months," replied Danny.

Tobias whispered to Danny, but his voice wasn't low enough as I caught some of it. "How about the other stuff...? Did you take care of that at least?"

"On occasion, when I was in the mood."

Tobias shouted, "You're a fricking guy! You should always be in the mood."

Danny said, "Sometimes you need a break from the same burger once a month. You know what I mean?"

"Once a month?!" Tobias shook his head. "And no, I don't know what you mean!"

Tobias whipped out his phone and began texting. I watched, wondering what he was doing. Suddenly, both my phone and Danny's beeped. I looked at it and saw Tobias's text. I asked him, "We're headed back?"

Tobias said, "Yup."

Danny whined, "Why are we giving up?"

Tobias replied, "Because you already did."

We all rendezvoused back at our spot. As we got closer, I noticed all the guys had returned. Just like me, they all looked confused and were waiting for an answer from Tobias.

Doc said, "What gives?"

Robert asked, "Did someone find her?"

Tobias was about to answer when he paused, giving Ryan a weird look. "Where'd you get a hot dog? But, the better question might be ... why?"

Ryan wiped his mouth with the back of his hand, "We were walking by, and there was a food truck that was still serving. And why? We were going on an adventure.... I figured we could use the sustenance for our long journey." Robert was next to him, shaking his head.

Ryan shouted back, "What if we kept searching and ended up starving? Then you'd have to look for both of us as well."

"It's only been...," Ken paused to check his phone, "twenty-five minutes, roughly."

Robert said, "Technically, you bought your first hotdog five minutes into our 'adventure,' Ryan."

Deciding to ignore Ryan, Tobias turned his attention to the one who had caused all this trouble. We were all watching Tobias as he came from behind Danny and put his arm around his shoulder. He said, "Listen, guys, this is Danny. Don't be like Danny." Danny narrowed his eyes at him.

Unperturbed, Tobias continued, "There's a lesson to be learned from someone else's mistake. When you have something precious, you take care of it and protect it. If you neglect it, there's only one person to ever blame. Yourself." He turned to Danny and seemed to solely focus on him "What did you expect, acting that way and thinking everything is awesome?"

Danny still didn't get it, "What do you mean?"

Robert chided, "I always said Danny was dense."

Tobias patted his shoulder, "At the end of the day, you didn't do your job. A relationship doesn't end once you find someone; it requires more work to maintain it. You, my friend, were a bad boyfriend, and I know it's painful to hear, but that's the fricking truth."

I stared at Tobias as I absorbed what he had to say. His words were the truth; they came from his heart, and I respected him for it. It was weird to think about it, but his tough guy exterior was hiding someone much kinder inside. I wondered if that could ever be drawn out.

"Love isn't a word, it's an action." — Kirin

Karaoke Night—Day 153

A week had passed, and our group texts were as annoying as imaginable. I'd leave my phone alone for an hour, and I'd be swamped with messages between the guys—and they all revolved around Danny's heartbreak. Basically, it consisted of Danny whining with what-ifs, and everyone else sharing from their own love life experience … uh, except me.

Even though it was declared that Danny's misfortune was a result of his own actions, we were all still family, and the guys wanted to cheer him up. So, Ryan's suggestion was to head out for a night of karaoke.

When I entered the room, I saw I was the last to arrive. In front, Tobias was already belting out a tune as the guys cheered him on. On a giant screen behind him, words on the bottom flashed the lyrics as the video highlighted the song selection. The room was filled with multicolored lights that hit every angle, and the loud music drowned out any background noise. The walls hugged several seats that connected with one another, forming a U shape with the guys positioned along it. Danny was in the far corner, seemingly sulking still from his heartbreak. I was kind of hesitant to do this because I had never sung a full song before, let alone done karaoke, but I figured Danny would be the main focus of the evening.

The guys waved me in and razzed me for being late as I took a seat in the corner. I hoped that here, away from the spotlight, they would forget I was even there.

Tobias was still singing and pointed to me as I made a face at him. He finally finished his song as they all turned to see his score: 93 flashed on the screen. He raised his fist in the air, "That's the high for today, boys and girls." He tossed his mic at Ken, who was up next.

I was seated next to Danny and bumped him with my elbow. "So, how's it going?"

Danny hung his head as Ken began to sing—or, at least, that was what I thought he was trying to do. "Bad, Kirin. All I can think about is her and how I screwed up."

I patted him on the back and tried to give some advice, even though I honestly had no idea about relationships in general. "Look, I'm sure it's going to take some time. So, everything you're going through is natural."

Danny looked at me, "Kirin, you're great at Wing Chun. You've improved faster than anyone I've ever known in the school, but you can't give dating advice when you've never been there."

Ouch.

Ken finished his last shriek and then handed me the mic. I held it out between my fingers, grimacing. "I've never sung before, guys. I'm not any good."

Robert said, "Did you just listen to Ken?"

Ken shouted, "Hey!"

"You can't possibly be any worse," added Robert.

They cheered me on, chanting my name over and over again. Ryan and Doc tried pulling me from my seat, but I resisted.

Doc let go of my arm and then made the motion to Ryan to do the same. He kneeled in front of me and spoke. "Kirin, I know it's natural to fear the unknown, but whenever I face a situation like this, I have a little something I say to myself."

I looked at Doc, "What's that?"

Doc replied, "I tell myself … I don't know what I don't know … and the only way to find out is to try."

I repeated his words, "I don't know what I don't know?" The question in my voice was clear as I still didn't quite get what he was trying to say. Doc was always the wisest of the group, and his words carried weight.

Doc explained, "The world is an incredible place, with unlimited things to discover … but if you shut yourself from the possibilities, that's on you … no one else. So, you may like it, or you may not, but you'll never know if you live in that bubble." He stood back up and reached out his hand.

I grabbed his hand and hesitated. "I don't know what I don't know," I muttered again as I allowed him to pull me up. I found myself walking to the center stage of the room. I was standing in front of the screen and said, "I don't even know any songs."

"You don't have to," Doc encouraged me. "Just read the words."

Honestly, I was nervous. This was something new, something definitely out of my comfort zone. My hands were sweatier than ever when I brushed back my hair.

Ryan shouted, "I'll help you out!" He grabbed the other mic and selected a song as he stood by me. He looked at me and said, "Don't worry; just have fun. You'll know the song, and just follow my dance moves."

"I have to dance, too?" I complained.

The music started playing, and I turned around to see the words. I had a sense of relief as I recognized the song. It was K-pop and in Korean. I turned to Ryan, who had struck a pose and wasn't even bothering to stare at the screen. He was oddly confident.

I asked him, "You know this song?"

"Duh, of course."

"But, it's in Korean."

"Kirin, I'm single…. I have a lot of free time."

"To learn Korean?"

"At the very least to memorize a Korean song. How's that for an answer?"

Fair enough.

As the music started, I struggled to work with Ryan and find my comfort zone. But, halfway into the song, I started getting the feel of the beat, I forgot the eyes that were staring at me, and I finally let it all go. The next thing I knew, I was dancing side by side with Ryan—or, at least, I thought it was dancing. The words seemed to flow out of my mouth, probably way off-key, but it was in Korean so no one really knew one way or another, other than Robert. I think Danny was in the corner still pouting over his loss, but I was having too much fun to worry about him. The rest of the guys kept cheering me on as I found out why karaoke is so beloved.

Big T offered, "There's only ten minutes left, Kirin. Since you came late, why don't you finish the remaining time?"

No arguments from me as I started chaining together one song after another. It really ended up being a ton of fun, and I wasn't even drinking, unlike most people who need it to settle their nerves.

Tobias put on the pressure, "Okay, take us home, Kirin. You got last song."

Robert said, "Kirin, I picked out a song. Sing this one."

I was so into it and having such a good time that I grabbed the mic and began singing out loud. At the end of the song, I hit the last note and then looked at the gang for approval. I landed on one knee with my hands high above my head, glazed in sweat and a proud glow from my accomplishment. For that very moment, I felt like a superstar.

I scanned the room for a reaction until my gaze fell on Danny. He looked at me, with puffy and swollen eyes, as he appeared he was about to burst. He leaped off his chair and dashed out of the room, bawling.

I was frozen in my pose and asked, "What gives?"

Tobias stood up, shaking his head, "Seriously, Kirin, how could you sing that song, 'Alone'?"

Oh crap. I had been so oblivious to the words and the meaning as I just sang whatever was given to me. "I, uh … didn't know." I finally stood up, and several of the guys went to see if Danny was okay. The room was silent, and I felt bad. However, in the corner and trying not to laugh, Robert was snickering like a rat.

It was the last week of November, and already snow had blanketed our city with white. Commuting was slower than ever, everyone seemed accident prone as they were getting used to the icy weather.

For us, this was our first real test of our new facility; could we really train there during the cold winter months. Big T worked his magic and had installed several solar panels to pull in some electricity. The test would be whether that was enough to make this a Gung Fu school as opposed to a skating ring.

I asked Big T, "It's Chicago weather. What happens if we don't get sunlight for a while?"

Big T flipped the switch, "See, this bar right here? We've got enough storage for at least one week of electricity. Obviously, we can't have the TV, lights, heater, and music all going at max. But, we should be good to go even if we stay dark for a while. Now one thing, though … obviously, I couldn't install these panels on the top of the roof because that would draw attention, so I positioned them lower toward the lake area. The main thing is we have to keep the panels clean, so when it snows, it needs to be shoveled off."

Ryan was quick to donate the torch, "I volunteer Danny to take first shift."

Danny was working with Tobias on a drill and said, "Shut up, Ryan."

Ken was doing a drill with Robert as he shouted, "Hey, can you leave the TV on this one time? Channel 33 for news."

"News?" I asked.

Ken was quick with the sarcasm, "Yeah, you know, where they report what's happening locally and around the world."

Danny stopped his drill and turned to Ken, "Why are you watching that crap? It's all fake."

Big T commented, "Fake news, kinda like the cops saying we'll be in your neighborhood right away."

"Yeah, what gives, Ken?" Chimed in Robert. "I know you're all gung-ho about land of the free and home of the brave stuff, but the crap they're reporting is no different from … the shit Kirin used to see in North Korea."

"Hey!" I shouted.

"Hey what?" Robert looked at me.

"Just confirming."

Doc stepped in and added his two cents. "All right, guys, this is still class. We can leave the TV on, but this is actually the perfect time to use this as a good example from a Wing Chun perspective. Something we rarely talk about is the spiritual side."

"I'll be in the corner," I announced. "Someone wake me up when this is over."

Doc grabbed my shoulder, "Kirin, stay right where you are and listen. There's no avoiding the spiritual side of Wing Chun. One day, you'll have to deal with it to figure out the art." He turned to Tobias and said, "Do you mind if I take lead on this subject, Tobias?"

Tobias gestured to Doc that it was okay. "Less work for me…."

I had to point out, "Tobias and spiritual? He's never once spoke about it, let alone showed it."

Tobias retorted, "Knowing and doing are two different things. Just because I haven't spoken about it doesn't mean I'm not aware of it. Besides, my actions are spiritual. I'm well aware I'm going to pay them back eventually." The guys chuckled at his comments, but I wasn't quite sure what they were referring to.

Doc ignored Tobias, "As human beings, it's easy to get emotional, but as Wing Chun practitioners, we train to keep that in control. If you lose control in the fight, then you won't be able to see things clearly. Thus, seeing news, fake or not, is no different because, if you understand the way of things, you'll realize that both exist in everything."

Ryan said, "So, you're saying that there's a little of both in everything ... regardless?"

Robert teased, "Kinda like how a donut has stuffing inside, Ryan."

Ryan shouted per usual, "Shut up, Robert!"

The group stopped practicing and surrounded Doc as the unusual topic had captured everyone's attention. Approaching from the side, Big T wiped sweat from his brow and said, "Can you give an example, Doc?"

Doc smiled, "I'll give you two, one from a Wing Chun perspective and the other an everyday example." Doc clenched his fist and threw several punches in the air. "What do you see?"

I grinned, "Some pretty damn good punches."

For some strange reason, Doc was embarrassed by my compliment. He blushed and replied, "There's actually more than just a punch. In fact, you see the *ying* and the *yang* happening at the same time. As Sifu said, you see the motion of the punch, which is the *yang*, but the power is the *ying*, which is hidden inside." He then released another punch, but this time it was quite different. He clenched his fist and over-emphasized the use of muscle. He said, "Now, as you can see, I did the punch, but I did the reverse of it. That time, you saw the muscle and power, but the motion was slower and less explosive."

"So, what's the point?"

"Is it still a punch?" asked Doc.

I thought about it, "I guess so, in theory?"

Doc pointed to the TV and said, "On the news, you hear one story, and you have one group go ape wild for one side and then strong arguments for the other. Who's right, and who's wrong? The truth is, if you understand that both right and wrong exist at the same time, it'll be easier to decipher what really matters."

Ken asked, "So, how does one do that?"

Doc thought about it for a moment, "I think, in the beginning, the easiest way is to try to argue both sides. Hmm, maybe that's not the easiest thing to do, but that's how I was able to look at things objectively without letting my emotions take control."

My nose wrinkled, and I tilted my head. "So, what do you mean?"

"When you can argue both sides, then you can take hold of your emotions. After that, you can allow common sense to look at the situation and make the proper decision. Most of the time, people argue not to prove that they are right or wrong, but to reinforce their belief because it is so weak."

Robert said, "That's all great, Doc, but let's face it. Something doesn't have to be true for people to think it is."

Ken countered, "Well, the truth is you can make a lie the truth just by repeating it, or even worse, just one statement can put doubt in people's minds, since people are cynical."

"How's that possible?" My curiosity was running wild.

Tobias sighed, "People are weak."

Danny stepped in, "What?"

Tobias looked at me and gave me a quick wink. He turned to Danny and said, "For example, I know I'm going to be in trouble for this, but Kirin told me she likes one of the guys she trains with here."

Suddenly, all the guys stared at me. Ryan rushed over and gave me a puppy dog look. His hands were clasped as if in prayer, "Please say it's me."

"Ah ha … I knew it!" Danny shouted, pointing straight into my face.

I looked at Ryan and punched his arm.

He rubbed it and asked, "Is that a yes or a no?"

I said, "That's a punch on your arm for being a dumb ass. It's not true at all. Tobias said he was just making it up."

"I don't know…," Tobias taunted. "I heard her talking about it with her friend, Gwen."

Big T came to my side and put his arm around me. "Seriously, little sister," he tried encouraging me as he pointed to all the guys, "which one of us do you like?"

I elbowed Big T in the stomach and walked away. "Will you cut it out? I don't like any of you."

"I don't know," Robert said. "You seem a bit more emotional than normal for someone who doesn't like any of us."

Doc jumped in, "I'd be a pretty good boyfriend, you know."

I saw Big T and Danny shift into gambling mode as they were trying to figure out the wager. A quick look at Tobias in the corner showed him holding back his laughter at my expense, of course. The guys began bickering as I narrowed my eyes and decided to end the commotion.

"I like Tobias!" I shouted. "We've gone on a couple of dates, and I enjoy his company. It's Tobias!"

Everyone immediately turned to Tobias, who looked like a deer in the headlights.

Doc frowned, "That is uncool, man. As our group leader, you always said in-school dating is frowned upon."

Tobias raised his hands, "Whoa, one second!" He pointed at me and said, "We've never gone on any dates at all."

Instead of replying, I arched an eyebrow and pulled out my phone, flashing the picture of me and Tobias at the lake front.

Ryan grabbed my phone and looked at it. "Dude, what the heck? You get all the girls, and you had to hit on Kirin?"

Robert came around and placed his shoulder around Ryan. "Tobias, that is so uncool, man. You can't let Ryan die a virgin."

"Screw you, Robert!" shouted Ryan.

Tobias grabbed my phone, "Guys, this was at her photoshoot, and I happened to stop by…. That's all. I swear."

"I guess Doc is right. There is some truth and some lie in everything." I kept my distance and watched Tobias squirm for a while as he dealt with the guys.

"If you can see both sides, you'll never be played as the fool." — Kirin

Section 2 Sifu's Journey Entry #5—The Real World

The Next Day

As instructed, Sifu stood at an isolated corner by himself and looked at the card's coordinates, which had led him to the very spot. He had no idea what he was stepping into, but he trusted his gut and the flow of the force as he found himself on a street where not many had ventured. He thought it must be close to 10 pm, but he had no phone to verify. The sudden sound of tires screeching from afar caught his attention. A maroon sedan with tinted windshields and a dent on the driver's door hugged the corner tightly. It began to slow down as it reached him and stopped right by his side. The rear door swung open as Nolan, the gentleman Sifu had kindly swept, peered out. He greeted Sifu and requested that he enter the car.

Sifu did not hesitate, giving in to curiosity. He entered the vehicle and made himself at home right next to Nolan.

Nolan pulled out a device shaped like a thin wand as he explained to Sifu what he was doing. "This is just to make sure you have nothing to be tracked." He waited for confirmation from Sifu before he proceeded.

Rick, who was seated in the front passenger seat, looked over to Sifu. "Uh, it's good that you showed up. I had a feeling you would." He hesitated for a second and looked at Nolan, who questioned his statement. "Okay, I admit it was a guess. You're a difficult man to read."

Nolan brought out a black hood and presented it to Sifu. "Sifu … uh, is it okay that I call you Sifu?"

Sifu replied, "It's okay."

Nolan added, "You'll need to wear this."

Sifu raised his hands and objected. "I'm not gonna wear that." The tone of his voice remained the same, but his intent was quite clear.

Rick sighed with desperation, "You have to wear this, or else there's no deal. Please understand, it's for our safety."

Sifu did not even take a second as he grabbed the door handle and prepared to exit the car. Both Nolan and Rick were caught in a bind, as they stared at each other, not knowing what to do.

Finally, the driver turned toward Sifu, which caused him to pause. It was the girl he had rescued two weeks ago. He knew in an instant as they locked eyes. "Hi, my name is Sindy, with an S ... but everyone calls me Sin. Thanks again for saving me from the ... you know, STDs."

Both Nolan and Rick chuckled as Sindy cracked a smile and squinted at them. She said in a stern voice, "Both of you, grow up. Not the time." Her voice held no sense of irony as she lectured both gentlemen who were her elders by a good fifteen years.

Sifu continued to look at her but didn't say a word. He waited, unsatisfied with her response.

As Sindy looked at Sifu's face, she could tell he needed more convincing. "Please, can you put the mask on? It'll only be a short drive, but, like Rick said, it's for our own protection. I swear, you'll be okay."

Weighing the feeling rather than the sound of her words, Sifu stared at only Sindy's eyes while Nolan and Rick waited and watched. Looking into her eyes, he searched into her soul and found no malice, so he finally released his grip from the door handle. He creeped back into the seat and positioned himself comfortably. He opened his right hand and reached out, requesting the hood, which he placed on himself.

Sindy strapped on her seatbelt and shifted the car to drive. "Shall we?"

Fifteen Minutes Later

The car pulled into a garage, and Sifu felt a jolt. He could hear the sounds of machines clanking and then felt the sensation of being lowered. He was definitely going underground as the mystery continued to grow.

Finally, Nolan spoke as their descent stopped. "We're here, Sifu. You can remove the mask, uh … yourself."

Sifu removed it and took a moment for his eyes to adjust. It didn't matter that he'd had his full sight restored since he was in a dark garage with nothing to really look at for reference.

Nolan said, "Just wait in here for a second." Nolan unstrapped his seatbelt and exited the car. He dashed around the rear end of the car and reached the other side to open the door for Sifu. Both Sindy and Rick exited the vehicle at the same time.

As Sifu stepped outside, all three of them stood in front. Sindy took the lead, "Please, Sifu, follow me." She headed toward the only door that was oddly positioned at the far corner of the room. The dimly lit room had a solitary light flickering above, making for an eerie 80's horror flick scene. Sindy opened the door and began walking down a long hallway. Again, the decoration was limited, and visibility was low, but Sifu continued to follow her with both Nolan and Rick trailing behind him.

She paused in front of another door and then hit it several times in a particular pattern. Afterward, she looked above where the camera was located and smiled. From the other side, the door unlatched, "We're here." Sindy entered first, holding the door open for Sifu. He walked in to find a long table in a drab and unflattering room with a gentleman seated at the far end. As Sifu approached him, he stood and made his way to greet him.

He extended his hand, "I'm sorry for all the secrecy. As I'm sure my associates explained, it is for our safety. My name is Damon … and, yes, that is my real first name, and I'd like to be sure it's okay that we call you Sifu?"

Sifu nodded and agreed again, but left him hanging.

He pulled out a seat and offered it to Sifu. "Please, sit down. I'll try to explain as much as I can to you in a short period of time. If you don't mind, I'll be glad to answer any and all your questions after my little speech."

Sifu sat down as Damon and his companions followed suit. He looked to Sifu and asked, "Can I offer you something to drink … water, coffee…?"

"No, thank you."

Damon nodded and apologized for his delay. "I'm sorry…. I forgot for a second that you like to be direct." He stood up and looked at his crew before he said another word. "What I'm about to tell you is difficult to accept, but what if I told you the world you live in isn't exactly as simple as it seems? Today, we think that the world revolves around governments either elected by the people or corporations lending out money to control governments. But, I'm here to tell you that both you and I are merely pawns and so are the countries that are run by the government in a game that a handful of the most powerful fully control."

Sifu said nothing, simply remaining silent and listening. For the next fifteen minutes, Damon went into more detail about this secret organization as all eyes were on Sifu to see how he was digesting this information. However, no one could tell as Sifu remained stone-faced.

"Trust me, it sounds crazy, but if you really look around and wonder why things are the way they are, nothing adds up. I was unaware. I didn't want to believe in this when I was first exposed to it, but eventually I saw the light. You see, Sifu, since that day you helped out Sin—I mean Sindy over there—we've been keeping a close tab on you. Our organization is always looking for individuals with a particular skill set to help us with our battle."

Sifu looked at them and chuckled. "You people are serious? You're expecting me to believe that there's a secret society or organization that's been controlling the fate of the world for all these centuries, and that a small group of rebels or whatever you guys are … are working to take it or them down."

"Like I said … I understand the difficulty in believing this." Damon nervously tapped his fingers together.

"Even if all this is true … I'm sorry. I don't see how I can help you." Sifu pushed himself away from the table and stood up, leaving everyone unsure what else they could do to convince him.

"If you don't mind …, I'd like to be on my way now," said Sifu.

Damon and the crew were frozen as Sifu seemed set on leaving. Nolan and Rick turned to Damon, who said, "Please, an opportunity has come about that'll give us a possibility of finally infiltrating this group, and we need your help."

Sifu was halfway to the door before Sindy jumped from her spot and shouted, "Your family's death was no accident! They were intentionally murdered."

Sifu paused in his tracks but didn't turn around. If there was one thing that could hook Sifu, it was this. Sindy had used the proper bait.

Sindy approached Sifu cautiously, unsure how potent the fuse she might have lit. Her voice trembled. "I'm sorry … I'm sorry I had to be the bearer of bad news, but it's true. All of this. I swear to you that your help is needed, and all that Damon has said is, in fact, the truth."

Sifu let out a little sigh and then finally faced Damon and his crew.

Sindy checked with Damon first as he gestured it was okay. She walked behind them and pressed a small button. From the side where Sifu stood, a black wall began to slide up, revealing a dark glass that reflected their image. Slowly their reflection disappeared as the glass became transparent. At the same time, Sifu's eyes widened, the very first hint of emotion. In another room, stretching as far as the eye could see, was an entire team of people working in the background. It was exactly as Damon had described: a small allegiance of workers who were busy with their tasks.

Sifu faced the glass and walked toward it. He pressed his hand against it, just to see if it was real.

Sindy's hand stretched out as she showcased her coworkers. "This is our rebellion…. This the Defiance."

"The possibility that we are living in a lie truly exist. Only the truth within can set us free." — Sifu

219

CHAPTER 6
Everything Ends

Several days ago, the deadline to announce her return had passed. News stations bombarded the public with the fact that Kirin Rise was not going to return for this season to the UFMF. The bombshell announcement stunned the world as gossip spread like wildfire. But, none of that mattered to Kirin, who was more focused on what the decision had led to.

Kirin sat next to Angelo in the rear seat of the limousine. The tinted windows hid the fact that it was night outside. Bryce sat perpendicular to both of them, tapping his foot. He had an unsettled look about him, which was quite different from his normal cool demeanor. Kirin tried to keep calm, but her mouth was dry, her nerves twitched, and her heart was racing. No one in the car could escape the tension.

Faced with mixed emotions, she didn't care what her gut was telling her, regardless of how loud it screamed. It was impossible for her to let go. Above all, she had to find out. She *wanted* this to be real. Every doubt, every question she could imagine was racing back and forth in her head. If the slightest possibility existed that her biological parents could be alive, how could she not do everything within her power to see this through, regardless of the cost?

She glanced at Angelo, who was surprisingly quiet and not his jovial self. He could not hide the tension on his face, but he forced a fake smile back at Kirin. He felt off, and so did everything and everyone around her. Her emotions made it difficult to see clearly. She thought, *Why the secrecy? Is this all necessary?*

They had been driving for a good twenty minutes, and all three of them had no clue where they were going or what destiny was about to bring. She had finally gotten to this point, and she placed her trust in Bryce, who had helped arrange this meeting.

221

The ride seemed to drag on for an eternity, but finally, the car suddenly slowed down and came to a complete stop. Both Angelo and Kirin looked at each other, wondering where they were.

Sitting erect as he loosened his collar, Bryce broke the silence though his voice lacked strength. "I think we're here."

Kirin gave him a wary look. "Where, exactly, is here?"

He shook his head, he was as clueless as she. "I have no idea. I'm just following the instructions that were given to me. Let's hope for the best."

Angelo jumped into the conversation, "I feel so naked without my phone."

Both Bryce and Kirin snarled at him. She replied, "Seriously, that's what you're worried about?"

"You know me. I always have to fidget with something."

"Honestly, Angelo, we've been driving around for god knows how long."

"Thirty minutes," he snapped back.

Kirin said, "The time is irrelevant. Not having your phone with you should be the least of your concerns right now. Don't you think?" Angelo didn't respond. No answer could be justified in a moment like this.

Feeling lost and helpless, all three waited inside the car for several minutes. Finally, they heard the sound of the driver's door opening and soon after footsteps circling around their vehicle.

The door swung open as the driver stood at the side and remained silent. His hat covered his face just enough that they couldn't get a clean view of him.

Angelo whispered, "Well, he's no social butterfly."

Kirin nudged him in the back, which caused him to blurt out, "Let me go first." Then he realized what he had just said, but could no longer take it back. Angelo hesitated before stepping out and then disappeared into the darkness.

Kirin combed her hair to the side, making sure her little scar wasn't exposed, her telltale sign that her nerves had gotten the better of her. Bryce placed his hand on her shoulder, which caused her to jerk, but his soft touch was comforting. He looked at her, "I'm sure everything will be fine. I'll be right behind you."

She waited for a second or two before finding the strength to step out. Kirin looked around, trying to piece together any clue of their location. To her far right was a long strip of hallway, wide enough for the car to have passed through. The room where the limo was parked was dimly lit by several decrepit old lights hanging eerily above. This place felt abandoned, as if it were lost in time. All the dust and cobwebs had found a home here. The wind howled through the room, sending a shiver down Kirin's spine. It scattered the dirt and any other foreign objects that were not securely in place. After her brief investigation, the answer to her question remained. Kirin was still none the wiser.

Angelo leaned over to Kirin and whispered, "Do you have any idea where we are?"

Kirin replied, "I can tell you this—it's not Disney World."

"No, it's not. It definitely isn't." He grabbed Kirin's hand, but she slapped it away.

"Quit kidding around."

"Who's kidding?"

Bryce signaled to both of them not to speak. "Hush up, both of you."

From the opposite end of the room on the other side of the car came a large crashing sound. The impact disturbed the dust again, sending it sparkling into the air. It appeared to be a large elevator creaking open. It struggled to do its job but finally revealed a piece of the puzzle. As the doors opened, six men, all dressed identically, stood in a two by three formation inside. They all wore masks, concealing their identities, which made the knot in Kirin's stomach tighten even further. Three of the men came out and stood shoulder to shoulder, forming a perpendicular line to the entrance, while the other three remained inside, blending in with the elevator wall. The driver gestured for them to enter and continued his silence.

Kirin muttered to Angelo, "This is getting weirder by the moment." She immediately sized up the men and was not sure what she would do if things went south. She hoped with all her might that it didn't come to that.

Angelo attempted some comic relief, "I don't recall this in the job description."

The driver continued to wait with his expressionless face, which gave everyone the creeps. All three of them exchanged glances as Bryce decided it was time to take the lead. He stepped forward, buttoned the top of his suit, and said, "Follow me." He began walking toward the elevator as Kirin noticed a bead of sweat dripping from Bryce's head.

Kirin thought, *What's the worst that can happen, right? It ends up not being my parents.*

As Bryce approached the entrance, one of the masked men held his hand up, causing Bryce to stop in his tracks. The driver took his cue and returned to his vehicle. A minute later, he began to pull away, but oddly his headlights never turned on, and the car quickly disappeared into the darkness.

Angelo muttered, "I guess we're going to have to taxi our way back home."

Kirin ignored him as any attempt to lighten the mood did not help.

Bryce was then signaled to enter, and Kirin and Angelo followed suit as all three of them crowded next to each other inside. The remaining three guards finished the sandwich formation, as they were now fully surrounded and placed in a rather claustrophobic position.

Kirin kept her head down as she did not want to make eye contact, but Angelo was quite unnerved.

Bryce whispered to his right, "Everyone stay cool."

Angelo was about to say something, but he pulled himself back and clamped up. Like everyone else, he was waiting to see how things played out.

From the far-left corner, one of the guards pulled the lever. Chains rattled as the motor strained to start up and began bringing them upward. The entire elevator shook, seemingly affecting everyone's center of gravity, except Kirin's. She felt even and balanced, maintaining her stance without even a thought. They went up several floors as Kirin tried to judge the distance. The number indicator located on the top no longer functioned. The rattling sound seemed to increase as they ascended even further. A few minutes later, a sudden jolt indicated they had finally reached their destination.

Kirin nudged Angelo, "This is the one time that I wish you had talked me out of this."

Angelo scoffed, "That makes two of us."

Everyone waited for the doors to open, but the elevator took its time. Kirin peeked at both Angelo and Bryce. Each one seemed even more tense, and now it was Angelo with a bead of sweat forming on his forehead. She kept her mouth shut even though the universe was screaming inside her.

The elevator door began to screech open, but halfway there, it fully stopped. Two of the guards got on opposite sides and had to pull them clear. A little elbow grease finally cleared the path for everyone to exit.

As Kirin took a step forward, her eyes widened as her breath caught. The vast space was dimly lit, and the twilight sky breaking through the top windows was the only source to aid in visibility. The high ceilings stretched far to the top, ending with boxed glass windows. Some covered and dirty but most of them shattered, the windows surrounded the entire upper area from corner to corner. The space was about the size of a high school gymnasium, stretching far and wide in all directions. As she took one step forward, the old wooden floors creaked, and she wondered about their strength. Outdated printing machines filled most of the room, forming a maze from one end to the other. Multiple pillars existed throughout the area, each one supporting a second level balcony that ran next to the walls hugging it. A small office room was centered on the furthest wall, overlooking the work area.

"What is this place?" asked Kirin.

Angelo replied, "Some kind of old abandoned warehouse is my guess. Looking at the equipment, maybe this was an old newspaper printing company."

Bryce wandered a bit, "I think this might be the old *Chicago Times*."

Angelo said, "Well, I can tell you this … this is just one notch less scary than meeting at a graveyard."

Kirin shook her head, "And you agreed to all this?"

Bryce reminded, "You said, and I quote, 'do whatever it takes so we can arrange a meeting to see my parents.'"

"Sorry, you're right," Kirin apologized as she regained her focus.

They continued to be led by the guards in front and finally stopped once they reached the center of the room. The guards kept their distance from one another, forming a circular barrier around them. Everything from the surroundings to the cloak-and-dagger meeting heightened Kirin's unease.

"This is beyond freaky," muttered Kirin.

Angelo nodded.

Kirin's gut was screaming, but she had to see this through. If ever she was going to go against Wing Chun theory, this was the time. The question remained if she was going to regret going against the flow. Her hands were clammy as she tried to wipe them down, but she could no longer stand the suspense. She broke rank and stepped forward. Bryce tried to stop her, but it was too late. She yelled, "I've done what you asked! We've agreed to meet here per your demand. It's time. I want to see my parents!"

Her heart raced as she was clinging to the small hope that this could all be real. She was prepared to give everything up just to see them, to touch them, to be together once again. Kirin clung to the hope of possibly making new memories and erasing the last image she had seen of her parents.

Her voice echoed through the room, but no immediate answer came. Her patience was thin. She began to open her mouth, ready to fill the room with another demand, when lights flooded the area, making everything more visible. Just as they had suspected, this was an old newspaper room. Now with visibility, they could all see the *Chicago Times* sign. Kirin held her ground. The time for answers was now.

From atop a ledge balcony within the dark office room, a light cast a silhouette of several figures. Kirin looked intently and wondered if any of them could be her parents. The door from afar swung open, and several people came walking out. Three of them were dressed in black suits and black ties. For some odd reason, they were wearing shades. The last man was decked out in a flashy pimp-like suit. His cocky demeanor and his slicked back, greased hair indicated he was the one in charge.

Kirin waited. As each person came through the doors, she hoped there would be a face she recognized, but after all four emerged, her heart sank.

"Where are my parents?" she demanded.

"Please, Ms. Rise, let us be a bit more cordial. First, I think introductions are in order. I am Yule." He spoke with a Russian accent, thick but clear enough that Kirin could understand what he was saying. "I'd like to thank you for taking the time out of your busy schedule for our little meeting."

"This is the last time I'm going to ask. Where are my parents?" She tried to dash forward as two of the guards restrained her by her arms. She shouted out in Korean, *"Um ma … ah bba! Naya Soo-Jin! Naayaaa!"*

"Patience, Ms. Rise … I do promise you one thing today: You will get an answer to all your questions. Now, if you will, allow me to speak further. You see, a great amount of time, money, and preparation," he raised his hands to showcase all that he had done, "was required for this very moment to occur. I must also say that you can add a sprinkle of luck." Yule chuckled at his choice of words.

He motioned to his men and spoke in Russian. One of his guards remained by him, while the other went into the office. Kirin watched intently as there appeared to be two more silhouetted figures in the office room. She held her breath as tears uncontrollably streaked down her face. She struggled from the grasp and shouted again, *"Um ma … ah bba!"*

As one guard entered the room, she watched the movement of the three individuals. The door popped open, and Kirin's face turned to shock. Hoping to see her parents come out, she was instead surprised as two guards dragged a beaten man she recognized right away. It was Quinn. His mouth was gagged, and his arms and legs were bound. They tossed him on the floor, where his face hit the metal balcony ground hard. He grunted in pain.

"Quinn?" shouted Kirin, who was wondering why he was even there.

He reacted to the sound of the voice but struggled to move from his position. When he tried to get up, one of the guards kicked him hard in the ribs.

Yule said, "I bet you weren't expecting that, were you, Ms. Rise? Now, please … just a little bit longer." He motioned to the guard, who rushed back into the office room. A few seconds later, the entire area began to darken slightly. Yule pulled a small device from his pocket and pressed a button. To the far left, a large beam of light hit the side of the wall as a video projector began to play. Everyone watched as an image of Kirin's parents began speaking from the recorded message. She watched with a hint of a smile as she felt a sliver of hope. They spoke in the voices she remembered and called out her nickname. Even their mannerisms were correct, and Kirin's entire body clenched tightly. She thought, *Please, please ... please be them*. Kirin continued to watch, but her smile soon disappeared as the image of her parents changed, and the digitized image showed the two actors pretending to play them.

She screamed out, "*Ahniyo!*" Kirin began crying and struggled from the grasp of the two guards. "Why? Why?"

Bryce and Angelo tried to come to Kirin's aid but were held back by the remaining guards.

Yule had not an ounce of remorse. Even with Kirin so distraught, he seemed to enjoy the moment of suffering. "First, you should be asking yourself: how? That's the beauty of it. Don't worry ... I'll reveal all of it to you before you die."

Kirin heard him, but the realization that her parents were actually dead drained her will to fight.

Yule continued, "You see, this was actually the easiest part. Creating digitized images of your parents was not difficult at all. Technology now allows us to mimic anyone's image and voice so perfectly that only a handful of experts would be able to tell who or what is the real thing. I bet you are wondering how we gathered all this information on them. The answer is simple: the universal language that everyone speaks ... credit, of course. So, it was quite easy to get information from your former neighbors back in North Korea. It took just a little digging. You might be surprised by how quickly they sell you out, just for a few measly credits and a promise of a better life. Then again, I can't blame them. Who wouldn't want to get out of that shithole? Unfortunately, once we got the information, we had to make sure all loose ends were … how do you say, taken care of."

Angelo wanted to help and shouted from afar, "I'm sorry, Kirin. I'm sorry."

Bryce called, "Kirin!"

Both men struggled from behind, in pain as they watched their friend suffer.

Yule said, "You see, Kirin, this is actually your fault. You were supposed to die the last fight, and you threw everyone's plans out the window. You cost me a ton of money, and now I have to do this job to pay off my debt. So, with the start of the new season, we had to make sure you were totally out of the picture. We figured, what better way to get attention for the new season than having the biggest UFMF star pass away tragically?"

Kirin's will kicked in, and the pain of the lie suddenly turned to anger. She hissed, "What makes you think I'm going anywhere?"

Yule chuckled and looked as his own guards, who followed his lead with dry laughter. "I've always loved your spirit, your 'spunk,' as they say in America. But, eventually, everyone has a breaking point, *dah*!" He stared Kirin down as he grabbed the railing and leaned against it. He could see that there was fire in her eyes.

Yule said, "I'm a man of my word. I said you'd know everything, so you shall. I want you first to know that we couldn't have pulled it off without your helpful assistant, Angelo."

Kirin turned to Angelo with a confused look. "What … what do you mean?"

Yule said, "How do you think we were able to keep an eye on you 24/7 the entire time? We hired him from the very beginning. He planted the devices where needed, and the rest was him keeping tabs on you and reporting back to us."

Angelo sobbed, "I'm sorry, Kirin! I swear I didn't mean to betray your trust, but I had to do it. I did it all for love … my love for Fawn."

Yule gave Angelo a confused look. He said, "Fawn?"

Angelo yelled, "I love him! This was all for him."

Yule barked out a laugh. "But … he's not gay!"

Everyone stared at Yule as confusion filled the air.

"What do you mean, he's not gay?!" Angelo asked. He recalled his past interactions with Fawn, which had led him to believe otherwise.

Bryce echoed, "Fawn's not gay?"

Yule said, "Yes, yes, he's flamboyant and all that, but that's all an act. Fawn bangs more babes then my guard Alexie over here." His bodyguard gave him a weird look that Yule ignored. "Now enough of your pitiful confession of love. You see, Kirin, in my business, knowing who to trust is costly." He strolled across the room and grabbed Quinn, who remained on the floor, by the hair. Quinn screamed as Yule pulled him halfway up. "I believe you already knew that Quinn had also betrayed you. Correct?" He pulled off the tape covering Quinn's mouth.

Quinn shouted, "Kirin, you have to run!"

Yule pulled him toward his knee as his head snapped back from the impact and came crashing down to the ground. "But, you see, he did tell you the truth. Can you imagine that? All the money he was promised, he turned down … for what? Love again."

He stopped to check Quinn's face. He pulled back his fist and punched him again as Quinn moaned in pain. "You see, Kirin. What wouldn't you do for love? Isn't that correct, Bryce?"

Bryce struggled against the guard holding him. "You bastard! You promised me no one would get hurt. This wasn't part of the deal."

Kirin slowly turned around and looked Bryce in the eye. He shook his head and teared up.

Yule said, "Of all the three who betrayed you, I can understand only Bryce's motivation. He's the one who slipped the drug into your water at the end of your fight with Justice. Isn't that right, Mr. Adams?"

Bryce looked at Kirin, who was overwhelmed with shock. "I swear I'm not a bad person, Kirin, but my daughter was dying, and they were the only ones with the means to keep her alive. I know I can't justify what I did to you, but you have to understand. What would you do for your family? I'm so sorry, Kirin. I swear to god, I'm sorry."

"The look you're giving now, Kirin...." Yule paused, chuckling dryly. "It looks almost exactly the same as the look you had in the ring when you stood there frozen and helpless."

It was just too much for any one person to bear. Her parents being alive had been nothing more than a lie, and now the people she kept closest to her had all betrayed her. Bryce's betrayal proved too much, and the fire in her eyes was extinguished.

"Kirin!" shouted Bryce.

Kirin flopped to the floor as the entire room appeared to spin in a circle. Her hope had died, and her trust was betrayed. At that very moment, her will was finally broken. Shattered into millions of pieces, she felt nothing. She was no longer crying. The words that Yule was

233

still speaking were simply that … words. She remained on the floor, distraught and despondent, not caring what would happen next.

Yule said, "You see, Ms. Rise, today we get rid of all loose ends. We eliminate you as well as all these Judases in one clean sweep." He signaled to his men, who moved without hesitation.

The guards who were holding Bryce and Angelo pulled out knives and in one smooth motion slashed each one across the throat. Bryce and Angelo crumpled to the ground, each holding his throat as blood poured everywhere. Kirin snapped out of her daze and sprang up. One of the guards tried holding her, but she pulled away quickly from his grasp while the other one stood and watched.

She ran to Angelo first as blood was oozing from his neck. She tried to put pressure on it, but the cut was deep. There was nothing she could do but watch. Kirin cradled Angelo in her arms as the guards kept a watchful eye and surrounded her. She hoisted his head up with her arm as his eyes struggled to stay open. He was quickly fading.

"I deserve this," he rasped as he coughed up more blood. "Please forgive me, Kirin. I should've never done what I...." He struggled to complete his final words as his eyes closed slowly. Kirin watched as Angelo passed away in her arms. That feeling of helplessness surrounded her; she knew it all too well. It had found its way back into her soul, calling it home.

Bryce rasped out Kirin's name. She lowered Angelo, giving him one last look. She crawled through the pool of blood on all fours, navigating her way over to Bryce. He grabbed her by her hoodie and drew her near. Tears still filled his eyes, blurring his vision. He was drenched in blood as he whispered, "Watanabe."

"What?"

"Waa … Watanabe." Bryce touched her face softly. "I'm sorry," he whispered as he faded away. Kirin was drenched with their blood. The smell of death hung in the air as she knelt between the bodies of her most trusted confidants.

"I have one last loose end to tie up," said Yule as he pulled Quinn by the hair.

Kirin was in a daze as she watched Yule hold Quinn. His face was bloodied and almost unrecognizable from the beating.

"I am a man of my word." He pulled out his knife, slashing Quinn's throat. He pushed him over the edge, and Kirin watched as his body flailed fifty feet to the floor below. The sound of bones breaking echoed, sending chills down the spine of the only person who cared.

She didn't even react. Emotionless and drained, she was covered with blood from Bryce and Angelo. Kirin was shocked and just wanted the nightmare to end.

Yule snickered and then laughed outright. "Pick the bitch up!"

Two guards dragged her limp body from the ground. Her feet dangled, leaving a trail of blood on the floor as her head hung. Her empty tears were all that existed. Two more guards remained behind her, keeping watch. The two standing in front at a distance awaited orders from Yule.

Yule smiled, "And now, the time has come. Your story will not have a happy ending, your name will be smeared in the press, and my debt will finally be repaid." He turned his back and began to walk away. "Finish her. Give her the end she so properly deserves."

One of the front guards nodded and turned around after hearing his orders. He pulled out a knife and was prepared to finish the job. The other guard grabbed her by the hair, yanked her head back, and exposed her neck. Kirin simply watched with hollow eyes as she waited for the end. *It'll finally be over*, she thought as she closed her eyes and took her final breath.

The guard cocked his arm back, ready to slash away. As his arm began to thrust toward Kirin's neck, it was suddenly redirected right back into his chest. His eyes popped open in shock as he looked down, staring at the hilt of the knife protruding from his chest. His body began to collapse, but the rogue guard who had disrupted the job came around the front and threw him at the two guards who were holding Kirin. They were bowled over, creating chaos.

The rogue guard charged to the left side of Kirin, and her hair stirred in the breeze. The two remaining guards further back were frozen in awe at the speed of the attacks. As the rogue guard approached, his right hand concealed a blade he'd taken from the first guard. Blood dripped to the floor as he slashed the blade across a guard's neck. The other guard approached, and the knife found its next target. It jabbed directly into the guard's neck, and two more had joined the ranks of the dead in a blink.

The rogue guard pulled the knife from the side of the dead man's neck and spun around. Flipping it, he held the blade's edge and threw it at one of the downed guards on the floor. His aim was true, hitting right through the socket of his eye, penetrating past the skull and into the floor. Upon impact, the downed guard twitched once and then laid lifeless.

The final guard turned to his downed companion, and a shiver visibly raced down his spine at the power needed to create such destruction. As death stared at him and began to approach, the lone guard breathed heavily. He panicked and stood up, as flight overcame the will to fight. He took a step, but was grabbed by a solid grip from behind and couldn't move. With his free hand, the rogue guard aimed directly at the upper center of his spine. At the impact of a single, open-palmed hit, his spine crumbled as the room turned dark for the guard. He was no longer one of the living.

In a blur, all those surrounding Kirin were quickly eliminated. Standing in a fog of blood and screams, she could not believe her own eyes for it was too much to process. The rogue guard moved with lightning speed and precision. Whoever this guy was, he did one thing exceptionally well.

Within ten seconds, five dead bodies were on the ground, and the floor shined blood red. No one was spared, no mercy given, and the smell of death permeated the night air.

Everything was a blur, and Kirin could not make her eyes focus. She was unable to comprehend the situation. The guard's motion seemed to be all too familiar, but that would mean the impossible. She thought, *It can't be. I must be dreaming.*

Yule watched along with everyone else and wondered what exactly was going on. He screamed in Russian as his remaining guards scrambled above in utter confusion.

The rogue guard turned around and began approaching Kirin. He stood in front and extended his hand, and Kirin paused in confusion. He pulled his mask off to reveal his identity.

"Sifu?" her voiced carried doubt. She gazed upwards and could only see a blur. Her eyes failed to confirm as her mind could not believe. All Kirin could feel was a warm presence.

Sifu waited as she was slow to respond. She reached out and grabbed his hand, and the touch of his skin told no lies. It was definitely Sifu. He helped pull her back to her feet, "Get up, Kirin."

"How is this possible? I thought you were still in jail."

"I'll explain all this to you later. For now, we need to survive."

Yule continued to spout a barrage of expletives in Russian. He paced back and forth on top of the balcony railing, raising his hands in anger. "What the hell is happening?" From the rafters, his men watched, not sure what their boss wanted them to do.

Sifu shouted, "The game ends now! I'm taking Kirin, and we're both leaving."

Yule was still speechless as he stared down at Sifu, unable to deal with his uninvited visitor.

Sifu held Kirin and was about to take a step, but he suddenly stopped and gripped her hand firmly. Sifu looked around, scanning the area from top to bottom.

"What's wrong?"

He did not respond but spun in a circle, searching. Kirin was confused by his behavior, and then he let go of Kirin's arm and yelled, "You can come out now! I know you're here. There's no point in hiding anymore."

Like Kirin, Yule and the remaining guards were wondering who Sifu was talking to. There was no one else in sight. Sifu waited and then focused his attention toward the east corner of the room. From the shadows, a figure crept out. The gleam of his eyes was the first sign someone was there, and then slowly he emerged to reveal himself. Far above the rafters, Justice looked down at Sifu. On the same level, Yule turned to his left, staring at him in surprise.

Kirin was in shock. "Justice?!"

Justice said, "Just as you knew I was here, I was aware that your presence would grace us tonight. And you didn't disappoint, Sifu."

Yule shouted. "Justice, what are you doing here?"

Justice scoffed back. "I think that's obvious. I'm here to make sure you didn't screw up—to clean up your mistake, but you are not my priority, Yule."

Sifu smiled, "I guess you are here to settle some unfinished business with me."

Justice gave a sinister laugh, "You've got that right. You were always right, weren't you, Sifu? Always wanting to teach the art, but never use it for its true power. Well, I'm going to put you in a situation and see even if you can avoid using it."

Kirin watched as Justice continued with his bickering about the past.

"What do you think, Sifu? Do you think now is the appropriate time to showcase one's skills? Or, maybe we need to raise that bar for my teacher just a little higher."

"You've always failed to understand the true meaning of the art, Justice. You wanted to abuse the power. All these years and you still understand so little."

"Tonight, your reign finally ends, and I will be the master," he answered with a deranged laugh.

"You'll be a master of nothing," said Sifu.

With his ego bruised, Justice smashed his fist against the railing, and the sound echoed. Suddenly, from all corners of the room, a trembling began to engulf them all. The sounds of many footsteps smashing against the wooden floor were accompanied by the battle cries of men that began drawing closer. Soon, row after row of men came charging into the area. From the top of the balcony to the floor where Sifu and Kirin stood, they were fully surrounded. Kirin and Sifu watched as the numbers seemed never-ending.

She recalled being in a similar situation with her gang at the amusement park, but these numbers were further from fair. It was just her and Sifu, and nothing looked good about this situation at all. Kirin's face painted the picture, the look of horror combined with concern. "Sifu, there's at least a hundred, if not more."

Sifu smiled and reassured Kirin. "Five people, one hundred, no matter … it's all the same."

"The numbers don't concern you? There's something else about them, Sifu," she muttered, noting a familiar look in their eyes as she gazed at each of them.

Justice called down to them, "This is the end for you, Kirin Rise … along with our Sifu." He walked along the side of the balcony as he added, "This is one of the greatest achievements mankind has ever conceived, and fortunately for you … you can lay witness to its true power."

"Shut up! Come down here and fight me, Justice!" shouted Kirin. Sifu put his arm across her, forming a barrier.

"I don't believe that will be necessary. In fact, I think you have something more important to deal with. I believe it's time for a demonstration."

Justice approached one of the men. "You see, here." He used his hands to showcase the man. "Imagine the ferocity of guards who don't know pain and who do exactly what they are told to do, regardless of the outcome."

He snapped his fingers and spoke loudly at the man. "I want you to go down there as quick as possible and kill those two people in front of you, no matter what happens." The man nodded as Justice leaned toward him and whispered a final command into his ear. Kirin and Sifu watched as he suddenly jumped off the balcony, landing on the wooden floor and breaking his legs. The sound of his bones breaking reverberated in the room, sending a chill down Kirin's spine. The pain didn't matter. The man did not let out a single whimper as he began crawling in an unnatural manner toward Sifu and Kirin with a demented look on his face.

Kirin squirmed at the sight, taking a step back. "Oh my god...."

Justice signaled to two of the men on the lower ground. His two companions surrounded the crawling man and doused him with gasoline. Finally, Justice pulled out a lighter and flung it into the air. It landed on the man, and a huge burst of flames swallowed him whole. He was being burned alive, but it did not matter as he continued heading toward Sifu and Kirin.

Yule stared in amazement, "Jesus. The power. I had no idea of the power. This is truly greatness." The flames of the burning man could be seen in Yule's eyes. He was beyond delighted at the sight of this.

The burning guard continued to crawl as the fires engulfed him further, but he was driven to get to Sifu and Kirin. For him, the goal was all that mattered. The sight of him was terrifying as the flesh peeled off with each motion he made. Finally, a few feet away from them, the man succumbed to the flames. He made no sound of pain, as death no longer concerned him.

Kirin screamed, "What the hell!" Her thoughts flashed back to her match with Diesel. She thought, *This explains what really happened.*

All this time, Sifu had been calculating an escape plan for them, but it would not be an easy task. Kirin was still stunned from what she had witnessed. She covered her nose as the smell of burning human flesh was overwhelming. The sight could not be unseen; as it would forever be seared into her memory.

Kirin looked at Sifu and said, "He didn't even scream. Not a sound. It's like he didn't even have a soul." His body continued to burn right in front of them as it twitched on occasion.

Justice continued his speech, "You've already seen those around you die. Why don't we end your night with you watching your Sifu die?" Justice gave a hand signal, and a group of his men responded.

Kirin stood behind Sifu, who did not react to Justice's threat.

Ten of Justice's men moved in at his command. They were faced square to Sifu and Kirin as they charged in without hesitation. The soulless beasts thirsted for their target, and their need had to be quenched. The sounds of their footsteps rained closer as Sifu stood with no guard, waiting for them to approach. He turned slightly to Kirin's side and gave her a quick wink with a smile. "It'll all be okay … I promise."

Kirin was shocked at his reaction, frozen at this point. As Justice's guards came charging in, she was unsure of Sifu's next move. In a flash, Sifu became a blur and disappeared from her side. Kirin's eyes widened. She had never seen Sifu move with such blinding speed. One second, he was standing still as ten of his oppressors were closing the gap toward him. Now, it was Sifu who had taken the lead and reached his opponents before they even realized it.

Kirin wondered how Sifu would handle it. They felt no pain. They feared nothing, which was the same challenge she had faced with Diesel in the championship. However, Sifu was being attacked by not just one, but ten Diesels all at the same time. Sifu launched the first attack on the closest of the ten. His timing beat his opponent to the punch once he entered attack range. With a single, effortless strike, he unified his motion with that of his opponent. The two structures had now become one. The attack looked like it was being done in slow motion, as a single punch shot square from his center and went directly into one of the guards. He held the fist in stillness, for that very split second his entire body forged a solid wall. The force he released went through the first guard's body from the point of contact and straight to the ground. The impact of the force rebounded back from the ground, returning to the source from which it was launched. It found no escape to either side and exploded within. It did not matter that the guard could not feel pain because Sifu had delivered instant death. Without so much as a whimper, his first opponent crumpled to the ground without a mark upon him. Sifu had snatched his soul from within and sent it on its way.

Kirin looked at Sifu, who displayed no hint of anger or emotion as bodies tumbled to the ground. It was as if he were relaxed and simply strolling in the park and enjoying himself. As each of the remaining guards approached Sifu, one by one, they met the same fate as the first. His motion blended so perfectly within the movement of the group that he eventually got lost within the flow. Within a matter of seconds, there was but one man left standing.

Kirin's jaw dropped as she, like everyone else, watched in awe. The hair on her arms remained standing. She shook her head in disbelief. As much as she had worked with Sifu privately, she now realized how much he had been holding back. She thought, *My gosh ... this is the highest level.* She whispered, "I have such a long way to go."

But, there was one within the room who was far from pleased.

Justice growled, "Let's make this more interesting. I guess I overestimated how challenging this would be for you, Sifu. It appears it'll be easier if you both die together."

Yule said, "Definitely, Justice. I'd like to watch the demise of them both."

"It's funny you should say that, Yule," Justice replied. "There's been a little change in plans. Like you said, today we are going to do away with all loose ends." He waved several men toward Yule. "And, you happen to be one of them."

Yule looked stunned by Justice's remarks. He grabbed his remaining three bodyguards to form a barrier around him. "You can't do this! This wasn't part of the deal." Several of Justice's men came charging in, and the swarm quickly overcame Yule's guards to capture him.

Justice grunted, "Get rid of him." With no hesitation at all, they threw Yule and his guards over the balcony and onto the floor. They lay motionless from the impact, and the body count continued to grow.

Justice motioned to several men at different locations. They scattered and uncovered several large canisters and began knocking them over. The smell of gasoline was everywhere, and all four corners of the room began to burn at Justice's signal. The fire spread quickly, becoming another enemy for both Kirin and Sifu to deal with.

Sifu did not take his eyes off Justice. As the room started to burn, the men surrounding Sifu and Kirin stood still. Sifu motioned Kirin over. He spoke quietly, "Don't make it too obvious, Kirin. Our goal is the east exit, the one with the double pillars. Do you see it?"

Kirin glanced over and saw what Sifu meant. She whispered, "Yes, I see it."

"We're going to fight our way toward that direction. Do you understand?"

"Sifu, there's too many of them."

"Remember how you broke Diesel in the fight?"

"Yes."

"You're going to have to repeat that. If things go south, you may have to go beyond that to survive." Sifu looked at Kirin and knew his student was not yet ready for what was needed. At the same time, he did not want Kirin to venture to the dark side. Her past combined with the current situation might bring her to an emotional state from which she may never come back.

Kirin asked, "Beyond that? How?"

Sifu said, "Suspend your heart."

"What are you going to do, Sifu?"

"I'm going to deliver these men to god."

Kirin stared at Sifu, haunted by his last words. He had always maintained a cool demeanor, but for the first time, that switch was off and now fully unleashed. She could feel it: death was standing right next to her. The realization caused her to shiver and take a step back. She feared even looking him in the eye. Her fear didn't shift focus as the threat surrounding them was not her concern; instead, it was the man next to her who was about to blaze a path of total destruction.

All eyes were on Justice as he raised his arm and then lowered it, shouting, "Attack!" His word echoed through the room as screams came from every direction. They charged. Heedless of the fire, they simply went through it. Nothing mattered to them, only the order that was given.

Kirin watched as everyone began to charge toward them. She scanned the room as ravaged eyes set upon her. Some of them jumped directly from above, crashing to the floor. Others were already set ablaze as they streaked through the room.

Sifu yelled, "Stay close by and keep moving … remember where we need to get to."

Kirin nodded.

Sifu took the initiative and led the attack as Kirin watched him pave a trail of devastation and destruction. She was playing clean-up mainly and was simply trying to stay out of the way and keep alive. Anyone he touched was dead on the spot. He held nothing back, and it did not matter whether they could feel pain or not. He was a human weapon, as every part of him was being utilized to the max. A fist could transform to either a punch, a chop, or a palm. The fingers were either penetrating eye sockets or grabbing foes before whipping them through the air. Kicks turned to knees, as the Achilles heel, instep, and bottom of the foot eventually found something to hit. The menu of death was here, and literally everything on the buffet was being served. This moment of pure chaos was poetic, showcasing skill that few possessed. For those not on the receiving end, it was quite a sight to see. Both of them continued to flow toward the east exit.

Sifu shouted, "Use anything around you to your advantage!" as he flung a chair into the air, toppling several men over.

Kirin listened to her Sifu and used her surroundings as well as anything within her grasp to aid her. The attacks were relentless, coming from every angle, always pressing. A single mistake could lead to their demise. Kirin and Sifu finally managed to get close to their designated area.

"Almost there, Sifu!"

Sifu was too busy to acknowledge her, but he was well aware that they were in range of the goal.

Right next to him, Kirin was doing her fair share of damage as Sifu had told her not to hold anything back. One of the guards grabbed her by the hair, but she went with the flow and regained her center. He took a swing as she threw her guard hands to intercept the attack, and she instantly flowed to the target and connected. She wanted him to pay, so she spun him around and kicked his support leg from under him. His exposure for a split second was all she needed as anger flowed through her. She was about to take a life when a fist came right past her, snatching his last breath right before her eyes.

She was surprised that Sifu had beaten her to the punch. Sifu said, "Not yet, little one," as she let go of the lifeless guard she'd been holding.

She said, "Sifu?"

"Watch out!" he shouted as a swarm came from above. She had no time for an explanation as bodies separated the two and attacks ensued. A guard lunged at her with both arms reaching, and she thrusted a front kick to the chest to clear some space. He flew from the impact, but the damage was not enough. Kirin thought, *There's so many of them.* She continued to throw attacks and counters. They were so close to the exit. From the corner of her eye, she caught a glimpse of Sifu, who was using everything he could as a weapon. A cup was smashed into the face of an opponent, a laptop was snapped into the throat, a pen stabbed directly into the heart of another. Sifu utilized his environment, turning anything into a weapon. The bodies continued to trail behind him as he never settled into one place.

Kirin looked at the chaos surrounding her. Savage men from everywhere continued to charge in, while the place began to crumble and burn. She felt overwhelmed by their determination to kill. The realization of their inevitable death began to swallow her whole. A quick punch sent one of the guards flying, but the next thing she knew she was pinned down to the ground by a swarm of three men. On her back, the weight of these men was significant, making it difficult to breath. With her free hands, she cracked one man's collar bone on both sides, rendering his arms useless. Kirin then grabbed the guard's ears and ripped them off. It had no effect as his blood poured on her, and she was taking damage from above from the other two on top.

She screamed in panic, "Sifu! Sifu!" as many more were about to jump on her. She did her best to fend off the attack, but she was in a dire position. The guard with no ears and no use of his arms leaned into her and took a deep bite of her shoulder. She screamed a horrific yell at the feeling of flesh tearing.

In a flash, all three were thrown away, and she was finally clear. Sifu was too busy to help her up. More surrounded them, and he continued to deal with the closest threat. Kirin staggered to her feet. She was injured but had no time to bleed. She covered Sifu's back side and took out two guards with a swift kick to their legs. They had a moment to breathe, but more were approaching.

Sifu looked above as the moonlight passed through the upper windows. He calculated a second possibility of escape. He had done a significant amount of damage, but even though bodies lay everywhere, the flow of people was never ending. He decided that, if they stuck together, there was no chance for escape. He had to delay the onslaught so that Kirin could have a chance to get out. It was time for him to make the ultimate sacrifice.

A new wave came charging in, guards from every angle, some of which were on fire. From above the top rafters as well as the ground, the swell of enemies continued. Kirin was preparing to attack as they had inched their way to the east side. She and Sifu stood between the two pillars. Caught off-guard, she found herself tumbling backward. She tried to regain her center but could not get it back. She felt like a ragdoll being tossed around as her back was pressed upon the ground on the other side of the door. She thought, *Damn, what was that?* Looking up, she searched for an answer, only to realize it was Sifu who had tossed her aside, leaving her confused.

Sifu stood between the two pillars and stared through the entrance at Kirin, who remained lying flat against the ground. From around his neck, he ripped a chain with a small object attached to it and threw it to her.

Kirin sat up and fumbled the catch, juggling it several times before her hand closed around it. She looked at it in confusion and shouted, "What are you doing? What is this?"

He replied, "You'll need the other half."

"What? I don't understand. What other half?"

As everything around him continued to burn and several men were closing in from behind, he managed to give a little smile. Even with all the death and destruction surrounding him, for that brief moment, Sifu looked at peace. He used his hands to focus his shout, cupping it in front of his mouth. "Run! Get out of here!"

Kirin said, "What are you doing?"

Sifu said, "I promise I'll see you again—if not in this lifetime, then definitely the next."

Kirin cringed at the thought. She had just gotten him back. She thought, *This can't be.* She staggered to get up and began to crawl toward him. She watched as Sifu kicked one of the pillars down. His kick was like thunder, cracking the support instantly and causing the structure above to collapse as he disappeared from Kirin's sight. The path between her and Sifu was now fully blocked by debris and fire.

She screamed as she managed to get back up on both feet. "No, Sifu! NO!" Kirin took several steps forward and approached the burning entrance, but the heat was too intense for her to get any closer. She turned to her right and ran a few feet, as another door down the hallway revealed itself. She did not hesitate and smashed it with a front kick right by the handle. She grabbed pieces of the door and tried to hack her way back into the room. It was no use; the barricade and the fire made it impossible to get back in. She stood there crying, wondering what else she could do.

Think, Kirin. Think!

But the ceiling above made a funny noise. Kirin looked up to see that it was about to fall. She faded back and stumbled to the ground as a piece of the ceiling came crashing down.

She turned around and looked down the hallway. Sections of the building behind her were beginning to catch fire. She had no idea how to get out. She screamed one last time in frustration, from the top of her lungs. "Sifuuuu!"

She took one last look at the barrier separating her from Sifu. Her face cringed and tears fell as the pain struck her through the center. She coughed several times, breaking her spell as the thin air choked the breath away from her and the smoke began to fill her lungs. She had to find a way through the burning inferno, or she would not make it out alive.

Kirin began to run, knowing her only goal was to head down the building. The heat was intense as different areas continued to burn around her, and smoke began to spread more abundantly than the fire, making visibility difficult. All the doors that existed looked the same with the unlit exit signs obscured by smoke. Kirin stopped for a moment and smashed a wooden chair. She took a single leg, wrapped a piece of her torn hoodie around the end, and then lit it, creating a makeshift torch. Now she could use this to see where she was going. She thought, *There's gotta be an exit somewhere.*

As she walked briskly down the hall and waved her torch around, she finally spotted a sign partially covered with dirt. She felt for the handle, which was still cool. Kirin opened the door, and out sprang one of Justice's men, who tackled her to the ground and knocked the torch out of her hand. Kirin was taken by surprise as he pounced on top of her and punched her right in the face. He took another swing as she shifted her weight, making him lose his balance. She punched him square down the center, but he didn't react at all. As the two struggled, the guard grabbed her by the neck and began choking her. She knew she was in trouble as she tried to reach for her torch, which was inches from her grasp. The room began to fade as he continued to choke the life from her. She stretched and clawed with her hand and finally got hold of her torch and jabbed the flaming end into his neck. He dropped immediately as she shoved him off her while she looked on in terror.

She began coughing, trying to get some air, but she was in shock. There he was, a lifeless soul. It was the very first time Kirin had taken a life. She reached slowly with her foot and tapped him once, retracting it quickly back. He did not react. She was hypnotized by the moment as the flames continued to rage. Her time was limited. The ceiling behind her crashed down, snapping her out of her daze.

Kirin got up and tapped the body one last time with her foot. As she entered the stairwell to the exit, she peeked over the edge. There was not much to see as the smoke rose to the top. She thought, *Four floors down. Hopefully.* Her visibility was short, and a ton of debris along with foreign objects made navigating down the stairs difficult. She tried to move as fast as possible, as the old building was not handling the fire well. Kirin descended the stairs as fast as she could. The goal was to get to the ground level, but she faced another obstacle upon reaching the second floor. The stairway was completely blocked to the lower level, making it impossible to go any further. To add to her problems, the exit to second floor had more wreckage blocking it.

"Crap!" she screamed. She thought, *There's no time to go back up.*

Upon examining the situation, she concluded that there was no way she could get a good kick without lifting the obstruction out of the way. Studying the door, she determined it was structurally weak and seemed to be unhinged. She tried lifting the objects around it but quickly gave up. She muttered, "There's no way. It's too heavy." She reached for the handle and tried shaking it loose, but she still couldn't pry it open.

Weighing her options, Kirin decided to take a gamble. She thought, *Maybe ... maybe I can cannonball my way through this.* She backed up several feet from the top of the stairwell and then paused briefly as the decision was questionable, but her options were limited. She took a running start as she leaped over the heavy objects, squeezed herself into a small ball and blasted through the door. It toppled over as she slammed down along with it. She moaned in pain and tried to shake the cobwebs after the impact. "Okay ... uh, that was not a good idea," as she rubbed her arm and back to try to soothe the pain. She struggled to get up, hoping her luck would eventually change—and it did. She finally heard the first sound of good news from a distance.

"Firetrucks," she whispered. Her attitude perked up with excitement. She thought, *I can still save Sifu.*

The dust and her own blood covered her, mingling with that of her former friends. She was a mess from head to toe. Kirin got up and was again disoriented. She tried to make heads or tails of where she should go next. She looked around the area and found a glimmer of light in one direction. She began running toward it, still unsure if she was headed the right way.

That has to be the exit, thought Kirin. Pieces of debris continued to fall around her, as the heat and flames had already reached the second level. As she made her way to it, several men burst into the hallway, blocking her path. The loud noise startled her, and she stumbled. She quickly got up and ran in the opposite direction as they began chasing her down. She knew that they were heavily juiced, she was injured, and time continued to count down. She covered several feet, but the footsteps were quickly approaching. She swerved to the right when a room presented itself, and once inside she slammed the door shut. She was breathing heavily. Panicked and unsure, she leaned for a second against the door to catch her breath. She was in a small office area with two large windows that made up a wall on the far side.

She dashed toward the window, waving her arm to clear the smoke while covering her mouth to breathe with the other hand.

Firetrucks and police cars surrounded the building and were definitely a welcome sight. She said, "Perfect." The door behind her began to rattle, breaking her moment of celebration. The sound of pounding and scratching forced her into action. She then realized she was still one floor up. It was a good thirty feet to the ground level.

"Dammit!"

She got behind the desk and began pushing it toward the door. Leaning into it, her tiny frame struggled against the weight of the desk, but somehow through sheer will she was able to barricade the entrance. In a frenzy, she tossed a chair on top to help further, hoping it would buy her some time. The pounding increased; it was only a matter of time before they broke through. She took several steps back, scanning for anything else she could utilize within the room. Kirin realized she had made the mistake—quite possibly a fatal one—of cornering herself.

The door burst open as two men came crashing through. They staggered through the barricade and fell onto the ground, clearing a path. The way they acted didn't even appear human anymore. The wounds on their faces and bodies weren't factors, and their only goal was for her demise. Through the door staggered another guard whose back was in flames. His look and the smell of his burning flesh caused Kirin to take several steps back.

The building shook, and the heat was becoming unbearable. Kirin had no time, very little space to navigate, and her will was hanging by a thread. As they charged into her, she gathered her strength by letting out a huge scream, knowing that this could be the very end. There was nowhere to run; her only option was to fight. The first guard took a huge swing as she ducked the attack, and he stumbled to the ground. She quickly turned her focus on the closest opponent as another attack flashed from her side. The guard's overextended arm exposed his elbow. She reached for his arm and used her shoulder as leverage, snapping it out of the socket. Of course, he did not react to the break, so she spun around and clubbed him in the head with a hammer fist. He tumbled over, running into his companion who had just taken the first swing.

Kirin looked toward the door as the sounds of more guards approaching drew near. The blaze of yellow and red intertwined with one another and began engulfing the outer entrance. More smoke continued to fill the room. Death was already there, patiently waiting. She had one person left who was set ablaze and still no route for escape. The other two were only stunned, and they would surely be on her soon enough. She thought, *Enough of this!*

The guard lunged forward and tried to grab her, but she did not give him an inch of solid ground. She took his lousy center of balance and began manipulating it to her advantage. Soon she felt in full control of his center as she began to spin him around in circles, gaining momentum. She spun several more times, knocking the other two guards to the ground as she caught a glimpse of the window, which gave her an idea. She thought, *Why not?*

The flaming guard leaned backward as Kirin pushed him hard, driving his momentum toward the edge of the window. She said, "Let's go for a ride … shall we?" She did not stop as she closed her eyes and forced out a yell, crashing through the glass window. Both Kirin and the burning guard fell the entire distance as she used him to cushion the fall.

She screamed as gravity and fear combined to make for a terrifying fall. "Aaaahhh!"

Wham!

Kirin landed violently on top of the guard. He was killed upon impact. She gasped for air as the fall had knocked the wind out of her. Bruised and beaten, she was surprised that she was even alive. She thought, *The great ideas keep coming one after another.* Exhausted, she rolled off the dead body and lay there briefly. Something inside her told her to get up, and she pushed up to all fours. The need for air was her priority. Her face was smeared with dust, smoke, and blood, making her almost unrecognizable.

She coughed, her lungs begging for untainted air.

She was drowning on dry land as she crawled several paces. She staggered, not knowing where she was. Each breath was a struggle as Kirin drew for more oxygen.

A hand grabbed her by the shoulder, and she swung wildly to knock it away.

"Ma'am … ma'am, I'm here to help you. It's okay," the stranger tried to assure her.

Kirin's eyes took a few seconds to clear up as her vision remained blurred. Slowly, she gazed upon the figure as lights surrounded her. Other men dressed like him were near the building. Their yellow suits began to take form as she finally realized who they were.

"Here, breathe this," said the firefighter as he gently placed the mask upon her face.

She took several breaths, trying to regain herself as she was being led away from the burning building. She was disoriented from the fall and continued to do what the firefighter instructed.

She heard one of the firefighters say, "Holy crap, I think that's Kirin Rise!"

"Please come this way. It's not safe by the building." The firefighter helped Kirin walk as another one placed a blanket around her. After several steps, Kirin realized what was happening. She spun quickly out of their grasp but stumbled to the ground, falling to her knees.

"Ma'am, what are you doing?"

"You don't understand … my teacher!" Her hand trembled as she pointed toward the building and fell into a coughing fit. She gasped, "He's still in there! I have to save him. I have to!" she pleaded desperately.

"We'll get him. We're doing everything we can, but you need to pull back to the safe area. Please … it's extremely dangerous for everyone." They helped her up and began leading her far from the building. She was too weak to resist.

She stood from afar, staring at the building, which glowed bright in the night. Pieces of the building began to crumble as flames and embers blew across the night sky. She never ventured to this part of town as the old abandoned newspaper building was right at the very edge of the lake. Most of the area had been laid to waste, and the lone building was the last of its kind. The other firefighter pulled her away, bringing her to one of the ambulances. Kirin watched as men struggled against the blaze. It looked like every firetruck in the city was out trying to battle the fire.

"Please, ma'am, you need to rest." One of the ambulance workers tried to persuade Kirin, but she continued to stand and watch as he did his best to dress her wounds. She continued to watch, feeling helpless. Her stomach began to knot as she felt something was off. She reached into her pocket and pulled out the object Sifu had tossed her. It was safe and still intact. *What is this?*

As she stared at the object, trying to figure out what Sifu had given her, an explosion rocked the area.

Boom!

On the far side of the building, a mushroom cloud of fire appeared on top. Kirin's heart stopped, and she took a small step forward as all eyes continued to watch.

Kaboom!

A second explosion rattled those around as the force sent shockwaves throughout. The entire building exploded like a bomb, leveling everything in sight. The sound cracked through the air for miles on end. The blast knocked her down along with everyone else within the vicinity. People around were scrambling away from the building as panic and chaos ensued. Pieces of the building and flames came raining down. Kirin was groggy and on all fours as her eyes began to water. She lifted her head and stared in the direction where the building had once stood. She saw only rubble and fire. For her, the world had just ended. Kirin remained on her knees and stared blankly into the night. Silent and lost, she was once again alone.

"The end is inevitable, but to start a new beginning is a choice." — Kirin

Section 1 Short Stories #6—Kirin's P.O.V.

K-pop Star—Day 195

Sweat poured from my head, stinging my eyes. I was just too focused to wipe it away. Positive that this time I would get it right, I listened for the start of the song to make sure I captured the beat and the move correctly. We were already an hour into practice, but I was struggling to get things just right.

I closed my eyes and bit my lip, and suddenly the music popped up.

One, two, three ... go.

As soon as I heard the song, I began to do the steps we had been practicing for the last week. It was a must that we all get it right, since we were going to debut this song and dance on stage by the end of the week. Perfection was demanded, anything less was not tolerated. Everything that we did was looked upon with a magnifying glass.

Things were going well, and we were halfway through the song when suddenly I heard a yell. It echoed through the dance studio where we were practicing. One by one, the girls turned toward me, and I became the focus of the blame. Ripley, Trina, and Jess all had piercing eyes. Only my closest friend Gwen stood by my side, without judgement.

Ripley rolled her eyes, "This is the fourth time, Kirin. You keep screwing up the same move over and over again!" She approached me, shoving me aside as she asked for everyone else to clear the dance floor. I took several steps back with the rest of the girls.

Ripley took the spotlight—she could never get enough of it. She posed in the starting position and looked like a perfect figurine. "Hit it," she said, and the music began to play. The other girls and I watched from behind. All eyes were on Ripley.

The music started as Ripley was looking down at the floor. She was in perfect sync as she burst into motion and began doing the steps flawlessly. It was so smooth, seductive, and it was no wonder she was the main draw to our group. Everyone watched for the entire length of the song. Normally after exerting that much energy, anyone else would be dripping with sweat, but, of course, Ripley was picture perfect, as if she hadn't done anything at all.

Jessica tossed her a towel, but Ripley walked by me and said, "I don't need this." She then threw it over my head. I was speechless. There was nothing I could do but eat the cake, as I stood there silent.

Trina walked by and tossed another towel on my head. "You could use two, Kirin."

"Thanks for the towel, Ripley ... and, uh, Trina." It was sincere because, even when I was just standing, I was in a ball of sweat.

Ripley clapped her hands at me, "Keep up with it, Kirin. You're already the least popular of our group, and you don't want to be labeled the weakest link as well."

Our manager TK clapped his hands, almost mimicking Ripley, and fortunately taking the focus away from me for a second. He began to shout in Korean ... well, he was swearing in Korean. All his words were directed toward me. I basically had to listen to him for the next several minutes, trying to find a bright spot in his, uh, constructive criticism. After circling around me like a shark, he finally headed back to his corner, his face beet red.

I let out a breath, "I swear I'll get it...."

Gwen came up behind me and patted me on the butt. "Kirin, you can do this. You know the steps. It's a matter of believing in yourself."

"I don't know what it is," I admitted. "I just feel like I'm a step behind."

Gwen leaned forward and whispered into my ear, "You can't think of the flow of the music; you just have to give yourself up to it. That's what practice is all about, repeating it till you don't have to think and you end up having the confidence to just do it."

I gave it a second as her words sunk in. I nodded, because I knew that Gwen was absolutely correct. I turned slightly and said, "Thanks, Gwen," as I flashed a smile.

TK shouted from the far corner, "Alright, ladies, let's get this right. We're not going to take a break until I say it's perfect." He raised his voice even higher and said, "Do you understand?"

The girls and I nodded, infuriating him. He shouted, "I CAN'T HEAR YOU!"

We all shouted, "Yes, sir!"

"Positions, ladies!"

For the next hour, we practiced nonstop. Gwen's pep talk made sense, but for the first twenty minutes, my mind was racing, and I could not quiet it. TK was standing in the corner, but I kind of preferred him yelling as opposed to his penetrating eyes and silent criticism. It took some time, but eventually I must have done the routine to his satisfaction, as he finally signaled to all of us to take a break.

The rest of the girls were on the ground exhausted, even Ripley couldn't escape it. I was about to join them when TK called me over. "Kirin, I want to talk to you in the other room." I glanced at the other girls before walking in his direction. None of them said a word, nor did I have any guts left to look them in the eye. TK led the way to his office at the side of the studio.

He entered first and left the glass door with his name written on it open for me.

I took my towel and wiped myself off as I followed him. I found TK seated on his chair, "Close the door, Kirin." I didn't dare look him in the eye.

I began reaching for the other chair when TK said, "I want you to stand." So, I pulled my arm back and awkwardly stood, fidgeting in front of my manager.

TK stood up, but again I avoided eye contact. "Kirin … do you love being a K-pop star?"

I did not hesitate to answer. "Of course. Of course, I do."

"Well, that's good to know. Do you know how we chose who would be the lead singer in the group?"

I thought about it for a second and replied, "I figured it was Ripley because she's the most talented in our group."

TK began walking around the room, "Actually, when we formed the group, we tested everyone's singing and dancing capabilities. I think it would surprise you to know that Ripley actually has the weakest of the vocals amongst all the members."

I was surprised if not confused by his statement. "That's hard to believe."

"It's true. She scored the weakest of all of you. But, the difference between you and Ripley is that she was willing to do whatever it took to be on top. Once she was willing to do that, the stars aligned, and she is where she is now: the lead singer of the most popular K-pop group, 6teen."

I thought about what TK was saying as he came uncomfortably close.

"Kirin, today was a pretty bad day for you, and I need you to do your very best for the sake of the group. Do you understand?"

"Yes ... I always do my best."

TK walked behind me and leaned over to my side. "Would you be willing to do anything to be the best?" He brushed aside my hair as I heard a sniff to my right.

"Of course, TK. You know I would." I continued to look straight ahead and avoid eye contact with him.

He came around and stood face to face with me. "That's good to hear." He reached out and lifted my chin as he stared directly at me.

Suddenly, he reached behind my head and pulled me toward his face. He pressed his lips hard against me and then grabbed my behind.

"What are you doing?" I tried to pull away as he smothered me.

"Kirin, you said you'd be willing to do anything ... didn't you? So, stop playing like you're a good girl and do what you need to do to be part of this band." He pulled my hair harder and pressed his lips against mine even as I tried to push him away.

"This is the price to pay. You know you want this, Kirin."

I continued to push away, pressing my hands against his chest. "No, TK! Stop it!"

"Either play the game or else, Kirin."

I closed my eyes.

Is this the price I want to pay?

Crash!

I tossed TK through the glass door, and he tumbled to the ground covered in shards. He lay there groaning as he held his back in pain, squirming around as everyone watched but no one came to his aid. I came through the door and looked at him as confidence flooded me.

"I guess I'm not willing to do anything, TK." The room was dead silent as I approached TK, who scrambled back, waving his hands in surrender. I stopped where I was, breathing heavily before I began to walk away.

TK shouted, "You're a nobody, Kirin! You can kiss your career goodbye. You hear me? A nobody!"

Several steps later, the last words from his mouth echoed in my head. I clenched my fist and ran back to kick him one last time in the groin. He withered like a dying flower and began sobbing in pain.

"TK … consider that my resignation."

Gwen came running toward me and grabbed me by the arms. She said, "Kirin … what are you doing?" She shook me, hoping to change my decision. "Kirin, Kirin, Kirin." She repeated my name over and over again until I finally responded.

I opened my eyes and found Gwen hovering over me. Gwen said, "I hate when you do this. You come over to my place to watch Korean drama and K-pop, and you always end up falling asleep." It took a moment to realize what was going on, but she was right. I had dozed off, just like she said. I rubbed my eyes.

These dreams are getting weirder each time.

"To be in the game is inevitably your decision, but what cost are you willing to pay to be in it?" — Kirin

Lonely New Year's Eve—Day 213

I was staring outside my window, but the low visibility made it almost impossible to see anything. The storm of the century had picked the perfect time to arrive, on the eve of the new year. The lights on the store front across the street barely cut through the snow. Not a single car had driven by for the last ten minutes as a winter weather advisory warned people not to travel. Even those most dedicated to enjoying the night's event had been grounded by Mother Nature.

I looked at Bacon, who was already dressed up and ready to go, but I knew it wasn't going to happen. "Sorry, boy, I don't think we'll be able to go." I pointed to the window, and he titled his head, trying to figure out what I was saying.

My TV was playing in the background, and this was one of the rare times I had the weather channel going. The new year was still several hours away, but if this weather continued to slam us hard, I would be celebrating the start of the year without my family. For the first time, I regretted my decision to move out on my own. At this very moment, my loneliness was amplified.

I reached for my phone and was about to call my mom when it rang just before I touched it. It startled me, but when I flipped my phone over, I saw that it was Mom.

"Hey, Mom." I already knew why she was calling and what she was going to say.

"Kirin, it looks so bad outside, and I know you too well."

"Mom … is everyone there?"

"Yes, but that's not important. I don't want you to try to drive here. Do you hear me?"

I could hear Kyle, Mark, Steven, and Dad in the background. I bit my lip, knowing I was going to miss spending time with my family. Then I heard…. "Mom, is that Jim in the background?"

"Yes, sweetie, it was to supposed to be a surprise. He made it into town."

"Mom…," I whined.

"Kirin, promise me you'll stay put and not travel in this weather."

I took a moment to think about it because I knew it was impossible to break a promise to my mom. "I promise, Mom."

"It's not a big deal, Kirin. We'll see you tomorrow … okay?"

"Okay…."

"I love you."

"I love you, Mom." I hung up the phone and looked at my only companion. "It looks like it's you and me tonight, Bacon."

For the next several hours prior to the countdown, I did as much as possible to kill time. I texted my friends and asked them what they were doing. I vegged for about an hour, scanning through all the channels. I killed another hour training my hand techniques along with some footwork. At one hour left before the start of the new year, I decided to make sure my backup meals of corned beef and spam would sustain me in the morning. Excited for the possibility, I opened the cupboard and was disappointed to find it was bare. I sprinted to my fridge and realized with horror that my end-of-the-world backup—my huge jar of kimchi—was empty. My stomach grumbled, just to remind me what I already knew.

I'm really doing a terrible job adulting. Mental note: need to go grocery shopping more.

I looked outside and found the snow was worse than I thought. In the distance, I saw the local Chinese place that delivered and decided to give them a call.

I waited for over a minute as the phone continued to ring. My belly would not go unsatisfied. Suddenly salvation, as a human voice answered on the other end. The possibility of hope finally shed light as the next several minutes would determine my fate. However, I quickly realized this was not going to go my way.

I pleaded, "It's a block away. Can't you come?"

"You only order 20 credits! No way we go out in bad weather."

"What if I ordered 25 credits' worth of Chinese food?"

The Chinese person replied, "What about our delivery guy? Too cold … too cold."

For some odd reason, I thought of Sage saying, 'If he dies, he dies.' "Wait, can't you send a drone to deliver?"

I heard him chuckling over the phone as he replied, "In this weather? Lady, you crazy…."

The conversation went back and forth for several minutes, but in the end, I was alone, hungry, and out of luck. I hugged Bacon, who was sitting on my couch sound asleep, and said, "I'm alone, and I'm starving." As self-pity overcame me, I sat crying with Bacon. He actually woke up and licked my face clean—well, at least that was what I thought he was doing.

With only five minutes left, I figured I might as well just go to sleep. I was about to get ready when my doorbell rang. I went over to my intercom and asked who it was, but I got no response. Figuring maybe the cold was making the system act up or someone just hit the wrong number, I ignored it and went to the bathroom to brush my teeth. Only a few minutes later, I heard a knock at my door.

I began walking to my door, glancing at Bacon, who did not seem to care at all.

I leaned forward and asked, "Who is it?"

The voice from behind answered, "Chinese delivery."

I looked through the peephole and saw someone covered in snow holding a plastic bag with Chinese food. I decided to open the door, since my stomach took over my sense of logic and safety.

Maybe my whining did the trick and they decided to deliver.

"I didn't order any Chinese," I told the snow-covered delivery man as my stomach grumbled.

From behind the bag, a voice asked, "Are you sure?" The voice sounded familiar, but I didn't trust what I heard.

It can't be.

Suddenly the person lowered the bag, and a familiar face revealed himself.

"Hunter! Oh my gosh! What are you doing here? And with Chinese food…." I was so happy to see him that I leaped up and gave him a huge hug.

He struggled to say, "I'm gonna drop the food."

I didn't care as I squeezed him tightly and didn't want to let go. "What brings you here? And how'd you get through this crazy snow?"

"I'm white…. That's our superpower, you know, resistant to hot weather or snow."

I chuckled and finally got back on my own two feet. I helped him dust off the snow from his coat. "You have no idea how glad I am to see you." I looked at him as he blushed. "Come on in. You must be freezing … I mean, if you were like us regular mortals."

He smiled, stomping his feet and doing his best to not make a mess before coming inside.

As he walked in, I checked the time. We had only moments to spare before the start of the new year. Hunter removed his coat, and I dragged him in front of the TV.

"Good timing, huh?" He grinned, still holding the Chinese bag.

"Will you put that down?"

"Where?"

"Anywhere, we've got less than a minute…."

I smiled and held his hand, not even worried, though I knew mine was sweaty. We both stood in front of the TV as they began counting down. "Five, four, three, two, one … Happy New Year!" A familiar song began in the background as Hunter and I looked at each other.

He grabbed me by the waist and stared into my eyes. I panicked, not knowing what to do, as he looked like he was going to give me a kiss. Instead, I beat him to the punch and hugged him tightly, resting my head on his chest. I didn't say a word; I wasn't sure what to do next. Then I felt a kiss on my temple.

I whispered, "I'm glad you are here with me, Hunter. Happy New Year, again."

"Same, Kirin. Same."

"It's as simple as yes or no, and then you move on. Just remember being in the friend zone is a choice that you made." — Sifu

UFMF New Reign—Day 230

For whatever reason, I found myself in familiar territory. I was close to my old school. Whether it was by habit or the force drawing me, I had wandered about two blocks away. At the corner, I faced a choice: go straight ahead and relive some old memories or go any other direction for a fresh start away from the past.

I wavered for a moment, trying to find the will to let go. Curiosity got the best of me as my weight shifted forward, and I took a step toward my old school. A few minutes later, I was back in my old surroundings, right in front of what was once Sifu's school. I saw the tree that still had the markings from someone driving into it. Its battle scars were the first sign I was home. A quick scan of my surroundings revealed that the school was the only thing left standing. Gone was the Korean dry cleaner to the right, and to the left was….

"Nothing," I muttered aloud.

Sifu's old place had a big UFMF sign plastered above the building. It glowed a tacky orange color that captured attention. Just the sight of it already pissed me off. It was evident to me that things had fully changed and that memories were all that I had from being here. I began to walk past it when I noticed activity through the window. It did not matter to me—what was done was done, and there was nothing I could do about it. That's what I kept telling myself. If I walked at a brisk pace several more steps, I would be safe from seeing the inside of the UFMF school. But, a quick flash from my side caught my attention, and I was hooked.

I brushed the window with my forearm and used my hands to shield the light. Inside were quite a few people training. At first glance, I did not even recognize the place as everything was stripped and redesigned from top to bottom.

"Wow, that's the most people I've ever seen! How can they fit so many?"

Near the window where I stood were two individuals in gear that were sparring. Further behind them was a group doing some kicking drills while others were down on the mat training on ground fighting. Even further to the back, I could see exercise equipment. Several people were weight training or sitting on some stationary bikes, working up a sweat.

Why's it look so different?

I took several steps back from the glass and looked from left to right, making sure I was really at the right spot. Then it dawned on me: they had torn down the wall to the left side and had expanded the size of the school. Home definitely was not home anymore. It looked nothing like it did before.

I should have never come back.

Deciding to take one last look, I leaned forward. Then a body smashed against the window, scaring me out of my curiosity. I shook my head in disgust and began moving away. I had had enough of this walk down memory lane. I was only a few feet away when I heard someone call to me.

"Hey, you there … you interested in joining the school?" This man in a gi waved at me and shouted again. "Don't be afraid! Come on in, and I'll show you around."

My emotions were torn as I was pissed and saddened at the same time. I did not have an ounce of interest in joining or in hearing what he had to sell. But, once again, something drew me back to my old school. I decided to play along and see what was going on inside.

He introduced himself as Drew and held the door open for me. As I walked in, everything was even more unfamiliar. Had I not known the history of this location, I would have had no idea that this used to be Sifu's school.

Drew asked, "So, what's your name?"

"Soo-Jin," since I did not want to use my American name.

"So, Soo-Jin, what brings you to this neck of the woods?"

"Nothing much … I used to live around this part of the neighborhood."

Drew said, "Well, that's great! Let me tell you about our school. Oh, by the way, have you ever taken any kind of fighting class before?"

"Oh, just a few classes here and there."

For the next ten minutes, he gave me a tour of the building. Everything had been gutted from the inside out. Not only was Sifu's school gone, but Drew also mentioned that the neighboring stores had lost their places. It appeared big business could not be stopped, as it engulfed all the mom-and-pop shops. He finally brought me back to the center of the school, where two students continued to spar.

I asked, "So, what was this place before you guys took over?"

As we watched the sparring match, Drew replied, "Oh, from what I was told, it was some shitty Kung Fu school that had been here forever."

I closed my eyes and began to breathe just so I could keep my cool.

Drew added, "Pretty impressive, isn't it?"

My ego got the better of me, "I don't know … seems kinda like they're playing tag."

Drew chuckled at my comment and said, "These guys are holding back, but believe me, if you were to go in there, you'd think differently."

I was about to let it go. I was just inches from shifting my weight to take that step and get the heck out of there, but something in me blurted, "I bet I could take either one of them."

I guess I said it loud enough that both of the guys sparring heard my comment. One of them stopped in mid-fight and removed his mouthpiece. "Why don't you come in here instead of yapping out there?"

Without hesitation, I said, "Sure. Why not?"

Drew looked surprised and rushed to say, "You'll have to sign a waiver."

"Done." I turned to the guy who challenged me, "I'll fight you, but I don't want to wear any of that gear."

He began removing his gloves and said, "Hey, it's your funeral."

I spent a second signing a waiver, and the next thing I knew, a small crowd of students had gathered around the mat to witness our fight. I looked toward the glass window with the UFMF sign glowing in front.

I really hate that sign.

Everything about this place got on my nerves, and whether I was doing this out of a sense of righteousness or simply for payback, I didn't know—and it did not matter to me.

Drew went over the rules as my opponent extended his hand for a handshake. I reached out to grab it, but he pulled it away.

Okay, that's how it's going to be. I smiled at him.

My opponent smirked as he got into a guard position while I stood several feet away in a casual stance. Like everyone else in the school who was watching me, he looked confused. He began hopping up and down and jumping in and out, as I waited for Drew to say the word. I had done this many times before, and I knew how I was going to play this game. Unfortunately for my opponent, I knew he was still stuck in sparring mode mentality.

You train that way, you lose that way.

I was watching my opponent the entire time when Drew finally barked out, "Fight!"

I wasted no time and closed the gap on my opponent. He was caught off-guard as I went in without hesitation, but I didn't launch an attack.

In his panic, he threw out a punch, hoping that would stop me from advancing. As soon as he moved, I knew he was done. Mentally, I thanked him for committing so soon. His focus was clearly on the attack as he surrendered his center of gravity to me. I easily captured it with the slight touch as he had nothing but momentum to support his attack. I wanted to give a lesson and was willing to eat the karma.

When I tossed him in the direction of the window, he shattered the glass and fell to the street, landing among pieces of the UFMF sign while the rest dangled by a thread. The school was silent; I didn't say a word. Instead, I knew the outcome even before it began and made my way out of the school.

I left silence in my wake. I did not look back as the rest of the school went to check on their classmate. Deep down, I knew what I had done was wrong, but for the first time, I felt a sense of accomplishment that my actions had a deeper impact on the world around me. I reached the corner and hugged it to take a minute for myself. As I leaned against the wall; I knew nothing was going to bring back Sifu's school. The reality set in for me as I broke down and cried.

"The soul will never rest till one finds its true path in the universe." — *Kirin*

Section 2 Sifu's Journey Entry #6—Your Role

Continuation

Damon had spent the next hour introducing Sifu to everyone and showing him their entire operation. Pleasantries were exchanged along with names from one station to another; however, Sifu was terrible at remembering them. As he was escorted through, Sifu could not help but be impressed by the small ragtag team of individuals at work, all bonded by a common cause. Even so, Sifu remained silent.

As Damon continued to point things out, Sifu finally stopped in his tracks. "I haven't agreed to anything, yet you've given me insight into all your happenings."

Damon nodded, retraced his steps, and came back to Sifu. "You know, Sifu, our little operation in this division has survived because of my ability to read people. And so far, with everyone here ... I've been pretty dead accurate. However, with you ... you're nearly impossible to read, but I'm willing to bet I'm right." He paused before adding, "My full name is Damon Lewis Mitchell." At that, he extended his hand again and waited. "I'm banking everything on the hope that I'll be able to convince you to help us. So, you could say I'm taking a leap of faith." Sifu finally reached out and shook his hand.

With a confused expression, Sifu said, "You said ... this division?"

"Yes ... while we are small in numbers, we have divisions throughout the world, all working for the same goal," Damon explained as he continued making his way through their headquarters.

Sifu said, "I take it this isn't your normal recruiting technique."

Damon smiled and shook his head, "This isn't our normal introduction, no. We're usually more cautious, but we couldn't just grab you and bring you down here like anyone else."

275

Sifu let his guard down slightly as he chuckled.

Damon reciprocated and added, "Does our story actually seem that far-fetched?"

Sifu answered, "I've been around, and one thing is constant … there's no underestimating the evils that men will do to one another."

"No truer words have ever been spoken." Damon waved his hand behind to all those working, "Everyone here, in some shape or form, can attest to that statement. It's what drives us and binds us together, the fuel to our soul that can never be satisfied."

Damon turned away as they both looked at a wall where several TVs were constantly playing the news. Chuckling, he shook his head. "This news that they're broadcasting … it's just to incite the people and divide them. I used to get sucked into these endless debates over nothing. I used to be one of those protestors hoping to bring about change, posting on social media, thinking my little call for action did something. I used to believe that my vote made a difference, but it was nothing but a stall to keep the machine of false hope alive. The never-ending wheel that we all live in." He had a look of frustration and added, "I feel silly believing that one side or another was actually concerned with our very well-being. But, like I said, this is all a charade as we are simply here for the handful to be entertained."

Sifu chimed in, "I get it. I understand that people get a sense of helplessness—that some action, regardless, is better than no action. Otherwise, the alternative is to escape reality by getting lost in fantasy or drugs…. Like I said, I do understand."

Damon continued, "I'm sorry we had to bring up your past to get your attention. I can't imagine the loss, but I believe we can help each other."

"I'm not sure exactly what you want from me. I don't think I can punch us to resolution."

Damon put his hand on Sifu's shoulder. "Look, we have a plan, and with your help, we think you can get this ball rolling."

"What is it?"

"The strength of the organization lies in its anonymity, but for the first time we may be able to flush out one of the five from hiding, or at least we believe the group to be that big. If we can do that, if we can reveal at least one of them, then that will be the lead we've been waiting for. It could have a domino effect and possibly reveal the others."

"I'm sorry, but I'm still not clear how I can help you."

Damon approached Sindy, who was sitting at her console. He tapped her shoulder, and she turned around and smiled at Sifu. She was glad that he was still there listening to Damon as she began typing away. Then he directed Sifu's attention to the monitor that Sindy was working on.

Sifu looked at it and saw a picture of Kirin.

Damon said, "You know her, don't you? In fact, she's your student."

Sifu nodded, stared at the picture of Kirin, but didn't say a word.

Damon walked closer to the monitor, "Well, she's been busy. The school you used to run has been lost to the UFMF. She and a handful of your students have been training in secret. Now our sources from all around say that whoever is in charge of the UFMF—and it's not Thorne—plans to make a drastic move to bring the UFMF over the top."

"What's Kirin's role in all of this?"

"They're looking for someone, someone special that will bring the organization to new heights. We believe your student is that someone, but in order to get noticed, she's going to have to enter a fight."

"You want me to ask her to join a fight?"

"No, it's not that simple. You've got to play a more secondary role as far as your involvement with all this. You see, we've been profiling her, following her, much like you. And we believe, given the right buttons, she'll enter a fight," said Damon.

"What's the significance of the fight?"

"She's been getting people's attention doing local brawls and cashing in on the credits. She's definitely skilled, as I'm sure you're aware. But, this is the fight that no one has ever been able to win. If she wins the fight, she'll make a name for herself with a little help from us as well."

Sifu managed to control his annoyance and keep from rolling his eyes, but couldn't keep from asking, "If...?"

Damon replied, "You seem confident that she would win?"

"Kirin winning the fight is not a concern but manipulating her to enter something is my issue. Her past has driven her from the start, and to fuel that fire ... I don't know."

"And doesn't it drive you as well? There's always a price to pay, people we love and care about. There's no one in this organization that's been immune to that.... I told you that's one common bond everyone here shares. But, this cycle of evil will be continuous if the few don't stand up against the powerful and restore balance."

The words were true and haunted Sifu as he looked away and pictured his family. He was about to speak, but Damon cut him off.

"I know this is a shock to anyone's belief system, and I've given out more to you than anyone else before…. But, you don't have to decide today. I'm going to give you some time to think about it, but keep in mind that time is short."

Sifu stared in Damon's eyes for a brief moment, "I wish I had an answer right now, but I'll need to think about it."

Damon nodded in understanding, "My associates will bring you back," He pulled a small device from his pocket. It was no larger than his thumb, and he brought it to Sifu's eye level. He demonstrated its usage by turning it and then pushing the button. Then he offered it to Sifu, who took it from him.

Sifu gave it a puzzled look. The image of Damon in the background became blurry as his focus was on this tiny object.

Damon explained, "Turn a full circle clockwise and then click the single button. It's that simple. Normal means of communication from an outsider are risky for us, so this will protect us from being traced, Sifu. I can afford you one week to think about it. If we don't hear from you, then it was a pleasure to have met you. Otherwise, one push will open you up to another world."

Sifu held the small device in his hand and gazed upon it.

CHAPTER 7
Secrets Revealed

After news broke about Kirin's incident at the newspaper warehouse, the days that followed blended together. Her absence from the UFMF season had dominated every form of media for weeks, but the deaths of Justice, Bryce, Angelo, and Sifu, not to mention the ties to the Russian mob and the unidentified remains ensured that the circus-like environment that followed was a spectacle in itself. She had spent most of her time at the police department, trying to explain what had happened. So far, no charges had been filed, but the paparazzi were relentless, as were the fans. Rumors spread as everyone wanted to know every detail of what had happened to Kirin.

None of that mattered to Kirin. She stood mustering up the strength to hold her balance, as her vision was blurred with tears throughout the day. No form of solace or words could comfort her, nor did she want it. The day matched her mood, and rain continued to pour, muffling the words being spoken at Sifu's graveside.

Everyone had gathered from all corners of the world. From long ago students to the community that Sifu had formed through his generosity, his presence had graced more than most people could ever imagine. A sea of black draped over the wet green lawn as the masses surrounded the casket. The priest tried to find words to soothe those around him, but they all felt the pain, immeasurable to many. Kirin's heart was broken, along with her will. She was riddled with guilt. The choices she had made played over and over in her head. She stood separate from the gang as she couldn't bear to look them in the eyes.

She had lost Sifu for some time, but this was different.... This was forever. She stood drenched by the rain, not wanting cover from the umbrella that was offered. Somehow, she felt she deserved this drowning. Deep down, she knew she needed to suffer. Though no one mentioned it, she could feel fingers pointed at her. She hoped the rain would cleanse her, but it fell short. Staring at her feet, she saw mud had covered her shoes. She hoped that she would wake from this nightmare. Her vision became blank, the sounds faded from a distant, and she was lost in nothing when a voice snapped her out of her trance.

Father Brannigan's words finally captured her attention. He stood towering over all those present, a gangly man, his pale complexion contrasted by his black priest garment. One kind guest struggled to keep an umbrella over him so he could deliver his final words. Kirin cleared her tears as he said, "I look around at the many faces who are here today, and I wish my words could soothe the pain I see. In times like this, we as human beings search for answers, but the reality is we may never find them. In fact, our only form of hope may rest solely in our faith. While I know it's easy to focus on the sadness of these events, I'm hoping to redirect you to what I see right before me."

"I see before me hundreds of people who have come from around the world for a single man on this day. How easily we forget the impact that an individual soul can have on so many lives. With the bustle of everyday life, we often fail to realize the greater power of one."

Kirin thought about what he said as she scrunched her eyes to hold back the tears.

"I've spoken with those who were closest to him, and they've told me it would be okay for me to refer to him as Sifu." He paused momentarily to weigh the response to his words.

"Sifu, I believe, will always be looked upon as a teacher first, but for those who are here, he represents so much more. We may no longer feel his physical presence, but his spirit lives on. His closest students will recall his words, 'Not bad, not bad,' as they remember their time training with him. But, his actions and words live in each and every one of you. I know it's difficult to think in these terms, but every beginning must have an ending, as this is the way of life."

Kirin finally looked up at Father Brannigan. His face looked kind despite his soaked beard. As he spoke, she leaned slightly to the side and scanned the many faces around her. All of them seemed to blend together, but one face stood out from the crowd. While she did not recognize many faces, this strange female captured her attention unlike the others.

She was small in stature, but thicker than the rest. While others had umbrellas open to protect them from the rain, she stood in the perfect position, and the rain somehow avoided her.

Kirin continued to study her, and this welcome distraction was the first moment she had not been filled with grief. Time drifted by until Father Brannigan concluded his service. One by one, people passed by the casket, placing a single flower on top of it as they said their final goodbyes to Sifu. It took some time as the people gathered began walking away. Kirin was the last one, and she stood at the foot of the coffin. She watched the workers begin to lower it into the earth. From the corner of her eye, she could see the gang watching her from a distance. They allowed her to have this moment with Sifu, although she could not say goodbye. The finality of it was too much for her.

#

After the funeral, many gathered back at Sifu's old shop. Inside, the mood lightened as everyone reminisced about old times with Sifu. Each person had a unique experience to share, and those memories helped ease the pain.

Kirin made idle chitchat with those around her but kept a constant eye to see if that one person she had spotted at the burial was here. For whatever reason, the stranger's energy had lingered in the back of her mind, and now she wondered if they would somehow meet. Kirin stood by the table and continued to scan the filled room. People stood shoulder to shoulder, and then one of the patrons accidentally bumped against Kirin. She felt Sifu's trinket press upon her, and she pulled it from her pocket and held it firmly in her hand.

She didn't want anyone else to see what she had gotten, but she took a quick peek just to ensure it was okay. She thought, *I still have no idea what this is for.* She shook her head. She had not mentioned it to anyone, nor did she have a clue what to do. Kirin put it back into her pocket and began searching once again for the stranger.

Kirin mumbled, "Hmm, I don't see her here...." She thought, *maybe she won't even show.*

A hand on her shoulder startled her. "You okay there, kiddo?" said Lance. "Didn't mean to frighten you."

Kirin grabbed Lance's hand but didn't turn around. "I'm hanging in there." She continued to look around and asked, "Lance, at the burial, did you recognize everyone?"

Lance thought for a second, "I knew most of them, but there were a handful that trickled in that I haven't seen before." He chuckled, "Sifu always said he was a social butterfly."

"I was wondering. There was a short, black woman with puffy hair.... She stood roughly behind Father Brannigan. Do you know who I'm talking about?"

Lance pondered Kirin's question. He caught himself before opening his mouth. opened his mouth. "Now that you mention it ... uh." He looked up and then snapped his fingers. "Hmm ... yeah ... come to think of it, I know exactly who you're talking about, but I don't know who she was. Never seen her before until then."

Lance and Kirin continued to talk as a path began to open its way to them. A figure emerged from the crowd, and Mike, Sifu's longtime friend, student, and lawyer, interrupted their conversation.

Mike greeted them, "Kirin, Lance, do you guys mind if we go to the back and talk in private?"

They both nodded, wondering why Mike was requesting privacy. They made their way through the crowds and passed the kitchen into the pantry. Mike entered first as Kirin followed, and Lance closed the door behind him. Kirin noticed that Mike was carrying a backpack but did not inquire as to what was in it.

"I know you guys might not want to hear this, but it feels so different here without him," Mike shook his head and let out a sigh.

Kirin provided solace, "It's okay, Mike. You're not wrong; it really does." She got lost in a daze as she imagined Sifu. They had shared so many good memories together, but all she could recall was the most painful one.

Mike continued, "I know the timing is never good for this, but can both of you come to my office on Wednesday?"

Lance and Kirin glanced at each other and then at Mike. They both said, "What for?"

Out of habit, Kirin quickly mumbled, "Jinx." Lance looked at her, confused. Kirin shook her head and said, "Uh, never mind … it's nothing."

Mike cleared his throat, "So, umm, I'll be going into more detail about this on Wednesday, but it's in regard to Sifu's trust. Obviously, there's paperwork that needs to finished, where you both have to dot the I's and cross the T's … but basically, Lance, he left you the entire shop and his place."

Lance shook his head, but didn't seem surprised. "That son of a gun."

Then Mike looked at Kirin and said, "As for you, Kirin, he left quite a considerable amount of credits."

Kirin looked confused. "Uh, credits? Why…? Wait … how considerable?"

Mike leaned over and whispered into her ear, "Let's just say at least seven zeroes' worth of credits, just to give you a ballpark figure."

Kirin looked even more confused as she choked to get the words out of her mouth. "Seven zeroes?" She turned to Lance, who gave a shrug. "Why would he do that…? He knows that I don't want that money, but more importantly, where'd he get all the credits?"

Mike waved her down to lower her voice, "It's been my experience that we should keep this kind of talk relatively quiet. But, like I said, I wanted to give you a heads up."

Kirin stood in shock, surprised that Sifu had so many credits stashed away all these years. She looked at Mike, "There's something else, isn't there?"

Mike nodded and began removing the backpack he carried. "Now keep in mind, this was all per Sifu's instructions." He handed the backpack to Kirin, who held it in her hands.

"What is it?"

"Go ahead and open it. My explanation is supposed to come after you see it."

Kirin began unzipping the bag, but her quick peek told her nothing. She reached inside and felt a cloth. As she grabbed it, she could feel the weight of the object inside.

"Oh, uh … be careful when you pull it out," Mike cautioned.

Kirin looked at Mike funny, ruling out the possibility it was a puppy. She reached further in to grab the cloth and removed the object from the bag.

"Please lay it on the floor so I can unwrap it for you," Mike made a gesture to ease it down.

She placed it on the floor gently and took one step back, following Mike's instruction. Even Lance was curious about what this could be as they stood next to each other. Mike got down on one knee and began peeling the cloth off. The light immediately hit the objects, blinding everyone from the reflection.

Kirin's eyes opened wide and Lance's jaw dropped.

Mike pulled out his phone, which had a specific speech written for him to read. He began to speak before anyone else could say anything. "So, what you see before you is a one-of-a-kind, custom-made Shinzuki *Bat Jam Do*, otherwise known as a butterfly sword. While you may not be familiar with the name Shinzuki, he is regarded as the greatest sword maker in the world. He is the sixth generation in his family of sword makers in Japan. The steel is made from ores that can only be found in the mountains of Japan in Seki City, which not only makes it the purest of steel, but also the strongest. Those who have a sword he created say the blade is unmatched. What's so unique is this is the first of its kind by Shinzuki, who took it upon himself as a challenge to create this butterfly sword. He went through several trials and took months before he finally achieved his level of standard. By fate, I...." Mike stopped and clarified, "These are Sifu's words ... I had been searching my entire life to find someone to make my swords, and good fortune shone upon me as my search finally ended in Japan. This Shinzuki sword is pure Japanese steel, it was designed for one purpose only. In short, after making it, Shinzuki himself said, 'what this touches, it will kill.' So, the responsibility falls in the hands of the individual. I've always thought that it would be cool to name your own swords, for now these remain nameless. That decision, I will leave to the owner who wields it ... and that owner is you, Kirin Rise."

Mike ended his speech and put away his phone. He pointed to the swords and nodded at Kirin.

She kneeled and grabbed the swords, delicately holding them like they were babies. In her hands, the blades felt solid in design, and the craftsmanship was unmatched, as the hamon was definitely one of a kind. Kirin saw the maker's stamp forged onto each blade, but it was the edge that made her cringe with fear. She looked around and made sure she had enough space before swinging one of the swords, cutting the air with a swooshing sound.

Mike warned, "Careful, Kirin," as he took a small step back.

Kirin flicked the other blade, which made the same sound. "I know what I'm doing, Mike."

Lance commented, "I think you just killed the air," as the breeze put a chill down his spine.

"Oh my gosh, I almost forgot." Mike reached forward into the bag and grabbed a piece of paper that was left untouched. He turned up to Kirin and asked, "If you don't mind, can you take one of your blades and point the edge to the top."

Kirin wasn't quite sure why Mike wanted her to do that, but she did as he instructed. One of the swords was now parallel to the ground with the edge pointing up.

Mike approached her and held the piece of paper several inches away from the blade. He looked at Kirin and said, "Don't move, please." She nodded, and he released the paper, which touched the blade. The sharpness was true and unmatched. With the help of gravity, the sheet split cleanly down the middle. Everyone watched as the paper, now in two pieces, floated gently to the ground.

Lance broke the silence, "Shit, that's one sharp blade."

The blades meant the world to her as she put both of them together and wrapped them carefully back in the cloth. This was the last reminder she had of Sifu. The swords were more valuable than all the credits in the world. Tears fell from her eyes as she turned to Mike and hugged him tightly. "Thank you."

#

A few hours passed and most of the guests had left. The only ones remaining were the gang and Kirin's friends. Lance was busy cleaning up while Gwen, Sage, and Hunter helped in the kitchen.

Kirin had remained relatively silent with the gang. Everyone was busy doing their part to tidy up the place for tomorrow. With the growing tension, Kirin felt she needed to break the silence. In her mind, she had lost everything already. Nothing really mattered as Kirin stood in the center of the room and shouted, "All right, who's going to say it?" No one responded as Tobias, Ken, Robert, Doc, Big T, Ryan, and Danny kept their heads down. "Even if you don't say it, I know everyone's thought of it. The fact is, this is my fault. Sifu's gone because of me."

Kirin's outburst caught the attention of her other friends as well, and Gwen, Sage, and Hunter hustled into the room. All eyes were on Kirin, though Lance remained in the kitchen and observed from a distance.

Tobias stepped forward and calmly said, "It's no one's fault. Everyone makes their own choices, and Sifu made his."

Danny stepped up and said, "We told you to leave it alone … that this is beyond what one person could do. Didn't we? But, you had to push it. Your crusade against the corporation is beyond what one person can handle."

Tobias shot Danny a stern look, "Quiet, Danny. You're talking out of your ass."

"No, I'm not going to stay silent. That's what led to this moment. Kirin kept quiet all this time. She was being blackmailed!"

"What would you have her do?" Tobias's voice raised.

Danny made a wild gesture. "Well, look around! Obviously, that wasn't the right choice. We warned her that she was in over her head, but did she listen? No! As always, she took it upon herself, and now Sifu's gone."

Tobias closed the gap on Danny and grabbed him by the shirt. "I said that's enough."

"I don't care if you beat me up." Danny didn't back down but stared Tobias in the eye. "At least I can see things straight. You're letting your feelings for her block your judgement."

Tobias dragged him in closer as Kirin jumped in, trying to separate the two.

"He's right. Time for me to eat the cake," said Kirin.

Tobias looked at her and, after a moment, finally let go of Danny.

Doc stepped in, "Everyone, let's chill. We're all emotional right now. The last thing we want is to say things we don't really mean."

Ken nodded somberly, "Doc's right. Let's all chill out."

Big T agreed, "Listen to the white guy. He's right. Stay frosty my friends."

"Why don't we gather around, make a campfire, and sing some songs?" Sage's suggestion went over like a fart in church.

When the group stared at Sage, he hopped up and said, "I'll go back and help Lance in the kitchen." He walked off, grabbing some plates before hastily scurrying away.

Ryan took the moment to hug both Tobias and Danny. "Come on, guys. We're all friends here—in fact, we're family. Don't ever forget that." Danny swiped Ryan's hand off his shoulder as Tobias turned his back, and they walked away from each other.

Hunter tried to defend Kirin, "There's no point in arguing. What's done is done. I know Kirin. She's not selfish."

Danny snapped at Hunter. "Friends don't keep secrets from one another. We warned her that what she does can affect every one of us. She dodged the bullet with her parents, but this time her luck ran out."

Gwen backed Kirin up, too, "No one here can put themselves in her shoes, not even remotely."

Danny continued his rant. "Irrelevant. So, who's next on the list if she keeps up her crusade?"

Tobias had had enough. He charged toward Danny and slammed him against the wall. Bowls came crashing to the ground as mayhem erupted. The guys moved in, trying to separate the two before it escalated any further.

Kirin stood shaking her head as she watched her friends in chaos.

She shouted, "Please stop fighting!" Several of the guys grabbed Tobias while the others held back Danny. She thought, *What else could happen on the worst day possible?* Just then, the doors flew open as police barged in, issuing a warrant.

At least a dozen men swarmed through the restaurant as the lead officer said, "Strip down this room first and then the kitchen." They began tossing tables and looking through everything with no regard.

Kirin charged forward, "What's going on here?"

The lead officer ignored her question and continued to direct the rest of the officers. Kirin opened her mouth, so he handed her a warrant to shut her up.

Lance came out of the kitchen and grabbed the warrant from Kirin. He looked over it briefly, "Someone call Mike, right away."

Kirin was angered as the officers were tearing the place apart, searching every inch of the restaurant. "What are you looking for?"

They ignored her again as they turned the place inside out. For the next fifteen minutes, they left nothing unturned until it appeared all their options had ended. The upper floor of the establishment was in shambles.

One of the officers came up to report their status. "Sir, we've searched everything, and we still can't find it."

Mike finally arrived, and Kirin dashed toward him. "Mike, do something!" She handed him the warrant, and he looked it over before shaking his head.

Mike said, "There's nothing we can do. Let them do their business."

The lead officer did another walk through the dining area and then the kitchen before finally stopping at the pantry, which his men had ransacked. As he continued to look all around, Kirin and Lance watched and tried to give no hint of Sifu's secret basement entrance. Finally, he began knocking on the walls. One by one, he tapped them and listened. He was about to approach the secret entrance when Kirin lunged forward. Two of his men held her back.

"There's nothing here. Look around! You've done your damage. Now get out!" Kirin shouted.

His hand reached out as he made a quick tap. Kirin watched and held her breath, not daring to look at Lance. The sound caught his attention, and he tapped it again. He motioned to his men, and a few ran off as they all waited. A few minutes later, his men came back with a battering ram.

He stepped away and said, "Break it."

Kirin stood in the way, forming a barrier. "Don't you dare touch that!"

"Your last warning, ma'am … move or be arrested."

Lance grabbed Kirin by the arm and pulled her away. She looked at Lance and hissed, "What are you doing?"

He held her arm tightly, and Kirin struggled briefly as Lance whispered, "Just look away."

She couldn't watch as they rammed the wall, smashing it into pieces. She knew how proud Sifu was of creating that hidden door. And just like that, another piece of him was gone. For the next thirty minutes, the officers searched every inch of the basement, leaving nothing unturned and stripping everything to the bone. The gang watched in horror as they ravaged through Sifu's stuff. An hour later, they left without speaking another word to anyone. When the doors closed behind them, everyone had a look of distress.

Lance said, "Land of the free, huh?"

Tobias asked, "What were they searching for?" Everyone exchanged confused looks, but the question remained unanswered.

Danny was still fired up, "I bet Kirin's got another secret."

Tobias turned to him and pointed. "Shut up, Danny!"

Kirin wasn't sure what they were looking for until she suddenly remembered what Sifu had given her. She looked at Gwen and then turned away.

Gwen called out, "What is it, Kirin?"

Instead of answering, Kirin walked to the door and locked it, shaking it twice just to confirm. She then motioned everyone else to lower the blinds on all of the windows. Kirin asked Lance to make sure the back door was closed. When he took off, she spun around and called out for Gwen.

"On your wheelchair, do you have that device for cell phones?" asked Kirin. "The one that allows for pure privacy."

She nodded. "I do, Kirin. Why?"

Kirin announced, "Everyone pull out your cell phone and give it to Gwen. Please power them down."

Lance returned from the back of the restaurant, "Back's closed … but, what's going on?"

"Please, just do it … your phones."

One by one, everyone removed their phones and gave them to Gwen, who gathered them all and looked at Kirin.

Kirin asked, "You're sure this is secure?"

Gwen closed the compartment on her wheelchair, "All right, Kirin. It's safe to talk. Now please tell us … what's going on?"

Kirin paused as all eyes were on her. She reached in her pocket and pulled out a small item, which she gave to Gwen.

She took a moment to examine it and then looked back at her. "Who gave this to you?"

"Sifu gave it to me in the warehouse, just before I escaped."

Gwen looked at it and immediately began studying the small object. It was no larger than her thumb, with imprints fully covering the outside. "Its coded, but from the looks of it, it seems incomplete."

"You can do something about that, can't you, Gwen?"

"I can try, but it's like half a map. Without the other half or pieces, I can't guarantee it."

Tobias ran his hand through his hair, "Well, this has to be what they're searching for."

Hunter stared at Sage. "Come on now. Half a map, the other one missing, and you're not going to toss in a quote?"

"I'm staying quiet," Sage answered. "I got scolded last time."

Gwen said, "Well, that's never stopped you before."

Kirin tried to reign in the group, "Guys, focus." She started to pace back and forth. "Where could this other piece be? Where do we even begin to look?"

"You see?" Danny continued his rally. "This is exactly what I'm talking about. More secrets."

Kirin pleaded her case. "I had no idea what this was."

"Well, that's just perfect," Danny muttered. "Now what are we going to do? It's not like the answer is just gonna walk in the front door and present itself."

The room remained silent as the group stood in place searching for answers. From the main entrance, a click caught their attention as the locked door began to turn. Everyone watched in wonder as Lance said, "I'm the only one with the keys." Tension filled the air as the gang prepped to spring into action.

Tobias looked ready to unleash all of his bottled emotion, "Whoever it is … they're going to be making the biggest mistake of their lives."

The door unlatched and began to swing open. Suddenly, the stranger from the burial walked into the room. She smiled and waved at everyone as if she had done no wrong. She pulled out her umbrella and placed it to the side. Both her and the umbrella were strangely dry, even though it was still raining outside.

Kirin took several small steps toward her and said, "You're that girl from the burial."

She let out a tinkle of laugh, "Well, I wish this was under better circumstances, but it's good to finally see all of you. Let me introduce myself. I'm April. April Welch."

Lance asked, "How'd you get in here?"

April sprang forward and gave him a hug, lifting him off his feet with ease. Lance didn't fight it, stunned by her actions and strength. She said, "Lance, your voice is just like I imagined it to be! And, man, his description of you was dead on." One by one, she rattled off everyone's name, greeting the gang as her charm was hard to resist. Then her moment of enthusiasm halted as she stared at Gwen.

"Hmm," April began to approach Gwen and spoke. "Sifu said I would know when the time was right…. This finally makes more sense." She reached into her pocket and then pulled out a piece similar to Kirin's. She handed it to Gwen, and the two pieces lined up perfectly.

Everyone turned to Sage and waited.

He hung his head down low, "You've broken my confidence…. I've got nothing."

April walked over and stood several feet from Kirin, who stood frozen. She had no idea who this stranger was, but she somehow felt a sense of closeness. April said, "There's no doubt I know who you are." She hugged Kirin tightly as she gasped for air. A few seconds later, April released her vice-like grip as they both were able to feel each other's pain. Kirin burst out in tears and gripped tightly onto April. "It's okay, baby. It'll be okay."

Several minutes passed, and eventually Kirin got ahold of her emotions. She pulled away and stared at April. "Be strong now…," April said, and Kirin nodded. "Well, let's see what Sifu was keeping secret, shall we?"

Everyone waited as Gwen worked her magic on her computer. Kirin leaned over and stared at the screen, "I have no idea what I'm looking at." Gwen pushed her away and continued doing her work, all eyes watched in anticipation. The room was silent except for the tapping of her keyboard.

April leaned in, pointed to the screen, and whispered something to Gwen. Gwen looked up, "Thanks, almost missed that."

April glanced at Kirin, "I know a little something about computers."

Sage moved behind Kirin and muttered, "Seriously, who is she?"

Several more minutes passed until Gwen stretched her arms high above, cracked her neck from side to side, and let out a little giggle.

Kirin asked, "What is it?"

Gwen looked up to her friends, "Let me put this in a way you guys can comprehend. It took some massive amounts of nerdiness to be able to put this thing together. I decoded the message, which took a little work, but I'm not sure what it means … and let me tell you, Sifu spent a pretty penny to make sure this wasn't easily cracked. This wasn't your typical hacker, with my connections maybe … maybe, I can think of three people who had the skill for this."

April cleared her throat, capturing Gwen's attention.

Gwen added, "Uh, quite possibly four."

Kirin thought, *Well, he wasn't hurting for credits.*

Tobias was the first to ask, "What did it say?"

Gwen hit a button and spun her computer around to show the message. On the screen flashed: 'My first love.'

Kirin wrinkled her nose. "My first love?"

The gang looked confused as everyone was trying to figure out what was going on. They began spewing out random theories for the meaning behind the message.

Gwen raised her hand and said, "There's a second message." She hit the screen again, and it flashed: 'Listen.'

Kirin was trying to piece it together, "My first love and listen, or is it listen and my first love?"

Gwen clarified, "There's no order indicated as first or second. That's all that was there."

Ryan said, "My first love … well, it has to be about his wife, Megumi, right?"

Robert countered, "I don't know. Was Megumi his first?"

298

Ken said, "Oh, come on now. Really? You're going that route?"

Robert shrugged and pretended to look innocent. "Hey, I'm just saying. Nobody really knows Sifu's dating history. For all we know, he was like Tobias."

"Hey!" called out Tobias.

Robert asked, "Well, am I lying?"

Tobias let his head hang, "No … but you don't have to bring it up."

Gwen interrupted the guys' pointless babble, "Maybe he's referring to one of his kids."

Big T and Danny began placing bets—Big T sided with Simo being the first while Danny picked the kids, and the usual twenty credits was placed on the line.

Kirin glowered at them, "Will you two cut it out?"

Doc chimed in, "Sifu always talked about balance: simple is hard; light is dark, thin is—"

Robert filled in the blank, "Ryan."

Doc said, "Was that really necessary?"

Robert answered, "Hey, I'm here to offend."

Doc replied, "Anyway, my point is this meaning must be deeper than its surface, right?"

Lance was nervously pacing, "Let's say we figure out what he's trying to say…. It still doesn't explain why the police tore this place apart for it."

Tobias's eyes darkened at the mention of the police and their destruction, "Lance is right, but first we need to figure it out."

Big T chimed in, "I think y'all are forgetting about the listen part."

Kirin replied, "Maybe something his first love said."

Danny added, "Great, if one secret message isn't bad enough. The listen clue is another headache."

"Listen, listen, listen...." Hunter repeated it over and over under his breath. "I got it."

Everyone turned to Hunter, who looked triumphant. When no one spoke, he said, "Listen.... Do you hear that?"

Robert said, "I don't hear shit."

"Exactly. That's because the smartest guy in the room hasn't said a single word."

Kirin looked at Hunter and then turned to Sage. "He's right. Sage, you're the genius. If anyone can figure this out ... it's you."

Everyone looked to Sage as he began pacing back and forth. He was the smartest of the group; in fact, calling him that was an understatement.

Sage turned around and then spoke. "I don't know Sifu as well as you guys, but each one of you gave a hint to the clue by your own response."

Kirin said, "But, we didn't really say anything."

Sage said, "That's not entirely true. Like Father Brannigan said, he lives through each and every one of you. There's truth to that statement, and your initial gut feeling gave me some insight. Words or statements have deeper meaning … and, as I often hear Kirin say, we must look to the source. Take the meaning of 'my first love.'" Sage paused, frowning slightly and muttering under his breath, "My first love … the Latin origin translates to *primus amor*. *Primus* doesn't necessarily mean 'first,' but first among equals. Now we take *amor*, and the Latin root word for love is *am*. It's natural to draw a conclusion that his first love is a person. But what if…? Hear me out now … but what if it's not a person, but instead a thing?"

The room stood silent after the words left Sage's mouth. Sage's last word 'thing' resonated for Kirin, "Holy sh…."

Tobias looked at Kirin and said, "What…? What?"

Kirin hugged Sage. "Geez, you are a genius … tell me the truth, can you move objects with your mind?"

Sage smiled, focusing his attention at the table as his hand stretched out and began to shake. He hung his head after nothing happened, "I wish I could." He adjusted his glasses and protested, "But, I didn't give an answer yet."

"Yes, you did. Sifu's first love is the thing he's had forever. I found it strange that he gave it to me."

Tobias snapped his fingers and then pointed at Kirin, "His wooden dummy."

Kirin nodded, "Exactly."

Sage shook his head, "I don't get it."

Kirin replied, "Sifu's had that dummy since he was in his teens. He's had it longer than you and I can even imagine."

Gwen added, "But, what about the dummy?"

"I don't think it's the dummy," Kirin clarified, "but maybe he left something inside the dummy. I don't know…. You know Sifu. He always kinda plans things out. He's always several steps ahead of everything or at the very least everyone. Why, after all these years, would he give me his dummy and then we see the police tear this place apart searching for something today? Coincidence…? I don't think so. Whatever he wants us to find, he needed to keep it somewhere safe. And that's probably it, the listen part." Kirin snapped her fingers and flashed a smile. "His first love will have a message for us. Thus, that's the only logical explanation I can come up with as to why he gave me his dummy last year." Kirin looked to Sage and waited, giving him the opportunity for redemption.

Sage smiled and appreciated the gesture. "When you eliminate the impossible, whatever remains, however improbable, must be the truth."

Gwen rolled to Sage's side and pulled him down to her level. She planted a kiss on his lips and said, "That's my man."

Section 1 Short Stories #7—Kirin's P.O.V.

<u>Storage Time—Day 250</u>

I gripped the handle firmly and lifted the locker door, hoisting it above my head. It was the small storage compartment that the guys and I had purchased to keep Sifu's stuff. This was the first time I had visited the place since we finally decided where to keep everything. In the back of my mind, I was hoping it would all be gone because it would be a sign that Sifu had returned and I was no longer alone. Upon opening the door, I was disappointed to find everything was still there, exactly how we had left it.

There was still a chill in the air as the spring weather was a good month away. I looked for the light and flipped the switch before quickly returning to lower the door three-quarters of the way down to keep the air from blowing in.

Honestly, I wasn't sure what I was doing there. For the last several months, I had felt like I was drifting from one place to another. For whatever reason, I was looking for purpose or answers, but I only felt lost. Standing in the center of Sifu's belongings, I looked at the most important thing to catch my eye. There, in the corner, was Sifu's dummy. It was his first love. He'd had that for many years prior to meeting Simo, but he had been able to leave it like it meant nothing. I approached it and touched its side, almost consolingly, as if we had something in common. I whispered, "I'm sure he'll be back … one day."

I decided to give it a couple of whacks, since I had always loved the feel of his dummy. It was perfectly made, and the smoothness of the wood and the craftsmanship were unmatched. I recalled that, when Sifu hit the dummy, there was a distinctive sound he listened for. I could not quite put my finger on it or replicate it on a consistent basis.

For the next fifteen minutes, I practiced the dummy form. Sweat began to bead down the side of my face as I began to welcome the slight breeze that entered through the lower crack. Instead of judging my performance, the dummy brought back memories of when I trained with Sifu. After a while, I had to stop. It began to hurt that the main component of my training was missing … Sifu.

I took a moment and leaned on the dummy as something in the opposite corner caught my eye. It was a little shoe box that I didn't recall seeing before. I walked over, making my way through the little maze of Sifu's stuff to grab it. Upon lifting it, I felt something shuffle inside, and I didn't hesitate to open it. To my surprise, I found a notebook—a journal, really—that looked weathered from the years. The black leather binder felt loose from many uses, and the paper within had lost its clean white look. I made my way to the cleanest corner in the room, dusted a small area, and sat down. I opened it.

Inside were handwritten notes from Sifu about the art. It went over the basics of the stance to the punch, with detailed sketches hand drawn by Sifu.

I didn't know he could draw.

I flipped toward the middle, which was filled with more information on the forms and theories. Some of it was fascinating; he went into greater depth than I had ever heard. A few pages from that, I found a section on the spiritual side and spent several minutes reading it, though it went completely over my head. Some of the notes were in Cantonese so I couldn't even read them.

But, then I noticed a slight crease at the end of the journal. There, I found notes on his students, more specifically on us. Curiosity had already gotten me this far, and I figured no harm could come from reading further.

#

Inside the Journal

Doc – The smartest of the group. Spends excessive time on theory of the art. Showed the most interest in learning the spiritual side of the art. Overthinks things and has a hard time relaxing. Needs to calm the mind. Do drills that are less set, especially when you chi sao with him. Be less strict on his technique to help him escape his rigidness.

Ryan – A natural quick learner, lazy. Always finds the easy way out, has the skill yet lacks the will. Must do drills to challenge him, even if he wants to quit. Need to find something to keep pushing him; otherwise, he'll slack. Not sure what motivates him other than food. Maybe girls … maybe.

Ken – Good at heart, maybe too good. Needs to know both sides. Has to work hard to get things, but never quits. Holding back on who he really is and only shows glimpses of his true personality. Need to tap into his dark side and bring it out. Without this balance, he'll lack the expression of the art and be boring.

Danny – Self-doubter, but has the potential to be the best teacher in the group. Creative in his approach when teaching others. Needs confidence and reassurance, which means more training. Current girlfriend will never last. Until he believes in himself, he will always settle for less than he deserves. Need to make him teach more so he can develop and trust himself.

Big T – Needs life experience, handy and innovative with his learning of Wing Chun. Loves the art, but is too casual in his approach. He needs to bleed for it and doesn't know how to push himself. Thinks with limitation and needs help to grow beyond that. Susceptible to being used by others.

Robert – Physically the most athletic. Extremely cocky, but that's because of his own insecurity. Need to balance him with less reward and more reality when he trains in order to control his ego. So greedy. Too much into technique and still can't let go to a more fluid motion. Afraid to go out of comfort zone, seems happy to settle. Hope he doesn't because his first wife would be a trouble. Not sure why I foresee that.

Tobias – Sure of himself, needs more spiritual. Sometimes pushes things to the edge. Too many girlfriends to keep track of. Needs to find a girlfriend who does Wing Chun better than him. It's a tall order as his potential seems without bounds. He needs to teach more but fears the responsibility of being a leader. I've repeated to him that, if he wants to master the art, he'll have to teach, but teach in his own way and not mine. Sometimes he thinks he knows better. Allow him to make that mistake and hopefully learn from it.

Kirin – Fueled, determined. Since my loss, I consider her my daughter. Can make a difference. How, I am not quite sure, difficult to see as emotions cloud one's vision. Something about her is special, but not sure what role she will play overall with the art. I still remember the very words she said to me when I asked her why she wanted to learn Wing Chun. 'I want to learn martial arts not to fight, but to control my desire for revenge.' I honestly don't know if I'm the solution to her problem.

I believe this core group will continue to spread the art, and it is in good hands. Even when my time comes, the art will survive.

#

I couldn't believe Sifu remembered what I said. I also couldn't believe I'd had the audacity to say that to him. I shook my head in embarrassment. I knew that was the truth, but my desire was far from controlled.

After reading for the next hour, I reached the last page, where a single quote caught my attention.

"The world will move on without you, unless you give it a reason to stop."

Blackout—Day 265

It was not our usual gathering that was required by Mom, but whenever she wasn't working and sent out a text that she had cooked, everyone would come. It didn't take much convincing for me to make it over. I still loved being with my family. Besides, since I had moved out, I'd found out how lazy I was with cooking for myself. There was no debating that a home cooked meal was impossible to beat, especially since it was free.

As she finally sat down to join us at the table, I asked my mom, "What made you decide to cook so much today?"

"Do I need a reason to cook?"

I shook my head as my mouth was already stuffed. The reason was not important at all.

Kyle mentioned, "It's raining kinda hard, don't you think?"

With my mouth half-stuffed, I managed to mumble, "You actually noticed the weather as opposed to all the food?"

My mom said, "Kirin, manners...."

"Is that a statement or a question?" Kyle immediately stuffed his mouth with food. He didn't really seem concerned with my reply.

"Up to you."

Kyle looked at me but did not answer, either by choice or because he could not clear a passage for words to come out.

"Hey, can you pass the rice, Dad?" Mark asked.

As Dad was about to comply, thunder rocked the area. The next thing we knew, the place was completely dark. Both Bacon and Butterscotch began barking under the table as I did my best to calm them down.

Mom commanded, "Steven, go get the candles and a flashlight."

Steven asked, "We have candles and flashlights?"

Dad took the reins, "Everyone, calm down. I'll go get the candles and a flashlight."

"I'll help you, Dad," I offered. "Is it still in the cabinet next to the sink?"

"Yes, sweetie," said my dad as we headed to the kitchen.

When we returned, my mom and I lit the candles and set them on the dinner table. We were at the tail end of dinner, and we finished our meal by candlelight. The storm was so bad it wasn't a good idea to be on the road till it died down.

Not that I planned to leave this delicious food anytime soon anyway.

Kyle said, "Thank god for my phone. Hard to say how long we're going to be down."

Kevin replied, "Hey, link up with me, and we'll play."

"Count me in," Mark added.

Then I looked at my mom and saw she had that look of determination. "Okay, this is actually perfect, I think now is a good time to turn off all technology and just hang out as a family."

Kyle whined, "Can't we hang out because of technology?"

My mom gave Kyle a look as he grabbed his phone and put it away. Before Mark and Steven could say a word, my mom added, "You could play video games anytime."

Mark groaned, "Mom…."

Mom put him on the spot instead, "Why don't you get us started with the conversation, Mark?"

Mark sat up in his chair and looked at me. I gave a quick smirk and giggled. "So, Kirin, what's it like to be solo?"

"Uh, nothing interesting. Just working on photography and getting more clients…. I totally miss the laundry service, Mom. Leftover meals seem to last for days, and I find myself eating out more than cooking at home. That pretty much sums up my day."

Can't mention the back-alley fights to help pay for rent.

Kyle, who usually was still eating and rarely entered conversations, said, "So, Kirin … now that you have your own place … do you have a boyfriend?"

"What?"

Despite my immediate response, it was too late. All eyes immediately locked onto me.

Mark prodded, "You heard him … a boyfriend?"

"I heard him." I squinted hard at Mark and gave him that look.

"You know, between that look and your stalling," Mark grinned, "it kinda makes me think you have one."

"I don't have a boyfriend, geez. I don't have time," I shouted back.

Steven jumped in, "Hmm, her anger makes me suspect that that may not be entirely true."

I rolled my eyes and chuckled. "Steven, you of all people are totally clueless. You didn't even know where we kept the candles and flashlight!"

Dad came to my defense, "Will you guys quit bothering your sister?"

"Thanks, Dad."

He nodded but then looked at me in the flickering candlelight. "Kirin … seriously, you don't have a boyfriend?"

"Daaad!" I looked at all of them in exasperation. "I'll repeat myself again. I do not have a boyfriend. I have no time for one, nor have I even bothered looking for one."

Steven said, "It's not a big deal, Kirin. We're all just trying to make conversation. I have a girlfriend. Mark has one also, this week, and I believe Kyle has three…."

I looked at Kyle. "You have three?"

Kyle finished what he was eating before speaking. "I'm only in high school, and I'm still trying to decide. I'm too young for commitment."

I tried shifting the focus to Kyle, "Mom, this is okay?"

My mom raised an eyebrow. "Kyle, these are real girls, right? Not virtual girlfriends?"

Kyle replied, "Mom, three real girlfriends and one virtual girlfriend. The virtual girlfriend I can customize fully to what I like."

Mom shook her head and glanced at me. "I'm glad he's actually interacting with human beings, instead of being on his phone or the computer all day."

"Dad?"

My dad leaned forward, "Let me see this virtual girlfriend."

"Dad!" I said.

"I'm just curious about his taste," Dad answered. "That's all."

My mom interrupted to ask, "Kirin, one last time … you really have no boyfriend?"

"Mom…."

She raised her hands in surrender, "I'm just trying to make sure. There's nothing wrong if you decide to go on some dates. You always seem to get wrapped up in certain projects that sometimes you forget to be … you know … social."

For the next hour, our family spent time talking about everything imaginable. It was enjoyable, especially to bond without any form of technology at all. Sometimes in our world, we fail to realize that even a few moments with the ones you love really gives you so much more than the quick hellos from a text or email.

Suddenly, the lights flared back to life. While no one said it, we were kind of sad when they did.

> *"Technology isn't a bad thing. Just like anything, there is good and bad that exist in all. We just need to find the proper balance in things."* — *Sifu*

Girlfriend Day—Day 290

I was constantly surrounded by guys. From my four brothers to the entire gang, I was the lone girl just trying to fit in the entire time. I didn't mind my situation, but Gwen was my solo attachment to the female species. Like any good friend, she made sure to remind me that, while fighting like a girl was great, it was also nice to be like a girl once in a while.

It was our day together. While we couldn't enjoy our typical activity of vegging the night away watching Korean dramas, we had the entire afternoon to ourselves. We were in the middle of lunch and were simply waiting for our meals when a strange silence formed between the two of us.

"Spit it out." At the sound of my voice, Gwen looked at me. "I know you got something to say."

Gwen hesitated before saying, "Kirin, you and I have been best friends forever, but there's one thing we rarely ever talk about. In fact, if Sage were here right now, he'd give me a percentage that would be close to 99.9%."

"You sure not 3720 to 1."

"Wow, how did you remember that?"

"Sage quotes that at least once a month at some point during our conversations. Anyway, what are you talking about?"

She shook her head, let out a sigh, and finally seemed a bit relieved as she spilled the beans. "We never talk about boys."

I took a sip of my drink as the topic was somewhat taboo for me.

Gwen pointed, "That is a perfect example of what I'm talking about."

She was right, and she did catch me. "It's not my fault. Everything else comes so easy, but when it comes to love and boys, it's just not something I'm comfortable talking about."

"I don't see why it should be uncomfortable," Gwen countered.

"Well, I can tell you one of the problems. You watch all that Korean drama, and your head is all messed up."

Gwen punched me on the arm. "Quiet, you. You know you love to watch it with me."

"Occasionally, I do, but you must realize that love doesn't work like that at all."

"In theory, some of it is possible."

"Seriously, you're going to go with the 'in theory' argument against me?"

Gwen said, "Let's cut to the chase … Ms. Wing Chun Direct. Name a single guy that you know that you don't necessarily like but you think might be attractive. Let's start with that first."

"This is silly. Why are we playing this game?"

"Just humor me, Kirin. As your best friend, I want to know."

"I … I can't think of anyone right off the top of my head. I mean, I'm not focused on that at this time."

"First of all, I know that's a lie … but, to help you break the ice, I'll toss in some names to help you get going. You hang out with all those guys you work out with." I could see her mind at work, almost filtering images of information just like a computer. She finally said, "Hmm, how about Tobias?"

"Tobias?" My eyes grew wide.

"Yes, Tobias. He's at the very least pretty beefy."

I began to blush. "I never really… thought of him in that way."

"I'm not asking for you to think of him in that way. Do you think he's beefy? That's all I'm asking," said Gwen.

"I'm not even sure what that means."

"You know, muscular, in shape, tight six-pack abs."

I paused and pictured Tobias for the first time in a new light. Gwen was right: from head to toe, he was somewhat "beefy". I wasn't sure why I'd never seen him that way before. Maybe I was afraid to.

"Well…?"

"Oh … I see. I guess you can say he is beefy," I replied.

Gwen tried to keep a straight face, but I could sense that she was pleased from me opening up.

"See, was that so hard?"

I thought about it and my thoughts didn't match my answer. "No, not really." But deep down, this was the one thing I struggled to deal with.

Gwen asked, "Look, I know this is tough on you for whatever reason. So you don't have to answer it. But, why haven't you given Hunter a second chance?"

I thought about it, but our prom night was still painful for me to reflect on. It was simply bad timing, what occurred on our night out together. "Hunter is such a good friend?"

"That's nice, but do you think he's boyfriend material?"

I wasn't prepared to answer that, and now I had the mental image of both Tobias and Hunter side by side. I decided to turn the tables on Gwen; it would be easier than dealing with the truth. "Now your turn. I want the name of someone you think is beefy or at the very least you might be interested in."

I watched for a brief second as Gwen was quick to throw out a name. "Corbin."

"Corbin, from our senior class?"

"Yeah, I think he's cute ... uh, beefy to be more exact. But, at the same time, I find brains sexier than brawn."

"Well, that's definitely not Corbin then. I'm surprised he can find his way home." I added, "Brains, huh? Well, if that's the case, why not Sage?"

Gwen made a face, "Sage? He's so goofy."

"True, but he's also the biggest brain that either of us has ever met."

"Look, Kirin. Love and boys or whatever aren't a difficult thing. You always tell me that Wing Chun exists in everything. So, why not explain relationships and boys according to Wing Chun? Humor me."

That statement took me aback. That was something I had never approached before at all, nor had I really heard Sifu talk about it. But Gwen was right: Wing Chun existed in everything. "I like that challenge, so give me a sec and let me think about it."

Gwen smiled and waited as she seemed genuinely interested to hear my answer.

"Let's keep it simple. Go with the flow, don't fight the force, and be direct."

Gwen replied, "So, how does that concern relationships?"

"Now keep in mind this is my interpretation, but when it comes to matters of the heart, I think Sifu would say to keep it simple. If you like someone, then be direct about it, but also be prepared to not necessarily get a positive response from it. He would say that's okay, because you start with nothing, you end with nothing."

Gwen smiled, "Hmm, that does sound like something Sifu would say. What else ya got?"

I thought about it some more. "He would say, I think ... don't play games. Love is very direct and we tend to overthink things. We make it more complicated than it needs to be."

"Give me an example. I'm curious," asked Gwen.

I laughed. "I know it's a Korean drama I'm referencing, but you know in the stories where she says she's not interested and they get back together and break up? And this is a recurring theme over and over again? I do recall Sifu telling me that he and Simo rarely fought. Now every relationship is different, but if you're miserable with that person most of the time, then it's a pretty good bet that that person isn't the right one."

"So, why stay together?"

I thought about it, "I think, for many, the fear of being alone is more painful than being with someone you can't stand."

Gwen rubbed her chin, "I guess you can use Wing Chun even in love."

"Obviously...."

Gwen looked at me, "You seem to have a good grasp of what to do. So, why no boyfriend, Kirin?"

This was not a difficult question because, deep down, I knew the answer. "Gwen, how many people have I lost that I cared about? It seems to me that, when I find someone I really care about, the universe finds a way to take them from me." That was the first time I'd ever said that out loud or admitted it to myself. It was true: my unresolved past still haunted me. Unless I figured out a way to deal with it, it would continue to play a role in my future decisions.

"Like all things in life, we make love more difficult because we fail to be honest with ourselves." — Sifu

Section 2 Sifu's Journey Entry #7—Letting Go

Four Days Later

Several days had passed since Sifu's meeting with Damon. His thoughts were lingering on a decision, which he had struggled with since the moment he left. Sifu kept a straight face, not wanting to burden anyone else with his problem. He looked at Lance, who was sitting across the room and tallying up the credits for the night. He smiled as the success of the shop continued, and for a brief second, he took a break from trying to decide. Sifu was at the tail end of cleaning up. He showed his human side as he used the shop as a distraction from dealing with a pressing matter.

Lance let out a big yawn as he watched his teacher finish the final task. "Sifu, you mind if I call it a night after I put away the credits?"

Sifu gave his signature warm smile, "It's been a long day. You can call it whenever you feel like it."

"What about you? You seem pretty wired still…."

"I'll close up for us, but I'll be heading downstairs and work out on the wooden dummy."

Lance covered his mouth and let out another yawn. "Sorry. Not sure why I'm so tired."

Sifu came by and patted his friend on the shoulder. "Go home. I'll finish up." Lance's eyes were heavy as there was no denying it: he was tried. "We can decide tomorrow if we want to open or not."

Lance said, "No worries?"

"No worries."

After checking the doors and lowering the lights, Sifu went to the pantry and pulled on the secret lever. The door opened, leading to the basement, and Sifu stood there and admired his handiwork. It never got old as Sifu reached for the switch and began walking down the stairs. In the far corner stood a wooden dummy. He'd needed another one after abandoning his first love, which he hoped had fallen into good hands. It had been quite some time since he had practiced on the dummy. His mind and heart had been battling for the last several days. He was torn in his decision about Kirin, as the lessons he had taught were being put to the test. He knew his past actions had resulted in his situation and that debt was his burden. But, his fire was fueled by loss and could not easily be put out.

Needing a release, Sifu began making his way to the dummy. Emotions were strong, and his mind was racing. He needed to empty it, so he could see the truth. Sifu walked in front of his wooden dummy and began doing the form. He bypassed the opening move to see the proper distance from the dummy. He had done this thousands of times, and knew exactly where to begin the form, so he simply stood in place. At first, it was just his standard moves with the same speed and same power. He finished one section, then the next, and kept his focus on the moment. But halfway through, as his mind achieved emptiness, visions of his family began to pop up. With each passing motion, Sifu was hitting the wooden dummy a bit harder each time. Finally, toward the end of the form, he was rocking the dummy along with everything else in the room. The sound of his hits was true, and the dummy's construction was put to the test as anger filled Sifu's heart. His last motion deterred from the form as he released a hit that echoed throughout the basement. He broke the arm of the dummy, which was almost an impossible task, but proof was laying on the floor. As he reached for it, there was a marking of its origin. *Made in China*, he scoffed.

He let loose a sigh and clenched the wooden arm. It failed to withstand his blast. Sifu hung his head over the fixture. Sweat poured down his face, mixed with his tears. He knew that, no matter what he did, there was no bringing them back.

A small sound caught his attention, and he glanced toward the desk where it originated. As he drew closer, he noticed that a picture had fallen—maybe from the impact of his hit, or maybe the universe working its mysterious ways. Regardless, he grabbed it and stared into it. It was a picture of him with his family, a split second of time when everything was perfect. He looked at Megumi with the twins and Hana always by his side, the image invaluable to a man who had lost it all.

He began speaking to himself. "What am I going to do? What am I going to do?" He paced back and forth in the basement, repeating those words over and over again. It was unlike Sifu to struggle with a decision.

Like all things, the answer was simple. Even with the new information about what had happened to his family, the past could not be changed. No matter what he did, his family would always be gone. Any action trying to mend his heart would dig him deeper into the dark. Now, he was being asked to help out an organization at the cost of his student—a student he had grown so close to that she was practically a daughter to him. Sifu knew, if he went down this path, this had nothing to do with making things right. He would be betraying the trust of his student. Once broken, it could never be repaired. He would be a hypocrite in light of his lessons about letting go and detaching from the past. At that very moment, it didn't matter. He had gone beyond the anger into a darker territory from which few could ever return. His goal was not to make things right. He wanted to share his pain with the handful of individuals who held the ultimate power.

He pulled the small device from his pocket and squeeze it firmly in his hand. He remembered the instructions as he twisted it once and placed his thumb on the button. He took a deep breath and closed his eyes as a last-minute internal debate took place. Moments later, he pressed the button and threw the device across the room. A decision had been made, a new path was created, and Sifu would have to live with his choice.

CHAPTER 8
To the Source

Late July 2034

Kirin fidgeted in the back of the taxicab as she stared out the window. The sun's rays made it difficult to look outside for long. Besides, there wasn't much to look at as stretches of abandoned buildings, shutdown malls, and tons of open desert space dominated the landscape.

The cabbie had been working nights and was at the end of his shift. Human nature set in, and the loneliness of the job reminded him that interaction was always needed. So, he glanced in his mirror, saw a lone girl, and broke the silence. He asked, "So, what you in town for, ma'am?"

Kirin pulled her baseball cap a pinch lower and avoided making direct eye contact through the rearview mirror. She muttered, "Just seeing an old friend ... nothing special."

"Is this your first time here?"

"Umm, yes, it is." Kirin realized that the cabbie was in chat mode, even if she dropped the subtle hint she was not. She lowered the window slightly just to feel the breeze hit her face. She thought, *Geez, even the air is hot.*

"Well, Tucson's a pretty quiet town. I'd have to say it's not like it was thirty years ago, back when I was much younger."

Kirin didn't respond and continued to look outside.

"You know ... you look kinda familiar?"

Kirin brushed the side of her hair like she always did when she felt uneasy. It caught her off-guard to see herself with blonde locks, as she had colored her hair just for the trip. She justified the look as a new beginning as well as to help her travel without so many people recognizing her. She quickly responded to the cabbie with a statement intended to cause some discomfort. "I'm Asian. We all look the same."

"Umm, okay." The cabbie felt awkward and focused his attention back on the road. "It'll be another fifteen minutes before we get there, ma'am."

Again, his comments fell upon deaf ears, for Kirin was distracted by her mixed emotions. She had heard stories about Sigung, but never had the opportunity to meet Sifu's teacher. She was excited and nervous and not quite sure what to expect. Her heart was still broken, and she hoped that Sigung could somehow fill the void. Kirin sobbed silently, hoping her driver would not hear. Just the thought of Sifu crushed her every time. She wiped her eyes and forced herself to look up; otherwise, she wouldn't be able to control herself.

As she stared out the window, Tucson seemed almost the same as Chicago. Many of the stores were abandoned, and people were living on the street. The only differences were the sand and the mountains surrounding the town. The sight was a constant reminder to Kirin why she needed to keep up the fight—all her suffering and pain were nothing compared to this. If anything, Sifu would want her to have resolve and continue the struggle without him.

It didn't take long for Kirin to fall asleep in the car. She had always had a hard time sleeping when traveling, but within a few minutes, she was out cold.

#

Kirin had finally gotten to her apartment. She'd told everyone that she should go alone. It would be too suspicious if they all went, not knowing if eyes were upon them. It had been several months since she had last stepped into her place, and once her door swung open, her jaw dropped. The place had been ransacked. She ran inside and scanned the entire area, but everything had been turned inside out, and nothing was left untouched.

"I can't believe this."

It didn't matter where she looked, as clothes were scattered everywhere and even her trash had been rummaged through.

Suddenly, she panicked as she remembered why she was there in the first place. She scrambled to the corner where she'd left Sifu's wooden dummy and breathed a sigh of relief. "Oh my god … it's okay." Kirin began to examine every inch of it, thinking that she would immediately find what it was that Sifu had hidden.

Ten minutes later, she was there staring at the dummy with empty hands.

"I don't get it," she muttered. "I've searched every inch of the dummy from top to bottom and nothing."

She took a deep breath and decided to invest more time. Another fifteen minutes passed with the same results. She scoured every inch of the dummy, removing the three arms and the single leg before replacing them. She shined a flashlight in the open slots, just in case she'd missed something. But, all her efforts had the same result: nothing.

"Ugh, Sifu, isn't this what you meant?" Kirin screamed in anger and then hit the dummy with her hand. The sound echoed through her place as frustration set in, and she slumped over the arms of the dummy.

She thought, *Your first love. Your first love, your first … first. Listen … first love. Listen.* She squinted at the dummy. "No way, this is crazy. He wouldn't." She shook the wooden dummy's arm and heard the sound. She thought, *Listen.*

It had been awhile since she had done the dummy form. There was a total of eight sections, each with a specific purpose. But, Kirin was fixated on the idea of first and quite possible the first section only.

"Here goes nothing." She began doing the first section of the form. Within a minute, she completed it and waited. "Well, that was horrible," she said. She looked around and still saw nothing.

"I wonder…." She took a deep breath and stood in front of the dummy. She recalled all the times she had done the dummy form while Sifu paid no attention to her, other than listening to the sound. She took a second and tried to calm her mind. She focused on trying to get her entire body working in sync. She needed that feel and the flow. She took one last breath and began working the first section again. This time, the sound rattled to a familiar beat as each motion was crisp and clean, and the dummy reciprocated with each move. She finished half of the first section, proud of her motions and hoping that a different outcome would result from it. Again, nothing happened. She hung her head in frustration.

Suddenly, she heard a sound from above the dummy and slowly looked up. A small piece of wood popped out from the top, falling to the ground as she quickly examined it. She said, "It's just a cover." She jumped up several times and saw a small opening inside. She tried clawing with her finger and felt something within, but she was unable to pluck out the object. She said, "Listen … my first love. It's not a message to listen to, but the sound I make."

Excited by the possibility, she got back in stance, took one quick breath, and then worked the first section of the dummy form again. She stared and waited as the seconds dragged. She leaned forward, hoping against hope this was what Sifu had intended. Finally, a tiny object began to rise from within. It was a USB drive with a piece of paper wrapped around it. She reached for it and grinned with a sense of accomplishment. "Why the cloak-and-dagger, Sifu?"

She unraveled the paper that was around the USB drive and read it: 'Gwen will know what to do with this, and you must seek the source to complete your training.'

Kirin clenched her fist and banged the dummy with excitement.

One final resounding whack echoed throughout the apartment.

#

Whack. Whack. Whack. "Ma'am … ma'am," said the driver as he banged his dashboard several times.

Kirin heard a faint voice and saw a vision of a figure in front of her. "Sifu?"

"Ma'am … we're here."

She quickly shook off her grogginess and sat up straight. "Oh, sorry about that. I must've dozed off." She wiped a hint of drool from her face and realized she had been dreaming.

"No problem, ma'am."

"Thanks again." Kirin grabbed her single suitcase and hopped out of the car.

No sooner did her feet touch the dirt she froze where she stood. "It can't be. Is this the…?" She turned around, hoping for some help, but the driver immediately pulled away leaving a trail of dust.

She dropped her backpack and suitcase on the ground and ran to the door. The front was all boarded up along with several of the glass windows. She pressed her face against a small crack in a window to see if she could see anything, but it was pitch dark.

"I don't get it," she said to herself. "It looks like no one's been here for years."

She took several steps back and looked around. The street name and her GPS confirmed the location. Then she turned to her left, remembering the ongoing joke that across the street from the school was a strip club. There it was, a glowing sign advertising the club

Viper, which had a parking lot that was already crowded by midafternoon.

She looked back at the school and said, "This is it." She took several steps forward and decided to try her luck, knocking on the door.

Knock. Knock.

She waited for a minute and then, frustrated, Kirin kicked the door. It shook from the force of it. "Why!" she screamed, tensing her entire body. She spun backward this time, kicking it with full force. It came crashing down with a boom and a huge cloud of dust mixed with the desert air.

Kirin paused, wondering if she had gone too far. She leaned forward and whispered, "Hello?"

Kirin thought, *No one's here ... unless there's a ghost.* She shivered for just a second and realized the absurd nature of her logic. *It's just the dark, Kirin,* she thought. She was more motivated than afraid as she forced her way in and began to explore. After ten minutes sifting through the place, Kirin had no clue where to look or what to do. The place was stripped to its bones, and there remained no hint other than the dilapidated sign out front that had remnants of the school's name with missing letters. On the floor she saw what appeared to be a business card. She dusted it off. "Curves Cabaret?" she read before tossing it to the ground, unsure what that was.

She shook her head and thought, *I got nothing. Maybe I should've called first.* She walked out of the old abandoned school and stared at the street ahead. She yelled, "Give me a sign!"

She looked up at the sky and waited, and suddenly her stomach grumbled. She shrugged and said, "Why not go with the force?" She looked down at her stomach and mused, "Now, where was that place

Sifu said he used to eat at…? What was its name? Oh yeah, Gus's!" She sighed and said, "Let's hope that's still open."

She pulled out her phone and decided to see how far it was from where she stood. "Oh my gosh. Maybe my luck has changed. It's still open and within walking distance." After trekking for the next fifteen minutes by foot in the hot Tucson sun, she finally got to the front of Gus's. *Geez, it always looks so much closer on the GPS*, she thought.

Out front, several cars took up spaces in the parking lot, a good sign in Kirin's mind that, at the very least, life existed here. She drew herself to the main entrance and pulled open the doors before walking right in. Her initial impression made her smile. It was a quaint little mom-and-pop diner, and it looked exactly as Sifu had described it. The L-shaped counter hugged the far wall, the back of the kitchen was visible with a single cook working the orders, and several of the seats were already occupied with customers. A small handwritten sign in the center was highlighting fresh pies for the day, as the smell drew Kirin further in. Kirin plopped herself at one end of the bar for a breather, and her feet dangled above the ground as she realized how short she was.

A lady behind the counter came toward her and asked, "What'll you have, sweetheart?"

"Can you give me a second to look at the menu?" Kirin peeked at her nametag and said, "Uh, Stacey."

"Sure thing, you look like a coffee drinker. I'm guessing just black?"

Kirin smiled, "Yeah. I mean, yes, please."

Kirin took hold of the menu and began reading her choices as the smell of good food surrounded her. After deciding what she was going to have, Kirin looked quickly around to see who else was eating here. Several local patrons were gathered and chatting amongst themselves, and one person she could not make out was hidden behind a menu. In the end, she concluded there was nothing special going on, just people enjoying their lunch.

Stacey came back and set down a mug of coffee along with a glass of water. She asked, "Have you finally decided what you'll have?"

Kirin spun around. "Oh yes, do you mind if I have the number seven?" Stacey took down the information. "Oh, I almost forgot ... a short stack of pancakes."

"What kind of eggs and toast would you like with that?"

"Over easy and wheat." She smiled and handed the lady her menu as she decided to relax and enjoy her coffee. It was the first thing that had gone right all day. *Let me enjoy this meal first and then figure out how to find Sigung.* With that, she took another sip, closing her eyes and hoping to catch a break.

Several minutes passed before Kirin looked down at the typical diner breakfast laid out in front of her. Her plate was piled with eggs, toast, pancakes, and on the edge, there was everyone's friend, bacon.

"Enjoy, sweetie. Can I get ya anything else?"

Even before Stacey could finish her sentence, Kirin had already stuffed her face with food. She simply smiled, shook her head, and gave her thumbs up. For Kirin, manners were a work in progress. As always, Sifu was dead on. The food was delicious and fattening, to say the least. Kirin savored the moment as she felt her luck had finally changed.

Crash.

The doors swung open, disrupting the peaceful environment. Several guys entered the diner, talking loudly. Each one was dressed in overalls and wearing a cowboy hat and boots. They looked like they came straight from the farm, bypassing the necessary shower. Stacey moved hastily toward the entrance and stood in front of them.

"Now listen, fellas, you can come in if you behave. We don't want any trouble like last time."

The tallest of the group came around. His beard was red and unkept as he took the lead and picked up Stacey, hugging her. "You know I'm all about behaving. Besides, is this any way to treat your ex?"

"Brody, we had one date. That was it. And, yes, it was the biggest mistake of my life."

"Well … challenge accepted. If you go out with me again, maybe I can top that." He spanked her on the butt and called for the rest of the guys. "Beau … Billy, come on, guys. I'm hungry."

Kirin kept her head down and cautiously began to eat. She noticed several of the locals had walked out immediately, and she wondered if she should do the same. Her stomach grumbled as she thought, *You're gonna get us into trouble again. Just eat fast and get the hell out of her.* Kirin began wolfing down her food when suddenly she could feel eyes peering at her.

"Well, what do we have here?" said Brody as he leaned to the side to confirm his hunch.

Stacey and two other waitresses stared at Brody and wondered what he was so hyped about.

Brody called out to the remaining diners, "We got us here a big-time celebrity, and you people don't even know it."

Kirin took her last bite and grabbed her backpack and carry-on. She tossed a credit to pay the bill and got off her seat in a hurry. She ignored his comment and took a route away from Brody as she headed toward the door. Billy stepped in front of her, blocking her path before she could leave.

"Look, fellas…. I just came here to eat."

Brody approached Kirin from the side and checked her out from top to bottom. "Well, that's kinda rude to just eat and leave. You think you're too good to talk to the locals?"

Kirin did not answer but tried to go around Billy as he stood right in front of her. She thought, *Don't do it, Kirin. You don't want to attract any attention.*

Stacey jumped in, "Please, just leave her alone, Brody."

Brody never let his gaze stray from her, "Well, how about you at least give us an autograph … Kirin Rise?"

As the words finally left his lips, those remaining in the room stared at her.

"Uh, you must have me mistaken for her … besides, I'm blonde."

"Oh, I don't think so. I've watched enough UFMF to know who the real deal is. Besides, just 'cause you dyed your hair a perrtty blonde don't mean you can fool a fanboy like me." Billy snatched her hat from her as she tried to keep her cool. Beau finally approached as the entire group was now around her by the register.

Suddenly, with all the excitement and commotion occurring, a little old man got up from the corner booth and began shuffling his way to the entrance. He seemed somewhat oblivious to all that was happening as he walked toward Kirin. Kirin looked at him strangely and wondered what was going on. She was not the only one giving him an odd eye.

He walked past Brody, his two friends, and Kirin as if they did not even exist. He pulled out his wallet and stood in front of the register.

"I was wondering if I can pay my bill now?" He spoke with a hint of accent.

Stacey was still several feet away behind the counter, "Uh ...," She stared at Brody and the rest.

Brody motioned to Billy to deal with the annoyance. He nodded and acknowledged the order before going right toward the old man.

"Hey, old man, don't you see we got something going on right now?"

The old man smiled at him and said, "My eyes aren't as good as they used to be. You know, I'm old and Asian." He adjusted his glasses and looked up to Billy.

The comment struck Kirin as odd.

"I don't give a shit what you are." Billy drew closer and hulked over the old man.

The old man approached Billy whose back was positioned toward the entrance. "My, my... you are big and strong." He gently patted him on the chest, admiring his physique. He suddenly grabbed Billy by his shirt and gave him a slight nudge as Billy began falling backward. As he lost his center of gravity, the old man pulled him back in with the same hand. As his weight shifted toward the old man, he clenched his fist, twitching slightly as Billy's entire body caved in before being blasted from that spot. In a blink, Billy flew through the doors, landing violently several feet outside. He lay motionless as the entire room froze.

"No way," Kirin whispered.

He spun around and faced the register. "As I was saying, can I pay the bill now?"

Brody looked at Beau and shoved him in the back. He yelled, "Get his ass!"

Beau came charging in with only a short distance to cover. He threw out a wild punch, hoping to connect and make a statement. Instead, the old man ducked out of the way, allowing his Beau's momentum to carry himself right into the wall.

Kirin stood frozen in total disbelief as she was now next to the old man, facing his back. She muttered, "He moved so fast."

Beau gathered himself and was now pissed. He was made to look like a complete fool. His eyes were seething as he cracked his neck and charged straight in. Within a flash, Kirin found herself being spun around, headed for the same direction as Beau. She lost complete control of her center of gravity.

She thought, *He's using me as a shield.*

Beau staggered as Kirin walled off his attack. She watched as everything transpired in slow motion. He stuttered to regain his momentum, and that's when Beau caught a fist to the face. His body went limp, but before crumpling, it was tossed like a ragdoll across the room. He crashed on a table and then fell to the ground, covered in plates and food.

Kirin felt a pull of her own center of gravity once again as the old man threw her to the ground. A fist came flying across, just barely missing her as he saved her from the hit. She watched from the ground as Brody stumbled forward. Before he could hit the floor, the old man yanked him back. Brody tried countering with a back fist, but the old man held his hand in place, as if he knew exactly the path his attack would be coming from. He stood there posing with his back turned to the old man and remained in the same position. The old man touched

335

his other arm, but it was not a joint lock or a grab, Brody simply looked like he couldn't move.

"What the fuck is this?" he screamed.

The old man released him and maneuvered him in a position where Brody was now on his knees, his one hand still extended but still unable to move.

"Oh my gosh … it can't be," said Kirin. She thought, *He's freezing him.*

Brody looked up to him, "I can't fricking move."

"I know," he said. "Choices you have ... Grab your friends and get out of here, or join them for a nap."

Brody looked at Beau, who was still out cold. Billy had never returned. The decision was easy as he nodded to the old man, who finally released him. He had motion once again as he crawled on his knees to pick up Beau, but he never took his eyes off the old man. He was still in shock and scared senseless. In his primitive mind, he was able to muster that it was either superpowers, magic, or alien abilities. He struggled to drag Beau past Kirin and eventually got to the register.

The old man turned around and said, "And another thing … pay for my meal as well as this young lady's … and don't forget about the damages you've done."

Brody nodded his head and reached for his wallet. Beau hit the ground hard as Brody couldn't prioritize.

The old man headed toward Kirin as she took a good look at him. He smiled at her but continued on his way. Still on the ground, Kirin did not move. She simply watched as he walked through the doors. She remained motionless for several minutes, trying to make sense of everything that had transpired.

She thought, *Move, Kirin. Move your ass now.* With that, Kirin shook off her trance and ran out the front door. The sunlight blinded her for a second, but she could not find the old man. On the ground was Billy, still recovering from his hit. Kirin looked at him and knew he wasn't getting up any time soon.

"He's gotta be here. He moves like a snail when he walks."

Kirin scanned the area and then saw the old man a good fifty yards away. "How's that possible?" she muttered. She began running toward him and stopped right in front of him, gasping for air as she bowed before him.

He looked at her, "You're welcome."

"Oh, yeah. Thanks again." The thought of thanking him had not immediately entered her mind.

His brief stop lasted for a second as he walked around Kirin.

She thought, *It has to be him. This is just too weird.*

As she stared at the old man, she couldn't believe how he kept ignoring her. Flustered, she shouted, "SIGUNG!"

Finally, it caught his attention, and he stopped dead in his tracks. His reaction confirmed what Kirin had suspected. She ran back toward him and stood face to face with him. "Sigung, it IS you." Kirin smiled, feeling a sense of relief.

"I haven't heard anyone say that in a long time," replied the old man. "So, I'm guessing that man was correct ... you are, in fact, Kirin Rise?"

"So, you've heard of me?" asked Kirin.

He shook his head. "Just heard of you then, never before," He continued his snail-like walk right past Kirin.

Kirin watched and wondered. She shouted, "Wait, Sigung! I'm a student of Sifu Bing."

"Bing," he muttered. "Hmm ... how's he doing? I haven't spoken to him in a while."

Kirin immediately teared up and trembled as she tried to answer his question. "Sigung ... he passed away recently." Saying that stabbed her in the heart.

Sigung put his hand on Kirin's shoulders. "How did he die?"

Kirin trembled, "From a fire ... Sigung. It was all over the news. Many people died in the warehouse explosion."

"And, he was buried?"

"Well, the place burned down, and basically there were only ashes remaining."

"Interesting," said Sigung. His reaction felt odd to Kirin, who gathered herself and wiped her tears. After she'd spilled her guts to Sigung, she was surprised he was walking away again.

"Sigung, I need to complete my training. You're the only one who can teach me."

This time, he stopped in place. With his back turned to her, he said, "Teach you? I haven't taught anyone in years. I'm retired, you know."

Kirin dashed in front of him, "Please, Sigung. Can't you ... uh, un-retire? You're my only hope."

"I'm very busy now. No time to teach."

"You're busy? You just told me you're retired. What could you possibly be busy with?"

"I need to go to the grocery today. Need to eat, you know."

"You can get that all delivered to you now. Can't you just use your phone?"

"Phone." He chuckled. "I don't even have one of those."

Kirin shook her head. She thought, *I found someone who's worse with technology than I am.*

"Sigung, please ... I need to complete the art. It's a matter of life and death."

"Me not getting my groceries is a matter of life and death also."

Kirin scratched her head in frustration. She took a deep breath and tried to figure out how to convince Sigung to teach her. She thought, *Don't fight the force.* She looked at him and pulled her emotions back.

"Sigung, why don't I help you with the groceries? You don't have to give me an answer right now, but just entertain the thought, okay?" Kirin knew to keep quiet and make sure Sigung was the first one to talk. Sifu had always taught her about the advantages of being passive.

He stood there with no emotion on his face and did not answer.

Kirin began to squirm, knowing that, if she opened her mouth, she would have already lost. The minute of silence felt like eternity, but Sigung gave nothing away. She thought, *He taught this game to Sifu, and I've got no chance to beat him.*

Kirin tensed up and could not hold it in any longer. She broke, "Please, Sigung?"

"Okay." He began walking. "Follow me."

Kirin blew out a sigh of relief, shook her head, and watched Sigung causally walk ahead.

#

Thirty minutes later, Sigung and Kirin stood in front of the grocery store. It was a typical corporate-owned food dispenser, which surprised Kirin. "You shop here for groceries, Sigung?"

Sigung looked back at Kirin and said, "Why not? Simple and easy." He passed through the sliding doors while Kirin stayed slightly behind, unfamiliar with Sigung's habits. He bypassed the fresh fruits and vegetables section and continued his stroll. She found it a bit odd, but he quickly approached the aisle with all the frozen food. He stood at a section and gazed upon the many selections.

"Uh, Sigung, what are you doing?"

"I'd say … I'm looking for tonight's dinner."

"You eat this?" asked Kirin as she scoffed at the food selection.

"Good food. Good food." He reached in and grabbed a handful of frozen foods. He then began tossing them to Kirin to hold. "Help an old man out, will you?"

Kirin glanced through the stack of frozen foods, each of which looked less flavorful than the previous one. She stared at the brand, Whiteman's Heaven. She thought, *Why is he eating this? Mac N Cheelicious, Meatloaf Mama, Whitey's MMM Nuggets, Blando Tuna Casserole?* She stuck out her tongue and made a face in disgust. Kirin recalled that Sifu had once said, "Tucson is a place where Asian taste buds go to die."

"That should be enough," said Sigung. "How many meals is that, Kirin?"

Snapping out of her daze, she realized that Sigung had just called her by her name. "Uh, Sigung, I have seven meals." She thought, *He actually said my name.*

"Perfect, that should last me the week."

"This is gonna be your dinner?"

He turned around and smiled. "Yes, it is."

Kirin had had enough. She walked back to the freezer aisle and began returning the food.

"What are you doing?" For the first time, Sigung looked doubtful.

"Look, Sigung, I know you haven't decided whether to teach me, but I can't let you eat this stuff. Tell you what, let me buy the groceries and cook you a real meal, and then afterward you can decide whether or not to teach me." Kirin extended her hand out and waited.

Again, Sigung remained motionless until Kirin looked uncomfortable with her arm extended. She fidgeted in place before Sigung smiled and finally shook her hand.

He said, "Fair enough."

Kirin thought, *Geez, just like Sifu. I hate when he does that.*

#

At Sigung's house, Kirin began to cook with the groceries she'd bought. He lived in a humble ranch house, not so far from where his school used to be, within a community that was less than desirable. Surprisingly, the house was neatly organized and well kept. The kitchen was spotless, and it appeared that it had not been used for quite some time. However, the little touches that Kirin spotted had to have come from a woman. *Definitely a woman's touch*, she thought. She kept the conversation light as his responses were short with an occasional grunt. For now, that was fine, as Kirin's focus was to make the best meal possible for Sigung.

Kirin continued to prep the meal while Sigung sat at the table watching her every move. How she stood, the way she wielded her knife, even the questions she asked all revealed her level of skill to the Wing Chun master. For the first time, he took the initiative and spoke. "Simo passed away about five years ago."

Kirin paused and then continued chopping away. Conversations about deceased loved were always difficult, especially for her. However, the timing of his question made her think. *How'd he know I was about to ask that?* She felt obligated to say something and blurted back, "I'm sorry to hear that, Sigung...," as she took a peek. Sigung looked stone-faced, even more difficult to read than Sifu. She added, "So, I'm guessing you live by yourself?"

"Yes, it's quiet around here. I like it like that."

Kirin added. "Any kids, Sigung?"

"Two boys ... both boys have their own families. One lives out of state, while the other one is all the way in Macau. They visit every now and then, when they can."

"I didn't know you had kids, Sigung. Do they practice Wing Chun?"

"They studied a little, but neither one got into it heavily."

Kirin was juggling several things at one time. This was the most cooking she had ever done. Everything was based off taste, as she never measured anything, just like her mom. Those lessons that were repeated forever eventually stuck. A fresh new scent began to permeate the room. Three of the four burners on the stove were finally being put to use.

"Mmm, that does smell good. Where did you learn to cook?"

"My mom. She taught me when I was growing up."

An hour quickly passed before Kirin plated the meals and set them in front of Sigung. She had prepared several Korean dishes. Considering the alternative from the grocery store, the odds were in her favor that he would like it. The table was overflowing with *tteok-bokki*, *bulgogi*, *kimchi*, fish cakes, and a set of Korean mini-appetizers. Kirin crossed her fingers, hoping that what she prepared wasn't too spicy for Sigung. During their meal, the dinner conversation expanded as Sigung began opening up to Kirin. He also brought about a sense of peace, much like Sifu, but different in his own way.

After one last bite, Sigung rubbed his belly and got up from his chair. "Thanks for the meal."

"You're welcome," said Kirin as Sigung had eaten literally everything she had prepared.

He walked away as Kirin found herself alone in his kitchen. She thought, *Well, this is odd*. Several minutes passed, and Kirin wondered if he was in the bathroom or if she should be clearing the table.

From the other room, she heard a sound as Sigung called out for her. "I'm waiting."

Kirin got up from her chair and slowly approached from the kitchen entrance. She peeked her head through the doorway and saw Sigung standing in the middle of the living room.

"Uh, what's going on, Sigung?"

"The best time to practice is after a meal; otherwise, you'll end up falling asleep."

Kirin had been so absorbed in the conversation with Sigung that she had forgotten her reason for being there. A smile formed as the first sign of good fortune was a relief for her. She asked again just to confirm, "So, you're going to train me?"

Sigung did not say another word but placed his hands in a rolling position, ready to do a drill. His actions spoke louder than words as Kirin ran toward Sigung. They touched hands for the first time and began her training.

"Keep in mind what may seem like random acts were set in motion from choices that we made in the past. The end result is cause and effect."— Sigung

Section 1 Short Stories #8—Kirin's P.O.V.

College Life—Day 305

After months of promising Sage I would visit, I finally ran out of my countless excuses and made it here, on campus with him. I was not alone because it had taken the efforts of my best friend to drag me along with her. We were at a prestigious university in Chicago. Only the cream of the crop got in, but the top 1% got a free ride, and that was my friend Sage.

Sage said, "I'm glad you guys finally made it here, even though it's almost the end of my first year."

I tried to absolve myself of blame, "It wasn't my fault. It's Gwen. She's always busy with her consulting work."

Gwen paused in her tracks and shot me a look. "You're really going to try to blame this on me, Kirin?"

I decided to continue to walk and hoped that Gwen would quickly forget my nonresponse.

"Mmm…."

I stopped side by side with Sage and turned around. "Yes, Gwen. It was me. Are you happy? Besides, I thought I'd give Sage some time to familiarize himself with the campus before he gave us a full tour."

Instead of answering me, Gwen decided to roll by us in her wheelchair, "Continue the tour, Sage."

Sage added, "I would've gone with the second excuse first."

I nodded.

The spring weather was a welcome awakening. The typical long Chicago winter had been tough for everybody. This year, the snow had hit hard and combined with the cold weather to serve as a painful reminder that we were slaves to the elements. But then, there was no point in complaining. Either you eat the cake, or you just leave. Choices are usually not as difficult as we make them out to be.

"I'm really impressed with all this, Sage." I was enjoying the time off from my daily grind.

"Don't be. It's all an illusion. Besides, I'm willing to bet your Stanford campus would've been a lot nicer than here."

"Why do you say that?"

"Fun in the sun, of course."

A quick breeze reminded me that there was no argument there. I turned to Gwen, "Gwen, how does this compare to your school?"

"Well, this is much nicer than my campus," said Gwen.

Sage said, "You actually go to school? I figured your consulting job made it hard to justify going to classes."

"It does," Gwen admitted, "but I still wanted a chance to experience what college life was like."

Despite all this talk, I had no regrets about my decision. The truth was the best part of school was simply hanging with my friends. At some point, we all had to grow up and couldn't always be together. You never realize that last day when it happens.

There was a food truck nearby where we caught a quick bite to eat. It was just too nice out not to take advantage of the day, so we picked a spot where many other students were hanging out. The grass was a mixture of green and dirt as spring was trying its best to remind us it was here.

"So, is college life that much different from high school, Sage?"

Sage said, "Honestly, for me, it feels about the same. I guess you could say there's more freedom, but there seems to be something off about the entire thing."

"What do you mean?"

"Look around. This represents the future, where hopes and dreams are born. But, seriously with unemployment at an all-time high … even though these guys graduate from here, statistically speaking, they'll all be leaving this school with a huge debt and no job."

Gwen somberly nodded, "Sage is right. I mean, whoever is on top pulling the strings isn't leaving many options."

"I hear what you're saying. Being away from school and seeing what everyday life is like working, I can't imagine how people make ends meet." I was speaking from my own experience as I was subsidizing my income with illegal fighting at nights. Without it, there was no way I could possibly live on my own.

Sage pointed to a girl who was eating on the lawn. "See that girl over there? That's Jill. She's working, like, three jobs and studying here. Not sure how she manages to do everything, but somehow she does. She's really smart, and I can see her making a difference, but if she represents the future, the way things are being run right now, I don't know if there will be one."

Gwen said, "That's a dime a dozen. When I go to class at my school, I hear the same things from my friends over there. Hard to make a difference when you get out that start gate, and your dragging all that debt with you."

"So, what do we do?" I asked.

Gwen chuckled, "Vote?"

I rolled my eyes. "I don't see how feeding into a system that doesn't work has any chance of making any kind of change."

Sage replied, "It's a fool's hope."

Gwen added, "You can't strip it fully away, or else there would be a total uprising."

"Remember: if you don't vote, you can't complain." Commented Sage.

Gwen continued, "It interesting how, if you say something long enough and pass it down from generation to generation, it somehow turns into the truth."

I reached down and plucked some grass, "So, if people do vote and things are still crap, do we blame the ones who voted? I mean, they were the ones who put those people in charge."

Everyone got a chuckle out of that comment, but it made sense to me.

"It seems quite flawed to put one's faith entirely in the hands of the government. In fact, the more logical approach is that it'll be up to you to make things better." Sage echoed some of his sentiments from his graduation speech.

Gwen smiled and shook her head, "I'd agree with you on that, but that would mean taking responsibility for yourself, and we already know most people would rather blame others than carry the ball themselves."

"I remember our debates in high school social studies class about this topic. In fact, if you think about it, that's really the problem."

Sage titled his head in confusion, "What do you mean?"

"People."

Gwen parroted, "People?"

I looked at them both, "People are so divided about anything and everything. You name a topic, from race to politics to religion. People live and die with their sides regardless of whether they are right or wrong."

Sage was unphased, "That's how it's always been."

Gwen added, "If that's how it's always been, then you'd have to factor that as a set standard. You can't make a change knowing that a given set of reactions will always be the norm."

"I think we're looking at it in the wrong way. Screw the system right now. It's not important, but the players involved are. The people are so divided right now. Nothing is going to change. The people lack focus."

Gwen said, "Hard to find common ground. It doesn't matter if you are right, people see things how they want to, regardless of facts or even the truth."

Sage agreed.

It made more sense that people were divided. If they were united and shared some common ground, then something could actually be done.

I spent the day seeing what I had missed. To me, it seemed like the world was an illusion. But, in order for the future to have a chance, in order to see the potential that could be harvested from this school and others, someone would need to blaze a path for them to grow.

"It doesn't matter how little it is, you need hope to get things started." — *Sifu*

Reaction—Day 330

It was Saturday afternoon, and the entire gang was together, training at out our makeshift school. It had been several months since we had made it our place, and this actually felt like home to me. Sure, a working toilet would be nice, but we were able to make our little area sustainable. We had lights, our training equipment, and, most importantly, we were able to endure the winter with our portable heaters.

At the end of the day, it served our purpose, and the best thing about home was that my Wing Chun family was together training. This afternoon, Tobias gave the lead to Doc. Every so often, depending on when he felt like it, Tobias gave everyone the opportunity to teach. Sifu had told Tobias, "You cannot be a student of the art forever. If you want to be good at the art, you also have to teach it." Even I had, on occasion, taught the class. Despite being the youngest in the art, the time spent one on one with Sifu made me feel on equal level to the guys.

Doc always took a more cerebral approach when explaining things, and this time he was making sure everyone understood one of the thirteen principles, which was reaction.

Doc shared, "Trust me, it's easy to say but even easier to confuse. We all think reaction is after the fact, but if you look at it that way, you'll always be one step behind."

Danny said, "Can you toss us an example, Doc?"

Unlike me, Doc never left things to chance, so he always took his time before responding. "If you look at our drills, they're not about memorizing techniques. Each one is more like a particular skill or something that Ken and Robert can appreciate ... a superpower."

Ken and Robert high-fived one another, and Tobias said, "That's why you two are king dorks."

Doc cleared his throat. "As I was saying, it's not too far-fetched to think that you are developing a power. Take, for instance, our stance. People take it for granted and don't realize how important it is. Sure, everyone says balance and stance are the foundation, but what does that really mean? So, what happens when you learn your basic stance and the next thing you know you are in a fight and end up standing like a fool trying to apply it?"

Ryan pointed at Danny, who shouted back, "It was one time, and I learned from my mistake!"

Ignoring them, Doc added, "The stance develops center of gravity control and awareness. So, in everyday use, for example, if you're walking and you hit a patch of ice, instead of falling on the ground like 99% of the population, you end up catching your center of gravity and not slipping."

Robert interjected, "Not slipping isn't the coolest superpower, you know, Doc."

"I didn't say that was all there was." He motioned to Big T. "If you will."

Big T approached Doc as he opened up his right hand. He said, "Big T, make a fist and put it upon my hand and push me as hard as you can."

Big T did as Doc had instructed. Doc was just standing normally without the stance. His hand was open as Big T's giant paw engulfed all of Doc's.

"Whenever you are ready," said Doc.

As soon as the words left his mouth, Big T used all his muscle and began pressing hard into Doc's hand. He was clearly trying, but Doc held his ground and did not waver. I'd seen Sifu do this before but never one of his students. I was actually quite impressed with Doc's skill.

Doc went on, "Notice how I stand. It's not the set stance but just natural. You'd never know that I was doing Wing Chun. We've talked about the difference between development and application, but this goes a bit deeper because there's a right way to react and a wrong way."

Big T finally stopped and took a second to catch his breath. He shook his head and said, "It's shit like this that makes it hard to justify doing sit-ups. All the muscle in the world can't overcome this structure."

Doc wasn't the least bit strained from the demonstration. "When it comes to reaction … Big T, please push my hand again."

This time, Big T did the same thing, but the results were different. Doc's stance wobbled, and he couldn't maintain his ground. He took a step back and quickly succumbed to the force. Doc explained, "Notice when he gives me force, I'm reacting to it and trying to make adjustments—like I said earlier, after the fact. Whenever that's the case, you'll always be playing catch up."

Ryan said, "Did you say ketchup?"

Doc shook his head, "Catch up."

Ryan asked, "Oh … anyway, what's the difference in reaction between the first and last example?"

"Big T, one more time." At Doc's request, Big T began pressing on Doc's hand, and this time he maintained his position. "This time, when he gives me force, notice how I'm automatically reacting to it without thought. That means there's no delayed reaction on my part, so when he moves, I move automatically."

Robert said, "That's impressive."

Tobias jumped in, "That's what you want to develop. You don't want to have a knee-jerk reaction to anything. But, by controlling yourself, you don't get the leftover response from whatever your opponent does. You want him to react to you and not the other way around."

I heard Ryan mutter, "Mmm, leftovers."

"A little more explanation?" I requested.

Doc smiled at me, "I'm not thinking of what he's doing. I'm thinking of what I'm doing, if that makes sense. By worrying about your opponent after he gives you a force, you'll always end up reacting to him. But, since I focus entirely on what I'm doing, I'm reacting to myself."

Danny made a gesture of his head exploding, and I noticed some of the other guys giving more thought to his words than normal.

I questioned, "So, focus on you?"

Doc tried to close things out, "I'll end it with this. Training is about finding out who you are and then, when you figure that out, being consistent to that truth. Never fade from the truth. Most people go through life being defined by others. When you let others define you, you'll always be a step behind, reacting ... making the world a very difficult place to live in."

I took a moment to think about what Doc said, which for me was rare.

Never fade from the truth.

"So, I guess you can say ... always be you."

"Remember that you define you. When you allow someone else to do it for you, you'll forever be owned by them." — Sifu

Symbols and Words—Day 350

I ventured to a part of the building that I had never been to before. Since we'd settled in our little school, I thought we might be able to expand it even further. This place was now our home, and I wanted to make it even more our own. Several rooms down the hallway, I found a section that looked quite decrepit. My first thought was that it would take too much work to rehab. Really, the problem wasn't the work, but the cost involved to make it work. However, something caught my attention from the corner of my eye. I stood there staring at it, a symbol universally recognized. Spray painted in red, a huge swastika took hold of one of the walls. It was about the same height as me and could not be missed. The color was somewhat faded, and I knew some graffiti must've occurred when the place was abandoned.

"Kirin? Kirin, what's taking you so long?" called Big T. When I didn't answer, he stopped right behind and saw what had caused my delay.

Big T said, "You know, we've been here for months, but I've never ventured off to any other part of the building except our main room."

"Same," I replied. "What do you think we should do about this?"

"I don't know…."

Doc called from a distance, and I shouted, "Big T and I are in here."

Soon, the rest of the gang came to see what had prevented us from returning. They all stared at the symbol, not speaking for a time as I wondered what was going through everyone's head.

Then Ryan broke the silence, "Nothing to see here, people. Let's get back and practice."

I shot him a look, "What do you mean, 'nothing to see here'?"

Doc nodded and begun to turn away, "For once, I agree with Ryan. Nothing to see here."

"How can you say that? Ken's right here, and you're not acknowledging how this might make him feel."

Doc gave me a gentle pat on the shoulder, "We all study Wing Chun. We're all better than this. We're not like everyone else, emotional creatures who get jolted by the sight of symbol, or a word, or some headline news."

I looked to Ken, "Ken…?"

Ken nodded his head in agreement, "I get it. I'm Jewish only in name, not in practice. But, yeah, at first, like Doc said, this would've bothered me. But, we as individuals give meaning to thing, like symbols or words. I'm not defined by how people label me or anything else. It's my own makeup that makes me strong. This, to me, is merely red paint and lines."

I asked, "How can you say that? We all know what this stands for."

Ken looked around, "Anyone have a pen or marker on them?"

Ryan handed him his pen, and Ken began drawing on the wall. When he stopped, the picture he had created looked very much like the symbol on the wall. He turned to everyone, "What is this?"

Robert said, "I'm surprised I can even tell, considering it's your drawing."

Ken glared, "Shut up, Robert," as he looked at it for a second and added, "Hmmm, that could be my best sketch ever."

I finally answered, "Looks pretty much like the other symbol on the wall, but slightly different."

Robert shook his head, "Fine. I'm going to contribute something other than an insult to this conversation. It's Indian."

Danny said, "Is that with a feather or a dot?"

Tobias punched him in the arm.

Doc chimed in, "To be more specific, it's a Hindu symbol. It basically denotes prosperity, if I recall properly."

Ken tried to make a point, "Notice how we as individuals assign meaning to things."

Danny said, "Kinda like the *S* on Superman's outfit. I thought it meant 'hope' on Krypton."

Robert rubbed his face and muttered, "Please be quiet."

Ken said, "No, no ... it's true Danny's an idiot, but that example is right."

Danny looked confused. "Hey!"

I asked, "But, what's your point?"

"My point is...." Ken paused before continuing, "Let's say we hear a word in a foreign language, and it's a bad word. Ryan give me a Japanese bad word."

"Uh ... oh yeah, *Kuso Kurae.*"

Ken looked at everyone's reaction and asked, "What's it mean, Ryan?"

"It means 'eat shit.'"

"Notice, not a blink from any of you because you had no idea of the meaning. They're just words that people have given meaning. It's up to you whether to accept that meaning or not."

Tobias said, "I remember Sifu talking about this. While I wish I dove deeper into the spiritual aspect of the art, if you think about it, it's all related to the stance."

"How so?" I asked.

"With the stance ... at the end of the day, what are you developing?"

"To be able to stand on your own two feet," I said.

"Yes, so no matter what outside forces come at you, they won't affect your foundation. So, no matter what's happening with the world around you, your foundation is strong enough that nothing can bother you at all."

Ryan scratched his head, "Wow, that's some profound stuff. I always looked at the stance from a physical aspect only."

Doc gave Ryan a pat on the back, "It's natural; we all do. But, the art always involves all three aspects, the physical, mental, and spiritual."

Deep down, I thought I understand what they were saying, but I was still unsure. "So, what do we do about this? Nothing?"

Ken smiled at me, "Honestly … it means nothing to me." He gave it one last look and began walking away. The rest of the guys followed suit, and I was left alone looking at the symbol.

#

The next day before the gang got there, I arrived with a small can of paint and a brush. I began painting over the entire wall. Several minutes later, I heard someone enter. I continued my work as I was focused on finishing it.

Ken stood behind me, "So, nothing we talked about sunk in?"

I put my brush down and turned to Ken. "You know what? Regardless of whether it bothers anyone, it still clashes with the look of the place. So, what's wrong with a fresh coat of paint to make our home look exactly how we want it?"

> *"Make yourself so strong that nothing from the outside world can ever throw you off your center."* — *Sifu*

Section 2 Sifu's Journey Entry #8—First Sight

Late July

Sifu left many disappointed faces behind him. Closing the restaurant had been a last-minute decision due to pressing matters. His group had informed him of an illegal fight match that would be happening, and they had reported there was a good chance Kirin might be there. The plan remained the same: figure out a way to convince Kirin to join Chum Night and remain in the shadows without her knowing.

He looked at his note and inputted the coordinates into his phone, so he could find the exact location. It was nearly 10 pm on a Saturday night. The location was a neighborhood, one of many that the government had left to rot on its own. From a distance, he saw an abandoned building with all the windows blown out, but inside a flicker of light could be seen.

This was uncharted territory for Sifu. He had kept an occasional tail on his students' whereabouts, but this was the first time he had physically ventured to see them in person. His decision was firm, and he was committed to seeing it through. He would somehow avenge a wrong, which he knew deep down was a price he had to pay.

As he walked into the abandoned building and made his way toward the only source of light, he began to hear the chanting of the crowd. Each step brought him closer to the first sight, but he stayed aware of his surroundings, making sure he didn't bump into anyone who might care. Finally, he reached the group of noisy, unsightly individuals gathered in the smoky arena. The smell all around was quite memorable and hopefully limited to the outer areas.

He took a moment to digest the situation and assess his current surroundings. He finally figured out what this building used to be. It was a grocery store, a famous chain that had gone out of business. The name escaped him, but that did not matter. Instead, he focused on the faces of all those who were watching. He was poorly disguised in a hoodie, much like his old student would wear, but he kept to himself and eventually blended in.

Thirty minutes passed before the first sign of activity appeared. Walking toward the center was the assumed ring leader of the event. He was decked out in eighties gear sporting a neon mohawk while wearing shades in a relativity poorly lit area.

"My name is XtoC. Gather around, boys and girls … I promise you that tonight's festivities will not only be entertaining but quite lucrative for those who choose wisely. Your pockets will be packed with more credits than you can make in a month's time. I have before you four matches this evening, each one better than the last."

Sifu continued to look around, making sure he did not bump into anyone who might recognize him. The crowd started building up energy as greed set in. The hopes of quick credits made it all so irresistible.

"All bets are final, and you must pay. Otherwise…." XtoC directed everyone's attention to the corner, where his associate who stood tallest amongst the crowd flexed his muscles and grabbed a large metal garbage can. He lifted it over his head and heaved it farther than anyone thought was possible as he let out a scream.

"And the scariest thing is he won't wash his hands after that." The crowd chuckled, and XtoC filled in the blanks for the remaining information. Everyone was anticipating the first fight, and even Sifu was on his toes, hoping that Kirin would pop up. But, as XtoC announced the names and the participants showed their faces, he saw no one he recognized.

Sifu let out a yawn and struggled to watch the first fight. He was the only one who looked bored, as the rest of the crowd was cheering on the battle. He waited through the drudgery for five minutes as the participants bludgeoned one another with fists and kicks. Looking away, he yawned again. Sifu could measure up each opponent with a glance and knew right away who would win. He thought, *This involves no skill whatsoever.* Finally, a wild swing connected, and the crowd let out a huge roar. The next several minutes were spent exchanging credits as XtoC began hyping up the crowd for the next fight.

For the next hour, Sifu shifted through the crowd, not staying static. He found it difficult to focus on the fight. While he normally worked during these late hours, he struggled to stop yawning. He looked at his phone and decided tonight was not going to be the night. He was considering leaving when XtoC began hyping up the final fight. None of the names caught Sifu's attention, so he began making his way through the crowd. He passed one of the first contestants, who was ripped from head to toe and definitely the largest fighter of the evening. He paused and watched as the crowd went wild and began chanting and jeering. He thought, *All the money must be on this guy.*

XtoC pointed to him and proclaimed, "Give it up for the most feared fighter of the evening. He is undefeated in his last seven bouts. One hit to rule the world, he is none other than the Fist!"

The Fist bullied his way through the crowd and walked right by Sifu. He began running and did a set of flips to make for a grand entrance into the circle. He landed in a superhero pose slamming his fist into the ground.

The crowd began chanting, "Fist! Fist! Fist!"

The Fist stood up and raised his arms in the air as bets began to fly around. He was the highlight of the night, the sure thing that everyone had been waiting for. As the Fist absorbed the crowd's adoration, XtoC announced, "Our last fighter has been making the rounds, scaring opponents, and has definitely earned the chance to prove their worth."

Sifu shook his head and decided it was time to go home. Just before he did, XtoC shouted, "Everyone, please welcome … Blink!"

The name had no meaning for Sifu, who was about to turn around. Just then Blink walked past him, and he felt a familiar energy. He turned to the fighter, and his eyes widened when he saw Kirin. Without hesitation, he ducked out of the way and got lost in the crowd. At that very moment, Kirin turned around but saw only the crowd cheering. She paused longer than expected but continued back toward her opponent.

As the formalities were finalized, the match was about to begin. Sifu made his way to the back of the crowd, ensuring that he would go unseen. He had a job to do and remained unemotional. She might have been his student, but for now it was just another match. Hopefully, it would be entertaining at least.

Both fighters kept their distance as XtoC stood between them. Kirin looked relaxed, much different than the last time Sifu had seen her. A sense of maturity overshadowed her, coupled with a resounding increase in confidence. Her opponent was jumping back and forth, shaking the nerves and trying to bait her into a stare down. XtoC took several steps back, waited for the crowd noise to reach its loudest, and then dropped his hand, signaling the match had officially begun.

The Fist stood there with his guard already up as Kirin sprang into action, charging directly into him. Her actions weren't the norm, as they never expect a tiny girl to be so aggressive. He let out a roundhouse kick to counter, but Kirin was already in. She planted a kick to his support leg, taking his structure out from underneath him. He fell straight to the ground and onto his face; humble pie had the taste of dirt.

The crowd cheered and enjoyed the moment, as Sifu clenched his fist, raising it slightly. He thought, *Not bad, but you have to hit the source of the attack to the centerline.*

The Fist stood up, shocked by what had just transpired. He dusted himself off and cracked the joints of several of his body parts. He clashed his fists together and returned to his fighting stance, looking even more determined.

Sifu shook his head and mumbled to himself, "Don't wait. Move in and finish him already." His body tightened, hoping that through thought he could will Kirin to do what he wanted.

The Fist moved in as Kirin stood there with no guard. He took a wild swing as she ducked the first attack and went with his flow. The Fist followed it up with a hard circular hook. Kirin caught the hook with a block and chopped at his neck at the same time. The force was strong, too strong for her block to deal with, but both fighters' attacks landed, sending each one back.

Sifu thought, *Dammit, Kirin, stop using technique.*

As Kirin tried to regain herself, the Fist was the first one to get up. One should never trade hits, especially with such a size difference. The Fist took the opportunity to see that Kirin was still shaken from his attack as he launched a kick to her ribs. She rolled several times from the impact and was gasping for air as the hit landed hard.

The Fist took the moment to celebrate, feeling confident that this match was pretty much over. As Kirin winced in pain, she pounded the ground and looked up at the Fist. Sifu couldn't contain himself as he shouted into the crowd, "Just ATTACK! Cut the B.S. and ATTACK!" He watched as her fighting spirit within her emerged.

A fire lit in Kirin's eyes. She had had enough. She wanted to wipe that stupid smirk off the Fist's face. As the Fist was enjoying his moment of celebration, she got back up and charged in hard. Her energy overwhelmed him even before she was in range. He threw out a straight jab to slow down her attack, but Kirin ignored the piddly attempt and merely shifted to the side. Her best defense would be her offense as she launched a punch right down the center just as he finished his jab. The Fist had no chance to block it as the impact was well timed and did severe damage. He held on to consciousness by a thread as the second hit connected with an uppercut, catching him square on the jaw. The last hit left no doubts as he crumpled immediately to the ground. Kirin stared him down, ready to unleash more.

And just like that, the crowd was stunned and silent. The Fist lay face down in an awkward position as his fortune shifted from exhilaration to embarrassment within a blink. Kirin stood over him as XtoC rushed in to raise her hand. Sifu cracked a smile as a sense of pride came over him. He, along with a handful of lucky souls, jumped for joy as he found himself high-fiving perfect strangers. The remaining majority hung their heads, knowing their pockets were going to be lighter than when they had started. Kirin's last charge performed the art to perfection, and there was no greater joy for a teacher than when his own student displayed it with such elegance. That sensation quickly fled as Sifu's heart felt squeezed. Thoughts raced through his head as guilt and shame soon followed. He had no answer to the question; how could he do this to his student? He hung his head in disappointment. Ashamed of his actions, he disappeared from the celebrating crowd.

CHAPTER 9
The Third Key

Late October 2034

For the last several months, Kirin had been training with Sigung down in Tucson. In many ways, the experience provided some comfort that helped her deal with Sifu's passing, but Sigung had his differences. Kirin came to accept the fact that there would be no substitute, nor did she think it was fair to compare her teachers. The days were long and extensive, and the training was unlike any she had undergone before. She would wake up first thing in the morning and invest forty-five minutes just on the first form, Siu Lim Tao. Sifu had always suggested that she do what she could when she could with the first form. For Sigung, Siu Lim Tao was a religion. He demanded that she do it first, before any lesson was even taught. At first, it felt like a chore, and Kirin found herself counting down the time until she finally finished the form. Over the last several weeks, the need to perfect every motion seemed to minimize. Instead, she was able to focus on a single thought, and somehow, through that, she found peace.

Kirin woke up first like always and had already completed her first requirement of the day. No, it was not the form—which she had finished—but Sigung's breakfast, though Sigung was still asleep and did not have a set schedule as to when he woke up. The agreement was simple: She would cook, and he would teach. Things were in perfect harmony for the time being.

She decided to turn on the TV and work on her sword form. Fortunately for her, Wing Chun did not require much space. Even in a little area, she was able to work with the swords that Sifu had left her. She was still enamored with the swords, and she felt a tingle throughout her body every time she held them. These were no toys, and they required an extra level of intensity and focus. She found it odd that Sifu had told her to name the swords, but it had been months, and nothing had stuck. She looked at it for a minute before blurting out, "Redemption … that's it! Sword of Redemption." She held one of the swords up in the air, striking a pose.

After letting it sink in for a few seconds, Kirin slouched back into position. "Ugh, that doesn't work." She took one deep breath and decided it was easier to practice than to come up with a name. Ten minutes quickly passed as the sound of the TV helped kill the monotony that existed in Sigung's house. From time to time, she would hear clips of the latest news, which consisted of everything that was wrong with the world.

During these long months, she had made minimal contact with her friends. Hunter would talk to her occasionally, making sure she was okay. Tobias was still trying to figure out how to vie for her attention. Only Gwen kept constant contact with Kirin, who had kept the original USB drive that Sifu had hidden within his wooden dummy. Gwen had made a copy and had been spending most of her days decoding the information that Sifu had gathered. Talks between them were coded, and Gwen made sure any exchange of information was fully secured.

Another fifteen minutes passed, and Kirin had built a significant amount of sweat with her swords cutting through the air. In between one of her motions, the TV flashed and caught her attention. She decided to take a break as she walked over to turn up the volume. It felt weird being on the other side of events, but Kirin didn't miss it. On the screen, she saw two familiar faces. She sat down in front of the TV, laying her sword on her lap as she began to watch.

Connor and Linkwater were discussing yesterday's match on the UFMF channel.

"Ripley Hawkins aka Whiskey has continued her streak in an impressive fashion, don't you think?" asked Linkwater.

"I agree. She has definitely taken the UFMF by storm, but you know, as fans, we are all cynical. As her fan base grows and her wins continue to pile up, it's only natural to start comparing numbers. Even though she's gone undefeated this season, she has yet to break any of Kirin Rise's records in the ring or the ratings."

"That is true, but the season's still young."

Linkwater said, "Have you felt this year to be different from the past two seasons when Kirin Rise first came on the circuit?"

Connor gave a slight nod, "There was definitely something magical about Kirin that captivated the imagination of the fans. Even though she's dropped out of this season, as you can see behind us, her huge fan base is still shouting for her return. In fact, despite her incident and her hiatus, her popularity has remained just as strong."

Kirin shook her head and thought, *Great, I'm sure Ripley is gonna love that.*

"There's definitely no denying that. The funny thing is I did notice our new star getting a bit testy in her last interview regarding Kirin."

"That is true, but I can't blame Whiskey. At some point, the comparisons will wear anyone down, especially if they keep asking you the same thing over and over again."

Kirin rolled her eyes, "Confirmed."

"However, getting back to your original question, I think that this season has been pretty much as expected."

Linkwater added, "With Kirin Rise, there was always controversy surrounding her over the last two seasons. This season, everything's been about Whiskey, and nothing shocking or surprising has really happened with her debut or the season in general. The additional three countries who entered into the UFMF this year—Russia, China, and South Africa—have provided a good mixture of new fighters, but no one in particular has separated themselves from the pack."

Connor said, "So, you're saying you miss Kirin Rise and her controversy."

Linkwater replied, "I think, in spite of everything, Kirin's unique fighting style was something we've never seen before … a breath of fresh air. So, in a way, I'm like the fans. I do miss her."

Kirin chuckled. "I can't believe it…. Now that I'm gone, they're finally saying nice things about me." She got up from the floor and decided to switch channels. The last several months, Kirin had enjoyed her isolation. After the whirlwind of events that happened, plain and boring were fine in her book. Excitement was the last thing she wanted.

She continued to swipe through several channels before stopping on one. The screen showed protesters forming a huge rally. They seemed lost as Bryce was no longer the voice and Kirin had decided to lay by the wayside and hide. On the screen, she saw a sign that read, 'Kirin, we need you!' Kirin watched as the cameras continued to film. Suddenly, the protest turned to violence, as police and STDs began beating and arresting the protestors.

Kirin clenched her fists, and anger began to boil inside of her. There was no escaping the responsibility. She was the voice, whether she liked it or not. While many looked to her, she had no answers. "Dammit," she muttered.

"Hmm, odd way to say good morning," said Sigung.

Kirin spun around. She had been so preoccupied with what she was seeing that she had not realized Sigung was there.

"Oh, sorry, Sigung. It's not you. It's what's on the TV." She gestured toward it. "Uh, good morning, by the way."

"Hmm…." He chuckled as he walked by Kirin and put his glasses on. "What's on TV that has you so wound up?" He stared for a second, leaning in and listening briefly. He shrugged his shoulders, "Waste of time."

Kirin didn't appreciate the comment, "What do you mean, Sigung?"

"Exactly what I said. Waste of time."

"How can you say that, Sigung? These people are sacrificing their time, effort, and possibly their lives to try to make a change."

Sigung began walking to the kitchen as he found the smell in there much more important. His voice trailed as Kirin watched him leave the room. "What they should do is go home and enjoy life, much like what I have planned for today. Better use of time."

Kirin followed Sigung into the kitchen, "Well, I'm sure they'd love to, Sigung, but it's kinda hard to enjoy life when the powers that be oppress you."

Sigung looked at her over his breakfast with a smile. "They don't oppress anyone. One ends up oppressing oneself."

Kirin thought about it but felt even more lost. "Explain, Sigung. I'm kinda confused."

"Kinda?" he asked wryly as he sat down, ready to eat breakfast.

"Okay, I'm totally confused."

"Why do people protest? Because they believe that they can make a change? But, to me, it's stupid. They aren't doing anything. Easier to bitch at outside forces than deal with the real problem. They lack the guts."

"Uh, still confused." Kirin hovered behind Sigung. "Guts?"

"Human nature always takes the easier way out. It takes guts to face your real problem."

Kirin nodded but still had a perplexed look on her face.

Sigung was about to reach for his breakfast before stopping himself. He looked at the food and then at Kirin and muttered, "You'll have to wait." He stood back up, approached Kirin, and instructed her. "Get in your stance."

Kirin looked confused and did not react right away, but Sigung's silence spoke volumes. "Uh, okay," she said as she got in her stance and waited.

He took his finger and raised it. "This finger represents the powers that be, understand? The outside source that you and everyone else wants to change." Sigung's voice carried an accent and was exactly how one might imagine a Gung Fu master to sound. He placed his finger on Kirin's chest as he tried to offset her center of gravity.

In the past, Kirin would have fought against the force, but she remained calm, allowing it in as she focused entirely on controlling her own center of gravity. She kept her spine straight and allowed the force of Sigung's finger to run from her chest all the way down to the ground.

"Hmm, good. It appears you have learned something." He removed his finger from her sternum.

Kirin replied, "I don't get it."

"Wing Chun is Wing Chun. It is not singular in application. What you apply in your training isn't limited to just fighting."

Kirin remained silent and looked at Sigung. She looked like a puppy dog tilting her head at her owner.

"How did you deal with my outside force?"

"Well, I remember a long time ago, I would push against that force. Now, I go with the flow. I deal with it by controlling myself and not worrying about that force."

"Good," he chuckled. "Good, in the end, any change that occurs are because the ones in power want them to happen, not because you caused change to happen. When your structure is strong, like your stance, you put yourself in a position of strength."

Kirin refused to accept Sigung's explanation. She was emotional about the topic and argued. "Sigung, I know you don't follow the news, but last year I led a protest. Millions from around watched and participated. For a single day, our actions brought the entire world to a standstill. So, I don't get it. I don't get how you can say that didn't do anything. We created a movement ... for the first time, big business was forced to listen. Is that not true change?"

"How long ago was that?"

"About six or seven months ago," replied Kirin.

"And was that your movement you saw on the TV that upset you?"

Kirin frowned and didn't have a response.

Sigung could not resist as he leaned toward the table and grabbed a bite of his breakfast. Kirin didn't say a thing. Their heavy discussion had not affected Sigung at all. He finished his bite, "Kirin, you can't force change. That totally goes against Wing Chun theory. That's not the way."

372

"So, what are you saying, Sigung? Are you saying do nothing and just eat the cake?"

"Eat the cake?" inquired Sigung, looking confused.

"It means to just take it."

He chuckled and repeated the phrase. "I'm not saying that either. How much of the spiritual side of Wing Chun have you dealt with?"

"A little here and there, but not much. Seems so religious."

"Spirituality has nothing to do with religion. That's a common misconception. You see, your physical and mental combine as one to bring out your spiritual side. It is your spiritual side that shows your true self, that allows you to always be you." He clasped both hands together.

For the first time, Kirin was intrigued by this side of Wing Chun. A certain mesh of words finally got through to her.

"Didn't your Sifu explain the spiritual side of Wing Chun to you?"

Kirin looked away, embarrassed. "He tried to, but every time … I kinda ignored it. I figured it wasn't as important as pulling off the punch at the right time."

"Everything in Wing Chun requires a natural balance. You fail to see the big picture. Wing Chun isn't about fighting, nor is it a system. What it is … is the universal truth of all things." He raised his hands in a circle. "You need to encompass all three—physical, mental, and spiritual—to figure out something as simple as pulling off your punch at the right time."

"I still don't get it, Sigung. How does the spiritual help me pull the punch off? And, on top of that, I still don't understand your antiprotest to protesting." Kirin made a face, wondering if what she said even made sense.

Sigung said, "Let's deal with one thing at a time. First, you want to punch, but you need the physical coordination to know the true path of that motion. So, you train that motion over and over again. Mentally, you have to know the way to do it; otherwise, the little details into making it work will be lost. So, the two have to work together and balance one another. Do, then think; think, then do. Eventually, there's no longer any thought, and the motion is just natural. But, to get to that form of harmony, you need to detach from all that you did to achieve that. Only if you can let go will it fully be yours."

"But, that's easy, isn't it? Just don't care, and you'll be totally detached."

Sigung chuckled. "Not caring isn't detachment, and if you're 100% detached, that means you're still attached to something."

Kirin shook her head as the words went in one ear and out the other. "Okay, Sigung, uh, let's switch subjects and go back to the protesting part. With that … I'm totally in the dark." In the back of her mind, Kirin was still clueless about the subject of detachment, but hearing more wasn't the key.

"This is difficult to hear and understand, but you looked at the TV and saw pain and suffering, and the first thing that jumped into your head was that the world isn't fair. But, I tell you that, in the big picture, everything is as it should be. The world is perfectly balanced, whether you like to believe it or not."

Kirin began to open her mouth, but Sigung raised his hand.

"Listen first, debate second. Remember, passive always wins…. Try to understand that two always exist. There is no right, and there is no wrong. Both are necessary parts of life, and we as humans allow our ego to favor one over the other."

Kirin cringed as that statement confused her even more.

"Human beings are emotional creatures, easily swayed by their own prejudices, whether they know it or not. So, when you see something, you naturally react right away. Regardless of whether you know the full story, you draw your own conclusions. Yet, you do not take into account the cause and effect. You do not consider that what you witness was generated by a past action that eventually had to be paid. What you are seeing is simply the universe in balance."

"Karma?"

"It goes a little deeper than that, but for now it's okay to say that if that's easier for you to understand."

"I'm still not seeing what you are saying, Sigung. Sorry...."

Sigung took a minute and tried to think of something that Kirin could grasp. "Okay, let's say you want to do a punch. You need to do it both the wrong way and the right way in order to figure out how to actually do it."

"The wrong way?"

"Absolutely, the wrong way."

"Why would I want to do it that way?"

Sigung said, "Think back when you first learned the punch. You listened to the instructions by your Sifu, and you spent time concentrating to make sure it was done right, correct?"

"Yes, I remember that."

"Now at that time, were you doing it right?"

"Obviously, I was doing my best to do it right, Sigung."

"Look back, were you doing the punch motion right or wrong?"

"Well, with what I know now, I can tell my punch was horrible. It was so off." Kirin cringed at the memory.

"Interesting … so I guess I'm curious as to whether or not that was right then or wrong now," stated Sigung.

Kirin's mouth opened as she was at a loss for words. She thought, *He's just like Sifu, all-knowing, so wise, and painfully enlightening.*

"Without one or the other, you'll never have the full recipe to complete the punch. When you do something wrong, you frown upon it and let yourself get eaten up by it, allowing the negativity to grow. On the other hand, you do something right, and you are ecstatic about it. So, in this case, you need right and wrong, yet wrong serves a good purpose in order for you to do the punch properly."

Kirin asked, hesitant not to sound foolish, "So, a good action isn't really … good?"

"Try to remember that always two exist in one. Always two there are. Whenever good is done, bad is also occurring simultaneously," said Sigung.

Kirin thought of her past and all those she had loved and lost. She could hear the words, but it was just too difficult for her to accept what Sigung was saying. She looked away feeling teary-eyed and did not want Sigung to see. She took a moment to gather herself as her eyes became watery. "And so in regard to the protest…." She managed to spit out the words without crying.

Sigung nodded. "Ah, yes, the protest. My finger represents the outside force. Did you change me or yourself in order to deal with it?"

"Well, I changed myself to deal with it."

"Yes, yes, but did you change the outside force? No. Because I still decided when to remove my finger from your chest."

Kirin grimaced still unsure about his answer. "Give me a little more, Sigung, please."

Sigung replied using hand gestures. "Imagine an ant and your foot. At what point does the ant dictate to the foot ... never."

His last example seemed to hit home, "So, how do I deal with changing the outside force?"

Sigung said, "Not necessary. Go with the flow and the outside force can't affect you. It is you who must adjust."

Kirin wasn't going to settle for that answer. She knew Sigung would have the right answer, if asked correctly. "Humor me, Sigung. I get what you say about going with the force, but let's say ... let's just say for the sake of argument, one wanted to destroy that outside force. Is it possible?"

"Of course."

"How then?"

"Just like Wing Chun, kill the source." Though Sigung realized the intensity behind the question, he still answered it and added, "The source is not my finger. Any change needs to be on equal ground. You have to ask yourself where the power comes from with my finger." After that statement, Sigung grabbed another bite, savored the moment, and walked away.

Kirin mumbled to herself, "Your stance." She had known it all the time—it was right in front of her. Now how did this translate to her current situation and problems?

Sigung muttered, "Kill the source. Kill the power. Claim victory."

Kirin stood still as a moment of enlightenment was fused with confusion. "Go figure, good with bad."

Sigung turned around before exiting to the living room. "Time to change topics."

"But why, Sigung?"

"Your cup is too full.... Let's go to the living room and train. Your mind needs to be cleared. No point in me talking more about something you can't absorb. Conserve my energy, store it until needed. Think of a different subject you want to dive deeper in."

Kirin was about to stop him and then pulled back. She let Sigung leave. His presence was a distraction, and she needed some distance from him to gather her thoughts. She spent the next several minutes standing alone, gathering her thoughts before finally seeing Sigung. She dashed into the living room once she realized what she wanted to go over.

Sigung stood in the center of the living room with his back turned. "Do you feel better now?"

"Huh?" She felt that to be a strange question. Then Kirin realized that her focus had changed so completely that she had forgotten what they were talking about earlier.

He added, "So, you decided you want to go over the freeze?"

Kirin was about to ask how he knew, but then realized it was Sigung she was talking to. Somehow, he was all-knowing, and she decided to let it go.

Sigung said, "Good, decisions should carry no doubt."

She asked, "At the restaurant, when you froze that last guy … it was unlike anything I've ever seen before. It was like magic…. Is it magic?"

"Not magic, just skill."

Kirin looked a little disappointed. She'd been hoping he would say it was magic. She finally replied, "Sigung, I've dealt with it before. I've tried to do it and counter it, but I need more explanation. How are you doing it? How do I unfreeze myself? How is it even humanly possible?"

Sigung winked, "So simple. The key is you freeze yourself."

"You what?"

"Come over here and make a fist."

Kirin walked over and made a fist as Sigung placed his hand on top. His hands were rough, but his touch felt solid. Even though he wasn't pressing on her hand, in an instant, she felt her body connected to the ground and felt frozen in place. The sensation was indescribable, something that needed to be felt to be believed.

"Good lord," she said. "How?" She shook her head but was in awe of his power.

"The moment we touch and you move, your move becomes my move. Thus, when I freeze myself, that automatically freezes your motions as well."

"In theory," said Kirin.

"First, I always need something to counter, which is your force; I always put myself in a passive state. Once you give me a force, I connect all three of my structures—hand, body, and legs—so they function as one. No matter how great that force is, it flows through me and to the ground. Once it hits the ground, it bounces back to you along the same path that it does through me. Thus, two structures merge and become one," said Sigung.

"Wow, so you're like water?"

"Like water?"

"You know, Sigung. You put water in a cup, it becomes the cup."

"Pffftt," scoffed Sigung. "I don't conform. You do that, you become someone else's bitch."

Kirin jerked back in surprise. That was the first time she'd heard Sigung swear. In fact, that was the first time Sigung had shown any sign of real emotion.

Sigung added, "I make them conform to me. That's how you get things to merge. Otherwise, you'll always be reacting to the outside force, like a trained dog."

Kirin nodded. She stood there, trying to feel what Sigung was doing. "What if I try to generate more force?"

"Try it."

Kirin tried to push harder but could not generate any force. "What are you doing?" The day continued to leave her puzzled and bewildered.

"To generate more force, you need to relax and let muscles shift around to get the momentum, right? Now, just to make my point, I want you to take a step.... Try doing that now."

Kirin was still in shock, "I can't."

"Why is that?"

She took a moment to feel the sensation as she squirmed from side to side. "I'm trying to, but my weight is so perfectly distributed that, when I try to lift either side … I can't." She was observing Sigung the entire time, but he appeared to be doing nothing. His control was incredible and effortless.

Sigung chuckled and then loosened his control on Kirin. "Can you step now?"

Kirin nodded in disbelief, "Yes, now I can step." Sigung let go of his control as she pulled away from him and stepped back. She thought, *This is more bizarre than what we were talking about earlier.* "Wait, Sigung, that's if I give force to you. How about if I try to relax myself and pull away?"

"Go ahead. Go lighter."

Kirin made a fist and reconnected to Sigung's hand. This time, she tried to pull away and relaxed her motion. But, even as she did, she felt the weight of Sigung's hand upon her, and she still could not move.

"How is this even possible? How are you controlling me like this?"

"Like I said, when you make yourself stronger so that no outside forces can offset you, you become more than you can imagine. And, to be clear, I'm only concerned about controlling me."

"Only you?"

"I control me. Only me. I don't care about winning or losing, but simply going with the flow of the universe. What you do is your own business. By controlling me, I can make you do what I want you to do. Thus, I'm never reacting to what you do. You, on the other hand, are reacting to me."

Kirin shook her head. "Sorry, Sigung. I just don't get it."

"Don't worry about it. More practice you need, and you'll get it … and hopefully you'll understand the deeper meaning of it, someday."

#

That night, Kirin's head was spinning. She lay on her bed staring at the ceiling, hoping the bland solid color could quiet her racing mind. The depth that Sigung covered left her mentally drained. The usual physical demands were a lot easier to handle. Thoughts continued to bombard her mind, and she could not sleep. She had tossed and turned for the last two hours but continued to struggle. Sigung was already asleep, so she kept as quiet as she could in order not to disturb him. She had to deal with her restlessness with the only cure she knew would work. Even though it was already close to midnight, she got into her stance and began doing the first form. She allowed the single thought to dominate her mind. Focusing on the breathing and letting the form run its course, she was able to finally quiet her mind. She was exhausted and checked her phone one last time. Kirin tossed it on her bed, where it barely caught the edge, and she flopped face down beside it. Within a minute, she was out cold.

Five minutes later, her phone dinged, waking her up from her sleep. She muttered a complaint about forgetting to put it on silent. *Who could be texting me at this hour?* she wondered.

She took a second to rub her eyes and then tried to focus on the screen. It was a text from Gwen: 'Found out what Sifu discovered. We need 2 talk ASAP. Also, I hv 2 tell u something. Promise me u won't b mad.'

"The ant is alive because the boot allows it. It's never the other way around." —Sigung

Section 1 Short Stories #9—Kirin's P.O.V.

Useless—1 Year, 15 Days

I was lying on my bed, using Bacon as my foot rest. Every time I tried to remove myself from that position, he would growl and complain. I thought spoiling a dog wasn't a bad thing, but sometimes I wondered if I was overdoing it. His last snarl led me to say, "Bad dog, Bacon," but he seemed to ignore anything coming from my mouth that was not food-related. I was held hostage for the next ten minutes until Bacon fell asleep, and then I slowly maneuvered myself out of the bed.

I grabbed my phone and checked through it, something I usually did only once a day, unlike most people. I prided myself on not being bound to technology, but that might have been because I was pretty handicapped when using it. I scanned through notifications and postings online and then struggled through five minutes of surfing through it all.

That's five minutes I'll never get back.

I made coffee and looked around at my loft.

This place is a mess.

But, the day was young as I enjoyed my coffee in one hand and continued to surf on the other. With it came choosing between doing something useful or something useless, I decided I felt like avoiding any responsibility.

I walked over to my TV and went through all the channels. Hundreds to choose from, but nothing that caught my eye. Between the TV and my phone, I quickly realized that an hour had passed since I left my bed, but I had done not one useful thing.

I glanced at my computer on the table and considered all the work I had to do this week. I had pictures to edit and appointments to schedule, and my place was a mess for a photoshoot. I made my way toward the desk and got a text from Tobias: 'Talk to me.'

I took another look at my adult responsibilities and weighed my options. I decided no on adulting. I began texting him back.

Kirin: I c you've been online all day
Tobias: same for u
Kirin: Anything good?
Tobias: usual stuff, funny posts but mostly useless, u?
Kirin: same as always, political rants
Tobias: get anything done so far?
Kirin: nope, I think I've been as useless as these posts
Tobias: C, more than one way to be useless
Kirin: y do people do it?
Tobias: ur do it might be different from mine
Kirin: u know, all these rants online
Tobias it's a voice. sometimes even if no one is listening, all u want is a voice
Kirin: sounds sad
Tobias: think about it - the world we live in. what is power?
Kirin: what u men?
Tobias: men?
Kirin: typo, mean
Tobias: all the things that are happening, the haves and the havenots
Kirin: I hate texting, can u just call me?
Tobias: k

The phone rang, and I put Tobias on speaker.

"Is that better?"

"Much. But, you're right—people seem powerless. I guess that makes more sense. Without a voice, it's kinda like you don't even exist or matter."

Tobias replied, "Truth is all that stuff is useless.... Besides, I find it even more odd that an eighteen-year-old like you is so up to date with current events."

"Well, most eighteen-year-olds don't have the same life experiences that I've gone through."

"You have a point."

I asked, "So, what's the alternative?"

"You see it already. I call it the investment into uselessness. It's kinda the reason you see people make money in nothing."

"What do you mean?"

"It's easier to get lost in fantasy than deal with reality. I mean, take a simple example of a professional video game player compared to a doctor. Who makes more money?"

"The video game player...."

Tobias said, "We're comparing a guy who plays games compared to someone who saves your life. Our values are skewed."

"Tobias, what would you do? If you could change the world, right now at this point ... what would it be?"

"I'd ... I'd find me a girl, and we'd get the hell out of here."

"What?"

"No, seriously. That's what I'd do. Find the perfect remote location, just the two of us, and just hang and enjoy life from a distance."

"I'm actually surprised by your answer."

"Why's that?"

"I'd thought you'd be more confrontational—like stand up to the man."

"It'd take a better person than me to challenge the man, to bring down the system."

I didn't say it out loud, but, deep down, I thought he was that man. We continued to talk for a while as light turned to dark before my very eyes. I stood up from my couch and asked, "Why am I so hungry?"

Tobias replied, "'Cause it's dinner time."

"Oh my god, we've been talking for hours, and I haven't done anything all day."

Weapons Training—1 Year, 45 Days

Tobias was barking out orders as we split the class in half. Doc, Ryan, Ken, and Robert were working on the sword form, while Danny, Big T, Tobias, and I were dealing with the pole form.

Tobias said, "Okay, guys with the poles, let's partner up. Ryan, oversee the sword form for your half."

Ryan tossed a thumbs up and headed off to the other half of the room with his group.

I partnered with Big T as we worked on a set drill that Tobias went over. We spent the next fifteen minutes working out to the clashing of poles. Every so often Tobias would go over some instruction and point out some finer detail that might have been missed.

Tobias said, "Remember, with the pole, it's about letting the body lead the motion. You want to move the pole and keep it balanced. You don't want it led by only the hands, but the body unifying the entire structure."

Big T asked, "All three structures?"

"You got legs, body, and arms … always."

He began demonstrating how he maneuvered the pole. His movement was so perfectly balanced and smooth, it reminded me of Sifu. Like all weapons when used correctly, they become part of the wielder. When he snapped the pole, I could hear the air crack.

"See, nice and easy. Notice how I keep adjusting my grip so that the pole is perfectly balanced, no matter what position. Throughout all this, I use the body to lead my hands in moving the pole."

Danny asked, "Why are we using the white wax poles? They're so much smaller than Sifu's regular poles."

Tobias said, "I'd think you'd be more comfortable with a smaller stick."

Danny argued, "I mean, it's okay, but—Hey! I know where you're going with that."

When the guys began to chuckle, I looked at them in confusion. "I don't get it."

Tobias ignored me, "To really answer your question, the white wax is perfect for training, and the difference is twenty credits per pole versus two-hundred credits for Sifu's pole."

Danny said, "Why not just use Sifu's poles that are sitting in storage?"

I spoke up right away. "No one touches Sifu's things ... got it?" No one questioned what I said, and not another word was spoken about it.

"My bad ... I forgot. My bad." Danny turned away, avoiding eye contact.

Big T said, "So, in a zombie apocalypse, what's your weapon of choice, sword or pole, Tobias?"

"Personally, I'd prefer the pole. Good for both long- and short-range fighting. I don't know if I want the splatter fest of the swords when zombies come charging in."

Big T rubbed his chin and thought about it. "You do have a good point about that."

Tobias turned to me, "How about you, Kirin?"

"That's a tough call. Are we basing this off what's most effective or what makes you look the coolest?"

Tobias smiled at my comment. "For now, let's just say what's most effective ... but I like that twist in your thinking."

"If that's the case, personally I think there's something about swords that makes their marks so final."

Danny agreed, "Yeah, 'cause if it connects, it's more than slice and dice."

Tobias said, "Guys, don't underestimate the power of the pole. Most people don't look at the pole as a deadly weapon, but it is, capable of snapping swords in half and taking away lives."

Ryan walked up to us with his half of the group, joining our silly conversation.

Robert asked, "So, the pole is to develop power while the sword helps with footwork?"

Tobias answered, "Yeah, that's correct."

Doc reminded everyone, "Remember, the pole *Lok Dim Boon Gwan* and the butterfly swords *Bat Jam Do,* both were never part of the original art. They were added later."

Ken said, "Oh yeah, I forgot about that."

Ryan asked, "Now, for a real question—and I'm being 100% serious about this. There's a total of eight of us, right? Eight of us versus one velociraptor. Can we take it?"

Doc asked, "Are we equipped with poles and swords?"

"Your choice of weapon."

Robert chimed in, "Wooden swords or real butterfly swords?"

Ryan said, "Of course, steel not wood. And, as for the pole, your choice of white wax or the real thing."

"Does any of this serve a purpose at all to our training?" Tobias glanced at me.

I rolled my eyes and gave him a little smirk. The guys were just having fun, so I decided to join in. "Do we get only one choice, or can we have both?"

Ryan thought about it for second, "Well, you can only use one thing at a time, so I guess only one choice."

Big T looked at Danny, "If I was a betting man, which I am … I'd say we could kill a raptor, but several of us would be dead."

Danny said, "Are you betting right now?"

Big T gave a single nod, "Now how do you figure we calculate this for real?"

Danny replied, "You have a point."

Doc gave his thoughts, "I agree with Big T. I think we could kill a raptor, but there would be casualties. I'd expect Danny and Robert to eat it."

Both Danny and Robert looked at each other, "What the…?"

Ryan was serious, "Yeah, that's true. I can see you two dying first."

Robert said, "I'm pretty sure the raptor would look at you as the tastiest."

Tobias shook his head, "Guys, why are we having this debate? It's something that'll never happen. If anything, wouldn't you rather see a battle between the pole and the butterfly sword?"

Ken smiled in agreement, "You're right. That would be more fascinating to see."

I said, "I don't know about you guys, but I'm thinking either the pole or the butterfly sword versus—get this—a samurai sword."

The guys nodded, agreeing that I had come up with the best challenge. We then spent another ten minutes debating which weapon would come out on top.

This is what makes friendships so beautiful, the ability to talk about nothing and enjoy each other's company.

Hide—1 Year, 90 Days

It was late Saturday night, and we had gathered to finish our training. The debate that had taken up most of the conversation was whether summer or winter was tougher in our school. Air conditioner or heat: that was the true question. It wasn't unusual for us to get into these types of discussion; in fact, useless discussion between friends always made for entertainment.

Danny came strolling back in carrying a stack of boxes. "Guess who's got the pizza?"

Robert looked at him, "You're the asshole who just walked in with pizza. What's there to guess?"

"It was figuratively speaking."

Ryan corrected, "Don't you mean literally speaking?"

Danny shouted back, "Don't be a grammar Nazi, Ryan."

Ryan replied, "That's unpossible."

Ken said, "Ease down, everybody. Just like you never bitch at the waiter, he's the guy holding all the pizza."

Ignoring the pizza talk, Tobias called, "Ryan, you're tech support. Do you have the projector set up for tonight's movie?"

Ryan complained, "I don't know why I have to be tech support."

Robert said, "You're Filipino, and you're asking why you're tech support."

"Shut up, Robert!"

Big T asked, "Hey, Danny, did you happen to get any colonizer sauce for my pizza?"

I asked, "What's colonizer sauce?"

Big T smiled and said, "Little sista, that's what I call mayonnaise."

I cringed at the thought and said, "On pizza?"

"Don't knock it till you try it."

Danny said, "Sorry T, I totally forgot to stop by the store and get it…. It's not my fault, my hands are full."

Robert stood up and showed off a pocket-sized sriracha that was attached to his pants. "Big T, this is the only way to go when dealing with bland American food … sriracha." He snapped it off and threw it at him

Big T looked at it, "Are you sure you are saying it right?"

"Do I question you on basketball?"

"No," said Big T.

"Then why are you questioning me on Asian pronunciation?" asked Robert.

Ken said, "Anyone else think Robert's being racist?"

The entire room raised their hands, laughing. In next thirty minutes, our little school was converted to a movie theater. We were all gathered around eating pizza and just enjoying the movie with each other as company. Ryan looked like he was barely awake, but he wasn't the only one struggling with the choice. Robert was on his phone swiping away, probably looking for a late-night date. Doc was on the ground, but he was practicing his hand motions. It appeared he was more focused on that than on what was on the screen. Big T and Danny were busy hogging the pizza.

Tobias was leaned over the side of the couch and sleeping. I watched as he was about to fall off and jolted himself back to the living. He looked around and realized he had dozed off. "Okay, who picked this movie?" he asked.

Ken raised his hand slowly.

Tobias said, "This movie blows."

"Hey, I can only go by the review rating…. Besides, they said it has a slow start."

Robert took a moment away from his phone and shouted, "It sucks!"

Ken defended himself. "It's not my fault."

Suddenly, our focus turned away from Ken and the movie as we all heard a noise. Tobias sprang up and made a signal to kill the lights of the screen. He waved everyone down and held his index finger by his lips, indicating everyone should be silent. He held his phone up and began to text the entire group. The text read: 'Spread out/quiet. Need eyes.'

I was next to Doc and whispered, "I thought we had sensors to pick up activity outside."

Doc palmed his face and leaned over. Keeping a low tone, he said, "I think when Danny came back with the pizza, we didn't reactivate it."

"Crap."

Danny whispered, "It's not my fault. Don't blame the pizza guy."

Tobias signaled to everyone to keep their voices down. We spread out, as we had briefly gone over this emergency scenario several times. However, this was the first time our plan was being put into action.

I checked my phone as Tobias texted our group: 'Front door closed?'

Ken replied: 'I'll check with Robert.'

Doc and I were on the opposite end, monitoring for any activity by our section. We waited several tense minutes for Ken's report. We knew what it would mean if the authorities discovered we were using this place to train.

I whispered, "Doc, who do you think it could be?"

Doc was leaning over the edge of the wall as he breathed, "Crap … Kirin, text everyone. It's a squad car about fifty feet away."

I leaned against the wall and sent out the message. Ken promptly replied to the entire group that the main door was, in fact, closed. I could see several lights flashing at the far end of the room. It appeared the cops were looking around for whatever reason.

"Frick!"

Ken texted the entire group: 'They're right outside the front door. What should we do if they try to come in?'

Tobias's text read: 'Everyone, prepare to take off. Ken Robert, start making your way back slowly. Don't make a sound.'

I texted back to the group: 'What about all our stuff?'

Tobias responded: 'It's only things. We can always replace it.'

His comments infuriated me.

Why do we have to live this way?

Doc extended his hand out, "Come on, Kirin. Be ready to run."

Ken texted the group: 'They're trying to open the door. Robert and I are staying put. If we move, they'll definitely hear us.'

Now I was in a panic. What would Ken and Robert do if they came in? I pulled Doc to me and hissed, "We should help out Ken and Robert, just in case."

Doc whispered, "You want us to beat up the cops?"

"I think the better term is 'stun.'"

Doc held my hand tight and stopped me from leading. We waited, wondering what would happen, as the next several minutes were unbearable. Finally, a text came through from Ken: 'Keep quiet still. They're walking away.'

I felt Doc tug at my arm as he went to take a peek. He finally let go of my hand, "Kirin, text the group. They're leaving." He sighed in relief and plunked himself down next to me.

Tobias texted the group: 'Everyone gather in the middle. Leave lights off.'

We all gathered to the center like Tobias had instructed. Even though the trouble was gone, tension still filled everyone's face.

Tobias let out a sigh, "We dodged a bullet."

Robert roughly pat Danny's shoulder, "Thanks, Danny."

"All I did was get the pizza." Danny held his hands up.

Tobias said, "It's all our fault. We got complacent and weren't thorough enough to set the alarms in place." He signaled to Ryan. "Ryan ... turn the lights on low."

Big T said, "You know I can modify the door so that, whenever we close it, the alarm detection will automatically go on."

Ken agreed, "Yeah, that's a good idea, less chance for human error."

Doc mused, "Maybe we can extend the range even further, not just the outer perimeter from the building but the driving pathway from Main Street."

Ryan added, "Maybe we can dirty the front more ... you know, make it less appealing."

Ken nodded, "That's a good idea."

I couldn't believe what I was hearing—our plan was to figure out a way to hide better. It made me sick to my stomach. As they continued to throw out ideas, I finally stood up and shouted, "All this is B.S.! Tobias ... look at us, cowering like rats as if we've done something wrong."

Tobias said, "Kirin!"

"Why do we have to live like this?"

Danny opened his mouth, "Well, it is an abandoned—"

"Shut up, Danny!"

The guys stood silent and stared at me. That feeling of being hunted brought back bad memories from my past. I wasn't about to spare anyone's feelings.

"You guys may be okay with this, but I'm not." I'd had enough with the compromising and stormed out of the school.

Section 2 Sifu's Journey Entry #9—Torn

Early August

Several days had passed, and Sifu had arranged a meeting with Damon. Just like in the spy movies, he found himself on one side of the bench feeding some pigeons. It was not his typical routine, but there were many individuals in the park, and Damon had picked the place to meet. It was mid-afternoon, and Sifu checked his phone, which read one minute prior to the arranged time, but there was no one in sight.

Sifu reached in his bag and tossed some more popcorn to the pigeons. Then, he felt a bump from the other side of the bench.

Damon was in a disguise and pretending to talk on his cell phone.

Sifu began the conversation, "Don't you think we look too obvious the way we're meeting?"

"I've been doing this for over ten years now. Can you have a little faith that I know what I'm doing?" Damon reached into his pocket and pulled out a small device. He placed it right on the bench, "This will only take a second."

Sifu looked at the device, "What is it?"

"It's a jammer. In our little fifteen-foot area, even if you tried to zoom in with a microphone, all you'd get is garbled language. Also, it renders are phones completely useless."

Sifu leaned over and gave some more popcorn to the pigeons. "Okay, now we're talking…. That's definitely some cool James Bond stuff."

Damon leaned back and continued to pretend he was on the phone with someone else. "So, I'm assuming the worst, now that you have me here."

"Sorry to call you out here, but I can't do it. After last night, I … I can't use my student like that."

Damon sighed and pulled from his pocket a small thumb drive, which he placed on the seat next to him. "I respect you, Sifu. I totally understand your position, but we've been waiting for years for an opportunity to flush out just one of them from hiding. And, when you get to this point, you ask yourself what you're willing to do and at what cost…. When do you go from the good guy to the bad guy just, so you can win? I struggled with this decision just as much as you've been struggling with yours. And the answer for me was … whatever it takes."

Instead of responding to what Damon had said, Sifu asked, "What is that?"

"May god forgive me, and hopefully you will as well. Inside is the entire case file on your family that we've been able to pluck. I have to tell you, it's not pretty, and what you'll also find is all the information leading to the day of the 'accident.'"

Sifu trembled, "Why?"

Damon stood up, "Because I believe in the greater good. To beat them at their own game, our intent has to be on the same level as theirs. If you're not willing to do that, then this cycle will forever continue."

Sifu tossed all the food toward the pigeon, emptying his bag as he stared blankly at the flock.

Damon hung his head, "I truly apologize that I had to go this route. I do feel your pain, just like everyone in our organization has at some point. If you can't find it in your heart to forgive my actions, then so be it. But, I am desperate, and you've become our only hope."

Sifu shouted, "Get the hell out of here!" The sound startled the pigeons, causing all of them to fly away.

Damon didn't say anything to Sifu as he walked away without another look.

Sifu shook his head and grabbed the thumb drive from the opposite side of the bench. He held it firmly in his hand as he looked around to see that Damon was nowhere in sight.

Several Hours Later

Sifu was back in his apartment. He had spent the first hour looking through the thumb drive at all the information they had gathered. It felt more painful now than when it had happened back then. For Sifu, it had been easier to stomach that it was an accident and the universe had dealt him a bad hand. He could accept that. But, knowing that it was no accident had left him battling between letting it go and unleashing the monster within.

He was on the floor, hunched against the wall as he stared at a picture of his family. Several bottles of hard liquor had been fully consumed and left empty. His tears had dried, but the conflict remained. He chuckled humorlessly. He'd tried to drink himself silly, but the alcohol had no effect on him.

Sifu looked at Megumi in the picture. "What would you have me do?"

He waited for a response, hoping for a sign from the universe, but the only answer he received was a call to the bathroom as he had to relieve himself from all the drinking. After he was done, he let the faucet in the bathroom sink run. After wasting enough cold water, Sifu splashed some on his face as he stared at himself in the mirror.

Damon's words and Megumi's were racing through his head. When he closed his eyes, he could picture his wife saying to let her go, that she was safe with the children and that he had to live once again. But, Damon's words were equally as powerful. The thumb drive had revealed much, along with the possibilities of what the UFMF might be planning in the future. He had finally decided that a sacrifice might be needed, that the cost would be his karma. He felt his pain needed to be shared with those at the very top, and he was willing to take it to the source.

As the water dripped from his face, he stared into the bathroom mirror. His eyes were glazed and reflected a distorted version of himself. Sifu said, "You're no master." He whispered again, "You're no master." As he jerked up to look at it, he flashed a punch and shattered the mirror.

CHAPTER 10
Unstoppable

Open entry to the Dome was happening tonight, and the entire world was watching. Crowds gathered, buzzing with anticipation. Were the rumors true? Would Kirin Rise make her triumphant return? The buzz had begun forty-eight hours earlier with stations speculating about the former UFMF superstar. She had been on hiatus for several months, with people claiming that they had spotted her at several locations throughout the world. Kirin was supposedly in Korea hanging out with the lead member of a K-pop group. Pictures went viral of her sunbathing on the beaches of Turks and Caicos. Witnesses swore that she was taking selfies at La Rambla in Barcelona. However, not a single lead was ever verified. All this time, she had been relentlessly training with Sigung in Arizona and, more importantly, making plans for her biggest adversary.

For the first time all season, ratings prior to the match had already surpassed any that had been set for the entire year. As much as the UFMF had promoted Ripley as their new star, Kirin brought in the crowds—and the ratings.

Once again, the odds were severely stacked against her. Kirin Rise would have to follow the path of last year's champion, Justice, through the Battle Royale. If she somehow pulled that off, the bracket for this year's tournament had increased even further, with the heavy favorite Ripley Hawkins at the center of attention. Only last year, the UFMF had implemented this one-and-done entry to the playoffs, and that had resulted in Justice as the UFMF Dome champion.

Every year the Dome Championship rotated from one of the four major city locations, as the same panel had gathered again for this huge event. New York was considered the grandest location as it was the birthplace of the UFMF's first match many years ago. Linkwater and Connor were the local favorites in the Midwest, while Stabler and Krenzel were considered the premier duo of the national audience. Finally, Grand Master Cheng was the martial arts anchor that completed the team. Even with the gathering of these experts, only those at the very top knew if the rumors could be true. The UFMF planned to keep everyone in the dark until the last possible minute.

The panel spent some time discussing the possibilities of what it might mean if Kirin did make a surprise return to the playoffs.

Linkwater started the show, "We are here on the eve of another historic event for the UFMF. For those of you not familiar with last year's format, the UFMF created an open division allowing anyone to duke it out in a Battle Royale. The winner of such a brutal event would earn the right to enter the Dome Championship tournament. These contestants were stringently tested for this all-out bash. The only change this year is that the number has been reduced to ten to ensure only the best of the best qualify. These men and women will enter at the same time, but only one will remain standing and have a chance to enter the tournament. Last year was a whirlwind of excitement because the open division gave us a new champion who defied the odds and won it all. Now, if things weren't crazy enough, rumors have been circulating about a possible return. Yes, folks, if you can believe it … Kirin Rise! The possibility of Kirin returning is the main reason everyone in this arena is excited. So, that raises the question: if Kirin Rise does somehow return tonight for this Battle Royale, can she do the impossible once again?"

Connor said, "Well, that's an interesting question, Linkwater, but first I think we need to talk about how Kirin returning could dynamically change the entire makeup of this tournament."

"How so?" asked Stabler.

Krenzel replied, "Vegas numbers are pretty interesting. I checked this morning, and they were quick to run hypotheticals…. If she somehow ends up winning this ten-person Battle Royale, she cuts the odds for the favorite Ripley Hawkins to win it all by more than half."

Stabler looked quite surprised. "I had my mental guess on those numbers, but I didn't think Whiskey's chances would drop down by that much."

Krenzel answered, "I was surprised as well. Kirin has gone from unknown underdog when she first stepped into this ring to one of the most respected fighters of the UFMF—and Vegas was quick to confirm that as fact."

Grand Master Cheng added, "I know many are excited and hoping for the possibility. But, knowing Kirin Rise, I doubt she'll have the guts to show her face back in the UFMF again. From the very beginning, I've always believed Kirin's reign would be short-lived. As an expert in Wing Chun with many years in martial arts, I guarantee there's no chance she's coming back, especially for this Battle Royale."

Stabler said, "Uh, thanks again for your expert opinion, Grand Master Cheng."

Krenzel interjected, "We've been scouring the arena both inside and out to see if there's any hint of her, but so far still no news. Everyone on social media has been posting possible sightings, but she's hid well for the last several months, and she's doing a fantastic job again tonight."

"Well, there are only ten minutes left till the final announcements of the contestants for tonight. I guess we're not going to find out till the very end—like everyone else here," said Linkwater.

Connor said, "Why don't we go down to the floor with our in-dome reporter Megan Mahoney?"

The camera switched to Megan, who was surrounded by fans. Her snappy, short red hair and pretty face helped her stick out from the crowd. She covered one earpiece to hear what was being said and tried to speak loudly without shouting to maintain a dignified appearance. "Thanks, Connor. You can see the anticipation for Kirin's possible return…. It is electrifying down here on the floor. I hope you can hear me speak. The crowds are acting as if this were the actual Dome Championship. This has been an exciting season with the debut of Ripley Hawkins along with the international expansion of the UFMF into three new countries, but all that is taking a back seat as everyone is crossing their fingers, hoping that rumor becomes reality, and Kirin Rise … well, I guess you could say 'rises from the shadows.'"

Connor asked, "Megan, can you find out from fans why they want Kirin to come back?"

Megan nodded and turned around. She shouted, "So, who here is a big Kirin Rise fan?" Almost everyone in her sight jumped up and raised their hands. Her experience led her to select someone she thought would appeal to the audience at home. "You over there … yes, you, the brunette with the Kirin Rise T-shirt on. Can you come here?"

The crowd was overzealous, making it a struggle for the teen to trek just a short distance. Being a veteran reporter, Megan put the effort in to meet her halfway. Everyone wanted to be in on the action. They screamed and shouted, hoping their antics would make them stick out. The teen with the short brown hair and braces looked surprised that she had been selected.

Megan reached out her microphone and asked, "Can you tell us your name and why you want Kirin to come back for this?" Megan directed her to look straight into the camera.

She nodded and spoke. "Hi, everyone. I'm Kimberly, all the way from San Diego, California. A quick shout-out to my friends at West Bay Side High School." The crowd cheered after Kimberly announced her school, as someone from the back shouted, "West Bay Side High." She quickly turned her attention back to the camera and said, "Anyway, I've always been a big fan of Kirin Rise. I think what makes her so special is that, in the movies and books, it's common to have a female hero who has superpowers or magical abilities … and don't get me wrong—that's great and all, but the truth is, you and I will never be able to fly or block bullets with our wrists or cast spells from a wand. I really believe everyone loves Kirin because she's real. She's like you or me. She has never claimed to be a great athlete, but somehow she's always defied the odds and beaten people with just … I guess her skill. I mean … I don't need to, like, fantasize about kicking butt. She's living proof that you can actually do it. And, for me, that's why I really hope she comes back tonight." She began to tear up but tried to wipe it away. "I love you, Kirin. Please come back … please. We miss you—and, most importantly, we need you."

Megan was about to speak when a section near the broadcasting booth began to erupt. All eyes were looking to see who was approaching the panel. "Guys, there's someone huge approaching you. I can't quite make out who it is. Why don't I send it back to you?"

Connor, Stabler, Linkwater, Krenzel, and Cheng all turned to see what was happening. From roughly twenty feet away, the crowd began to cheer as they cleared a path toward the booth. Surrounded by several huge guards and waving to the crowd, the mystery guest finally appeared.

Stabler took the lead and stood up, welcoming their surprise guest to the booth. "Well, this is truly an unexpected honor! Not the guest everyone was expecting, but one we definitely welcome." He extended his hand to greet the guest, but she bypassed it and leaned to kiss the side of his cheek. Stabler blushed and lost his train of thought as he stared at Ripley, who was just standing there. She smiled before he realized she needed a seat. He offered a chair, which she kindly accepted and positioned herself in a line with the panel. They received only a friendly hand wave from a distance, as a hint of jealousy could be seen on their faces. "Ripley Hawkins, you definitely caught everyone off-guard, but we're happy to have this year's favorite join us."

Ripley replied, "Thanks for having me." She turned around and waved to the fans as they began cheering her name out loud.

Linkwater handed her a headset and mic, so she could join their team before the introductions.

Krenzel asked, "This night seems to be filled with surprises. What brings you along before the start of the Battle Royale?"

Ripley said, "I'm just like everyone else. I'm excited that the season is reaching its end … and, like last year, it's very possible I could be running into one of these contestants during the tournament. So, I'm curious…." She gave her trademark little smirk to the camera.

Connor added, "So, this is just scouting out your possible opponent?"

Ripley replied, "I think people don't realize that life in the UFMF is 24/7. It's not just training your body and mind. You also have to know your opponent better than they do." She turned around and waved to the fans who continued shouting out her name. "See, boys and girls, learning doesn't stop after school. Sorry to tell you the truth."

Stabler said, "You've done incredible for your first year in the UFMF, and I have to say, you seem like a natural in the booth as well. What's been the biggest learning curve for you since entering the UFMF?"

Ripley smiled into the camera, "It's weird…. I was used to training prior to joining the UFMF, but balancing the demands outside of fighting has been the biggest learning curve."

Linkwater said, "I'm sure, like everyone else, you're aware of the rumor's been spreading like wildfire of the possible return of Kirin Rise tonight. What're your thoughts on that?"

"You know, I've said in the past that Kirin and I were very close friends at one time. I know she's had a difficult year with the incident and all, but I'd welcome her with open arms."

Grand Master Cheng added, "Like I said, this is all just rumor. I don't think there's a chance in hell she's returning."

Stabler scoffed, "Thanks, Grand Master Cheng. I think your contribution has been more than enlightening."

Krenzel snapped back toward the main arena. The sound of the crowd was deafening as everyone grew frantic. Brock Sherman, the announcer, began his introduction, his words revving up the crowd as the stadium shook.

Krenzel nodded to the arena, "It's about to start."

Stabler looked at his pad and scanned the information. "We already have the names of nine of the contestants he'll be announcing, but number ten is still a mystery."

Brock began his announcement. One by one, he gave a little introduction to each contestant as each fighter walked down the aisle, waving to fans and striking their own signature pose. Nine stood in the modified ring of the UFMF as they waited to learn who the last contestant might be.

Stabler said, "Any of those fighters mentioned so far catch your attention?"

Krenzel took a look around, "Brandon Hayes aka the Giant is just a physical specimen. He towers over every fighter around him. He's got the height of a basketball player with the build of a muscle man. Just by looks alone, he's the most intimidating."

Connor threw his thoughts in the ring, "I'd have to say, of the two female fighters, the feisty Brazilian Jiu Jitsu expert Theresa the

Terror is who I'm keeping my eye on. She's got her signature chokehold, which she officially named the Gagger."

Ripley added, "It's going to be difficult to apply that in a group setting and—"

Grand Master Cheng interrupted her. "Tyrone is shaped like a black Juggernaut."

Stabler said, "Uh, okay … that's an … interesting choice of words, Grand Master Cheng."

Ripley eyed Grand Master Cheng for a moment but knew the cameras were on her. She gave a quick smile and pretended to listen to his words intently. Inside, she didn't like being bypassed by the group.

Linkwater elbowed Connor in the side, "This is it. The last fighter!"

Brock waited for his final signal to read off the last name on the list. His voice echoed as he screamed into the mic. "Now … for our final fighter of the Battle Royale…." He frowned down at his pad, looking confused as he read the name. He muttered it to himself, just to make sure he said it right. "Our final fighter for tonight's main event is … Soo-Jin Park!" He spun sharply and directed everyone's attention to the far center as the lights aimed at an empty space. The crowd began to grumble in confusion as they stared at the empty entryway.

Stabler looked to his panel of associates for assistance, "Soo-Jin Park?"

Connor commanded, "Someone look up who that is."

Grand Master Cheng muttered, "Probably a Chinese fighter."

In the booth, there was a mad scramble to gather more information. The panel of experts used their resources to try to find a quick answer.

Grand Master Cheng seized the opportunity, "I knew it. It isn't Kirin. I was right!" He shook his fist high into the air as the cameras focused on his celebration.

Seconds passed that felt like forever before a figure small in stature walked up to the lights with a hoodie pulled down low. The cameras zoomed in, but the fighter's identity remained hidden. A handful of diehard fans recognized the name, but their screams were drowned by the mutters of confusion from the rest of the crowd.

The fighter's hand reached for the top of the hoodie as all eyes watched. Slowly, the hoodie came off, and the light shone off locks of blonde hair. The fighter looked up with determined eyes, ready to do business as she began the long march toward the ring. The crowd erupted into pandemonium, sending a shockwave that caused the stadium to rock. The anticipation became a reality, much to the delight of all those there. The guards worked feverishly, trying to keep the path clear and maintain order amidst the chaos.

"Oh my god, it's Kirin Rise!"

"It is…. It's her! It's really Kirin!"

"We missed you, Kirin!"

Connor looked down on his screen and realized what had happened. "Talk about a surprise entrance. Kirin Rise used her birth name to be announced, and now she's sporting a new color for her hair. Wow, I'm close to speechless."

Linkwater jumped in. "Like I said, when it comes to Kirin Rise, she's always shocking…. There's never a dull moment when she's involved."

Stabler added, "Guys, let's put things into perspective. It's great she's back, but she still has to win this event in order to advance. Keep in mind we don't know what she's done to maintain her training, if anything. It's not like you can just walk in off the street and win this."

"I think the world and everyone here—correct me if I'm wrong—is … stunned," Krenzel interjected, "but we definitely want to know what you think, Ripley."

Ripley turned a hint of green and replied, "I, umm … umm … I … I can't believe she colored her hair blonde like mine."

The members of the panel exchanged glances, confused by her remark.

Connor said, "I think she actually looks good with this fresh new look. Can you imagine it? This year's UFMF Championship could be a battle of the blondes!"

Ripley was far from pleased by that comment. Even for her, it was difficult to hide her true emotions. She flashed a fake smile and imagined physical harm upon Connor.

Linkwater stepped in, "Everyone, hold onto your seats. This roller coaster ride is about to get bumpy. We are just minutes away from the beginning of this Battle Royale mayhem. Remember, we have ten fighters, and last year was the first time we showcased the Battle Royale. What we saw was literally every man or woman for themselves. So, it'll be interesting to see how this plays out and what new strategies they developed. Remember, there is no time limit for this Battle Royale. Once that bell rings, the last one standing is the winner. And, while the ring has been expanded to accommodate the number of fighters, if you fall off or get thrown or knocked out of the ring, you are gone from the fight."

#

Two worlds appeared to coexist. On one side, all that mattered was the electricity of the crowd, the anticipation of the fight, and the outcome of the Battle Royale. And then there was Kirin Rise, who knew the importance of this match. In order for her plan to work, this was only the first step toward a larger goal, but she had to deal with this hurdle first. Kirin stood stern-faced and did not make eye contact with the other nine contestants. The referee was spouting out the rules as Kirin stood apart from the group. To her, it did not matter; she knew what had to be done. The referee screamed out the last rule and then ordered the fighters to take their positions. He would remain in the ring to try to maintain some form of order.

All the fighters began to take their places, forming a circle near the outer edge. Kirin picked her spot and joined the rest of the fighters spaced equally apart. The referee found the only empty spot, which was the center of the ring. Everyone there was thinking the same thing: how would Kirin perform after such a long absence?

Stabler commented, "This is an odd formation by the fighters. Last year, they were scattered throughout the ring."

Grand Master Cheng added, "I'm not quite sure what the strategy is behind all this."

"That's a first for you," said Stabler.

All eyes were on the referee, waiting for him to start the match. Several of the fighters stood out from the crowd. The tallest fighter, the Giant, was true to his name and towered over the rest at about 6'6". Tyrone—the one Grand Master Cheng referred to as the Black Juggernaut—took the scales to the max, weighing in at about 305 lbs. Theresa the Terror was hopping up and down in the ring; she was the only one sporting a traditional gi. Cyborg the female muscle bound Muay Thai fighter was showing off her kicks. Thus, a total of three female fighters including Kirin made up the battle royal, with the remainder of the group consisting of men. Everyone got into some kind of ready stance, preparing to charge one another, except for Kirin, who maintained her causal position.

This was Kirin's first fight since returning, and she felt more prepared than ever. She did a final scan of all her opponents and took one last breath. Normally, at this point just before the fight, she would remind herself of the words, "Center, target, own it." Instead, her mind remained completely empty and at peace.

The referee's hand cut through the air in a downward motion. "Fight!"

Kirin's intensity spiked. She was ready to deal with whatever came her way. Instead of the mad rush she expected, the remaining fighters gathered in the center of the ring, forcing the referee to step out of the way. The crowd—and Kirin—looked confused.

Connor stood up from his chair in disbelief, "What's going on here?"

Stabler joined him by his side, knocking over his chair in the process. "I believe they're forming a team, from the looks of it."

Krenzel observed, "I think you're correct. But, they're all facing in only one direction, and that's at Kirin."

Ripley cracked a smile but didn't say anything.

Linkwater asked, "Is that legal?"

Stabler said, "The rule is pretty much anything goes. In the Battle Royale, there's no rule against teaming up."

Connor couldn't hide his disbelief, "But, that makes it nine against one!"

Linkwater said, "I know I sound like a broken record, but this keeps getting more interesting."

"Grand Master Cheng," Stabler began, "if you were in this situation, what would you do? This seems almost impossible for her to win."

Grand Master Cheng replied, "For her, yes ... but, for me, this would be a walk in the park. Personally ... strategy-wise, she should stay by the edge of the ring so that she can use her positioning to her advantage. Then she'll have to deal with only those in front of her. Remember the rules: if you go out of the ring, it's game over. You see, you have to have a certain level of awareness of your surroundings as well as your opponent. My years of experience have taught me this."

Kirin looked at the rest of the fighters as she stood a mere ten feet away from the edge of the ring. Any other fighter would deem this to be impossible, but nothing could be worse than escaping the warehouse. She still had the battle scars on the outside and the pain of loss forever burning inside.

The other fighters were talking amongst themselves, plotting their move against her, when Kirin decided to charge in.

Stabler was shocked, "What's she doing?"

Krenzel replied, "She's crazy."

Ripley muttered to herself, "Kill her."

Kirin went straight in, catching everyone by surprise. To the naked eye, she appeared to blur. She paid no attention to the opponent's size or sex—whoever was closest and in her line of attack was going to have a bad day. Kirin got into range of her first target and locked on. Her action created a chain of events as her opponents shifted and adjusted.

She flashed a smile when her target stood frozen for just a second. She did not hesitate and launched a punch straight down his center. There was nothing fancy about it, but she hid her intention until the last second, and he could not react. The punch was true and landed square on his chest, making his head whiplash from the impact. The intent was not to kill him but to knock him back, bowling over several of her opponents. The Giant, who was at the rear of the group, stumbled to the ground, giving her some much-needed space to deal with the others.

A hook came to her right side at full force. Catching it from the corner of her eye, Kirin had to use an emergency technique to deal with it. Both her hands shot up in a circle, protecting her center and catching the attack at the very last second. The simultaneous block was combined with an attack, as the chop to the fighter's neck connected. The fighter was stunned from the hit to the carotid, and Kirin's block hand flowed to another chop to the opposite side of his neck. This time, she drove the force of her hit all the way to the ground, nearly snatching his life away. She shifted her weight and threw his limp body toward the other fighters approaching her left side from behind.

For the first time, she was seeing things differently as long as she kept her emotions in check. She felt the natural flow of the universe, and she was simply enjoying the ride. She could feel the intent of the others all around her as her senses felt heightened. She felt a pull of the force to spin around and focus her attention once again on her closest target.

Another fighter cried out, launching a front kick, which she ignored. The range was too close for her to even worry about, so she shifted to the side and leaned in, using a *bong sau* punch, drilling him in the face. His head hit the ground, making a cracking sound, and his legs lifted from underneath, knocking him out. The entire crowd gasped.

The fighters kept coming in as the one closest to the recently KO'd fighter leaped over the body and led with a left cross straight toward Kirin. Her guard hand intercepted his punch, and she yanked him forward, making him lose his balance. As he continued to stumble forward, Kirin kicked his shin from under him, taking out his base. He felt the pain, cringing from the hit. Kirin threw him toward the other fighters, forming another barrier.

The biggest of the bunch, Tyrone, shouted, "She's mine!" as he pounded his chest several times. The others paused and watched as he charged in like a football player at full speed.

Kirin cracked her neck from side to side as she stood and waited. All eyes were on her, but even with the threat she appeared calm. Tyrone wanted blood; he wanted the spotlight. He rushed in and lunged with both arms open, intent on tearing her apart. He committed too early, leaving his center fully exposed. Kirin sank to one knee and delivered an uppercut straight to the groin. Her force braced by her stance and his force combined with the charge led to an explosion upon impact.

The pain surged throughout his entire body, but his face captured the devastation of the blow. Somehow those watching knew exactly what Tyrone felt, but Kirin was not done. She chained three more hits in the same area. He crumpled to the ground, cupping his shame, knocked out from the excruciating pain.

As Kirin looked up at the other fighters, her eyes appeared to be changing to the look of death. Theresa, the sneaky fighter with a bitch face, had circled around undetected during this chaos. She tackled Kirin from the side, catching her off-guard, and tried to apply a clench. With Kirin on the ground, Theresa scrambled to secure a body part to put into a lock.

It did not matter to Kirin, who went with the flow of the force. It was all the same to her whether she was standing or on the ground. She did not bother wrestling with Theresa, and her hands remained free and close to her opponent's face. She dug both her thumbs into Theresa's eyes, as the Brazilian woman let out a haunting scream. Kirin did not stop as she raised her opponent's head from the ground and then smashed it again, digging even deeper. She stood up and watched as her victim fluttered on the ground in agonizing pain. Blood covered Theresa's face and poured into her mouth, making her gag. Kirin's hands were dripping with blood, and her thumbs had pieces of eyeball clinging to them. Kirin looked almost annoyed and delivered a swift kick to the back of her head, just to keep her quiet.

The audience squirmed from the punishment, and some even threw up. That last act of brutality was something no one had seen from her before. Kirin was emotionless as she looked up at the remaining fighters, who began setting up a new formation. She brushed her hair to the side with a quick blow of breath. Her new blonde locks now featured streaks of blood.

Linkwater said, "I've seen Kirin Rise in action, but never like this. Before, she was putting on a show. Right now, this almost seems like an execution."

Connor added, "The old Kirin Rise was emotional in the ring. This new Kirin with the stone-cold face absolutely gives me the creeps."

One of the fighters yelled, "Attack her at the same time, you idiots! Don't stagger in."

Three fighters looked at each other and nodded before charging together. Kirin waited until the last second before shifting her weight to one side. She saw them all commit to it, but her center was still dead even. She quickly went the other way and initiated the attack. Fists were flying from all directions. There was no time to block and then attack. Instead, she used everything to her advantage. Her offense was the best defense as her focus was simply their centers of gravity. Regardless of the attack, all she saw was the source of the power. In the back of her mind, she repeated Sigung's lesson: kill the source of the power, and you destroy everything.

After several exchanges with the three, Kirin stood alone. They lay on the ground, broken and knocked out. All that stood in her way to victory were the final two fighters: the Muay Thai female fighter called the Cyborg and the Giant.

Even with the evidence of Kirin's dominance lying around, the Giant decided to antagonize her. He decided talking trash would goad her out of her flow. "Look familiar, Kirin? Looks just like the warehouse that burned down with your Sifu, doesn't it?" He laughed and high-fived the Cyborg, as they both chuckled.

Throughout the entire fight, Kirin had maintained her cool, but their taunting broke her. Her vision shifted, and the flow she had sensed was gone as the fire inside was ignited to the max. Her anger raged as a teardrop formed and fell to the ground. She screamed and ran straight toward the Giant. He took a huge swing that led into a roundhouse kick toward her. It looked like a tree stump being thrown in the air. She didn't even bother to block it. Instead, she kicked his supporting leg from under him, breaking it like a branch. The distance from top to ground was great, and he crashed to the floor, slamming his head. He was out cold, but that did not stop Kirin from continuing her attack. She got on top of his chest and rained down punch after punch as blood splattered everywhere. He lay unresponsive as she reached with both hands around his head and snapped his neck. His body twitched for the last time.

Krenzel squirmed. "Oh my god! Did she...?"

Stabler said, "Holy sh...!"

Kirin stared at the last opponent, who watched in horror. Before she could react, Kirin sprang from the ground and chased her down. There was no turning Kirin off; she was going to finish the job and be the last one standing. The remaining fighter's courage quickly melted as she turned around and ran the other way. Kirin was relentless, and her pace outmatched her opponent's. At the last moment, the Cyborg decided to abandon all hopes of entering the Dome. She threw herself out of the ring to avoid Kirin's wrath and breathed a sigh of relief as she reached the safe zone. It was over. Kirin stopped her charge as she stood alone in the ring. The referee began to approach her to signal her victory.

Bodies were clustered around her; some were moving while the Giant remained motionless. She was still focused on the Cyborg. That look of relief on her face needed to be wiped off. She stood there breathing heavily as anger consumed her. Kirin pictured the Cyborg's high-five with the Giant as she started a charge. Darting past the referee, she jumped out of the ring. A surprised Cyborg could only watch as a flying kick came at full speed to her face. The impact was so great that she flew into the stands and was out cold. Kirin landed on the ground outside of the ring and struck a superhero pose.

Connor exclaimed, "Good lord," as the entire panel felt exactly the same.

Stabler reiterated, "I didn't think it was possible … that Kirin could leave me speechless once again."

Linkwater added, "What a beast…."

Kirin had again done the impossible, and the proof was in the ring lying on the ground. One remained lifeless. The crowd was cheering as the scene of pure dominance left them fully entertained. Kirin was breathing heavily and shaking with anger as adrenaline pumped through her. She took a minute to gather herself and then spun around. She climbed back into the ring and walked over several bodies before reaching the center where the referee stood. He looked terrified as he tentatively reached for her hand and lifted it.

The crowd began chanting her name, but she ignored them. As the medical staff was busy dealing with the injured, Megan Mahoney finally made her way into the ring. She held her mic up to Kirin and said, "Congratulations on the win, Kirin! It was definitely a surprise to see you come back, and I'm sure all your fans are grateful. Did you think the Battle Royale was going to end up like this?"

Kirin did not respond as she continued to search through the crowds.

Megan pointed to the giant screen and tried to get her attention. "Kirin … Kirin, we're on live."

Kirin finally looked up and saw the entire panel on the screen. Her face darkened as she spotted Ripley with the rest of the broadcasters.

Megan asked again, "Kirin, is there anything you want to tell us about the fight?"

Kirin grabbed the mic from Megan, who looked shocked. "I do have something to say." She took several steps forward and then turned to Megan. "Can the panel hear me?"

Megan nodded as it was impossible to talk over the crowd.

Kirin said, "This is for Ripley Hawkins." She faced the camera, smiled, and lifted her middle finger, thrusting it forward. Megan looked stunned as the camera caught Kirin's rude gesture and Ripley's reaction at the same time. Kirin added, "I'm coming for you!" She dropped the mic and walked away. The split second of silence was quickly drowned by the thunderous roar from the fans—everyone was shouting.

"Kirin! Kirin! Kirin!"

"That moment where you get to shine, is when you realize why you trained so hard." — Sifu

Section 1 Short Stories #10—Kirin's P.O.V.

<u>Distracted—1 Year, 105 Days</u>

I was huffing and puffing as I took a quick glance at my phone. I had only ten more minutes to spare. I couldn't believe my alarm clock hadn't gone off—or maybe I'd hit snooze. Regardless, I had to make it on time for the fight. I would've blamed Bacon for making me hit deep REM sleep, but he was just too damn cute, except for all the farting.

I stopped at the corner and looked at the street sign crossing. "Irving and Pulaski … god, why am I so awful with directions?" I pulled out my phone again, consulting the map, which helpfully told me to go northeast from here. Spinning in a circle, trying to align myself with the arrow on the phone, I finally screamed, "I don't even know where the heck north is!"

Then, I distantly recalled what Chun had told me: to look for the abandoned printing company on a far corner. From there, he'd said I would take the back alleys and the way would be obvious—even for me.

"Go with the flow, Kirin. Go with the flow." At last, I decided to pick a direction and ran hard and fast for the next minute. Looking straight ahead, I saw an abandoned print shop, just like Chun had described. I stopped to catch my breath.

Holy smoke, that actually worked!

When I checked the time, I discovered I had a few precious minutes to spare. I was about to turn into the alley when I stopped in my tracks. I looked around from side to side and then behind; for some odd reason, I felt like I was being followed. It was late, just past eleven, which probably added to my unease. I brushed it off, thinking my imagination was at work. Besides, why would anyone want to follow me? Anyway, I was running out of time as I booked down the alley and caught sight of Chun.

"What the hell, Blink? Where have you been?"

"Sorry, I overslept."

"Overslept? You're a fricking teenager! At that age, you guys don't need sleep."

Chun grabbed me by my arm and started to pull away, but I stopped. I turned around again to see if anyone was behind me. When I saw no one, I assumed my imagination had gotten the best of me.

"Blink… if you want to get paid, we gotta go NOW!"

"I can walk myself. Just lead the way," I huffed as I followed close behind him. The light down the alley grew brighter, and the sound of the restless crowd became louder as I followed Chun. I was unconcerned with the setting; to me, the fight was just a paycheck, plain and simple.

Chun mentioned, "You'll want to be careful with this one. He's—"

I said, "Let me guess, rough and tough and muscles upon muscles. Chun, every opponent you set me up with is all the same."

"Hey, I'm just warning you…. That's my job."

"No, your job is to get me work. My job is to kick ass."

"Yeah, yeah … just don't get cocky."

"Does he have a silly nickname?"

Chun smirked and nodded, "Of course … he's called the Warrior."

"I swear these guys spend more time coming up with silly names for themselves than training, but this one really lacks imagination."

My comment caused Chun to chuckle.

"So that's it, 'the Warrior.' Does he have a real name?"

Chun replied, "Nope, he only goes by the Warrior."

"Okay, enough of that, on to more important things. So, what's the inside scoop on the bets?"

"If the fight last over two minutes—and, yes, they're still betting against you—it's an extra five hundred credits for you in addition to the main pot."

"Sweet … signal me when it's two minutes, right?"

Chun gave a single nod, "I got your back."

He continued to walk ahead of me, cutting through the crowd. I could see very little around him until, at last, I spotted my opponent standing at a distance. From my quick glance, I could tell he was no different from any other opponent I'd fought in the past. To me, everyone looked the same as my focus was always their center.

The usual formalities were completed, and the gambling stakes were set over the next several minutes. I stood still as I watched him, noting every motion and action that revealed exactly what he favored. The Warrior began bouncing up and down, a simple tell to get rid of the nerves, but once he saw me, his expression grew more confident. He began beating his chest, as if that did anything. I chuckled at the fragility of the male ego. His right foot took the lead as he hopped around, telling me he was definitely a striker.

I whispered, "Center, target, own it."

My focus was solely on my opponent until I felt it again—that itch between my shoulder blades. I scanned the crowd as that feeling wouldn't leave me.

What is that? Is someone watching me?

I shook it off. Of course someone was watching me—there was an entire crowd focused on me. It didn't matter. I had business to deal with.

The referee gave the signal, and the crowd let out a huge roar. My opponent did not dash right in. I was sure he knew how I fought since I was now a regular in the circuit.

All those muscles, and he's still a wuss.

I remained motionless, since he was far from striking range. I had to beat this guy, but I couldn't do it too quickly. The extra five hundred credits was much needed.

Finally, he went for a front kick, but he was well out of range. I hooked it with my hand and stepped back, forcing him into an awkward split. I couldn't resist, and my foot planted back. I used that to spring forward and lunge into his face with a knee. The hit was on mark, ending with a solid connect.

Oh crap!

I landed on top of his chest. He looked like he was out cold, and I cursed as I realized my overzealous mentality would cost me five hundred. There was no signal to say the match was over, so I decided to rain slaps on his face to try to wake him up. I hit him several times, and then I saw one of his eyes pop open.

"Get up, you!" I went for one more slap, and he reacted and blocked it. He thrusted upward, bouncing me off his chest. I rolled several feet away from him, sparing a quick glance at Chun, who held his hand up to signal that there was a minute to go.

My opponent finally rolled up and took a moment to shake off the cobwebs. He seemed to have no idea that he had been knocked out. I could tell he was still wobbly in the knees, so I decided to slap him to extend the fight.

He lunged forward and went for a huge haymaker, a clear sign of desperation. I ducked underneath it as he exposed his back. I slapped him in the back of his head as he took another random swipe. He kept dancing around and hitting only air, growing more heated as several more of my slaps landed.

I looked at Chun, who finally gave me the signal. My opponent was frustrated and let out a roar as he bulled straight in. I was not going to back down from this joker—he was no match for me. The Warrior reached out with both arms as I angled myself lower and did an uppercut ginger fist to his chin. The impact stopped him in place. As he whipped back, I sprang straight up and finished him off with a kick.

My opponent was down, and I was ready to knock him out and collect my credits. That sensation returned, peering eyes at the most inopportune time. I looked up. There he was amongst the crowd, watching me—Tobias. I hesitated as the shock froze me in my stance. "Holy sh…."

The next thing I knew, pain exploded in my gut. I was on my back, looking at a fist flying right at me. Seconds felt like minutes before I was being dragged along the ground. I stared up blankly to find that Chun had me by the side.

He was saying something to me, but the crowd's noise drowned his words. Finally, the buzz from my head cleared away as I heard him say, "What the hell happened, Blink? You had him dead and stopped!"

I shook my head. My face felt raw. "What did you say, Chun?" I winced as my head was ringing.

"I said, why'd you stop? You had that match and a big payday with it."

I was about to answer when I felt someone lift me from the other side. A familiar voice said, "I'll take over from here."

Crap. Confirmed.

Chun stopped and asked, "Who are you?"

"I'm her brother."

He paused and looked at Tobias from head to toe. "I don't quite see the resemblance."

"In the art, not by blood," said Tobias.

Chun squeaked out, "Art class?"

Tobias ignored him as his strong grip hoisted me to a sitting position. I heard someone call my name.

"Hey, Blink," my opponent razzed me from afar, "you're not so tough now, are you? What's it like to be on the losing end?"

He was right: this was my first loss. I had to eat the cake. There was nothing I could say.

Tobias looked at me and then faced Chun. "What's your name?"

"Chun."

"Hold her for a second, Chun," He pushed me into Chun's grip.

"You want a piece of this?" my cocky opponent taunted Tobias.

"You really gonna trash talk after you were getting your ass handed to you?"

"I got the victory, bitch! Besides, that Kung Fu shit don't work. That's why I'm known as the Warrior."

Tobias had a look in his eye I'd seen before. It meant only one thing, bad news for his opponent. He removed his jacket and tossed it to the ground as he began walking toward the Warrior.

The Warrior spread his arms open, "So, you want a piece of this."

"There's going to be pieces of you."

"Bring it, bitch. You'll be joining your little girlfriend on the ground soon enough."

I watched Tobias who didn't respond and took his time by casually walking toward the Warrior. I remembered Sifu saying to me, "I don't fear the barking dog. It's the silent one that will attack you."

The Warrior got into a fighting stance as Tobias casually walked in.

What's he doing?

The Warrior threw a high roundhouse kick to Tobias's head. He didn't move in like he should; in fact, he barely moved. He raised his elbow in the direction of the kick and allowed the Warrior's leg to run into it.

Crack!

The Warrior hobbled back, clenching his leg. The pain was written on his face. It must've been like kicking a wall. It looked like there was a good chance he had broken it. Tobias continued to move in slowly, allowing his opponent the chance to attack as I watched the match progress.

The Warrior screamed, summoning some strength as he launched a wild circular hook at Tobias. He allowed the momentum to carry as he moved into the shoulder area of the swing. The Warrior ended up popping his shoulder out, and now he stood awkwardly as half his body was useless.

Tobias approached him and grabbed his shirt by the collar. He screamed, "I am the Warrior!" With a last-ditch effort to snatch victory, he leaned back and with full force went for a head-butt. Tobias merely shifted to the side, and the Warrior's head cracked into Tobias's shoulder. The force rocked him back as he crumpled to the dirt floor.

Tobias looked back at me and then focused his attention on his opponent. "So, Warrior … what's your real name?"

The Warrior blurted out, "Eat shit. Asshole!"

Tobias mashed on his broken leg as he howled in pain and asked, "Name?" There was no remorse or hesitation in his movement.

"I'll tell you. I'll tell you. Please get off my leg."

He stepped on it harder, and the Warrior finally blurted out the answer. "It's Sheldon. Sheldon Witherspoon!" Upon hearing the name, Tobias finally took away the pressure from his leg. Tobias exuded a confidence that was different from mine, as his presence alone brought fear into the hearts of his opponents. That was something I still needed to develop.

The crowd was stunned silent by the demonstration of destruction. Tobias looked around, pointing at everyone in the crowd. With a loud and commanding voice, he declared, "This," he pounded his fist to his chest, "is Wing Chun Gung Fu!" He pointed into the crowd. "Know it! Fear it! Are there any doubters?" He stared directly into the eyes of everyone present, but they all shied away from him. The area was silent as he turned back and walked toward me.

Chun asked if I could sit on my own, and I nodded. He muttered into my ear, "Your boyfriend is bad ass."

"He's not my—" I began, but Chun ignored my words and walked away.

He approached Tobias, "Hey, I can arrange for you to do these matches, too … you interested? Big credits for your skill."

Tobias didn't answer Chun as he grabbed me from the ground and lifted me up into his arms.

"Silence is more terrifying than noise." —Kirin

Argument—1 Year, 106 Days

A block away, we found an abandoned building that didn't smell like a urinal. "Can you stand?" he asked. I nodded as he finally put me down on the ground.

Back on my own two feet, I leaned against the wall. My head was killing me, but I didn't want to show any sign of weakness, so I kept my mouth shut.

"Let me look at your face." Tobias began to reach for it, but I swiped him away.

"What's your problem?" I could feel his blood boiling again, and I rubbed the top of my eye to help soothe the pain. I watched him as he began pacing before kicking a pile of garbage on the floor. He let out a scream that echoed and made the rats run away.

431

"I knew it. I knew it!" He began his rant.

Here we go.

"The math just didn't add up. I knew you couldn't afford to live on your own. It made no sense your place was so much bigger than mine," as he waved his hands around in frustration.

"That's not true," I countered.

"You want to continue to keep lying to me or yourself?"

I shouted back, "You have no idea what you're talking about!"

"So, you're doing this for ... for what, fun?"

"Hey, camera equipment can be expensive."

"Don't bullshit me, Kirin. You're talking to the master of it."

"Oh, now you're a master."

"Don't go that route, Kirin," he warned.

"Why don't we just put it all out on the table and say what we want to say?"

Tobias said, "I'd rather you do that than continue your ball of lies."

"Fine, let's do it!"

"Fine!"

"You're afraid? Big, bad Tobias is afraid to deal with the truth. You want the truth? I'm tired of how we're living. We're hiding in shame studying our art as if we're doing something wrong. I've lived my entire life like that, and I will not stand for it anymore."

432

"So, what are you going to do, punch your way out of this?" he said in a condescending voice.

"I don't know," I admitted, "but I'm tired of living like sheep. I came to this country thinking things would be different. Instead, it's like déjà vu."

"Well, whatever you're thinking—and I *hope* you're thinking—you're not going to solve the world's problems in the back of an alley."

"Action is at least action."

"There's gotta be a goal. There has to be a target. You can't just randomly do something, hoping it'll lead to some random better thing. It's like chasing hands."

I shook my head in frustration and disgust. "You're not Sifu, and you're a far cry from him."

"That may be true, but I'm here! I stayed, Kirin."

I didn't know what to say, as the truth couldn't be argued.

"I never said that I was his replacement. No one in this universe could be that … dammit! I never wanted the job, but I'm it. I'm all the group has to keep it together. So, unlike you, I stood up and did what had to be done. Ask yourself what you've done."

"Pretending that things are okay doesn't cut it," I retorted. "Playing like you're the master and running drills doesn't change the fact that he's gone."

"Yeah, you're 100% right, but putting our school in jeopardy by doing these fights, when I clearly said not to, is downright stupid, Kirin!"

I began to get angry and then stopped. My head was killing me, and the throbbing was getting worse. I paused in my tracks and looked away.

Tobias approached me, "You need to put some ice on that."

I mumbled to myself, "You need to shut up." Then I raised my voice and said, "Look, I'm feeling like crap. Unless you've got something important to say, I'm gonna head back home and take care of this."

Tobias was silent. I didn't even bother to turn around to face him. I knew he was right: I needed a better plan. But, I couldn't think of a better route, and I kept hoping a way would present itself. The time wasn't right, but I knew I would find a way.

"If you listen more and talk less, a way will present itself." —Kirin

Lose Control—1 Year, 113 Days

It had been a week since our argument, and I knew today Tobias was planning on running a class at school. I wanted to train regardless of my current feelings about him, and I wasn't sure if he had mentioned the incident to the other guys at the school. My drive to improve my skill ate my ego, and I decided that my goal was what really mattered, even if it meant facing him. Still, I carried on an internal debate for about five minutes as I sat in my loft with Bacon. No matter how I looked at it, I had little choice. Either I would have to do something, or everything would stay exactly the same.

"Screw it. Let's train." I sucked in my pride and made my way to our school. I was halfway through the door when I realized that I still had a bruise on my face. If I went to class that way, I knew that would end up being the center of discussion. I took a detour to my bathroom and used makeup to cover it up. Five minutes later, I checked the mirror and decided I'd done a pretty good job hiding it.

Thanks for the lessons, Gwen, and then went on my way.

#

Twenty minutes later, I was outside our building, sneaking toward our entrance so that no one could see me from the outside. I walked in and found that class was already in progress. Tobias was in front leading the drills, and I could feel his eyes on me, but I had no intention of returning the favor.

I walked past Doc, who left his hand out for a shake, and I got a couple of head nudges from the other guys. They were halfway through the first section of Siu Lim Tao, so I got in my stance and joined them.

Tobias said, "Focus on the placement and positioning of your *tan sau.* Notice how the elbow naturally moves in. You shouldn't force it. Now, when you practice this, the triangle is your guide. You stay within the triangle, and everything will be fine. If you venture outside the triangle, then you put yourself in harm's way."

I wasn't exactly sure, but it seemed like those remarks were directed toward me. I remained focused on looking straight ahead and not giving him the satisfaction of reacting to his comments. The first half of the form was defined as standing meditation. It was slow for a reason, and it allowed a person to reflect on a single thing. I could feel myself relax and the anger subside, but whenever I heard Tobias's voice, my blood boiled. Deep down, I wasn't sure why I was so mad. Maybe it was because his arguments were right, or maybe it was because he led me to my first loss.

Fifteen minutes later, we finally finished the form, and the room immediately filled with useless banter.

Ryan approached me, "Hey, what's up with that shiner?"

"What shiner?"

Ryan reached for my face and started rubbing off my makeup.

I slapped his hand, "What gives!"

The next thing I knew, the rest of the guys surrounded me and began bombarding me with questions.

Big T asked, "Little sista, what happened?"

Robert added, "You know your makeup job is pretty crappy."

Danny chimed in, "Damn, Kirin. Did someone beat you up?"

"Guys, will you stop being so nosy and give her some space?" Doc came to my rescue.

Ken looked concerned, "Does it still hurt, Kirin?"

Tobias walked up to me and didn't say a word about my eye. Instead, he said, "Okay, everyone, let's partner up and chi sao. I'll be working with everyone." By the way the guys reacted, they knew something was up, but they went along with it and didn't push the situation any further.

I partnered first with Robert, who was strangely silent while we worked out. The chi sao drill was simple: one person attacked while the other one only blocked. Much of the focus on the art led to blocking. The idea behind it was simple: if you no longer feared the attack, you could simply focus on the target.

One by one, I worked with the entire gang. I was doing my best to avoid working with Tobias, but we had an even number, so it was inevitable that we would run into one another. Each time we switched partners, Tobias barked out some instructions.

"Remember, when blocking, don't chase the hands. Focus on the target. As for the attackers, don't give up your structure just for the sake of the attack. A true attack should have killing power and not just be able to tag your opponent."

I spent some time working with Ken, and then I heard Tobias say, "Okay, last round. Switch partners. Make sure you worked with everyone."

Ken thanked me for the time and walked away from me. Always the nice guy, he offset Robert's level of annoyance. The rest of the guys started partnering up while I stood alone until Tobias walked up to me.

"You want to block or attack?"

"I want to attack." Here was my chance.

He got into his stance and put his hands forward as we began performing the chi sao drill. We began rolling and testing one another's structure. I decided to do my first attack and lead with a punch that flowed into several more attacks, all of which he blocked. Everything seemed cool as we continued to roll again. He gave me a push, and I felt my structure rock. I caught myself and regained my balance and decided to go in. This time, I changed angles and went with a palm strike. He blocked it, and that led me to flow to several more attacks to his center—all of which he easily blocked as well.

Tobias said, "When you're disciplined in your structure and don't go wild, you can block anything."

I didn't respond to his comment and began attacking again. I started noticing that, no matter what my attack was, he held his ground and would not step back. Tobias was copying what Sifu did when he wanted to make a statement. He was trying to prove his superiority over me, and now it really pissed me off.

I took a moment during our roll to calm down. My focus was no longer on the attacks, but on my stance. I quieted my mind and was determined to maintain my vertical at all cost. We began to roll again, and things felt different this time. Unlike before, I could feel glimpses of openings as my solid stance made everything more sensitive. I tested his structure and, for the first time, felt something slightly off with his center. That was when I unleashed my attack. He countered it, but I didn't care. I continued to concentrate on my own stance.

He looked at me in the eye, "You're not going to move me, Kirin."

A spark flared within me. It did not matter whether my opponent was Tobias or Sifu—my determination could not be matched. I began launching the attacks to the flow of every motion with the goal of getting to the center. The guys formed a small circle around us and began to watch, but I was too busy to care. I was single-minded in my determination. It didn't matter if my moves were countered. I would go to the next motion right back to the target.

Attack after attack came raining down, but Tobias would not budge. Every so often, I would feel his center, a slight motion here and there, but he was solid. Finally, in a blink, I found his center off and, instead of pushing him back, I pulled him toward me without hesitation. When his center of gravity came forward, I did not attack. I held my structure, and he bounced off me and finally took a step back. I heard the guys make a sound. I heard a slight muttering all around me, as they were surprised just like me by what they just saw. That was the first time I'd ever seen Tobias take a step back. Once that occurred, I started my chain of attacks, and I could feel my confidence along with my intensity growing. I just *knew* I was going to get through, but my emotions got the better of me as the greed increased and my focus on my center lessened.

I went for a heavy attack, and Tobias caught my center and yanked me forward. The pull was harder than I'd ever felt before, and I found myself on the ground looking at Tobias from below. I let out a yell, got back up, and began to charge in, but Big T and Danny blocked my path as someone grabbed my arm.

It was Doc who pulled me away, "Why don't we take a breather, Kirin?"

I was breathing heavily as I looked at Tobias, who stared me down. He'd kept his cool, while I had lost mine.

Not today ... but one day.

"A good fighter isn't the one who hits hardest or can take the most hits. It's the one who can keep their cool and always maintain control." —Kirin

Section 2 Sifu's Journey Entry #10—Against the Flow

Late October

For several months since making his decision, Sifu had maintained what seemed like a normal life. He and Lance would open up the ramen shop late at night and serve meals to the long line of fans. On occasion, he would also work with Lance and continue his teachings with his student. But, while everything on the outside seemed normal, he had been observing, plotting, and studying Kirin for some time.

He had tried to steer her toward the Chum Night fight without making any contact, but it seemed Kirin was satisfied with her late-night battles in back alleys and abandoned buildings.

Now that he was part of the organization known as the Defiance, he had arranged another meeting with Damon. Sifu learned about how the world really worked and that evil never rested. He had already known the greed and lust of men were difficult to quench. With tension on his face, Sifu sat at the desk across from Damon.

Damon said, "We're nearing the end of the year, Sifu. Our sources say that the UFMF is still looking for that star to showcase. They have one girl, but she's not quite ready yet. I was hoping we could make the decision for them. I've let you call the shots on this, since you know her better than any of us, but you have to give me some progress."

"I've tried several ways indirectly to get her to fight, but she's stuck to a pattern. It's human nature to get comfortable, you know?"

Damon replied, "That's the problem, and that's also my fault. In the last several months, you've learned a lot about what we are dealing with, and I have learned so much from your teachings as well. I believe you told me that, if you don't hit the source, you're simply putting a bandage on the situation. The route you've gone is unchartered territory for you. It's too indirect."

Sifu did not respond. He knew Damon was right.

"I know I've put you in a difficult spot." Damon looked into Sifu's eyes. "What's her source, Sifu? Deep down, you must know what it is."

When Sifu remained quiet, Damon stood up from his chair, "When it comes to deciding, there is no easy choice. I'm sure that, even though you've agreed to help us, something must be tugging at your heart." He went to the door and opened it. "Sin, you got a second?"

Sindy came walking into the room, "What's going on?"

"I was telling Sifu that everyone involved has made choices—difficult ones, things I'm sure that some of us regret. But, at the end of the day, we all know what we are fighting for, that it goes beyond our own personal feelings."

Sindy nodded, "Sifu, it's true. How can we win if our enemy will do whatever it takes, but we won't?"

The last comment resonated with Sifu. He knew that one always needed to match intent in a real fight.

Damon explained, "Our window … our chance to flush out one person is upon us. Now, Sin was kind of in a similar situation when I found her, just like with you and Kirin. How old are you again, Sin?"

"Just turned seventeen."

"Maybe you can help Sifu out. Any ideas you can think of that would motivate you if you were in Kirin's shoes?"

441

Sifu looked at Sindy and waited.

Sindy said, "I did the case file on Kirin. She was adopted, right, Sifu?"

Sifu answered, "At the age of eight or nine, I believe she moved to the States from North Korea."

"She lost both her parents as well?"

"Yes, it's always haunted her ... but then again, what person wouldn't be?"

"You know, from my own experience...." Sindy's voice cracked before she cleared her throat. "When I lost my parents, it felt like the entire world crumbled before me. Finding any resemblance to what I could call home was the most important thing."

"Well, that applies to almost everyone, don't you think?"

Sindy agreed, "Yes, but for Kirin, it's even more important. Sifu, your school's been shut down since the beginning of the year, right?"

"Yes, you wrote the reports and the incident that led up to that."

Sindy gave it some more thought. "That doesn't make sense...."

Sifu asked, "What do you mean?"

"So, why continue to fight?" Sindy began to pace, her mind rolling. "What's driving her to fight? I mean, before, your students were using the money to keep the school open, but that's no longer the case. She's the only one who's continued fighting ... but why?"

Damon watched Sindy pacing as he thought aloud, "Something's motivating her. Whatever that is, all it will take is just a little push from our side to get her over the top."

Sifu stood up and circled the table before turning to both Sindy and Damon. They were busy brainstorming with one another. He caught himself before revealing his thoughts. Once in the open, there would be no going back. He fumbled with the word, before finally spitting out, "Home."

Sindy was so preoccupied with her own thoughts that she didn't hear Sifu. She added, "Her fights. It's not money motivated or to test her skill, is it, Sifu?"

"Home," Sifu repeated. "It's all about her home. It's about her family. She fights to protect it, and anyone who threatens them…." He trailed off as his words appeared to be falling on deaf ears.

Sindy got up, "You know she's still out there looking for you, Sifu."

Damon raised his hand, "That's enough, Sin."

Sifu said, "Don't you get it? We take away her home and link it to the source. That'll be the motivation to enter Chum Night."

Damon looked at Sifu as he finally realized what he was saying.

Sindy repeated what Sifu had said, "Home…."

Damon's gaze was intense, "Are you prepared to do that?"

Sifu remained silent and did not answer. He felt torn apart, knowing what it would mean.

CHAPTER 11

The Showdown

December 14, the Night Before the Tournament

For the third year in a row, dinner at the Rise household was a somber affair on the night before the Dome tournament. Kirin sat between her parents, who remained relatively silent before the meal. Both of Kirin's parents, Kevin and Diane, had again refused to watch their daughter's match. Her brothers were restricted from the dining area as her mom and dad wanted to speak with Kirin alone.

Diane looked at her daughter, who refused to make eye contact. She knew that this was a struggle for Kirin as well. As a mother, this wasn't about proving who was right or wrong, but finding a middle ground, which she knew was impossible. So even though the pain ran deep, her thoughts were still on her daughter's feelings. With a tender voice, she spoke. "Kirin, I think I know you well enough to know that, no matter what I say, you're still going to go through with the fight tomorrow."

Kirin knew this was difficult for her parents. She tried to keep the moment as painless as she could. Kirin mumbled, "I'm sorry, Mom," knowing that nothing she could say would alleviate the pain her mom was feeling.

"Your father and I have been talking, and I'm asking you for one thing. I pray for your safety, but I'm more concerned I'm going to lose you."

Kirin looked up, "You're not going to lose me, Mom," but her voice lacked confidence.

Diane shook her head and stared down at her daughter. "It's not that kind of loss, sweetie."

Kyle shouted from the other room, breaking their conversation. "Are you done yet? I'm starving!"

Diane shouted out, "One more word from you, Kyle, and you won't eat all week!" All three of them waited and sat silently for a moment.

Kevin broke the silence as Kirin continued to avoid any eye contact with her parents. "Your mother and I know that your past will always haunt you. We've tried everything we could, to the best of our abilities, to help you. But, I think we've come to realize that the driving force cannot be quenched by logic or reason."

Kirin looked up with watery eyes, "Dad…."

Kevin replied, "I want you to hear what your mom is about to say." He signaled to Diane.

She placed her hand on Kirin's. It was a warm touch, and she could feel Kirin shivering. She held it tightly, trying to soothe her daughter's nerves. "I've heard about your fights that you've done recently to get to the championship. You're driven, unlike anyone I've ever seen before. I want you to remember that, at the end of all this, if you go beyond yourself … it's not going to bring you happiness or resolve. You may feel like you're willing to do whatever it takes to win, but if you destroy what you hate the most, you won't like what you'll become." Diane's voice trembled as she got on her knees and laid her head on Kirin's lap. She sobbed as any concerned mother would over her daughter.

Kirin brushed her mom's hair and kissed her on the top of her head. Her dad put his hand on Kirin's shoulder as she looked up to him, and he shed a tear. She leaned forward and whispered into her mom's ear, "Mom … I love you. Promise me that, no matter what happens tomorrow, you'll try your best to understand. I know I'm asking a lot from you, but whatever you see or hear tomorrow…." Her mom sobbed on her leg as Kirin squeezed her hard, trying to comfort her.

Forgive me, she thought. *Forgive me.*

The night that all fans had been waiting for was finally here. The two weeks of the round robin tournament had gone exactly as everyone had expected as both Kirin and Ripley had been dominant in their matches. Each elimination brought the possibility of this final battle closer to fruition. The ratings were astronomical and continued to break records after each match. Tonight, the world would stand still. Even those few who were not UFMF fans were drawn to tonight's match—it was the biggest spectacle of the year. Beyond the already extraordinary hype, this historic event for the UFMF's Dome Championship would be featuring two female fighters for the first time in history.

Fans were divided on who they wanted to win, while the experts were busy trying to offer their opinions on who would come out victorious. Both Ripley and Kirin were extremely active after their matches. They gave interviews and went on talk shows to hype the event. Not a second went by that they weren't on some media format.

For Kirin, that display was over tonight. She had already entered the arena and remained extremely low-key. No one was allowed in her dressing room area as guards were on high alert. Even the cameras that normally caught the fighters prior to their matches were denied by Kirin's camp.

Fortunately for the UFMF, Ripley was more than happy to hog the spotlight in Kirin's absence. The camera was on her as she was just warming up and preparing for the biggest night of her life.

Megan Mahoney was in Ripley's dressing area, trying to get a few last words before the match. "Ripley, how are you feeling before this big match?"

Ripley gave her signature smirk to the camera. "Megan, I'm actually feeling really good and confident about tonight. I know this is the biggest match of my career, but I prepared for this the same way I did for all my other matches."

"Do you find it strange that this fight is kind of being promoted as the friends-to-enemies battle as well as the battle of the blondes?"

Ripley shook her head. "I really have no comment about that…. That's what you guys have been pushing—or maybe it's the fans. All I can say is that people change, and I'm fine with that. If Kirin Rise wants to make this a blood match, then I'm more than prepared to give her exactly what she wants. Oh … and by the way, I'm really blonde."

Megan was surprised by Ripley's comment and looked into the camera. She turned toward her and asked, "What do you think is your opponent's biggest weakness?"

"It's hard to say. If I had to take a guess, it might be her overconfidence. For the last two weeks, she's been shooting her mouth off, but the day of the fight, she's become camera shy, if not totally silent … kinda strange, if you ask me."

Ripley's trainer cut in, "Sorry, Megan, the match is about to start soon. We need to get Whiskey ready."

Megan looked back into the camera. "Okay, good luck, Ripley. That was our final comment from Ripley Hawkins prior to the match. Stabler, I'm sending it back to you and the crew."

The panel spent the remaining time talking about all possible outcomes of the fight with each announcer offering some final input. The decision was split amongst the panel, as each made a convincing argument. At the end, they all agreed that it could go either way and only the fight itself would determine the outcome.

Stabler said, "We are now about to begin the introduction of the fighters. They did a coin toss earlier, and it will be Ripley Hawkins walking in first, followed by Kirin Rise."

"Some facts and tidbits while we wait for that moment," Connor broke in. "Well, I'm not the expert on fashion by any means, but Ripley will be sporting a pink fighter's outfit with black highlights created by the famous designer Jacklyn McQueen. While on the outside it sports a simplistic look, if you can zoom in with the camera, the custom hand-stitching took over three months to finish."

Linkwater added, "I'm sure our viewers might be wondering why her outfit is such a big deal. If you haven't been paying attention—or if you're like Connor and fashion's not your thing— whatever Ripley wears has been selling out immediately. Ripley also stated that, after the match, her fighter's robe will be given up for auction, and 100% of the proceeds will be donated to charity."

Krenzel said, "Any last thoughts? Besides fashion, I mean." He spared a glance for his colleagues.

Stabler replied, "Did you see the look in her eye? I know she said she's not taking any comments from Kirin personally, but she looked determined to make a statement tonight. To make a mark in history."

Instead of responding, Linkwater said, "I think this is it. We're about to begin...."

Brock the announcer became the main focus as the camera and the crowds awaited. The lights were on him, and beads of sweat glistened on top of his brow. His distinguished voice bellowed out, "Ladies and gentlemen, tonight we are gathered here in New York City from all corners of the globe for a very special event. This battle is a long time coming as the UFMF is proud to present the 2034 Dome Championship...." He trailed off and remained quiet for a few minutes as the crowd in the arena roared, drowning out his voice.

Brock began spouting some stats about Ripley and then added, "The most dominant fighter of this season, going undefeated in her rookie year. She is beautiful and glamorous, but most importantly she is a deadly blonde with a killer fist. I present to you Ripley Hawkins aka … Whiskey!"

The spotlight flashed toward the main entrance, and the music blared. The crowd seemed hypnotized as they roared in unison to greet their gladiator. Whiskey gave her signature pose at the beginning of her walk down the aisle, and the hearts of many fans melted when she began to strut her stuff. Several bodyguards surrounded her so no one could get near, but she flaunted her God-given assets openly to all rather than wearing a robe like other fighters.

Her team reached the center of the circle where she and Kirin would do battle. Ripley loved the attention and didn't want to share it. This felt like home for her, and she wanted more. She began jumping up and down, shaking her head from side to side. She was ready to finish the fight they had begun several years ago. Ripley closed her eyes for a moment, remembering the past. She could see herself once again at the theme park as chaos surrounded her and Kirin as they stood opposite each other, ready to do battle. This time, their fight wasn't for the deed to the school which Kirin wanted so badly, but something greater. It was Ripley who was longing now, wanting to take the spotlight from Kirin. She knew what was at stake. Kirin was the only thing standing in her way to complete fame and fortune. Ripley snapped out of her trance and opened her eyes, waiting to see her opponent once again.

Receiving a signal to introduce the next fighter, Brock said, "Two years ago, she shocked the world and became the first ever female Dome Champion. Last year, she fell just short of obtaining back-to-back victories when an unknown rose from the ranks of the Battle Royale and stole it from her. She has returned this season by winning the Battle Royale in dominating fashion, and she has been steamrolling her way through the tournament for this very moment.

Ready to claim victory once again, I give you the fighter who needs no introduction. Lend me your ears and give me a hand for the reason everyone wants to fight like a girl ... Kirin Rise!"

Kirin stuck to the same theme from her two previous championship fights. The gang was all there, dressed in their modified hanbok that Gwen had newly designed. They carried a banner with a new message waving high in the air. It read, 'Always B U.' A cheesy eighties song that Sifu used to listen to supplied them their beat. This time, however, each one of them kept their hoodies on, not revealing their faces. Kirin was at the very end of the line, waving as fans yelled out her name. She had remained hidden from the cameras up until now, and this was the first glance that anyone could get of her.

Stabler said, "At the beginning of the season, I don't believe anyone could've predicted this was going to be the main fight." He glanced over at Grand Master Cheng, who didn't make eye contact and looked away.

Linkwater said, "There's a ton of mystery involved with tonight's fight. We still have no idea why Kirin has so much animosity toward Ripley. It's like she's been waiting for this night for payback ... but why, no one knows."

Kirin entered the circle as both camps kept their distance. Ripley got into position while the referee prepared to tell both fighters about the rules. The gang cleared space for Kirin as she made her way toward Ripley. Her hoodie remained in place, letting the crowd get only a glimpse of her golden locks. Both fighters stood inches apart from one another. Ripley tried to stare her down, but Kirin wouldn't bite. She stared at the ground, refusing to make eye contact. Then Ripley took a whiff and made a strange face. She got even closer to Kirin, who was still avoiding eye contact, and smelled again.

Ripley said, "What's going on here?"

Kirin offered no response as the referee asked Ripley if she understood the rules.

Ripley ignored him, "You don't wear perfume. Ever!" She squatted down, trying to get a peek at Kirin from below. Her frustration mounted, and she snatched Kirin's hoodie from atop her head.

Ripley yelled, "What the hell! What in god's name is going on here?"

There she was, in full glory—the exact likeness of Kirin, but not Kirin at all. Ripley reached over and grabbed her by the robe and pulled her in. She yelled, "Explain!" and tossed the Kirin lookalike to the ground.

Gavin fell to the floor, holding his hands up to protect himself. He squeaked, "Please don't hurt me! I'm just a little bitty cosplayer. Don't hurt me!"

The cameras focused on Gavin, the Kirin Rise cosplayer who was now on center stage. The rest of the gang pulled off their hoodies, leaving Ripley gaping. Each cosplayer looked like some slightly wrong version of his or her counterpart.

The crowd was confused. The stadium was in shock. No one knew what was going on.

Stabler said, "What the heck is happening? Where's Kirin Rise?"

Krenzel said, "It appears nobody on Team Kirin Rise is who they should be. Especially Kirin."

Connor helpfully added, "I have no idea what's going on."

Ripley began to tremble, and a vein bulged from the side of her head as she clenched both her fists. Ripley, enraged shouted, "Kirin!" at the top of her lungs into the crowd.

#

Thirty Minutes Prior

Zipping through the streets of New York in a stolen van, the entire gang raced toward destiny. Each one was dealing with the tense situation in their own way. Everyone there knew what was at stake, what they were willing to risk and possibly lose. Since Kirin had returned from her training, she had been planning this for weeks. Getting back into the UFMF tournament and winning the Dome Championship was never her goal, but just a piece of the puzzle necessary for her ultimate target: bringing down the UFMF from the inside, once and for all.

Kirin leaned over the side of the driver's seat and grabbed the back of the headrest firmly. Her voice trembled from nerves. "What's ... what's the ETA?"

"About fifteen minutes, sweetie," said April, whose attention was on the radio station instead of the road in front of her.

Danny rocked from side to side on the inside floor of the van. His nerves—and April's driving—were getting to him. "I think I'm going to be sick...." He grabbed a bag on the side and threw up as everyone squirmed away.

April chuckled as she continued to fidget with the radio. "This car is old school. It still has knobs and a cassette deck!" She seemed to be unconcerned with their current plight. She took a peek in the rearview mirror and shouted, "Don't be such a baby, Danny. I told you guys I'd get you there in one piece."

Hunter, who sat on the floor of the van, raised his hand, "Umm, is that in one piece or many pieces?" He checked for a seatbelt and sighed. Discouraged by the realization that there were none, he said to April, "Couldn't you have stolen a better van?"

April replied, "I liked this one. It spoke to me."

Hunter mumbled, "You sure that's not the voices in your head?"

"What was that?"

"Uh, nothing," Hunter stammered hastily. "I said how did it speak to you?"

April said, "To be honest, it was the license plate. It read, 'mel mel.'"

Tobias sat in the passenger seat next to April. Even he was fearful of how she was driving, and he was lucky enough to have a seatbelt. "Is there a reason you're driving down the street like it's an asteroid field?"

"That's because she's driving like it's through an asteroid field." Gwen's fingers were clenched firmly onto her wheelchair, and she'd made sure its wheels were locked in place.

Kirin said, "Aren't you supposed to be less suspicious? You're kinda driving like a maniac."

"So, how should I be driving?"

Kirin thought for a second as the question confused her. "I don't know," she admitted. "Drive … casual."

Sage caught the movie comment but decided to enjoy the moment to himself.

"I'm driving in New York City. I'm pretty sure this is the norm. Besides, I'm making good time." April rolled down the window and stuck her hand out, flipping off another driver before she honked several times.

Kirin rubbed the bridge of her nose and shook her head.

"Obviously you are, at this speed…." Doc checked his watch.

Ken, who was standing up holding onto a grip attached to the van, asked, "How fast is she going?"

April caught wind of the comment and turned around to look at Sage, who couldn't resist the opportunity. They both smiled and said in sync, "Twelve parsecs?" She turned around and double high-fived Sage.

Kirin shouted, "Hands on the wheel!" She gave Sage the look.

Doc replied, "You know, that's not really a unit of time, but distance."

April swerved hard right, which jarred Doc as he hit the side of the van. "Ouch," he muttered as he rubbed his shoulder.

April said, "Thank you, Professor Killjoy."

Kirin shouted, "Good lord, will you keep your eye on the road? I swear you've spent more time looking for a song than you have looking straight ahead."

April replied, "I'm looking for 'Let's Go Crazy.'"

Kirin said, "How about … let's not go crazy?"

April replied, "Kirin, can you fight blindfolded?"

Surprised by the question, Kirin hesitated before answering, "Uh, yes, but what does that have to—"

"And yet you don't hear me bitching to you when you do that." April made another hard turn just to switch lanes.

Kirin rolled her eyes. She was starting to second-guess their decision to bring April. But, if Sifu had trusted her, then Kirin knew there was a purpose behind it.

Tobias said, "If she goes any faster, we're going to get a speeding ticket."

That comment got April's attention, and she turned to Tobias. "Really? Really! You're worried about a speeding ticket? We're all about to break into the UFMF headquarters, hack their computers, and dump all their information to the public. And you're worried about a speeding ticket. I repeat … really?"

Tobias looked at April. "Well, to be honest, I've never gotten a speeding ticket before."

All eyes turned to Tobias. The gang looked surprised and expectant, as if they needed some kind of explanation.

Big T broke the silence, "The bad boy of our group is an angel on the road."

"Hey, I didn't say that. All I'm saying is my record is clean," Tobias protested.

Danny replied, "Kinda like how your karma is clean."

Tobias gave Danny a look but didn't respond.

Kirin said to April, "Just a reminder: We've got two other vans behind us ... which happen to hold the rest of the team. Can we not lose them?"

April tapped her communicator, which was on the left side of her chest. "Team Eskrimadors and Team Bokken, you guys still behind us?"

A few seconds later, a response came through her communicator.

Freddie, the leader from Team Eskrimadors, said, "We're good."

Trevor, the leader from Team Bokken, said, "Right behind ya."

April replied, "Copy that." She glanced back at Kirin and slammed on the gas pedal, which cause Kirin and everyone else to jerk backward.

Freddie's voice came through the communicator again. "By the way, you're kinda driving like you're in an aster—"

"Sorry, bad connection." April tapped her communicator and hung up.

Always the voice of reason, Doc said, "I know everyone is feeling the tension, and while these conversations are enlightening ... to say the least ... don't you think we should go over the plans and double check all our gear and equipment?"

Robert pulled out a smoke, "Knock yourself out."

Ryan said, "Wait, you're gonna smoke in a van full of people? That's why you're King Dick, and I'm not talking about size either."

Robert replied, "Hey, man ... let's be real about this. What we're doing is no walk in the park. Even if we can prove them wrong, the burden falls upon us." He lit his cigarette and enjoyed his drag. "For all we know, tomorrow, I'm in a jail cell with a guy named Bubba, hoping he doesn't find my K-pop ass cute and that there's enough lube to go around."

"Might as well enjoy our last hurrah," Ken agreed. "If nothing else, we're in for one hell of a night." He lowered his window to let out the smoke. Ken reached out his hand, gesturing to Robert. "Can I bum a smoke?"

Robert looked at him. "You sure?"

"If tonight's gonna be my last, I can at least scratch this off the bucket list." Robert handed him the cigarette and lit it for Ken.

Big T turned to Danny, hoping to set up some bets, but Danny was slumped over looking nauseated.

Lance had remained silent the entire time, examining the action of his team as he stood in the back. He had done this before, the real thing, and he'd lost men as well as his leg in the process. His experience was invaluable for helping organize this mission. He cleared his throat and spoke. His raspy voice brought a calmness to all those there. "Listen up, everyone. I'm no speaker, so bear with me as I try my best. First, let me say I've never been more proud working with a group of guys and gals than I am right now. If Sifu were here...." It was rare to see emotion from Lance, but he choked up for a second and then regained his composure. "Umm, if Sifu were here, I'm sure he'd say ... 'not bad, not bad.'" He got a chuckle from those in the van; for a brief moment, Sifu's spirit seemed to be there with them.

"For the first time, I'm about to embark on a mission that's being done for the right reason. I'm not doing this because my government said so under the guise of freedom or protection, when it was really just for the corporations and their greed. Everyone here knows what we're about to do. We know the UFMF is plain wrong and evil ... and when good people such as you and I do nothing, how can we pass judgement on anyone else? Because of what we know, we bear the burden. We may be labeled as rebels or even terrorists, but I believe deep down that our fight goes way deeper. I believe that, for every man, woman, and child on this living planet, we carry the last hope for this and future generations. It'll be up to us to bring balance back to those who desperately need it. One day, they will look back and realize the impact we're about to have in history. Who knows? Maybe they'll write stories about us." He banged the side of the van several times. "Alright, everyone, let's make sure our watches are in sync. Check your gear one last time, and we'll go over the general plan."

April shouted, "ETA … twenty minutes!"

Kirin looked at everyone inside the van. She knew that these twelve brave souls were about to make a mark on the course of history. Very few out there actually back their talk, since that would involve them sacrificing something … something they were never willing to risk. But, these were her friends, who stood by her side and rose when she needed them. She closed her eyes, hoping for the best.

The gang all got together to check their equipment and watches to make sure they were in sync. Tobias leaned over to check on April. In disbelief, he said, "We need to be perfectly in sync with one another, and you have a Hello Kitty watch!"

April just laughed. "You guys didn't specify what kind we needed. It's digital down to the seconds. Besides, this is a lot more fashionable, don't you think?" Everyone was wondering how April could be so relaxed. Tobias looked at Kirin, who simply shrugged her shoulders.

Tobias replied, "You know—" His head snapped back, preventing him from finishing his sentence. He rubbed his neck and looked at April.

"We're here!" The car halted, jarring all the people inside. "I just parked along the side about a hundred yards away with the rest of these cars … and see, all in one piece, as promised." She wiped her hands at a job well done.

Danny threw up again. Everyone kept their distance, except Big T, who patted him on the back and made sure he was okay.

Lance shook his head and began barking out orders. "April, kill the engine. Sage, engage the main communicator so that Teams Eskrimadors and Bokken can hear and see everything that's going on. Tell them to keep distance between the vans. Everyone gather around."

April turned off the van as the gang assembled, forming a circle and leaving a space in the center. All eyes were on Lance, who made eye contact with each and every one. He paused when he looked at Ryan.

Ryan asked, "What?"

"I get that Gwen was kind enough to create customized outfits for everyone, but this is your fashion of choice?" His comment directed the gang's attention to Ryan, who was dressed in black with multi-colored stripes like some kind of Japanese anime sword fighter.

"Hey, it's comfortable! Besides, look at Kirin … she's got the same red hoodie, jeans, and Cons on. That's lack of imagination."

Kirin looked at Ryan, "It's not the same." Hanging from the side was a scarf attached to her hoodie. She flung it around, and it partially covered her face.

Ryan nodded in approval, "My bad. Digging the assassin look you're sporting."

Robert added, "Problem is everyone will know that it's her."

Sage interrupted their conversation and gave him a thumbs up as the remaining teams in the other vans confirmed that communication was a go.

Lance said, "We all here?"

"Team Eskrimadors present."

"Team Bokken here as well."

Lance nodded, "All right, as you all are aware, we picked tonight because this is our best opportunity to break into the UFMF. All eyes will be on the fight that's not going to happen, and there will be a search for Kirin afterward. So, that buys us some time to do what we need to do. The UFMF building is a state-of-the-art facility. It's the testing ground for all new technology within the UFMF. However, it's what's buried inside the heart of this building that requires our full attention. The main facility is known as the Cube, rightfully so because of its shape, but this small section could literally be shut off from the rest of the world and be self-sustaining. It can create its own energy, it has its own communication, and they even can grow crops in that son-of-a-bitch place."

Robert interrupted Lance, "The Cube? This state-of-the-art facility, which has all the bells and whistles, and the best name they could come up with is the Cube?"

Ryan said, "If our adventure tonight ever becomes a book or movie, calling it 'The Cube' is just some bad writing. Everyone watching would just be like, 'Lazy, stupid writer, couldn't come up with anything better.'"

Lance cleared his throat, wanting full attention again. "Anyway, entry into the Cube begins at the sixty-sixth floor. It's built like a nuclear bunker. It could take a blast and keep on smiling. Fortunately, due to the Dome Championship, security will be at its lightest. At the very least, they'll be distracted like everyone else should be tonight."

Ken said, "So, what's the goal?"

Lance pointed to Gwen, who reached into her specialized wheelchair, which was decked out from top to bottom. With Big T's help, she had constructed a new wheelchair that was literally a portable communication center on wheels. Everything she needed for tonight was in there, financed with the credits Sifu had given to Kirin—which had also helped to buy everything else the team needed for this operation. A few seconds later, she used an item in her hand to flash a holographic projection on the ground. The image of a building began to appear from the ground up, illuminating the entire van inside.

Gwen clicked her communicator and said, "Teams Eskrimadors and Bokken, are you seeing all this?"

Team Eskrimadors replied, "It's all clear."

Team Bokken said, "Crystal."

Gwen said, "Good ... what you see before you is the UFMF headquarters. As Lance mentioned earlier, it's built like a fort ... correction, the Cube is built like a fort. The rest of the building stands a hundred floors high. Each floor is roughly the size of a football field, and the very top is uniquely shaped as a triangle. The sixty-sixth floor is the only access point for the Cube. Thus, getting into it will be the first obstacle. Only those with authorized security have ever ventured into that area. From what we've deciphered from Sifu's information, there are three levels. The first will be the server room. It's massive like everything else inside the UFMF building. You'll see row after row of diamond-shaped servers suspended off the floor." The image changed and highlighted the floor plan Gwen had described.

Gwen continued, "Team Eskrimadors, pay close attention. Once we're in, you're gonna have to set up our neural network grid." On the screen, a ball appeared, circling around so that one could see from every angle.

Ryan chuckled. "It looks like a Pokémon ball."

Gwen chuckled and corrected him, explaining "It's a neural network drone, to be exact. There are a hundred of them for each team, with several spares just in case. Team Eskrimadors, you'll need to launch all one hundred of these drones. They'll automatically scan the area and create a grid formation. You see, it's one thing to access the UFMF computers, but if they see any unusual activity, like me just randomly downloading petabytes of information, they'll assume some form of unauthorized usage. These neural drones will hover over a grid of servers, making it seem like only one server is being accessed as opposed to, say, fifty of them. Thus, depending on which server I need to work with, you'll be responsible for their positioning."

Lance said, "Explain what else they can do, Gwen."

"They'll be a visible cloud for us. Our communicators won't work inside the Cube. The UFMF will realize our presence is unauthorized and automatically jam our signal. But, we'll be setting up these three grids on each floor so we can communicate with one another. As long as we are physically underneath the grids, regardless of obstruction, we can us these to communicate. You got that, Eskrimadors?"

Freddie with Team Eskrimadors said, "Sounds like it should go without a hiccup. All fifteen of my guys and gals are up for this. Aren't we, Eskrimadors?" In the background, Kirin's gang could hear them clashing their sticks together.

Gwen continued with the plan. "Okay, Team Bokken, you're on floor two, where the power grid is located. Once I hack the main computers, you'll need to physically reset the power so we can reboot this baby so that the changes will take effect. Without this boot up, we're screwed. Do you understand?"

Trevor from Team Bokken replied, "All twelve of us here are up for the challenge." Then Team Bokken shouted in Japanese, "*Kakatte Koi yo.*"

Gwen said, "Perfect. I'm sure you guys will do great. Finally, it's Team 6.5. That's you guys," she added as she looked at everyone in her van. "The third floor isn't so straightforward. It's broken down into two sections. The first section will be the research facility. I have no idea what this will look like, since it was the one thing from Sifu's info that was vague. We need to make our way through that quickly, and then we'll finally see the command center. Team 6.5, Lance will be your lead, and Doc will oversee the tech details, but you're going to have to locate where exactly they make the drug SSP761 By the way, that's the holy grail. This is supposedly the enhanced version of the drug that Diesel used when he fought Kirin. Remember we can't just fabricate a video. We need actual physical evidence they have such a thing. Tobias, Hunter, April, Sage, and Kirin will be with me. I'll have the two biggest nerds with computers helping me out while I'm busy hacking away."

Sage said, "Hey!"

Gwen replied, "I'm sorry. My very cute boyfriend and Lead Foot over there."

April started snorting out a laugh as everyone was watching.

"Now, three floors don't seem like much, but we're only thirty strong. It's going to take some time to get through the facility, and time is not on our side."

Doc said, "So, once we break in at the ground level, I'm assuming the alarm sounds, and it's on total lockdown."

Gwen said, "That's correct, Doc. Any incident in the building will have it on complete lockdown. That means, from the ground up, no one can get in or out of the entire building for two hours."

Ken said, "Two hours?"

Gwen replied, "That's a set default of two hours for the outside perimeter of the building, but inside it's fully controlled by whoever has access to the command center. Hopefully, that'll be me."

Big T asked, "So, how do we bypass all these lockdowns? I mean, we get to floor sixty-six and then what?"

Gwen held up a little thumb drive and said, "This is what Sifu did for us. Through Watanabe's son, who happened to be involved with the early setup of the place, before he went bonkers ... long story, no time to tell ... we were able to decipher a back-door entry into the entire system that no one even knows exists. Usually, a creator of any system allows for this kind of fail-safe."

Ryan was calculating things out in his head, "Sixty-six floors? Uh, by elevator, right?"

Gwen shook her head. "Hey, Slim, looks like you're working on your cardio tonight."

Ryan gawked, "Oh my god. You're kidding, right? With all the stuff we have, you want us to trek sixty-six floors? Why can't this be done remotely?"

Gwen said, "That's what makes this so difficult to hack. Like I said, anything can be hacked. However, any outside source trying to even take a peek into the facility is immediately chopped off. I have to literally be inside that room to hack and take over the computers. Don't you think I would've done this already if I could do it from a distance?"

Ryan raised his bags, "Luckily, I came prepared. I packed us some snacks." He shifted items in his bag to make sure he was all set. He took pride in his preparation.

Everyone looked at Ryan as Robert said, "This isn't a fricking camping trip. Did you bring some goddamn s'mores?"

"This requires energy! Food is energy. Just remember to thank me when you find yourself starving or lacking in sustenance."

Robert poked him in the stomach, "I'll be thanking you from the sixty-sixty floor while you'll still be on the twenty-ninth."

Tobias looked to Gwen, "Walk us through once we get to the main entrance…. I'm figuring whatever security they have in place will have to be dealt with."

Gwen nodded, "Well it's twofold. I'll hack us into the entrance, and the other security is up to you guys. I'm sure we'll be meeting some form of physical resistance with the number of guards they have up there."

Big T said, "Fortunately for us, the UFMF is a stickler for following their own laws, 'cause guns be trouble, if you know what I mean."

Gwen said, "It's not going to be that simple, and it's not just hand to hand, Big T. You see, they don't have guns, but they are armed with this."

Gwen clicked a button, and the projection changed from the building to a picture of a glove. It began spinning in all directions as the gang examined it.

Ryan said, "It's a glove. What are they gonna do, slap us?"

Big T added, "Looks more like a gauntlet."

"This glove or gauntlet will slap you with about 50,000 volts if it touches your ass, and I can guarantee you that every single guard is going to have one."

Ryan thought about it. "That'd be kinda useful with the s'mores."

Robert looked confused. "Wait … you really did pack s'mores?"

"I told you I was prepared, but I only brought enough for one each."

Kirin said, "Focus."

Doc agreed, "Can we focus and get back to the glove-slash-gauntlet that'll deep fry our asses?"

Gwen said, "I've asked Tobias to bring your counters, and now you know the reason we're called Team 6.5."

Tobias scooted his way through the van to a long duffle bag on the floor. He yanked on the zipper and began to unravel it, pulling an item out. "Here, we have our counters … six-and-a-half-foot white wax poles. We've all trained with these before. They're smaller than the real poles, but that'll give us room to maneuver. Team Eskrimadors, you've got your *escrimas* or sticks, and Team Bokken, you're armed with your wooden swords."

Robert rolled his eyes, "So, they've got gloves from the future that can fry us while we've got primitive weapons to counter them like cavemen."

Gwen let out a chuckle, "Makes for a more interesting battle, don't you think?"

Tobias interrupted Gwen and said, "You brought that insurance policy I told you to put in your chair, right?"

Gwen nodded.

Kirin asked, "Brought what?"

Gwen muttered, "It's not important."

When Kirin looked at her best friend, Gwen whispered, "Trust me."

Tobias gestured to the building, "Okay, we get into the main area, and we deal with the resistance with…?"

Sage said, "Friendly negotiations."

Tobias replied, "Can't you at least quote good movies?"

Sage smiled at his own taste, "I'll go to my grave saying that the prequels were better than the new ones."

Tobias gave a glum look, "Well, let's hope that doesn't happen tonight."

Frowning, Sage looked concerned, realizing that possibility did exist. "Agreed."

Lance jumped in. "That's where your fighting skills really come in. You guys can't have a kill mentality. I know it goes against everything that you've been taught, but we can't prove the UFMF guilty if we leave a trail of dead bodies. So, hit so we can bind them and not bury them. We clear on that?"

Team Eskrimadors replied, "Copy that."

Team Bokken said, "Roger that."

Ken barked out, "Boo-yah."

Lance looked at him funny, "It's ooh-rah."

Ken muttered, "Yeah … yeah, I know. I got a slight cold. That makes me sound nasally…. Uh, anyway, how do we know how many people we have to deal with?"

Gwen shook her head, "We don't. Not until we make it to the sixty-sixth floor. The terminals within the Cube will give me low-level access. Everyone who works at the UFMF has built-in trackers. I can scan through the entire building and pinpoint their location, and with that we should have a total head count. But, remember: the goal is the command center. That will give me full access to the good stuff."

Sage said, "You said earlier we have two hours. What happens if it takes longer to find what we need and broadcast it out?"

Lance said, "Let's go by the worst-case scenario. We know the entire building goes full lockdown for two hours. During that initial time when we try to take over the building, they'll be calling everyone from the police to the STDs. Once they're involved, the police are no big deal. It's the STDs with the guns that could be cause for concern."

Big T said, "How are we going to deal with them once they get in?"

Lance looked to Gwen, "Hopefully, by that time, you'll be in the command center. You can control who comes in or out of the Cube. If that doesn't happen, then we could be toast."

"Simple breakdown: command center within two hours. We need proof of SSP761. Play Kirin's message and broadcast the proof to the world." Instructed Gwen.

Lance said, "We all clear on that? Once we have access to the command center, we need to play the chosen one's message right away."

Kirin shook her head in embarrassment. "Please don't call me that, Lance."

"Sorry, I thought it was appropriate."

Tobias nodded in agreement. He asked, "You said earlier a reboot is necessary?"

"If Gwen does her job, then a reboot is needed for it to take effect." Lance confirmed.

Gwen scoffed, "If? Thanks, Lance, you are correct. *When* I have full control of the main computer, we'll have to force a reboot for the changes to take full effect."

Kirin said, "Seriously, all this state-of-the-art, and you still need a reboot?"

"Yes, so Team Bokken's job is pivotal because I can hack it, but we need that reboot."

Kirin wanted a better explanation, "Are they gonna just pull a giant plug?"

Doc replied, "It's a bit more complicated than that, but Gwen should be able to access the schematics and guide them through the process."

"Not to be a stick in the mud, but can we go over our escape route? I hear prison year-round isn't a place we want to visit." Said Hunter.

Doc asked, "I'm with Hunter on this. This is definitely up for discussion. If we can broadcast the truth to the people from around the world and solidify the proof, then how do we get out without landing in jail and not collecting $200 for passing go?"

Lance said, "As we stated, Kirin's message has to go out, and if history is any indication … the masses will gather right outside the UFMF building. Once we have them gathered, they should slow down the police and the STDs, and hopefully we can use those numbers to get lost in the crowd."

"By the way, all these outfits you created for us, Gwen … you outdid yourself." Kirin smiled with gratitude.

"I do like the personal touch. At least if we go down, we go down in style." Robert struck a pose.

Sage grinned ear to ear with pride, "Only my girlfriend is capable of outfitting all of us with some form of mask and still making them fashionable."

Danny said, "That's all fine and dandy, but raise your hand if you think skydiving off a building like I originally suggested makes more sense?"

Hunter raised his hand. "I'm with Danny. Jumping off a building is definitely the dumbest option he's ever come up with."

Danny crossed his arms and sulked like a child in the corner.

Lance replied, "I've calculated our way out. This is the safest way for us to escape. Afterward, we all meet back at our rendezvous point where we all stay low until the dust settles. Okay, that's it for me … any last words?"

Always the group leader, Tobias stepped forward and extended his hand out. One by one, everyone joined him as one hand was placed on top of the other. He waited for the circle to be fully complete and said, "The hours, the years, the sweat and tears … if you ever wondered why we trained our entire lives, it's for the skill we have to be used at this very moment. Leave it all on the line, give me everything you got … and whatever happens, whatever it takes, when it's all said and done, I want you to be able to look yourself in the mirror—"

Kirin cut in and whispered, "No regrets."

Tobias locked onto Kirin's eyes, and this time she said it louder. "No regrets!"

Tobias nodded and silently agreed. Giving a moment for her words to sink in, he looked into the eyes of everyone there. He said, "One, two, three … no regrets."

"No regrets!"

For the next ten minutes, the group finalized the plan. April was driving again and circling near the UFMF building. The radio was on the UFMF station, which was broadcasting the announcement of the fighters. It was nearly time.

#

As they approached the building April turned around in her seat. She asked, "I know you've been game planning this entire thing, but you're gonna try sneaking in and not be direct? I've listened to how we get into the main building, and there's a chance we may not all get inside in the first place."

Gwen said, "Yes, I mapped it all out. There's no such thing as foolproof, April."

April narrowed her eyes. "Let me be clear on this, just for my own sake. Once it goes on full lockdown, you can still hack your way through to the command center area, right?"

Gwen looked cautiously at April. "Uh, yes, why?"

April looked slyly at Gwen. "Change of plans." She slammed on the gas and started charging toward the front of the building entrance. Everyone was caught off-guard as they staggered to get their grip. April tapped her communicator and said, "Team Eskrimadors and Team Bokken, wait for my signal before you follow in."

Gwen shouted, "What are you doing?"

"Punching it," said April as her grip tightened on the steering wheel. She was determined to drive the van straight through the glass entrance of the UFMF building.

Sage growled. "Whhrraaagh!"

Crash.

Their van cracked through the glass, shattering it into thousands of pieces. There were only four security guards in the main lobby, and they fell off their seats in shock. Immediately, alarms automatically sounded as confusion descended. The radio broadcasted a similar chaos as everyone was wondering where Kirin Rise could be.

Gwen shouted, "Are you insane?"

April raised her hands up, "Look, I got you inside and just bypassed the several steps that you were going to take that were totally unnecessary."

"Weeks preparing for this!" shouted Gwen. "Weeks!" She turned around and asked, "Is everyone okay?"

April argued. "The way I see it. A group that sticks exactly to a plan never, ever succeeds. So, by taking the initiative and changing the plan, I've just ensured a higher chance of success."

Gwen looked confused. "What are you smoking?"

"What the hell...?" Tobias muttered, still shaken up from the crash. "How old is this car? There's not even airbags in it!" Tobias's voice trailed off as he noticed movement on his side of the van.

Kirin leaned toward him and saw the security guards scrambling their way. "Heads up … security's coming!" She turned to the driver's side and realized April was no longer there. "What the…?"

April was already outside, waving her hands and screaming, "My bad … my bad! Lost control of the car when I heard Kirin Rise is missing. Can you believe that?"

The guards actually stopped charging in. They empathized with her plight, and their mood toned down as they began a conversation with April.

April said, "Where the heck could Kirin Rise be?" She acted faint, spinning slowly in a circle. The guards surrounded her and lowered her gently to the ground.

Lying there, she murmured, "I'm sorry about your window."

One of the guards said, "It's okay, ma'am. We'll contact the ambulance."

The other guard replied, "Chuck, it's protocol to immediately set us to lockdown; besides, if we don't do anything, we've only got a minute to override it."

He answered, "You want to deal with someone who's injured for the next two hours? Besides, look at her shirt!" Everyone looked down and saw she was wearing a shirt with a picture of a huge heart and the UFMF logo on it.

April grabbed hold of the collar of one of the guards and asked, "Where's Kirin Rise? Do you know? Do ya? Kirin…?"

One of the guards held her hand and said, "We all just heard it now. Everyone's looking for her. It'll be okay."

April whispered, "I think I know…."

"Know what, ma'am?"

"I think I know where Kirin Rise is…."

The guard asked, "Where could she be?" All the other guards were staring at her, wondering if she really had the answer.

She waved them in closer, and they leaned over as she looked kindly into each of their eyes. "I think … I think she's right there."

The guards looked toward the van as the door sprang open. Kirin stood there, shocking all of them as the rest of the gang charged out. April hit her communicator, "Team E and B move in."

Within a minute, the four guards were easily subdued, and Teams Eskrimadors and Bokken drove their vans in. Suddenly, the entire lower lobby began sealing itself from the outside. It caught everyone's attention as a massive titanium wall covered the broken area and then secured the lower lobby shut.

April was still on the floor, watching the events unfold. "Well, that's impressive. Most impressive."

Kirin looked at Tobias, "Why the delay before it secured the lower level?"

Lance replied, "Probably because of the guards. While they didn't sound the alarm, it's common to report back to their post on a timed interval. I'm assuming since they didn't check back in, it automatically locked down afterward."

Kirin walked over to April and extended her hand. She was still lying on the ground, almost as if she were relaxing and enjoying the moment. April grabbed Kirin's hand and stood. "I guess that worked?"

April said, "Of course it did. Shall we…?"

As everyone was preparing for their trek up the stairs, Kirin pulled Tobias aside.

"Hey," said Kirin. She grabbed him by the shirt and pulled him close to her. She stared him directly in the eyes and said, "Don't be reckless." Then she gave him a big hug. Her aggressiveness caught Tobias by surprise. It took him a moment to react before he squeezed her tight.

He mumbled, "You know me."

Kirin nodded against his chest, "I know."

He pulled away and started getting his gear in place. Hunter stood at a distance. Having to watch the affection between the two caused a little tug in his heart. Old feelings still existed, even though Hunter had a girlfriend.

Kirin turned to her close friend and rushed in and squeezed him hard. "I hope Annie doesn't mind this one-time hug. You've always been there for me to back me up. You've done more than enough … so, tonight, play it safe so we all make it out of here." Kirin shed a little tear.

Hunter hugged her back as emotions surfaced from the past. "You be careful, okay?"

Kirin shrugged, "You know me."

Hunter replied, "I know."

The groups stood at the front entrance of the stairs, ready for the long journey up. It was time. Destiny was unavoidable.

> *"People confuse the perfect plan as being the goal, when in fact it's to go with the flow to achieve the goal." —Sifu*

Section 1 Short Stories #11—Kirin's P.O.V.

Escape Room—1 Year, 187 Days

After the incident between me and Tobias, Doc thought a team-building event would help the morale of our group. We had all gathered at the escape room and listened as the host, Gary, gave out the final instructions. The entire gang was there in a circle around the dimly lit room. It was oddly decorated with a desk stuck directly in the middle, several bookshelves hugging the wall, and a corner bathroom stall as part of the props. Old and decrepit was the look they were trying to obtain, and they nailed it.

Gary said, "Any questions about the game? You have one hour from the moment I say the game begins."

Danny raised his hand. "So, if the zombie touches you, you're out of the game, right? Do you get another life?"

"That is a negative," Gary replied. "Keep in mind that, every five minutes, the zombie's chain gets longer, and you'll have less room to maneuver. And, remember this is just a game. You cannot touch the zombie actor at all."

I looked at the female zombie, who was covered in makeup, and then I noticed several eyes on her. Ryan had his love-struck look, while Danny and Big T looked like they were discussing something other than betting. I rolled my eyes at their lack of effort to disguise their intent.

Doc called out, "I just want to be clear: three keys to open the door?"

Gary confirmed, "Yes, you must find three keys to unlock this door. As you can see, it's built like a rock. There's no way to kick this baby down." Gary walked by the door and knocked on it to prove its toughness. He looked at the group one last time and said, "Since we have no more questions … let's begin!"

Tobias took the lead like he always did in every situation. "Guys, split up in groups of three and search the entire room for clues."

"One group has to be a pair," Ryan pointed out.

Doc jumped in, "I'll team with Kirin."

I smiled at Doc, figuring I'd be the brawn to his brains and have to do zero mental work. "Perfect, Doc."

In the past, I'd battled with my gang, and I knew how my team worked. Everyone has certain characteristics in moments of pressure. In the far corner of the room, Ken, Robert, and Ryan were grouped together. Ken was always the hero type. He would put his friends before himself, no matter what the situation. Even though he hated the label, Ken was honestly what one would call a nice guy—certainly nicer than the rest of the group. Robert had an edge about him. He would test the limits of the rules but never quite go past the gray area. I remembered Tobias mentioning to him once that his assholeness would get him in trouble. I chuckled as I glanced away from him to look at Ryan, who was gifted but lazy. It might seem like that combination would not work in the real word, but take any situation and the lazy guy will find the most efficient way to resolve it.

Ten minutes passed, and the zombie's chain extended further. Our group was solving riddles and working together as best as one could expect.

As Doc was busy working on one of the puzzles, I watched my closest friends interact with one another. The fact was I was just pretending to look busy; these puzzle games weren't exactly my strong suit. And, even though this was a game, my mentality was that we should just kill the zombie, problem solved.

Doc asked, "Kirin, any thoughts on this?"

"Doc, I'm terrible with this kind of riddle."

"Fine … just keep an eye out for that zombie if it's getting close."

I did as he said as the zombie was wandering around, being a distraction every now and then. I finally got bored and decided to see if I could possibly help Doc. Several minutes trying to read the riddle over and over again, I said, "I don't get it."

Doc looked at me, "Put some effort into it, Kirin."

"You're the smart one, Doc."

"Uh, Kirin … no one's going to believe you playing the dumb girl role. No one in this room can say they turned down a full scholarship at a prestigious university."

"The fact that I turned it down may be my argument against that…."

A scream from our actor zombie broke my concentration. Tobias had just got bitten—well, not literally.

Tobias shouted at Danny. "You had one job!"

Danny yelled, "It's not my fault!"

Tobias repeated, "One job!"

Big T said, "I'd bet against that."

Danny pointed back at Big T and did not say a word.

Gary said, "You guys have thirty minutes remaining. You're down one member, and you still haven't found one key yet."

So far, this team-building thing isn't going too well.

Doc advised, "Guys, let's shuffle it up a bit. Ryan work with Kirin, Ken with Big T, and Danny and Robert with me."

Robert said, "I know the weak link in this...."

For the next five minutes, we worked with our new groups. The guys began to move faster as our time was running out. Big T made a comment, and the next thing I knew, we had finally figured out where one of the keys was located. Big T might have been our gentle giant, but his handy skills with building had helped solve the first riddle. Big T high-fived Ken and shouted, "The ebony and ivory duo are the first with a key," as he waved around the first key.

Within the next twenty minutes, the team did their best to work with one another. Somehow Ryan and I unearthed the second key. I'd bet on pure luck as opposed to any skill involved. But, during that stage, we lost Big T, Doc, and Ryan to the zombie. I calculated out that we probably had less than five minutes remaining, but I wasn't sure.

"I got it!" Robert shouted, waving the last key.

"Behind you, Robert!"

The zombie lunged forward to tag him as he held the key with pride. I watched from a distance as Ken pushed Robert out of the way and got tagged by the zombie.

Gary called, "You've got one minute before everyone loses."

Robert tossed the key toward Danny, who was standing right by the door, waiting. The key floated through the air as we watched. With only three of us remaining, we might still be able to salvage a win.

480

Danny reached for the key, but it slipped through his fingers. Everyone watched as it bounced several times on the floor and slid underneath the bookshelf. I watched in panic as Robert began to reach for the keys.

Danny looked in shock as Robert shouted, "You had one job!" as he continued to get the key.

Robert began crawling away from the zombie, who had the full extension of her chain to tag everyone.

Danny gulped, "We're gonna die."

The zombie pretended to crawl for us, and it looked like there was no hope of escaping.

Gary said, "You got thirty seconds…. You have to get that last key."

I analyzed the situation. There wasn't enough time even if he got the key. As I stood by the door, the zombie was to my left, coming fast, and my friends were on the right, busy trying to get the last key, which Danny had dropped.

I shook my head and said, "Screw it." I wound up and made sure I aimed at the main part of the door.

Bam!

The door tore free and fell straight down to the ground.

"We're free! Everyone run!"

Gary and the zombie looked at each other in shock as the rest of the gang headed out.

Outside the room, Danny, Robert and I had survived. The three of us gave one another a high-five. I knew what I had done was crazy because this was just a game—but I had to do what I had to do so we could survive.

"Either find a way or make one." —Kirin

Betrayed—1 Year, 201 Days

I was sitting in the corner taking a break from practice. The guys were gathered that night, and the weeks that had passed had smoothed out the relationship between Tobias and me. Everything appeared to have blown over, as time and short memories helped ease the situation. I had already worked out with everyone that night, even Tobias, who appeared like nothing had happened between us. I never asked him, but I didn't believe he'd ever mentioned the incident to the rest of guys.

Everyone was busy with a simple drill that Tobias was overseeing. It was nothing more than testing out our stances, but I continued to listen in, making sure I didn't miss anything. Over the last several months, Tobias had become more creative, as he invented brand new drills to help explain Sifu's teachings.

"Listen up, people ... if there's no questions, I'm gonna switch gears." Tobias waited and received no response from anyone. "Okay, when it comes to attacking, any fool can do that.... The key is control. Unleashing an attack on an enemy beyond what you can handle leaves you vulnerable. So, it's all about securing your motion in the end. How much of it can you back up?"

As I listened, every now and then it felt like his words were directed toward me. The rest of the guys continued to practice as I sat by myself. After Tobias gave the last of his instructions, he strangely planted himself next to me.

We sat silently for only a minute, but it felt like we both wanted to say something. I decided to break the silence. "Interesting lesson you have tonight."

Tobias made me wait as he took a moment to answer. "Sometimes lessons need to be repeated over and over again before they can be understood."

"How many times did it take before you understood this lesson?"

He turned to me, "Still a work in progress for me, like all things."

His comment caught me by surprise. Tobias was always so confident, never showing a hint of doubt. This was one of those rare moments where he opened up to me. I said, "I uhh … wanted to say…."

Tobias interrupted me, "Everyone, quiet! Something's wrong." I shut my mouth as Tobias jumped up from his position and pointed to Doc. "Doc, check out what's going on."

Doc immediately scrambled to our monitors, and the tone of his voice said it all. "Holy shit! We're surrounded."

Tobias asked, "I thought your alarms would signal if someone was in the proximity!"

"I swear I tested the alarms," Doc responded, "I have no idea why they didn't go off."

"The entire place is surrounded," shouted Ryan, as some of the guys began to approach the monitor.

Tobias began barking out orders, and it was a good thing we'd gone over what to do since the last incident. "Everyone get into your designated areas. Once we're positioned, kill the lights. Remember, let them rush in and do not engage. Everyone meet at our rendezvous point and spread apart. Do you understand?"

Ken held up his phone, "Don't forget your phones ... kill the sound."

Doc nodded, "Cover up as well."

Big T scrambled to the monitor, "They're getting ready to come in."

Everyone had their own designated area to get to and took off. Once confirmed, the lights shut off. I made sure my face was covered because the STDs wore body cams, and there could have been drones hovering outside. It was dark, but a source of light to the exit was my guide. I went down a hallway by myself, and I could feel my heart pounding. From a distance, I heard a pair of men walking by as I hid behind the very wall that I had painted several months ago.

Listening to their movement, I could tell they were on the hunt. I closed my eyes and concentrated on the sound of my own breathing. Tobias always said to focus on yourself and don't worry about any sounds that you may hear. I heard his voice in the back of my head: *Make sure you escape.*

Once the two guards passed me, all I had to do was dash for the exit. It was a mere sprint for me, and I lucked out. There was literally no resistance in front of me. I could hear them walk past me and waited until they headed off to the main room. Afterward, I could make my move.

Tobias's voice popped into my head again: *Avoid any conflict. Just run.*

Leave 'em alone. They're just following orders.

I faced the exit and was ready to take off when my legs went the other way. Before I could realize what I was doing, I found myself charging toward the STDs. Whatever was pent up inside me was about to release.

484

I targeted the guard on the left, yanking him from behind. His weight from the gear and his lack of balance allowed me to toss him backward. Once there, I delivered a swift kick straight to the head; even his helmet didn't protect him from the impact. As the other guard spun around to see what was happening, I was waiting down low for the opportunity. I caught his momentum and tossed him against the painted wall. He landed hard, and I rushed up to pummel him some more. He was already knocked out from the impact, but their presence angered me. I punched him several times over and over again, until a flash of light from the outside reminded me what I needed to do.

Kirin, run!

I finally got up and ran toward the exit. I made sure I was covered so no photos or video could capture me. My only hope was that the rest of the guys got out safely as well.

Decision—1 Year, 209 Days

A week had passed since the raid on our school. The pain felt worse than when we had lost Sifu's school, and talk amongst ourselves was limited. I had canceled all photo appointments for the last week, even though I knew I needed the money. Deep down, I felt like nothing mattered. Empty inside, I sat by my kitchen counter with a cold cup of coffee that had been sitting with me for the last thirty minutes. Bacon was at my feet, hoping for me to drop a treat. He pawed at me, but I ignored him.

My phone beeped several times. I flipped it over, and my eyes widened slightly as I saw activity on our group chat for the first time since the raid. I read several of the texts, but nothing was important. More time passed, and the emptiness filled my soul. I could not think of anything that could make things right again.

The TV played in the background. It sounded like static to me, the words meaningless. Then suddenly I saw an ad, another one for the UFMF. I usually ignored them, but this time, I turned toward the screen and watched.

"The UFMF is here to make your life better. Every day, more and more UFMF schools are opening up. You want to learn self-defense? You want to gain confidence? Then stop by and try a week of free lessons at your local UFMF school."

I'd had enough. I was so angered, I threw my cup at the TV, where it shattered and fell to the ground. Bacon saw that I was agitated and began barking.

Then I got a call I wasn't expecting. I let it ring several times, but the caller could not take a hint. Finally, after the fifth ring, I picked up the phone, scowling at the name on the screen.

"What is it, Chun? Can't you take a hint?"

"I got something for you ... something big," said Chun.

"I'm not interested ... not now, Chun."

"I heard about your school, Kirin."

I stood silent, stunned by his words.

"Kirin, did you hear me? I said, I'm sorry about your school."

"How'd you know about my school, Chun?"

Chun replied, "It's me. I'm a hustler. Word on the street spreads fast about what went down a week ago."

I paused, considering my next move. He probably didn't even have the answer. "Chun, someone ratted us out somehow. Do you have any clue who that might be?"

486

I heard him chuckle before he said, "It doesn't take a rocket scientist to figure this one out, Kirin. It's the UFMF. They're everywhere."

"What do you mean? We were just training on our own. We weren't recruiting new blood for the school. Why would they care?"

"You don't get it. They want to control everything, and the truth is, nothing is going to stop them."

I took a deep breath as the words got my blood going. "Chun, why'd you call?"

"I got something for you."

"I told you I don't want any fights right now."

"It's not a back-alley brawl, Kirin. This is a lot bigger … and, besides, I'm offering you an opportunity to stick it to the UFMF."

His last word caught my attention. "UFMF?"

"Yeah, UFMF. In a way, if you do this—and the payout is *huge*—you can kinda stick it to them."

I said nothing as the thought of getting back at the UFMF snared me in. I wanted to do something; in fact, I needed to.

"Kirin? Kirin … did you hear me?"

"I heard you."

"If you are interested, come down and see me in thirty, and we can talk about it."

I looked at my cracked TV—and, lo and behold, there was another UFMF commercial blasting away. Whether it was a sign or not, it didn't matter. I had made up my mind.

"What'd you say, Kirin?"

I heard him but didn't respond.

"Kirin?"

"Chun … I'll see you in a half-hour. I'm in!"

Section 2 Sifu's Journey Entry #11—Betrayal

Mid-December 2031

It was early Thursday evening, and the winter night quickly consumed the light. Sifu had already told Lance that they were going to open later, and he'd asked Lance to begin prepping before he got there. From the outside, everything seemed like a typical day, but Sifu had made a decision—a difficult one, at that—and now he was prepared to see the entire thing through.

Sifu was dressed in all black, hiding on top of the rafters. He had to be there. He had to make sure that, in the end, everyone would be okay. The plan was simple. If carried out to perfection, this would not only hit the source, but begin a chain of events that would set things in motion. He checked his watch as he patiently remained hidden within the shadows. He had aid from his group to break through the sensors and disable them for later.

He was at his students' training facility, an abandoned building still quite intact. They gathered there several times a week and spent time preserving the very art he had taught them. Since his school had been shut down by the UFMF and replaced, this was what they now considered home.

Suddenly the sound of a door slamming was followed by several voices chuckling from afar. Footsteps approached from below as several lights brightened the room. He watched from above as familiar faces began to appear. Tobias the ring leader came out first, followed by Danny and Big T. Ken and Robert were joking around with one another, and Ryan was offering Doc something to eat, which he kindly turned down. He leaned forward and listened, but he did not hear a girl's voice.

Sifu wondered, *Where is she?*

The door slammed again before another set of footsteps approached. Finally, he saw Kirin join the group. In her hand, she had a bag as she waved to the group and showed off her prize.

Kirin explained, "Snacks for later."

Ryan, with a meal already in his hand and food in his mouth, muttered, "Thanks, I'm starving."

Robert looked at Ryan. "Starving? Do you really understand the meaning of that word?"

The rest of the gang chuckled, and everyone began to partner up. Tobias gave out instructions as they began to work on some structural drills with one another. Kirin was in a corner, seated and observing the rest of the gang. Far above, little did they know their teacher was watching their every move. Sifu finally pulled out a small device and placed his thumb on top, but he hesitated. He admired the dedication his students were putting in; however, he was only delaying the inevitable.

In his earpiece, a voice said, "Sifu, this is Sindy. I need confirmation from you before I send them out."

Sifu did not respond.

"Do you copy?"

Sifu yanked his earpiece out. During this time, he was mentally correcting their mistakes, but he watched as everyone worked together in harmony. He closed his eyes as guilt hit him. He held the device in his hand and struggled for a brief moment before he finally pushed the button with a tight squeeze.

He reached into his pocket and put his earpiece back on.

Sindy said, "I just got the signal. I've sent notice to the STDs, and I'm tracking them. They'll be there in less than ten minutes. Make sure you are out of there."

Sifu repositioned himself so he could see the outside of the building. He moved stealthily through the upper rafters and was now keeping watch. Ten minutes passed before a swarm of cars pulled up outside of the building. Once there, uniformed STDs rushed out of their vehicles. Within minutes, they had surrounded the entire building.

He checked back on his students and saw their mad scramble within. He watched and listened to their actions.

Tobias was animated, yelling at Doc. "I thought your alarms would signal if someone was in the proximity!"

"I swear I tested the alarms," Doc responded. "I have no idea why they didn't go off."

Ryan confirmed, "The entire building is surrounded." He was looking at the monitor and doing a number count.

Danny had a look of panic on his face. "Look, we can say we were just hanging out at the building, right? What's the big deal?"

Ken rubbed his face, "It's the STDs. They don't call them in for small shit like this!"

Kirin was dumbfounded, "Someone ratted us out?"

Tobias stood in front and gathered everyone's attention. "We can debate about this shit later. For now, everyone cover up. I'm sure they have their drones and body cams on, we don't want to be physically identified."

Robert asked, "Doc, you got control of the light?"

"I got it," Doc replied.

Big T was looking at his monitor. "They're about to move in."

Tobias barked out some final orders. "Let them move in. When they rush in … kill the lights. Everyone spread apart and meet at our rendezvous point, just like we practiced. Do you understand?"

Sifu listened in as the panic was amplified. He wanted to make sure that everyone did escape, and no one was harmed. Suddenly, from several areas of the building, crashes simultaneously occurred. The STDs began shouting, trying to cause fear and confusion.

"Don't move! Don't move! Freeze!"

As the chaos began, his students shut down the lights and scrambled for several exits.

He heard Robert shout, "Shit, they got night vision!"

Sifu ran toward the rafters at the center of the room and reached into his bag. He dispersed several balls which landed in multiple directions on the floor. Suddenly, they blasted a beam of light, momentarily blinding the STDs.

From his perch, Sifu watched to determine whether everyone escaped.

Then he heard from the far corner one of the STDs shout, "I got one!"

Sifu began running to that side on the very top. He looked below and saw that two STDs had one of his students. He couldn't quite make the figure out clearly, but then he heard the voice. "Let me go, you bastards!"

Sifu thought, *Figures. It's Danny.*

Sifu found a pole and slid down quickly as Danny struggled to get free. But, now he was being dragged by the two STDs toward the center. He had to move quickly. Once in the middle of the room, it would be too difficult to deal with the entire group. The last thing he would want to do is leave a body count. Sifu seized one of the STDs from behind and threw him against the wall. He shouted in shock, not knowing what was going on as he slammed onto the floor. Danny's back was still toward him as the other STD spun around. Sifu delivered a kick so hard that it cracked his helmet. Before he crumpled, the STD was flung on top of his knocked-out companion.

Danny stood up realizing he was free. "Holy shit, what the hell just happened?"

Sifu ducked into the shadows and out of sight. He thought, *Fly, you fool.* Almost as if Danny had heard him, he took off and escaped.

One of the STDs finally got hold of the power and switched the lights on. For the next several minutes they searched the entire building, only to discover two of their companions laid out in the corner. They were unable to arrest anyone; the gang had successfully escaped. Sifu was back on top of the rafters as he watched silently from above. He thought, *I hope this was worth it....*

CHAPTER 12
Enemy Territory

Of all the things that could go wrong with this mission, it appeared that the simplest task, climbing up the stairs, would be the greatest obstacle. Adrenaline quickly drained from their souls as the first several flights proved exhausting. The entire group was now wearily trudging up the stairs. Time was nagging, as they knew they were racing against the clock to get to the Cube. Other than a few commands barked by Lance, the trek upward remained relatively silent. Their energy was expended to deal with the extra gear and Gwen's wheelchair. Even with the modifications to help with the transport, sixty-six floors up were still quite a challenge.

Lance wiped the sweat from his brow. Just like everyone else, he could feel the burn of the climb, but probably more so due to his prosthetic leg. He turned around to look at his comrades, well aware that any sign of weakness would lead to a domino effect on their morale. There was only so much room per exit floor, which made for cramped quarters and edgy moods.

He stood tall above the rest and scoffed at them. "You all need to add more cardio to your Wing Chun training." He shook his head in disgust, picking the right words and the proper attitude to motivate his team. "Come on, you pussyfoots. You're all in your twenties! I'm twice your age, *and* I have a fake leg!" He stomped his fake leg several times on the metallic floor, just to emphasize his resolve. He had everyone's attention, with one exception.

Ryan lagged at the tail end of Team 6.5. He had several steps to go, which seemed like miles before he would set foot on the sixty-sixth floor. He could feel Lance's judging eyes as he slumped over the side of the railing, too tired to care about what anyone thought. No one looked more exhausted than him as he whipped out his inhaler for the second time. He struggled to speak, wheezing, "I say we camp out here for the next ten minutes and replenish our energy."

Lance pointed to his watch and then raised his foot. "I'm going to replenish your energy with my foot up your ass. We're already fifteen minutes behind."

Ryan pulled rank, "Hey, Lance, I am your Si-hing, you know ... a little respect, please."

Lance nodded and apologized sarcastically, "Sorry about that, senpai ... oh, I mean Si-hing.... Now get your ass up and signal the two groups behind you!"

Robert, always the critic, could not pass up this opportunity. "Yeah, Ryan, don't be so selfish. Think of the groups behind you that you've terrorized with your fat ass for the last sixty-six floors."

"Shut up, Robert!" Ryan was about to lift his middle finger, but exhaustion won over as he decided just to rest.

The two groups behind Ryan grumbled in agreement. The view to the top was, in fact, only Ryan's ass.

Ryan snapped back, "Quiet! I could let one loose right now." It was always difficult to determine if he was serious or not, since Ryan had such a gentle soul.

Tobias got tired of the useless banter and snapped at his group. "Zip it, guys!"

Kirin waited by the fire door entry/exit, ignoring the minor squabble amongst her group. She had grown quite accustomed to their bickering. Her feeling of unease was growing. The burden was on her. She was not concerned about the goal, but about protecting her friends during the mission. She brushed her hair to the side, making sure her little scar was still covered as she looked down at Gwen. Her BFF was fast at work, typing away on her computer. Her focus on the job at hand could not be shaken. Kirin leaned forward, anxious for action, and asked, "Gwen, can you open—"

Click.

"—the door?" Kirin finished.

The sound of the door opening, while small, echoed throughout. The entire group, even those at the very end of the stairwell, felt a small sense of achievement. Gwen flashed a smile directly at Kirin. Her wizardry with computers was finally being put to good use. Her physical limitations bound her to the chair, but her knowledge and skill with technology made her dominant. The computer was her Gung Fu, and it freed her soul.

She gave a quick nod to Lance, signaling it was time for action. He gestured back at her to give the command. Surprised by his response, she did not hesitate to take the lead. Gwen squeezed her insides to bring out a deeper voice, "Let's move out." With a sense of pride, she looked at Sage, who happened to be standing behind her. "Gosh, I bet you always wanted me to say that."

Sage leaned from behind and could not resist planting a kiss on her forehead. The moment was too perfect. He didn't pull away, but instead spoke loud enough for only her to hear. "Let's move in together." She blushed and grabbed his arms, wrapping them around her. He whispered into her ear, "I always wanted to say that," and placed one more kiss on her cheek.

Danny watched from afar and made a timeout signal, breaking through the ranks. "Not the time for love, boys and girls. Besides, think of the single people in your group like Ryan."

Ryan looked up from his position and shouted, "That's by choice, you jerk!"

Robert coughed, "Just like weight gain?"

Ryan gave Robert a look as the gang chuckled, easing the tension.

Lance clicked on his communicator so that everyone could hear. "Team 6.5, we move in first. Eskrimadors and Bokken, wait for our signal; otherwise, we'll bottleneck this opening." He grabbed the door handle as he signaled with his hand to follow him. He made a silent count with his hands. After three, the door swung open.

Within seconds, Team 6.5 stormed the main hallway and filled the room in military fashion. Lance felt a moment of pride as the weeks of training seemed to have paid off. To the right were several elevators—six, to be exact—which caused Ryan some anguish upon seeing them. But, it was the metallic doors, circular in design and engraved with the UFMF logo, standing tall and daunting over everyone that captured the group's attention.

Gwen spotted the glow of the computer screen to the side of the UFMF doors. It drew her like a bug to a porch light. This was the first major obstacle that she would have to overcome. Before they could reach the computer, they had to deal with the two janitors who were caught off-guard by the ambush. They were in the middle of the room, blending in perfectly with the environment. As Lance began to approach them, the thin Asian janitor began shaking and dropped his mop where he stood.

The other janitor quickly fell to his knees. His cap fell to the ground as he rolled up in a fetal position. He cried in a high-pitched voice, "Don't hurt us! Oh please, please, kind sir."

Lance stood over him, giving him a pathetic look. "No one's going to hurt you." He looked at the other janitor, "Your coworker?"

He nodded, embarrassed for the both of them, but did not say a word.

Lance took one more glance at both janitors, "Stay in that corner, and don't say a word. Otherwise, it's duck, duck...."

Hunter stepped forward, stretching out the duct tape, which made a distinct sound. "Goose."

The standing janitor nodded and picked up his coworker, who was still groveling on the floor. They both sat down in the far corner and got out of their way. The high-pitched, animated janitor kept his head low and did not make eye contact with anyone.

Kirin took several steps toward him and tried to get a better look at his face. She thought something was familiar about his exaggerated actions. However, Gwen rolled by her, breaking her focus, as she moved directly to the main console system. Intensity covered her face as she got ready to work her magic. The remainder of the group turned their backs on the janitors to focus on more pressing matters.

Lance began dishing out orders as he pointed to the four cameras that surrounded them from above. The remaining group finally marched into the hallway and joined them. Like those before them, they were awestruck by the entrance.

Kirin gestured with her head to the cameras, "They know we're here."

Lance nodded, "I know, but they don't need to see how we're going to set up."

Several of the guys gathered material from their backpacks as Tobias said, "Hunter, you're up."

Hunter mumbled to himself, "I never pictured myself using my baseball skills for something else." He grabbed the small, balloon-shaped item and threw it at each of the cameras. One by one, the goo from inside the balloon blacked out the view as it dripped down each camera.

Lance said, "That's a good arm, son."

Hunter turned to Lance and said, "I doubt they have a baseball league in prison."

Robert chimed in, "They do. Just make sure you don't get drafted by the Butt Pirates."

Ryan grabbed Hunter from behind, clamping his hands on his shoulders. "Not that there's anything wrong with it." Ryan's touch, more than the thought, made Hunter shiver.

April was busy watching over Gwen's shoulder. "Sweetie, you really need to open these doors. Even if they can't see us visually, I'm sure they still know how we're set up by some kind of thermal sensor."

Gwen was focused as she ignored April and continued to type away on the console.

Tobias told the rest of the gang, "Arm up, guys … uh, and gals."

Kirin held a pole in her hand as she stood next to Tobias by the entrance. She whistled to Tobias and tossed him his pole. The rest of the guys began lining up evenly behind Tobias, ready for whatever was waiting beyond the doors. Team Eskrimadors armed up with their sticks, and Team Bokken whipped out their wooden swords. They were all ready to do battle as their game faces turned on.

Tobias smirked to himself, "This feels just like old times, just like when we fought at the Greatest America theme park."

Kirin bumped his arm, "How'd that work out for us?"

Tobias ignored Kirin and watched the doors. He was ready to spring into action.

Lance looked at his watch, "We're almost at the one-hour mark…. Gwen, any time now would be great."

Gwen turned around, "I'm not online shopping here, Lance." She was typing at a blazing speed as she added, "I bet they're thinking there's no way we can get in."

Lance thought, *I'm wondering that myself.*

Sage said, "Are you in?"

Gwen looked to the door and then pressed the last button. The door shook, and the light above turned clear. It began to slide open as they heard a commotion from the other side. The entire group was ready to charge in, each one holding their respective weapon. By the console—Gwen, Sage, April, and Hunter stood next to each other as Lance stood guard.

Voices from the other side continued to shout as footsteps could be heard scrambling.

"Holy shit, they're getting through!"

"How'd they break through our security?"

Kirin turned reminding the group, "Hurt mode, not kill mode … remember." She then looked to Lance and his group. "Tie up the ones who are down." Lance nodded in acknowledgement as he prepared for action.

The doors slid open as five guards rushed through in a side-by-side formation. They were gung-ho and beaming with confidence. Each one flashed their electric glove in front of them in an intimidating fashion, but they soon realized the numbers were not in their favor. Tobias held his pole to his side and hammered it down twice. He then grabbed it and posed in fighting position as the rest of the gang followed suit in a hypnotic fashion. The Eskrimadors clashed their sticks together behind them, slow at first with the rhythm increasing with each passing second. At the very end, Team Bokken raised their wooden swords high above their heads, slicing through

502

the air as they assumed their guard stance. The screams of the entire group shook the inner part of the entryway as the sound echoed, sending a chill down each guard's spine.

The guards looked at their opposition and then at one another. They quickly reached a unanimous decision. One by one, they threw their glove onto the floor and raised their hands above their head. Surrender was the easiest—and smartest—option.

Tobias snickered and moved forward. He walked with a swagger, holding his staff by his side in an intimidating manner. He pointed to the ground and shouted, "On your knees … now!"

Big T and Danny chuckled, acting like kids.

The team moved with precision and secured the guards in place. The main area was just the security clearance, but what lay ahead was even more impressive. Several steps in, the group began to realize the daunting task at hand. All eyes widened as they looked above. They entered the main server room, which revealed row after row of data servers as far as the eye could see. Suspended in the air, the servers were shaped like metallic teardrops. Roughly thirty feet in length, they glowed from top to bottom, almost appearing like living creatures as panels would open and shut to ventilate. Everything was state-of-the-art, as no expense had been spared. Limitless information was being transferred at the blink of an eye through the servers hanging above them.

Sage's breath billowed white when he spoke. "Incredible … all this information."

Big T sputtered, "Damn, it's cold in here," as he hugged himself.

"It has to be," Sage replied. "These servers are running nonstop."

Ken chuckled and hit Danny on the side.

"Hey, what gives?" Danny as he rubbed his arm.

Ken leaned forward, "It probably has your porn history, Danny."

Danny hesitated before whispering to Ken, "You really think so?"

Big T placed his hand on Danny's shoulder, "Someone's been bad."

Danny knocked his arm away, "You should talk."

Ignoring them, Lance took the lead, "Welcome to the Cube."

As the teams gathered inside, Gwen was busy hacking away at another terminal. She admired the excessiveness that the UFMF displayed with their computer system. Gwen's mastery showed when it came to this technology. A handful got caught up in watching her deal with the intricacies that only she could understand.

Gwen said, "It looks like we have ten more individuals that we have to deal with inside the Cube. Like Lance said, everyone was watching the match…. It must be a skeleton crew. Check your communicators. I'll send the location."

Lance began instructing the teams and dishing out assignments, making sure everyone knew what they were supposed to do in their designated area. "Okay, it appears we still have several groups to deal with, but the numbers are in our favor. Team Eskrimadors, this is your area. Prep your drones and report to Gwen to have them enabled. Setup is priority. Do it as quickly as possible." Freddie signaled to his group as they listened to the final instructions from Gwen.

Lance knew in a battle situation that communication and organization were key. It was easy for people to get lost and confused in the chaos, so he made sure his orders were simple and direct. He went over and prepared the next groups. He shouted, "Time to split up, boys and girls! Team 6.5 and Team Bokken, you're headed up with me to the second level. Once we're up there, Gwen does her computer magic to control the power grid, and Team Bokken will secure it and prep it for reboot. Remember, each team has to get their drones up and flying so we can communicate with one another. Team 6.5, you're going on a scavenger hunt through the research facility on the third level. Priority is the drug SSP761. That's our proof. Once we're there we'll split up, Doc you're in charge. I'll stay with the eggheads, along with Kirin, Tobias, and Hunter at the command center."

Sage frowned at Lance as he didn't take too kindly to the comment, but April chuckled.

Exasperated, Lance asked, "Are you a computer dork or not?"

Sage thought about it for a second and then sought confirmation by looking at April. Sage made a gesture to Lance. "Continue."

Doc stepped forward and examined the opening hall of the server room. "Look at the size of this place! This is going to take some time."

Ryan's shoulders sank, sulking, "It looks like more walking."

Lance gave Ryan the look and then glanced at April. "Time?"

April waved her Hello Kitty watch and said, "Fifty minutes and thirty-seven seconds, sir, yes, sir!"

Lance circled his hand in the air, "Secure your levels first. Gwen has forwarded you the coordinates of the remaining opposition. Get that communicator set up ASAP. That is priority number one. Remember, we've got another hour and ten minutes. An hour and ten, people, and then we'll have more company if we don't take control of the command center. I'm sure the police and STDs are waiting to get through to the lower level, and we can't handle those numbers. All in all, I'd rather not deal with them."

Lance pointed to Gwen, who swept her hand forward and above. "Move out, people!"

#

As impressive as the rest of the Cube was, it paled in comparison to the command center. The earlier schematics hadn't done it justice, and the main group, led by Tobias, were in awe. It appeared fairly large, even though it occupied only a third of the top level of the Cube. In the center of the room stood a rectangular table three times the size of a normal dining table. Above it a projector flashed downward, displaying an overview of the UFMF building in a holographic image. Kirin approached it and touched the image, amazed to find she was able to manipulate the interactive display. At the far end centered in the middle wall was one towering screen, standing close to twenty feet in height and width, with two slightly smaller screens accompanying it. *This would be a gamer's dream*, she thought as the team of computer geeks approached it and felt dwarfed beside it.

Gwen ordered them into position and immediately got to work. Ten minutes of extreme hacking led by Gwen finally got them access to that area. However, her work was far from complete as she typed feverishly to get full control of the UFMF's system. Sage was in charge of maintaining communications between the three teams, while April searched through their servers for proof of SSP761 and anything else she could possibly dig up.

Hunter was exploring the area when he came across a small isolated room that stood behind the main consoles. Situated at the rear, its fancy bells and whistles would have almost gone unnoticed. He called for the group to come see what he had discovered. "Jesus, check this out!" he hollered. "How's this even possible? Look at the size of this."

Tobias walked over at the other entrance of the room and took a quick peek. "What is it?" he asked as Kirin joined the party and peered over his shoulder. Lance shortly followed.

Hunter explained, "It's an XL4000-3D printer … but if I'm looking at this right, this isn't a device, this entire fricking room is the printer!"

Kirin asked, "How do you know that?"

Hunter pointed to the name that was etched on the side of the panel. "This shouldn't even exist. I remember reading that a prototype was in development but not expected to release for another three to five years. Yet, here it is, and here we are."

Kirin cocked her head, "What's the big deal?"

April chimed in, "The big deal is it's possible to print and assemble a working car with that … in roughly fifteen minutes."

Kirin's jaw dropped, "Say what? A full car?"

April corrected, "A fully *working* car, at that."

Hunter snapped back, "She's right. It's like a Green Lantern ring. If you can imagine it, this baby can make it … and at lightning speed."

Kirin looked at April, "Hey … shouldn't you be working on the console, searching for secrets on the server?"

April pointed to a corner of the room, "What's that?" Kirin spun around, and April dashed away and headed back to her work.

Just on the opposite side, Gwen called for everyone to return. She was shifting back and forth in her wheelchair. Lights were flashing in front of her as if it were the Fourth of July. "I think I need another fifteen minutes, but things are looking good."

Tobias glanced at his watch. "That'll give us about thirty more minutes before the lockdown ends or you have full control."

Gwen nodded, "Let's get to work then." Gwen was seated at the main computer screen, while April and Sage were plugged in at her side. Hands were clicking away, swiping at the screens and breaking down the server walls so they could have total control. As the three computer geeks worked on their task, Gwen cried out, "Holy crap!"

"Did you crack it already?" Tobias asked eagerly.

"Almost there, but look on the screen," Gwen pointed.

Kirin asked, "Who's that?"

Gwen responded, "With the data that was gathered by Sifu, this was the constant unknown factor in literally page after page of information. I present to you the final piece of the puzzle …our mystery man, Youshiro Watanabe. He is the head of the head of the UFMF."

Kirin was still staring at the screen, "I repeat, who?"

Gwen said, "You know your bestest of friends, Thorne? He's simply the president. This is *THE* guy who hired him, who I'm sure calls all the shots. He is the guy behind the scenes otherwise lurking in the shadows."

Tobias replied, "Speak of the devil."

Gwen smiled and said, "All the info we had, now I finally have a face to go with it."

Sage shouted, "Boom! We're networked together. I've got connection to Team Eskrimadors, Team Bokken, and Team 6.5."

Gwen gave the command, "Remind everyone they need to stay underneath those drones for our coms to work. Until I have full access to this place, that's the only way we can communicate with one another."

Kirin was staying out of the way of the tech geeks, but she noticed that April was particularly quiet and busy working at her station. She walked toward her and leaned over to see her screen. There was just too much code and too many lights to make heads or tails of what she was looking at. April said, "Wow, there's just so much here!" Then she fell silent, and Kirin noticed a change on April's face.

"What is it?" she asked softly.

April looked up and, for the first time, hesitated before speaking. "It's a file on Sifu ... but, more importantly, on Sifu's family."

Kirin's expression changed too, "Pull it up."

April began unearthing the information about Sifu and was clearly distraught. "I can't believe what I'm seeing." Kirin leaned over April's shoulder and began reading. April said, "The early stages of the SSP761 drug had some severe side effects." As she continued reading, she stumbled upon information about Watanabe's son. "Well, this makes more sense. I know Gwen explained it further, but ... wow, this is cray-cray."

Then April was caught off-guard. She gasped. "Sifu's family's car accident was far from it. Seems the drug caused one of the subjects to go haywire and crash his car into them."

Kirin held her hand over her mouth in shock. Her eyes scanned the information, and she saw pictures from the accident scene. Tears began to pour down her face, and she felt the pain all over again.

"On whose orders?" Kirin chocked out.

April said, "It appears it comes from the very top … the very top of the UFMF."

Kirin turned away. She had seen and read enough. Shock quickly turned to anger as she clenched her fists. It wasn't an accident. In Kirin's mind, a wrong could no longer be corrected, but only avenged. She wiped her tears and walked away.

Ten Minutes Later

Gwen growled and slammed her fist on the console. "We are fricking in!" She held the little item Sifu had given her and kissed it before pointing to Sage. "Baby, tell Team Bokken it's time to reset the power grid."

Sage nodded and began giving instructions to Team Bokken.

Tobias asked, "How much time will that take?"

Gwen said, "Five minutes to reset, give or take…."

Hunter was pacing, "Do we have enough time?"

Gwen paused, calculating it out. "Three minutes to spare," she said as she flashed a smile. The entire group waited as Gwen stared at the screen. "They did it." She began working on the computer as all eyes were upon her. The room was silent, the team holding their breath in anticipation. It appeared they had somehow pulled off the impossible. She raised her hand in an exaggerated manner and pressed a single key. "Total control … I'm in."

The crew was busy celebrating as Tobias waved them down. "It's too early to celebrate. Everyone, chill." He paused and realized a face was missing. Tobias dashed around the command center as everyone was wondering what was wrong. "Where's Kirin?"

Sage searched for her face but then confirmed, "I don't see her."

Tobias nodded to Gwen, "Gwen, focus on your job. Do what needs to be done and broadcast that message."

Hunter left to search the entire room but came running back after a minute. "She's not here."

Tobias shook his head and slammed his fist. "God dammit."

Sage ran back to his terminal and began looking at the screen. He hunched over, studying the screen before his eyes widened. "Shit … shit!"

Gwen scrolled over and looked at the screen. "Dammit … she's headed up to the top. She's going for Watanabe."

Tobias ran over and checked out the screen, finding the dot that represented Kirin. He looked at Gwen, "I'll need the backpack … now!"

Gwen reached into her wheelchair and pulled out a backpack for Tobias.

He put the backpack on and began heading out of the command center. "Gwen, contact Lance. Tell him to come here from the research area and cover you guys." Seeing that Gwen was worried about her friend, Tobias wanted to reassure her. He spoke with his eyes as an aura of confidence always followed him. "Don't worry…. I promise I'll bring her back."

One on One—June 20, 2034

Sifu had underestimated the resolve that Kirin's enemies would have to destroy her. He knew he was responsible for her safety, so he decided to buy her some time and hoped she could escape from the blazing inferno. He quickly spun around as several of the henchmen were closing the gap on him with haste. Another quick glance above revealed an exit that would face the lakeside. He thought for a brief second that maybe there was a way for him to escape as well. Maybe this would not be the end for him if he could make it there.

He grabbed one of the pieces of burning wood and quickly swung it in a circular motion, wiping out several opponents with a single blow. It was not enough. More moved in on him, and he had to get to the top. A stairwell would get him there, as anyone within his range was immediately snuffed out. While his skill preserved him for the time being, the numbers at some point would be overwhelming.

Pieces from the roof began falling onto the floor, and the smoke made it difficult to breathe, as if his challenge wasn't great enough. The environment played no favorites in who it burned as it ran its path of destruction randomly throughout the building. After making his way to the top of the staircase, Sifu saw a clear path for a brief moment. He coughed several times, waving the air around him. Sifu took several brisk steps forward and stopped in his tracks. Cutting through the smoke, his former student appeared in front of him, blocking his path to escape.

More guards came from all directions with a trail of them rushing up the staircase Sifu had used. Behind Justice, at least a dozen stood by, ready to carry out Justice's previous order. From every angle, Sifu was fully surrounded with the biggest obstacle standing in his way.

Justice screamed, "Leave him! Everyone, back down … now!

He's mine." At his orders, the henchmen backed away from him and Sifu. He stared Sifu dead in the eye. With a hollow look, he shouted, "Go now. Hunt down Kirin Rise. Make sure she doesn't escape this building." His command echoed throughout the room as Justice's henchmen swarmed away from them, leaving them to face each other one-on-one.

"Noble as always, Sifu. Saving your student while once again being a coward and trying to find a way to run."

Sifu walked toward Justice, never breaking eye contact. "Justice, don't do this. There's no way you'll win."

"You think this is all about winning? Look around. We've already lost. You created this, long ago, when you kicked me out of the school and decided to do nothing." He pointed at Sifu.

"What are you talking about, Justice?"

"I warned you. You had no interest in preserving the art. You believed that somehow the universe would balance itself. You let the entire UFMF spread like a plague and kill everything. The skill should've been spread, but instead you decided to hide in the shadows and not share it with the world."

Sifu's voice toned down as he realized what Justice was saying. He could feel the pain in the voice of his former student. "The universe doesn't work that way, Justice. The art will live on, long after we're gone. Its principles will live on forever."

"Don't give me that B.S. spiritual junk, Sifu. I've mastered everything you've taught me: from the stance, twist and lock, and even the freeze."

"You've mastered only my teachings and never made it your own, Justice. You'll always be a distant second."

Justice shook with rage, "My skills and understanding of the art have surpassed even yours. I'm no longer your student, and I'll do what you were so afraid to do."

Sifu shook his head with a sad look on his face. "You choose to fight, you pick your path. Just remember that." Sifu took a quick glance behind Justice, noting he was a good thirty feet from the outer escape exit. If he could get there in time, before the entire building burned down or collapsed, there might still be a chance.

"Don't think I don't know what you're planning, Sifu, but where I stand is a wall you won't be able to get through. You want out? You'll have to go through me."

Time was short, and Sifu did not hesitate. He moved in on Justice until both men were in striking distance of one another. Though Sifu may have taught Justice, both men knew this game. Now it was a question of who executed it the best. The first to commit to an attack would be at a disadvantage. However, Sifu made the first motion and entered into range, hoping Justice would bite, and he did. Sifu could feel his intent, his anger surging through his body. Justice was already mentally off-center. He wanted to make a statement, to show his teacher he was far beyond him.

Justice threw out the first punch, and the battle between the two ensued. The advantage swung back and forth, attack meeting counterattack as the two men followed the force. In a flow of three, Justice attempted to chain several attacks, trying to get to the heart of Sifu's core and land the punch that would end it. As the third attack came close to landing, Sifu froze his motion for a brief moment. From the point of touch all the way to the ground, Justice was stuck, no matter how he tried to counter it. Suddenly, Sifu released the hold and centerline punched him in the chest, sending him several feet back. Justice's head hit the railing hard, cutting a gash on the side of his head. Sifu's intent wasn't to kill his student, but to push him back to get to the entrance.

Justice slammed the metal railing floor, "That's impossible!"

Sifu took several steps further from Justice, "Clearly it can't be, since it just happened to you."

The snide remark didn't sit well with Justice. He rushed up as the space between them lessened, making a motion to throw out another attack. Sifu did not care about the attack. He had spotted Justice's motion prior to the punch. With the shift of his center of gravity to one side, he had already given away his hand. Justice's attack was still winding up, when suddenly it was interrupted by two hits to Justice's center, which caused him to sail further back.

Sifu realized he had only ten more feet to go. Was he prepared to kill his student in order to escape? The thought swallowed him whole. "If I wanted to end this, it would already be over. Stay down!" Sifu commanded Justice.

Justice screamed, "This can't be happening…. I'm better than you!"

"I'm sorry, Justice. Like I said, you can't win. There's no way you can stop me. You always failed to understand the lesson. It has nothing to do with beating your opponent."

Justice looked at Sifu as blood poured down his face. The realization that he could not beat Sifu tore inside every fiber of his skin. Deep down, the truth hit hard. He knew Sifu's hit could've ended him right there. It would've been more suiting to have died at the hands of his teacher, instead of receiving pity from him. However, Justice had a backup plan and was prepared to win at any cost. He said, "If I lose, we all lose." He pulled out a small device and raised it over his head. Finding his last ounce of strength, he pressed the button.

Sifu took a swing and knocked the device from his hand. It crashed to the ground, as Justice smiled. "Too late." Sifu heard explosions begin to rumble from the building below.

Sifu breezed a kick across the face, knocking him out. He jumped over Justice and then dragged his limp body on the ground, trying to make a wild dash for the upper exit. "Looks like I ruined your plans again."

> *"A true master never calls himself that, those around him do because of how he carries himself." —Kirin*

Reverse Intervention—October 9, 2034

I waited outside in my car until I could confirm that everyone had arrived. I used an alias and rented a place for the next several days because it was less suspicious than renting for one day only. The third-floor apartment was mainly used by outsiders visiting the Chicago area. It would be the perfect place for our little meeting. The gang was the first to make it, followed by my closest friends, Gwen, Sage, and Hunter. Several minutes passed before Lance and April straggled along, making the final count complete. I grabbed a quick sip of my coffee, placed my hoodie over my head, and exited the car before crossing the street.

I walked up the stairs and stood outside the doorway, where I listened briefly to see if I could catch their discussion prior to making my entrance. I leaned in and gently pressed the side of my face along the door.

Tobias said, "Did someone plan another intervention for Kirin?"

Robert held up his phone, "Everyone got the same text, right? Meet here at noon … urgent."

"Wait, this is a meeting?" April complained. "I thought it was a get-together for eating."

Ken asked, "So, whose place is this anyway?"

"Wait, there's no food? What are we doing here then?" cried Ryan.

Lance said, "Something's not quite right about this meeting, and I have a feeling we're about to find out what this is all about."

Upon hearing that, I swung open the door and popped in on everyone, catching them all by surprise—except for my mole in the room. "I'll tell you what we will be doing. If everyone would be kind enough to grab a seat, I'll need your full attention." I turned around and closed the door, locking it from inside.

I held a small device up and began scanning the entire room. "Excuse me ... excuse me," I muttered as I began checking every nook and cranny possible in the room.

Danny crossed his arms, "What's with the James Bond meeting?"

I ignored Danny's question and then pointed to Gwen as I continued to scan the room. She moved forward in her wheelchair, placed a small device on the table, and then waited for my signal.

Sage stood up, "Gwen, you knew about this?"

"I am her BFF. Kirin will explain all of this soon enough." Gwen gave him a quick smile.

Robert punched Sage's shoulder, "I'm surprised you didn't piece this together, Sage."

I said, "Shut up, Robert." I was smiling during the quick exchange before I turned back to Gwen. "Gwen, please play it. It's clear."

For the next ten minutes, the group sat quietly watching the video that Gwen had put together along with all the data we were able to gather. I watched as no one lost focus, and I could see their shock and disbelief written all over their faces. I knew it was a lot to take in, as my initial reaction to the truth had been no different. Finally, the video ended, and the lights came back on. Silence continued to dominate the room until I finally broke it.

Everyone was waiting for me to say something, so I said, "I brought you all here today because I need a team … and a team can only work if every member on it is someone I can fully trust. My brothers in the art, I've known you guys forever. We've battled side by side since I can remember. Sage, Gwen, and Hunter have been my friends from the very start. Through thick and thin, you've always been there for me. And Lance, you've been the closest with Sifu for some time." I paused as I turned my attention to April.

She chuckled, "You've known me the least, yet here I am."

I paused before answering, "If Sifu trusted you with that final piece, then I trust you as well."

Tobias stood up, "What are you proposing, Kirin?"

"Well, the details still have to be worked out, but in a nutshell … I need a ragtag team to help me break into the UFMF building, hack their main command center, and expose all their dirty little secrets and lies to the entire world."

April raised her hand. "I'm in."

Danny's eyes were wide, "Kirin, this isn't some video game we're about to venture into. There are repercussions to such actions." I bit back a smile. I had known that Danny would be the first to oppose my idea, and I was okay with that. This was the time to air things out and make sure we were all on the same page.

Sage said, "I'm glad that you trust all of us, Kirin, but … you're asking people to sacrifice their future."

"And, quite possibly, their lives," Ken said quietly, giving voice to the reality that we'd all have to face.

"I know that, and that's why I'm asking to see who would actually join me to do this."

Gwen nodded, "You know I'm in."

Sage moved behind Gwen and said, "Gwen, you sure?"

Gwen nodded again, "I only showed the group a short clip of all the stuff the UFMF is doing. I can't sit around … well, maybe I should rephrase that." Her little comment got a chuckle from the group. "What they plan on doing, the evil … I can't imagine, nor can I imagine knowing all that I do and not doing a thing about it."

Lance said, "I've traveled the world doing missions and meeting many people. There's one thing that's a common core: the evil of men has no limits."

Hunter added, "I know everyone's worried about their future, but after seeing all this … I'm with Kirin. What kind of future do we have if we do nothing?"

Big T said, "You know, in the movies, the black guy is always the first to—"

"Big T … this isn't the movies, and I want to make sure everyone understands the risk involved." I tried to explain.

Doc said, "Kirin, you are my sister in the art, and we've battled before. But, what you ask … that's a sacrifice that each one committing must be clear on." He stood up and paced back and forth. "The intel you gathered, it's 100%, right?"

I nodded and looked to Gwen for confirmation.

She turned and faced Doc. "It is."

Danny stood up and appeared most agitated from the group. "Let's say you are right … and imagine we live in a fairytale word where we prove everything about the UFMF correct. What then? Does our sacrifice carry some reward?"

Robert said, "Always thinking about credits, aren't you, Danny?"

Danny replied, "If not me, then who? I mean, let's get real here, people. We're looking at insurmountable risk, with … what reward? I mean good karma doesn't pay the bills."

I took a deep breath, "I don't have that answer for you. I have no guarantees about anything, but every fiber in my body says that something has to be done."

The room was silent as more people began voicing their opinions. Even as discussions became heated, we were still able to talk things through together.

Tobias made a fist with his right hand and punched his left palm, "You can bet this is only the beginning. You know I'm in."

I smiled at Tobias. I had never doubted that he would help me out. "I know some of you have made the decision, and I don't want it to be made off emotion. So, I'm going to give you several days to think about it. No pressure, regardless of what you decide. If you want in, meet back here on the third day at the same time." I started walking out the door and was halfway through it when I turned and looked at my closest friends, who were all watching me. "I don't want to be a hero. Nobody does. But, if not me, then who?"

"Bitch less. Do More" — Kirin

A Call to Rise—December 15, 2034

This was the broadcast that was played when Kirin and her friends took over the UFMF building.

"If you are seeing this video, then you've come to discover that the fight between me and Ripley Hawkins will not be happening tonight. For that, I apologize, but instead a more important battle is taking place as I speak—one that goes beyond the ring and affects each and every one of you. For those who don't know, I am Kirin Rise. I was the underdog two years ago that shocked the world and became the first female fighter to win the Dome Championship. I defied the odds and, through my actions and examples, you the people have chosen me to be your voice.

"I'm here again fighting for what is true, what is right, and what is just, and I ask those that feel the same way as I do to finally rise. Rise from the lies and push beyond your limits. Join me tonight to make the millions become one. Haven't you waited all your life to find a reason to fight? Well, tonight, I give you one.

"Right now, I'm here at the main headquarters of the UFMF. Everything you've been told, everything you've seen has all been lies. When you watched me fight Diesel two years ago, you witnessed something quite unusual—a man who was able to withstand incredible amounts of pain, no matter the damage. Then, just last year, when I fought Justice, I stood frozen even though I knew he was about to attack me. What you don't know is something that I've just discovered. The UFMF has created a drug that led to all this. This drug was originally designed for our soldiers, but the UFMF is taking it to the next level. Their need and lust for global domination isn't only from a corporate standpoint. They want to control each and every one of you. This goes beyond the laws they create. They plan to use this drug—this *mind control* drug—to make the perfect society of obedient citizens.

"What will you do the moment history asks you to act? Will you be part of it with me or stand to the side, wishing and dreaming your lives could be better? You have the power to forge your life now. This is the moment for you to decide. This is something that will actually lead to change.

"You ask me why I'm doing this? I'm giving the world a reason to stop. I've experienced more tragedy than most people will ever know in a lifetime. I need you to help me help you and to bring a balance once again to the world we live in. Come to the UFMF building and see the truth for yourself."

Millions throughout the world watched Kirin's broadcasted message. As it ended, her words moved those who were in New York to come to the UFMF building. There, the masses gathered, hoping that finally her words and their actions could put an end to the injustice facing all.

Section 2 Sifu's Journey Entry #12—The Circle Is Complete

Friday, January 2, 2032

At the entrance of the ticket stand, he flashed his phone and was scanned in. He was quickly ushered in as the crowd seemed particularly energetic for the first fight of the year. His seats weren't too terrible. They weren't nosebleeds but were common enough to blend in with the rest of the crowd. This was quite different from the handful of matches he had witnessed in the past. No longer at an abandoned building or in a seedy back alley, this was definitely a step up.

Several matches flew by as Sifu found observing the crowd's reaction more entertaining. The crowd nearby was focused on one match that drew everyone's attention. He kept hearing whispers of a fighter named DJ and tried his best to listen in. Next to him was a gentleman who looked like a regular. He was busy keeping tally of his night's winnings. He wasn't drawn into the hoopla of the others that were there.

Sifu surprisingly struck up conversation with him and broke through his defense by stroking the stranger's ego. He asked, "You seem to know what you are doing?"

"I do okay…. You win some, you lose some," was his modest response.

Sifu responded, "It's my first time here. What's the big deal about the match with DJ?"

The gentleman looked at his score card and then adjusted his glasses. "Ah, DJ. He's the fan favorite, a fighter past his prime, but incredibly deadly."

Sifu asked, "Isn't that typical with all the fighters? I mean, they are going up against all amateurs, right?"

"That's true, but it's not him so much that they are drooling about. It's the GP he's matched up against."

"GP...?" Sifu frowned, having no clue what the acronym stood for.

"Ah, you're a newbie. It means 'guinea pig.' You know, the worst of the worst with zero chance of winning. It's set up for total entertainment for the crowd. It's like a human sacrifice."

"Sounds kinda cruel, don't you think?"

"Definitely, but this is how society is. They want to see that sinking boat or car accident on the road. I guess, in a way, they want to know that someone has it worse than them. By the way, my name is Abe," the man extended his hand out to Sifu.

"Oh, my name is Bing," Sifu said as he shook Abe's hand firmly. "Thanks for educating me."

Just then, the announcer began exciting the crowd; they seemed to hang on his every word. It was clear to Sifu this was a man who needed to be the center of attention. His actions were deliberate and calculated, and the crowd appreciated his showmanship. He finally settled them down so his words could be heard. He said, "Our next contestant ... from parts unknown, weighing in at ... one-hundred-five pounds?" The announcer paused, seeming genuinely surprised and, for the first time, unsure of himself. A few seconds passed as he tried to confirm if the information was correct before he continued, "Again, at one-hundred-five pounds, style unknown, the fighter known as ... BLINK!"

Sifu and the rest of the crowd followed his gesture to see the spotlight on an empty area.

Abe nudged Sifu, distracting him for a second. "This is the GP, but I've never heard of one this small. You want some friendly advice? This is a sure thing to bet on."

Sifu looked around as people were scrambling to electronically enter their wagers. Sifu turned to Abe, "You sure?"

Abe replied, "This is as close to 100% as you can get next to death and taxes.... Besides, the last two fighters that DJ met up with, he ended up killing. I can't imagine what he's going to do with this fool."

Sifu felt a hint of doubt followed by a pinch of guilt. While his student was skilled, this might be asking too much, even for Kirin. His actions had put her in this very spot, and now he was second-guessing his decision. As Kirin walked toward the ring, she appeared so tiny and lost in the crowd. They were relentless with their jeers and snide comments. Sifu's mind was racing as he came to a decision. If things went bad, he would jump in to save Kirin.

The introduction of DJ was a spectacle to see as the crowd was finishing up their wagering. Sifu's nerves were on edge. As he studied Kirin, he realized she looked different. Unlike her fight in the alley where Sifu first saw her, she bore an air of confidence that he noticed. The more he saw of her, the less concerned he felt.

There's something different about her.

Abe broke Sifu's concentration and nudged him on the arm. "Did you finish putting in your wager?"

"I don't really gamble."

"This isn't gambling. This is a sure thing." He showed him the wagers on the phone as Sifu took a glance. "The money's guessing how quickly DJ destroys this fool."

"What's that last bet with the knockout?"

Abe took back his phone and stared at it. "Oh, that." He chuckled. "That's a sucker's bet."

"What do you mean?"

"Bing, that bet is saying that this Blink character can knock out DJ in the first round. Not only is that impossible, but in the history of Chum Night, no amateur fighter has ever come close to winning. And, remember: this Blink fool's not just an amateur. He's tonight's designated GP."

Sifu inquired, "How do I take that bet?"

"Seriously?"

"Seriously."

"I can enter it for you through my phone," Abe couldn't help but give Sifu a side-eye.

Sifu nodded, "That's fine.... How about one thousand credits?"

"A thousand credits!" shouted Abe as fans around them took notice of the bet.

Sifu asked, "Is that too little?"

Abe shook his head. "That's a thousand credits that you're throwing away."

"That's why it's called gambling, right?"

"It's your money, my friend," Abe said as he entered the info and Sifu gave him the credits. After hearing the bet, others around them wanted to take the wager against Sifu, and he gladly accepted. The frenzy increased as Blink finally revealed that he was a she. Sifu quickly became the center of attention, which was not what he wanted, as he hunched himself in the center, trying to stay out of the spotlight.

The fight finally began as DJ maneuvered himself in the ring. The crowd, including those around Sifu, were ready to cash in on their bets. It would appear that Sifu was the only one to pick Kirin to win the fight. Sifu watched and waited. As DJ charged in, Kirin also closed the gap with her opponent. He could see it perfectly, unlike the rest of the crowd, which was about to be in for a shock.

WHAM!

DJ was out cold on the mat, stunning his camp and shocking the crowd. It was total mayhem in the arena. All around Sifu, no one could believe what they had just seen.

Abe was shaking his head in astonishment, and the rest could not believe the amount of money they had all lost. While this was all going on, Sifu felt something else, a presence he recognized. He began scanning the arena, which was a difficult task considering the number of people there. But, as Kirin would be the target, he tried to place himself at a location where that person might be. Whoever it was would be going against the flow of the moment. He closed his eyes and silenced his mind, giving a moment for everything to sink in. He took a slight breath and opened his eyes, causally glancing around the arena. Just like that, he found the source of his feeling. He saw Tobias making his way through the crowd. It seemed he had caught the tail end of the fight, but from the looks of it, Kirin had no idea he was there.

As several minutes passed, Sifu collected his winnings and was about to head out. But, then he heard Kirin's voice.

She shouted, "My name is Kirin! This … is Wing Chun Gung Fu!"

He watched as Kirin threw the microphone toward DJ and said something he could not make out. He was still out cold and being looked over by the physician. Everyone stood shocked, not knowing what was going to happen next. Sifu watched as Kirin studied the credits in her hand. He already knew what she was going to do before she threw all the credits into the air. Pandemonium broke out, and greed and lust took over the crowd. At that very moment, with that single action, Kirin placed herself dead center in the game.

For Sifu, right and wrong were now blurred, but his fuel for revenge could not be quenched.

And so it begins.

CHAPTER 13
From the Ashes

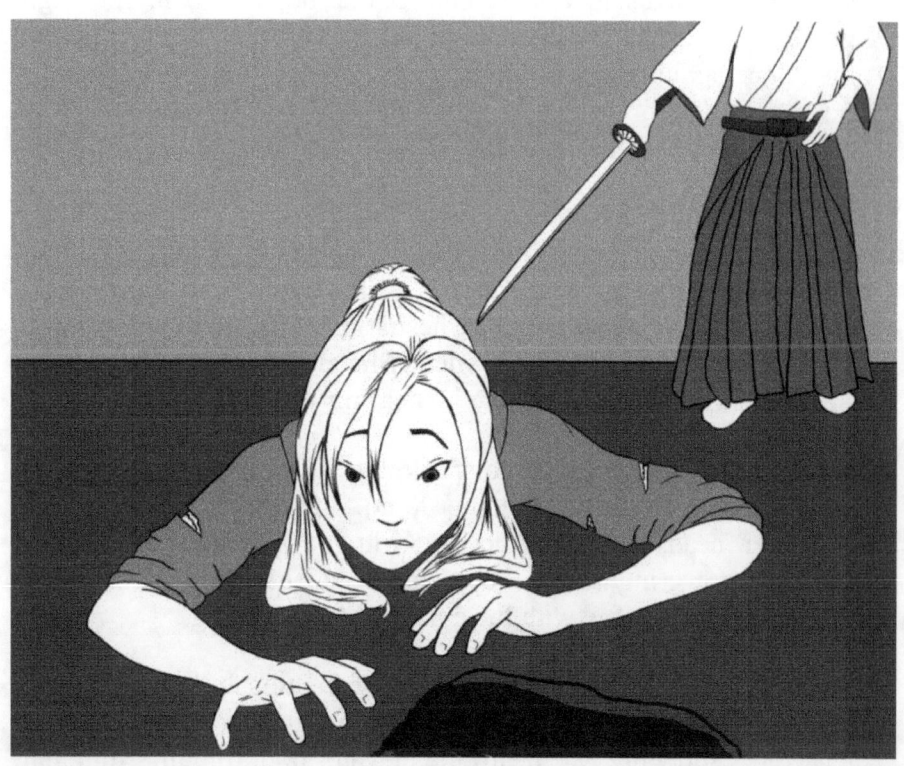

Kirin had one thought in her mind. It was not about getting justice, but all-out revenge. She didn't care about bringing balance to the world. The pictures of Sifu's family haunted her. She knew there would be a price, but she didn't care what that cost would be. Fortune had presented her the source, and now it was time to eliminate it. The elevator doors opened as she reached the very top of the UFMF building. From a distance, she could see the end of the hall. The bright lights laid out a path as she felt the silence surround her for the first time. Once again, she was alone, and it was up to her—and no one else—to resolve this. She took a step forward and continued her walk straight ahead. As she reached halfway, the view began to present itself clearer.

Three secretaries continued working behind their desks, not acknowledging her presence at all. It didn't matter to Kirin as she continued toward them without hesitation. She finally got within speaking distance but remained silent. She turned to her right and saw a single door, which appeared to be her only option.

She opened her mouth to speak, but all three secretaries raised their arms in sync and directed her to go. They never paused in their work, their heads remaining down. Kirin got the hint and proceeded toward the towering doors; they made her feel small. That appeared to be a recurring theme with the entire UFMF building.

She began to open the doors as she cautiously looked back to see if the secretaries would do anything, but they continued on with their work. Suddenly, she heard the elevator door dinging from afar. She turned to see who it might be. Kirin felt it odd that her path to the top had been met with zero resistance. She clenched her fists, ready to spring into action, but her emotions quickly changed as she saw Tobias emerge.

Tobias shouted, "Kirin!"

Kirin let go of the door handle and stood to the side. Tobias began running toward her and made it three-quarters of the way to the hallway. A breeze rustled Kirin's hair as all three secretaries ran by her. They formed a wall, striking a pose and preventing Tobias from getting to Kirin.

Wearing a look of confusion, Tobias stopped in his tracks. He stared at each one of them, pausing to admire the view. "Hello … what have we here?"

They all spoke in harmony. "She may go, but you may not."

Tobias snickered and then, being Tobias, ignored their order. "I do what I want."

He approached them, ready to unite with Kirin without considering that they could possibly pose a threat. They approached him from all angles and seductively surrounded him, causing him to freeze in surprise. One of them pressed her hand firmly on his chest and ran it slowly to his navel area while another one hugged him from the side and began nibbling on his ear as her breast caressed his arm. Finally, the last one approached him square on, stopping just shy of his lips. She licked hers and pressed them firmly upon his. Tobias did not resist as he wasn't sure what to do.

Kirin rolled her eyes and turned away, annoyed by his reaction and determined to go on her way.

In a flash, pleasure turned to pain as they maneuvered in unison, catapulting Tobias to the ground. He looked up to see the center secretary holding a side kick position, which had landed on his chest. The other two focused their attention on Kirin, silently warning her not to move to aid him.

Kirin shouted, "You deserved that!"

Tobias sighed, "No argument from me. I deserved that."

He stood up with his ego slightly bruised and began to dust himself off. He shook his head and took a moment to gather his bearings, surprised to find a footprint on his shirt. "That's a pretty strong kick for a girl."

"You deserve another kick for that!" Kirin called.

Tobias did not respond as the three secretaries melded into their singular formation, recreating a wall. They spoke again in unison, "She may go, but you cannot."

Tobias looked at Kirin and shouted, "Go ahead. I'll be right behind you. This won't take long."

Kirin hesitated, unsure what was the right thing to do. Tobias removed his backpack from his shoulder and slid it across the hall toward Kirin. The secretaries did not contest the action, so Kirin grabbed the backpack, but she decided not to look inside.

He shouted, "Go … now!" His commanding voice jolted her out of her indecision. She took one last look at Tobias and did not speak a word as she scurried on her way to find Watanabe.

Tobias cracked his neck and began approaching the secretaries again. "My bad. Definitely my bad for underestimating you beautiful ladies." They stood silently and did not move as he drew closer.

"I always dreamed about having two girls at one time, but to have three…. Now, this isn't exactly how I imagined it, but you ladies need to move out of the way or be moved." He began walking toward them, this time at full attention and ready to spring into action.

They stood still until he was in range. Each one looked exactly the same to him, almost as if a single girl were moving in a blur. He made a concerted effort to first use his blocking skills to avoid getting hurt as well as dishing it out. A fist flew straight at him, and he caught it and decided to toss her away from the group. She rolled unharmed to the ground and was frustrated that she had missed. The other two went for two kicks at different parts of Tobias, but he maneuvered again out of harm's way, allowing each of them to kick one another by accident. They staggered to the ground, upset that he had been able to break through their defenses.

Tobias took their time of disorientation to sprint for the end of the hallway where the door stood. He pulled on it several times, trying to open it. He was about to attempt to kick down the door when he saw all three secretaries lined up a good fifteen feet away. He ignored them and unleashed a front kick that landed solidly on the door, causing it to shake, but not to break.

"What the…?"

He launched a second kick that was even cleaner in motion and generated a greater impact, but still the door didn't budge. He shook his head in surprise as he turned toward the secretaries. The middle secretary reached into her dress, specifically her cleavage, and pulled out a little device. As she began to open her mouth, the rest followed once again to remaining in sync.

They said, "In order to get through the door, you're going to need this."

Tobias shook his head, "I guess there's no Mr. Nice Guy for me today. Looks like I'm going to have to serve you ladies some cake."

The secretaries formed a new sexy pose together and said, "Like we said, she can go, you cannot."

Tobias mumbled to himself, "They're just girls … hot, gorgeous girls. It's okay to hit them." He charged in, hoping to inflict minimum damage as his goal changed to getting the device that would open the door. Several exchanges went back and forth as he used an open palm to deliver slaps instead. When he found himself suddenly placed in a headlock, he went with the flow and decided to palm strike her at her lower part. Upon contact, his eyes opened up and his hand instantly pulled away. He felt her off balance as he tossed her in the direction of the other secretaries. They collided with her, and all three fell to the ground. Tobias stepped back and looked at his hand. He had a look of horror on his face as he took his sleeve and wiped his mouth vehemently.

He spit first and then looked at them as they began standing up. "What the fuck? You're a guy?!"

The three secretaries reformed a line and spoke. "You don't find us beautiful anymore?"

Tobias pointed, "That one over there … Is a guy."

"Correction." They spoke together once again. "We are all women, but I believe the term you are looking for is transgender."

Tobias wiped his brow and shook his head in disbelief. "Well, now it's not gonna be a problem whipping your ass." He paused for a second, wondering if his choice of words was appropriate.

Tobias cracked his knuckles, "My patience just left, and you're all no match for me."

#

Kirin ran through another long hallway. This time, she had a sense of finality. She could feel it. Through these doors would lie her last challenge. She took a deep breath, preparing to do whatever it took as visions of Sifu clouded her mind. A tear ran down her face as the thought pained her even more. *For Sifu*, she thought.

She prepared to kick the doors down and make a smashing entry, but the door crept open, welcoming her in. Surprised, she hesitated before entering. From a distance, she could see her target: an older Asian man sitting at a desk at the far end of the room. She had reached the top of the UFMF building, so this could only be the one and only Watanabe. She was ready to face him and make him pay for his crimes. She took several steps, unconcerned with her current surroundings, though she noticed the other individual in the room. To his right stood a beautiful lady with blonde hair and glasses in a classy business suit. Her arms were crossed in front, and her face was stone-cold.

As Kirin continued moving forward, another figure emerged from behind Watanabe's chair. He revealed himself while Kirin stood frozen as if she had seen a ghost. With a smug smirk on his face, Justice looked directly at her.

"No … no, it can't be," she whispered as she took several steps forward.

"Welcome, Kirin. We've been expecting you." The woman gestured for her to approach.

She took a quick glance at her surroundings and noticed very little was in this fairly large office area. She turned toward the entrance and wondered where Tobias was. *What's taking him so long?*

"By the way, my name is Kristen, and I'm quite pleased to make your acquaintance. I wish it was more on mutual grounds … but I'm sure at this time you're hoping to make our first meeting your very last."

She ignored Kristen and continued to look at Justice.

Kristen realized that her words were going unheard. "Oh, my apologies. I'm sure you are wondering about Justice…. Justice, would you be so kind as to fill in the blanks for our guest here?"

535

"As you can see, unlike Sifu, I survived the blast." He pointed to his face, "I can't complain. The scar gives me some character. Besides, there's no greater satisfaction than beating your teacher."

Kirin pointed to the ground and said sternly. "Right here, right now. We have unfinished business."

Watanabe finally spoke, trying to gain control of the conversation. "I must commend your little attempt on my corporation. Brilliant, in fact, and some things even I initially over—"

Kirin interrupted Watanabe's speech as she began charging in from across the room. She dropped the bag that Tobias had given her. She didn't care what Watanabe had to say. She wanted Justice, and nothing was going to stop her. As Kirin moved in, Justice jumped over Watanabe's table and began closing in on Kirin.

Kristen cried out, "Sir?"

Watanabe held his hand up to Kristen and did not stop the two. He sat back to watch what would transpire.

The gap closed quickly, and once Kirin got within striking range, she launched her first attack. Justice smiled. Having Kirin make the first move just made it easier for him to counter. However, once they made contact, Justice went for the counterattack, and that's when the smile vanished. Kirin immediately went for the freeze as her touch traveled from his hand through his body and down to the ground. For that split second, he couldn't move until she threw an attack that connected squarely onto his chest.

Justice was stunned, unaware that Kirin now possessed the same skill. He took the brunt of the first hit, and his body buckled as it sprang back from the impact toward Kirin. She used that momentum and pulled him in for a second attack, connecting a chop to his neck. She flowed into a final attack as she grabbed him from the back of his neck and landed an elbow to his face. Justice fell to his knees as Kirin quickly snapped his neck. His limp body crumpled to the ground.

Watanabe clapped his hands in approval. "Well, someone's been practicing." He genuinely admired Kirin's work as he reveled in Justice's demise. "Good … good."

Kristen, who was next to Watanabe, was in shock. She held her hand in front of her mouth, unable to hide her emotions. She had thought no one could best Justice and was surprised by Watanabe's behavior.

The adrenaline was pumping through Kirin's veins as she continued to stare at Justice, but she felt no satisfaction. She was breathing heavily as her intent finally shifted gears. She took a step, shifting her focus back to Watanabe, ready to dash for him.

Watanabe raised his hand, a signal that caused Kirin to hesitate and hold her ground. "Please, Kirin. You'll have your chance. I promise. But, I'm sure everything that you've seen tonight is difficult to process…. Allow me to at least explain myself."

Watanabe got up from his chair and began to walk toward Kirin. The triangle-shaped office didn't seem appropriate for the largest and most powerful corporation in the world. Empty except for a few key items, it was underwhelming in a way, though few ever visited or had the rare opportunity to see it. However, as Watanabe continued his stride toward Kirin, the windows began to transform, and the inner surroundings began to flash live scenes of the chaos occurring at the UFMF Dome. For the first time, the office finally began to flex its technological advancements as it almost appeared that both Watanabe and Kirin were in a live VR display of what was being shown on the news. From the ceiling to the ground, she was surrounded by another location.

Kirin began sizing up Watanabe. His English was quite good but carried a slight accent. His movement showed he had some training, but she was unclear as to what.

Watanabe drew closer. "Impressive, isn't it? All this." He raised his hands to showcase his work. Kirin looked around, reluctant to admit she was impressed by what she was witnessing.

"I understand your pain, Kirin. I understand it all too well. And, yes, for progress to occur, mistakes must happen. As you are well aware, there is no escaping both success and failure. Throughout all this, you and I have had to make sacrifices."

Kirin said, "All I know is what you've done. I'm here to make sure you pay."

"Don't get me wrong, Kirin. I admire you. In fact, in all the scenarios that were run, the chances that you would pick this to bring me down were astronomically small. Yet, here we are. Two people with similar goals, but with vastly different opinions on how to achieve them."

"What are you talking about? You're a monster!" Kirin felt insulted by the comparison.

"From a certain point of view, I could say the same about you."

"Enough talk. I'm here to end it for you—the corporation *and* your reign of evil. I'm going to expose the UFMF for what it truly is."

He turned his back to Kirin and began to speak. "You … and you alone?" He chuckled, "What about your friends?"

She looked surprised by Watanabe's comment.

"Oh, yes, your friends. You sure put a lot of faith in your friends. But, then again, I could say that your friends put a ton of faith into your misguided plan."

"What are you talking about?"

"I'm well aware of your intentions. I'm well aware that you and your friends are going to try to spread the … truth. Right now, they're in the command center, believing that they've hacked through our system and will begin transmitting to the world all of the atrocities we've committed when, in fact, it'll never leave the UFMF building at all."

Kirin didn't respond but had a look of concern, as her breath and heart rate increased.

"Your skills are impressive, Kirin Rise … but you fail to understand the true power. It's not the UFMF, but something beyond. You didn't realize that, when your Sifu was off to obtain information about the UFMF, I was well aware of what he was trying to do. I knew he was pestering my son, who had no will of his own, to give information about us. But, I let that all happen. So, now we can finally end this last bit of hope that you and your people foolishly cling to." He pointed to the screen, which showed several of Kirin's friends who were working in the command center, the power grid, and the server rooms.

Watanabe said, "You see, you and your friends have walked into my trap." Kirin watched as a video showed Gwen at the command center. There she was seated in the center of the console with Sage and April at her side. Team Eskrimadors was on the lowest level of the server room, and Team Bokken was in the central power grid. All of them were carrying on with their business, unaware of the eyes upon them.

Watanabe said, "Look at your friends, Kirin. You can watch it all now and enjoy it in the process. As soon as they reboot the system, they'll believe they have access to the entire site when, in fact, what they broadcast will never leave this place."

Kirin shook her head in confusion, "Why are you showing me all this?"

Watanabe turned to her, "To be so close and lose it all … tears at the soul and creates its very own prison."

Kirin watched with Watanabe as her friends reset the main system and celebrated. They began transmitting a live stream, believing they were reaching the entire world and finally exposing the truth about the UFMF.

Watanabe said, "You see … a moment of hope. And now you'll see that the true power was never the UFMF … but, in fact, what hid in its shadows."

Kirin could only watch, as she had no idea what Watanabe had in store for her and her friends.

#

Hunter was beside himself as he paced behind the group, "I can't believe it. We did it! We actually pulled it off and did it." He shook his fist and smiled, joining in on the celebration with high-fives.

For the first time, April had a concerned look on her face. She was the barometer that everyone seemed to hang on. Gwen noticed it too and asked, "What's wrong?"

April bit her lip, "That was too easy."

Hunter looked at both of them, "What are you talking about, too easy? Do we need a recap of tonight's events? Besides, I'm looking at the screen…. We're broadcasting, aren't we?"

Gwen went back to the computer and started looking through things. She said, "We're definitely broadcasting. Hunter, do me a favor. Go over to that screen and turn on one of the networks."

Hunter rushed over and did as Gwen requested. He pulled up a channel, "It's just regular news. News about Kirin missing tonight's UFMF fight."

"Check through all the channels … now!" commanded Gwen.

He began scanning through each channel, but not a single one was broadcasting them at all. Hunter shook his head, "I don't get it." He continued to scramble as worry began to settle on his face. "Wait a second. It's all about Kirin. There's no news about the UFMF building at all. Nothing about our broadcast."

Gwen slammed her fist onto the keyboard, "It was too easy."

Hunter said, "I don't get it. We're still in lockdown at the lower levels, but the police and STDs haven't been notified … and not one story about us."

Sage looked at April and then at Gwen. "It's a trap," they all said at once.

Gwen confirmed, "We're broadcasting, but it's not leaving this building." Suddenly, the screens flashed as all the lights went off inside the command center. The only light source was the glow of the computer screens. "What's going on?"

April looked around. "Everything just flashed for a second. That can't be good."

Hunter began nervously biting at his nails, "When April's worried, I'm worried."

Lance got on his communicator and spoke. "Everyone, report in."

Trevor answered first, "It's pitch dark here."

Freddie replied, "Same here. Can't see nothing."

Doc responded jokingly, "What you guys break?"

Gwen scoffed, "Nothing. I'm turning on all the lights on your drones above you, but this will eat away at your battery life."

April said, "I have a bad feeling about this."

Sage shouted, "Everyone, check out this screen!"

Gwen moved over to Sage's workstation and stared at the screen. "What is that?"

Sage pointed to the screen, "We've got movement. Lance, get over here and check this out."

Gwen said, "It's probably just Kirin and Tobias."

Sage shook his head, "It's not. There's too many of them."

Gwen looked closer and said, "That's impossible." She checked the screen and saw two figures at the very top. "That's gotta be Kirin and Watanabe." Then she looked again at the layout of the Cube where the remaining guards they had captured were still registered and intact. "Lance, what do you think this is?"

Lance stood silent and tried to process what he was seeing.

Sage said, "It's coming from everywhere."

Hunter said, "Outside the sixty-sixth? Right?"

Gwen replied, "No, it's inside the Cube. It's not a mistake … it's definitely from inside!"

April said, "She's reading it right. Whoever or whatever this is … they're coming."

Lance hit his communicator and said, "All teams, we've got a problem."

Freddie said, "Team Eskrimadors is here. What's up?"

Trevor replied, "Present."

Doc said, "What's going on, Lance? Talk to me."

Gwen clicked her communicator and said, "We're broadcasting, but it's not sending out. I've just double checked and confirmed. You should have lights now from your drones."

Doc replied, "We got lights now. Confirmed. But, how's it possible you're not transmitting?"

"Something's blocking our transmission, and I need to figure out who's doing it," said Gwen.

Lance picked up the communicator, "We've got bigger problems. We've picked up activity throughout the Cube. There are quite a few dots amassing."

Freddie asked, "What is it? Are you sure it's not just us?"

"Copy that," said Trevor. "I'm with the rest of the guys. I don't see anything."

Rather than arguing, Doc asked, "What do we do?"

Lance covered his communicator and leaned toward Gwen, "Isn't the building still in lockdown?"

Gwen gave a solemn nod, "It is, but I didn't override the original command for it. We're in lockdown because someone wants us to be here."

#

Tobias was having his way with the secretaries. As skilled as they were, he had an answer for all their moves. His cocky attitude and disrespectful ways didn't sit well with them. He threw the last one to the ground near her companions. They slowly got up. Unhappy with the results so far, they dusted themselves off and tried to collect themselves for another attack.

Tobias flashed a smile, "It's been real fun, ladies … uh, or gentlemen." He was still somewhat confused on what to call them. "But, either you clear out of here or no more Mr. Nice Guy for me."

The three did their best to move in sync, as their outfits were torn and their faces bruised. They looked at Tobias and lined up, next to each other once again.

"You can't say you haven't been warned," Tobias smirked.

The lead secretary stepped in front, as the other two slid behind her, making a triangle formation. Without a word spoken, they all reached into their right-side pocket and pulled out a tiny object that sparkled in the light. Each one appeared to be a small talon that fit right over the index finger. They all smiled, even with their current beat down, as they pointed the talons toward Tobias and then held them against their faces. The two secretaries from the sides spun in a circle and positioned themselves behind the main one in front. They were perfectly lined up to appear as if they disappeared from sight.

The main secretary in front spread her arms, and the remaining two formed a unique hand position behind her. From Tobias's perspective it now appeared there was only one secretary with multiple arms dangling about in front of him. They began moving in a hypnotic manner as he stood for a moment and gazed at the spectacle.

Tobias cracked his neck, "You see, now it's going to get messy." He charged in with no intent of messing around. As he neared the secretaries, they split from their group and surrounded him. It didn't matter to Tobias what they did or whether they were armed. The closest one was always the target and the greatest threat, so he dealt with her first. Bodies and attacks were flying from every angle as Tobias navigated his way through each one. He dished out the pain and didn't hold back until he was the only one standing.

He looked at the three secretaries who again were on the ground. Tobias made a snide remark, "Déjà vu."

One of them stood up, cleaning the blood from her mouth. "Are you sure?"

Tobias checked himself and noticed a scratch on the side of his arm. "All that effort, and you only managed to get a little scratch?"

The secretaries smiled and said together, "A little scratch? Oh, it's more than that."

Tobias stared them down, "You're not going to beat me…."

"We weren't planning to beat you."

#

The screens all around were broadcasting the events that were happening inside the Cube. Kirin watched as her friends were unaware that they were being observed. She turned to Watanabe and asked, "Who are you?"

Watanabe kept his distance, "It seems only fitting to reveal the truth to you, Kirin. Is that not what you seek?"

Kirin didn't answer as she slowly tried to shorten the gap between them.

Watanabe placed his hands in the pockets of his finely tailored suit as he began to speak. "I hate wearing suits. Did you know that? But, I thought tonight it would seem fitting to dress in proper attire. For seventy-five years, we have stayed in the shadows, the clan sworn to secrecy from the outside world by our founder. And, as fate would have it, the night of the Dome Championship is the time for our unveiling."

Surprised by his comments, Kristen interjected, "What are you talking about? Clan … sir?"

Watanabe's focus was on Kirin, and he seemed somewhat annoyed by Kristen's questioning. "I'm sorry," he said incongruously as he looked over his shoulder at Kristen, who remained behind his desk. "You've been a loyal worker, Kristen, but you were simply a necessary piece of the puzzle."

"Sir?"

Watanabe straightened his arm, and a single dart fell perfectly into the palm of his hand, hidden from sight. In a flash, he spun around, whipping it toward Kristen. It hit with precision straight through her eye, penetrating her glasses. She slumped over and collapsed as blood slowly poured onto the desk.

In shock, Kirin stared at Kristen and then looked over to Watanabe. His face was smooth as glass, showing not an ounce of regret.

"You monster!" she screamed. She had seen and heard enough. She charged at Watanabe and closed the gap within a heartbeat. She was almost within striking range when he threw a small, circular object on the ground. It exploded upon impact as smoke filled the air, causing Kirin to stop in her tracks. She spent a moment waving her arms, trying to clear the smoke.

As the air finally cleared, Watanabe was nowhere to be found. She spun around, checking every possible location, but he was gone. She thought, *Where is that son of a—?*

Her ear caught wind of his voice, which caused her to turn around and focus her attention on the samurai suit. Nestled in the far corner several feet from his main desk, it was the most colorful item in Watanabe's office. Watanabe appeared from behind, silent in his movement as he emerged from the shadows. The video of her friends continued to play in the background, and she knew time was limited.

He finally spoke, breaking the silence. "Kirin, Kirin … I would be a fool to go hand to hand against you in combat. But, what you see before you is something very special. This suit has been in my family for generations. Often, people's concepts of the ninja are misconstrued, trivialized by TV and movies. People fail to know the true history and the role we played. The samurai were looked upon with honor, but little did people know that we, too, were samurai, serving the leaders and doing their bidding without them knowing our role in the shadows. But, that time has passed, and now we bring forth the possibility of something even greater as we shine new light from the darkness."

Kirin noticed that he no longer carried an accent when he spoke. "You're crazy."

Watanabe grabbed a sword in a scabbard decorated with fine colors. He had yet to reveal its blade. He said, "This sword is what I'm most proud of." From the way he held it, Kirin could tell that he was no stranger to the sword. In fact, this was the first thing that was distinctive about him and not hidden. In a blink, he pulled it from its scabbard and sliced through the air in one clean cut. He said, "The souls of hundreds of men, women, and children have been taken with this blade, and now, unless you choose wisely, your name will added to the list."

Kirin began creeping toward Watanabe, planning some kind of counter to the man holding such a deadly weapon.

Watanabe said, "Join me. Join us, and I will show you the truth you seek."

His words froze her in place, "Join you? You're everything that I despise."

"I understand it's difficult for you to see. You feel the world has wronged you. You feel that you are here to bring about justice and balance, but I'm offering you the very thing you seek."

Confused, Kirin inched nearer but refused to speak.

"You believe that people should have a choice, that they need freedom. But, I'm telling you that is the greatest lie of all. I remember your banner, the illusion of choice. The real truth is that, if you give people exactly what you believe they want, they'll run from it. They fear it—a fact that has been proven throughout history. Mankind has always chosen the easy way out. That instinct has been bred into the very fiber of our being. If you get what you want right now and defeat me, I guarantee you nothing will change."

"That's a lie."

"A lie? I think that you're lying to yourself. Mankind wants to be subjugated; in fact, they choose to be. Look around, they can't even face their very own demons, so they would rather be lost in the fantasy than deal with the truth. Those with the power will forever take advantage of this fact because they know it all too well."

"That's you," she accused as she pointed at Watanabe.

"No, far from it. You think you understand how this world is run." He chuckled with disgust. "If I told you the truth, you would be in shocked. You believe it's run by politicians or corporations, when they are merely pawns for the few who play the game. What I'm offering you is to finally have a world of peace and order."

Kirin shouted, "By brainwashing people!"

"How is that any different from the man who has free will and chooses to bury himself in his work? To buy things that he doesn't need or impress others just to feel better? At the end of the day, he still feels empty and unhappy. Who do you blame for that, Kirin?"

"Who are you to decide the fate of man?" Kirin asked as they continued to circle one another.

"If not me, then someone else will. What I'm offering you is a chance to join me. If you do, I will spare your friends. See, Kirin, for the first time, you have true choice: choose your cause and allow your friends to die or join me and I will show you the truth behind that which you despise. It is far uglier than you could ever imagine."

Kirin continued to inched nearer to Watanabe. She knew she was at a disadvantage as his steel could end her life with a single touch. Her surroundings offered her little coverage: Watanabe's desk, a table with small items on it near the center of the room, and the samurai suit where he stood—with a smaller sword peeking from the bottom. She thought, *Not much for choices.*

Watanabe asked, "So, what shall it be, Kirin Rise? I will offer you this chance only once."

"I choose death," Kirin declared as she charged in.

"So be it. Death shall fall upon you!" Watanabe charged in as he held his sword at his side. Kirin didn't back down but was well aware of the danger. Behind Watanabe was her target, the smaller sword lying by the feet of the samurai suit display. She had to make him commit first; otherwise, the risk was too great. Watanabe took a swing as Kirin kept her distance and dodged the blade, sliding underneath it. He followed up with another slash but caught only air.

She fell short of the distance and scrambled on her knees to reach for the smaller sword. Kirin grabbed it and pulled it out of the sheath, her hand trembling nervously. She held the sword in front, trying to keep Watanabe honest and give a decent separation between them.

Watanabe laughed as Kirin flashed the sword at him. "Even with your skill, you think you can just fling that around?"

Kirin held the sword, which was half the size of Watanabe's weapon, in front of her. It felt like death, but she had no clue how to wield it. It was awkward in her hand as she tried to wield it like a Wing Chun sword.

As Watanabe held his sword in front, showcasing its blade, he continued to talk. "Do you even know what that sword is? It's a wakizashi…. It's usually used for close quarters combat and beheadings. It almost seems fitting that now you are holding it … as its last use is for *seppuku*, a ritual of suicide."

Everything he said was true. This blade was far from the equalizer she had hoped for, but something was better than nothing. Watanabe charged in as his sword disappeared in a blur through the air. Kirin went for the block, and the impact knocked her back, sending her to the ground.

She stood back up and edged her way to the main desk. There, slumped over his table, was Kristen lying in her own blood. Kirin began circling around the desk, using what she could for cover.

Watanabe's eye looked twisted, he chuckled devilishly, "There's no hiding here, Kirin. Nothing can save you now. Nothing can save your friends."

Watanabe's dominating presence began to overshadow her. His confidence with the sword was intimidating, and Kirin lost her focus to the target. He took a swing as Kirin blocked the attack, but he had captured the feel of the other sword and dislodged it from her hand. Kirin's wakizashi flew into the air, knocking over a jar filled with small items that scattered to the ground. He took a second slice at her and caught the side of her arm. She cringed in pain as she maneuvered to the other side of the desk.

Kirin looked to the door, hoping that Tobias would pop through. More than ever, she needed him. It was going to require both of them to defeat Watanabe.

#

Within the Cube, tension filled all three levels occupied by the group. Everyone was on high alert as they looked for the extra individuals that were supposedly in the room with them. Gwen was busy, hacking away on the computer, trying to figure out why they didn't have full control of the command center. April and Sage were on their terminals, assisting her. They were also busy communicating with the other groups.

Sage shook his head in panic. He stared at the screen as he was counting the number of individuals who were inside the Cube. "Shit, we've got close to a hundred individuals unaccounted for inside the Cube. They're not supposed to be here…. Lance, let's call everyone back into the command center."

Lance nodded, "April, Sage, tell them to haul ass!"

April and Sage gave Lance matching confused puppy dog looks. Finally, he realized they didn't understand the term. He said, "Tell them to return quickly."

Sage hit his communicator. "All teams ... I repeat all teams, please proceed to our command center ASAP!" He turned to Gwen and asked, "Gwen, can you at least get access to the auxiliary controls so they can have light?"

"Trust me. I'm already working on it."

April pointed to her screen, "Whatever those things are, they're moving now."

Lance leaned over and huddled by the screen. "Gwen, can you get us back up?"

Gwen yelled back, "What do you think I'm doing?"

"Whatever it is, do it fast," said Sage, who was searching for an extra light in his backpack.

The only lights that were being shed were from the huge monitors, as the rest of the room was covered in darkness. Gwen didn't miss a beat as she typed away on her terminal.

"Here we go!" she said suddenly. "I figured out what's happening, but I've got three obstacles to crack before we really have control of this command center ... or anything." She glanced up. "April, Sage, both of you control the drones and start guiding the teams to the exit so they can make their way up to the command center."

Hunter came out of the shadows to ask, "What should I do, Gwen?"

Gwen pointed to another computer, "Take over Sage's job. This one monitor has the layout of the entire building, keeping track of all the movement occurring in the Cube. I'll set up a second one next to it. You'll be the eyes and ears for all the teams. You'll be able to see what the drones are seeing from above." Hunter dashed toward the console and put the headgear on.

Hunter stared at the monitor in shock, "Are you guys seeing this? The numbers are increasing."

Gwen hit her communicator again. "Everyone, head back to the command center. Stay under the drones, which will provide lighting. Sage and April will help guide you on your way here...." She trailed off as everything became quiet in the command center. Something was off. They looked at one another as Hunter stared at the screen.

Then he screamed, "Run!"

Lance gathered behind Hunter, who was watching the screen, as everyone continued to listen to their coms.

Freddie from Team Eskrimadors shouted, "What the hell is that?"

The dots were too many to count as they surrounded the teams and swarmed in. Screams echoed through the coms as the group watched the screen in horror. The view from the drones made it difficult to see what was happening. All they were sure of was that chaos had erupted.

Lance called into his com, "What's happening people? Report … report?"

First Floor, the Server Rooms Several Minutes Prior

After hearing the order, Team Eskrimadors began backtracking to the main entrance. They were the furthest from the command center and cautiously moved at a steady pace. Everyone was on high alert as they stayed under the lights that the drones provided. They were uneasy—the lights provided visibility but also put a big target on all of them. Every one of them could feel it: they weren't alone. Eyes were peering at them … eyes they couldn't see.

Freddie stood in front, making sure he was the focus of the group. He kept his game face on, hoping his demeanor would keep his teammates in check. As the team leader, he gathered his group in an orderly fashion. Their goal was to get back to the main entrance and climb up two additional floors, hopefully reuniting with the main group at the command center.

Freddie's younger brother Fergus and his second-in-command Scott stayed close behind as they were watching from every angle of the server room. Their warm breath combined with the cold air created puffs of frost for everyone in the room.

Scott suggested, "We should run for the entrance. We're halfway back."

Fergus nodded, "I agree."

Freddie said, "No, we shouldn't. We're being hunted." He stopped in place and banged his sticks several times. "Ready to cross sticks!"

Scott repeated his order and made sure everyone heard. "Cross sticks!"

The Eskrimadors got into formation. Well trained, they had done battle before, but this was something they did not expect.

Fergus asked, "Are we still in hurt mode?"

"Negative." Freddie scanned the room and shouted out, "*Yahay … yahay!*"

Fergus turned to his brother and breathed, "Holy shit!"

Scott now knew this was for real. *Yahay* meant 'do what you must.'

Freddie kept smashing his sticks as the beat kept increasing. He screamed out, "Fly like the king eagle, Eskrimadors. *Balintawak*!"

Every single member clashed their stick as well and screamed, "*Balintawak! Balintawak! Balintawak!*" The tribal cheer was created to put fear into their enemy, as the rhythmic sound echoed throughout the server room.

Freddie commanded, "Fight under the lights, and watch your brother's back."

Team Eskrimadors' roar was broken by sounds of shuriken whistling through the air. Smoke billowed in random places, and death hovered from atop the servers, hidden in the shadows. One of the Eskrimadors slowly looked up as a dark shadow fell on top of him. All he could see was the blade that sunk straight through his body as he cried out.

Scott yelled, "I don't see them!"

Freddie couldn't find the enemy either as his head jerked from side to side, searching. No matter where he turned, there was no one to be found. Then he paused and slowly looked straight up. "Above!"

Several members were already down as the members of Team Eskrimadors looked to the top of the servers. There hanging from above were assassins, visible only by the reflection of their swords. Then the dark assassins began to rain down on them.

Freddie screamed, "What the hell is that?"

Second Floor, the Power Grid

Trevor from Team Bokken screamed into his communicator, "They're goddamn ninjas!"

Confused, Lance replied, "Did you just say ninjas? Confirm?"

Trevor said, "Ninjas, assassins, warriors of the night … it doesn't matter what you want to call them. That's what they are!"

Freddie from Team Eskrimadors shouted, "There's too many of them. They're slicing us apart."

Trevor's team was almost to the exit of the second floor when wave after wave of hooded black warriors poured in from every direction. Several bodies were left on the ground, some of which were sliced into pieces.

Trevor was next to one of his students, and he did his best to protect her. He held up a ninja sword he had taken from one of the fallen opponents. He shouted, "Reiko, get up! You have to fight!" He continued to scan the room as weapons and enemies were coming from every angle.

Reiko was holding one of her companions. She pulled out a shuriken that was lodged in his head and then laid him gently on the ground.

Trevor grabbed her and forced her to stand up. "He's gone. Forget him. Either you fight, or we all die." He threw her to the side as a star clipped him on his left shoulder. The ninja came in right afterward with a swing from overhead. Trevor immediately blocked the attack from above and countered with a slice across the belly. His opponent fell to his knees as his innards came gushing out.

Reiko screamed into the communicator, "There's too many of them! We're going to die!"

Third Floor, Research Facility

Doc was giving out orders as the rest of Team 6.5 was heavy into battle. Their numbers were the smallest amongst the group, but each one was armed with a pole.

Robert swatted at the ninja's sword from the side, shattering it in half. He knew exactly the weak structure of the sword, and Team 6.5 was armed with the perfect weapon to deal with their blades. He used the bounce of that break and flowed right into his enemy's throat. As his opponent laid on the ground, Robert pole vaulted on top and stomped him with his foot, clenching his fist and making a face. Three more popped up behind him as he swung around the pole in a huge circular motion, knocking them all to the ground. He took a second to relish in his victory by striking a Bruce Lee pose.

Ken shouted, "Hey, asshole, nice moves … but now is not the time."

Robert replied, "Hey … when in my lifetime can I ever do my idol's move—who, by the way, is one of my own—in a real-life situation?"

Ken said, "One of your own?"

"Yeah!"

Ken threw out a punch right down the chest of his opponent and said, "He's not Korean."

Robert argued, "His last name is Lee."

Ken replied, "He's totally Chinese, dude!"

Robert swung his pole over the head of his opponent. "Oh my god! I don't believe it."

Big T was on one knee, staggered for a moment as he was removing a shuriken from his arm. Hovering right in front of him was another ninja ready to slash him during his vulnerable moment. Doc took a running start and slid behind him, toppling him to the ground. As he got back up, he spun his pole and hoisted it above his head. His smashed the end into the ninja's face. He extended his hand out to Big T, "No time for breaks. You gotta keep moving."

Big T nodded, "I owe you one."

Doc snapped back, "Just stay alive."

Ryan had several cuts on his arms and leg as the bodies began to pile up around him. "I swear," he gasped, "if I make it … out alive, I'm gonna … start cardio … tomorrow."

He was kicked from behind as he lost grip on his pole. For the first time, fire lit in his eyes as he snapped back. He closed the gap like a gust of wind as his assailant was attempting to draw out his sword. Ryan cracked a fist straight down his solar plexus, sending him back. As his weight tilted backward, he grabbed him with both his hands and pulled him in. He thrusted his belly out forward as the ninja flew backward.

Several more surrounded him, but he was a man on a mission. Ryan unleashed the full arsenal from kicks and knees to elbows and punches. Every part of his body was a weapon. He was a bolt of lightning cracking everything within his path. Grabbing the last ninja with a single hand, Ryan looked at him and head-butted him straight to the floor. Finally, he had gotten back to what he needed most … his pole. He grabbed it and said, "Damn ninjas, without my pole, I had to do more work." He wiped the sweat from his head and hugged his pole tightly.

Ken dashed to the side and pulled Danny away from a strike. He shouted, "Watch your six!"

Danny replied, "Is that am or pm?"

Ken gave him a weird look and shouted out loud. "Not the time. Your back!"

Big T shouted, "Six is probably the number of kills you've got. I'm five ahead of your ass."

The reminder from Big T that he was running behind on their bet seemed to motivate Danny. He stepped up his game and became more aggressive. Danny was small but scrappy, and his natural speed worked well with the art. He jabbed the pole right into one of the assassins and then shoved his body toward Big T, who picked him up over his head and then smashed him across his knee.

"Thanks for that kill!" Big T kicked the pole back into his grip.

Danny shouted, "That's my count!"

"Nope, the ending is what counts," Big T insisted as he looked at the body lying below him. "Besides, assist don't count."

"Quit your gambling, you two!" shouted Doc as he motioned to the group. "We're headed downstairs!"

Big T said, "Gwen said to head back to the command center."

"I'm in charge, and I say we need to help out the other teams," Doc argued. "Did everyone hear that?"

Everyone on Team 6.5 looked at one another and reached a silent agreement. They began making their way down to the second floor, battling ninjas and moving like a fine-tuned machine. The years of training and their camaraderie gave them the advantage. They anticipate each other's moves without speaking a word, as they all knew each other's tendencies.

Doc spoke into his communicator. "Eskrimadors and Bokken, meet us at the exits. We're on the way down to assist."

#

Gwen wiped sweat from her forehead and continued typing. Only April and Sage could appreciate the amount of multitasking she was tackling while she worked. "I've cracked the first layer, but still no control on general auxiliary. It'll have to be all three."

Lance yelled into his communicator, "I repeat, all teams come back to the command center." He moved over to Hunter's terminal and looked at the screen as he tried to make heads and tails out of what he was seeing. "Talk to me, Hunter."

Hunter shook his head. "Their dropping like flies. Team 6.5 went back to help the other teams. Team Eskrimadors is down to four people, and Team Bokken has five remaining on their team."

Sage overheard Hunter and asked, "So, the rest of them are…?"

Lance slammed his fist into the console. "Doc, talk to me. Status?" He waited as silence descended, making seconds feel like an eternity. Lance took another breath, waiting for the faintest of sounds to finally penetrate the mic. Gwen was the only one to continue her work, as the rest sat and listened.

"Doc here, reporting."

Lance said, "You guys should be back at the command center. What's taking so long?"

Doc replied, "Made a call. Went back to help the other teams. We're bunkered at the stairway entrance of the third level. All teams are present … or what's left of us."

Lance said, "I can see that.… We'll talk about following orders later. Gwen's still working on cracking the system. We'll open the doors into the command center once you get here."

Doc huffed out, "Lance, you got eyes? Give me numbers of what we can expect?"

Hunter spoke into the communicator. "All teams listen carefully. I count roughly fifty-seven remaining. You've got thirty-nine on the second floor and eighteen ahead of you before you get to the command center."

Lance barked out, "Roughly? What about the first floor?"

Hunter said, "Something must be wrong with the sensors. It's not showing anyone."

#

Ken and Big T had barricaded the entry level to the third floor. They stood guard while the remaining group caught their breath. The door continued to thump as everyone exchanged doubtful looks. Ken stated, "Whatever we're going to do, make it fast."

Fergus wiped sweat from his bow, "Japanese steel is too strong. We're getting carved up out there."

Freddie had a quick meeting with his team, "Remember, our goal is to defang the snake. Don't go head to head with them.… We can't."

Ryan was sitting next to Reiko of Team Bokken. As she was holding her sword and examining the quality of her blade, he noticed she was cute. He decided to close the gap and strike up a conversation with her. "I know this is not the time or place, but considering that I might die … I figure screw it."

Reiko looked at him, "You're a good fighter."

"How do you know that?"

Reiko replied, "Because you're still alive."

Ryan took it as a compliment, "At least I got one thing going for me. Anyway, if we both survive this, would you be interested in going out for some coffee or something?"

Robert couldn't pass on the opportunity. "Really, Ryan?"

Reiko did not answer right away and put her sword back into the sheath. She turned to face him and planted a kiss on his cheek. She stood back up and walked away.

Ryan looked at Robert, "That's a yes, right?"

Robert shook his head and placed his palm over his face. "Kill me now."

Danny said, "That may actually happen."

Doc turned around and examined the team. It wasn't difficult to assess their situation. They were all shell-shocked from the fighting and dealing with an enemy no one had a clue would be there or, for that matter, even exist. Most were tending to their wounds or wounded companions. He decided to take charge. For the sake of their existence, they needed a leader now more than ever. He stood at the top of the stairs and gathered their attention. "Listen up, everyone. We're going to split the team in a run formation. Got that? Danny, Ryan, and I will lead the charge once we open these doors.

Eskrimadors and Bokken, you'll carry the middle, and finally Ken, Big T, and Robert, you cover the rear."

Robert said, "We're not going to battle it out?"

In a commanding voice, Doc said, "People are injured. We're down numbers. We gotta regroup in the command center. The goal is to get there as fast as possible and avoid any conflict or casualties." Doc paused and asked, "Command center, are you catching all this?"

Through the communicator, Sage said, "There's a bit of a breakup, since you aren't directly under the drones, but I caught most of it. Doc, if you will, I have an idea."

Doc replied, "I'm all ears…. What are you thinking?"

Sage said, "We've got the…." His voice broke off in garbled static.

Doc said, "Repeat that again, Sage."

"Comm … rones … communication drones."

"What about them?" Doc stood as close as possible to the main entrance of the third floor.

"Can you hear me, Doc?"

"Yeah, I'm in a better position."

"Good. While their main function is for communication, they're still drones. We can form a set pattern around you guys as a shield all the way up to the command center. Like I said, right now they're sitting directly above your entrance. As soon as you guys open the door, I'll control them, so they can at least make it more difficult for them to focus on you guys. Remember, there's only so many of these drones."

Doc agreed, "Great idea, Sage. That should help run some interference for us."

Hunter added, "Doc, I'll do my best to give you a play-by-play on the ninjas' location."

"Sounds good."

Doc faced the remaining group and gathered them together. He filled them in on the details that he discussed with Sage. He started positioning the team in their designated areas. As he worked, he gave each individual some words of encouragement that they'd be able to see this through.

Doc said, "Sage, we're all set."

"Roger, that."

Hunter chimed in, "Doc, they're spread throughout the research facility."

Doc commanded, "Sage, set the drones now!"

The doors swung open to a pitch-dark area until lights flashed from above and from the sides in a pattern. Doc led the charge to the command center as everyone followed him for a mad dash. Just like Sage said, the drones came hovering above and all around, forming a shield. A quarter way to the goal, the drones were doing their job. They ran interference for all the teams, and shuriken weren't hitting their mark. However, they were quickly beginning to dwindle in number.

Armed with his pole, Doc continued to run as they had reached the halfway point to the command center. Suddenly he noticed that drones were no longer being taken out. They met little resistance as the enemy drew back in surprise. They were within striking distance of the opening of the command center.

Doc hit his communicator as he panted. "We're halfway there."

Hunter shouted on the coms. "They're all positioning themselves right at the main entrance of the CC!"

He waved his hand and shouted at the group, "Keep running."

Hunter added, "Doc, the barrier from the second floor broke. They'll be coming from your rear soon."

Doc clicked his communicator and shouted, "Sage, position all the drones in front of us now like a wall. At my signal, I want you to flash the light at full beam right toward the main entrance."

"At the main entrance?"

"Yes, main entrance."

"Got it."

The drones started changing their position, just as Doc had requested. Behind him, he couldn't see his team as all the lights were focused directly in front of them. Suddenly, he caught visual of the main entrance and shouted, "Sage, now!"

The lights that were focused on the floor leading a path to the command center switched directions and beamed toward the entrance. The lights were blinding, and anyone in that direction would be hard-pressed to see their targets.

At Doc's side, Danny was sprinting. "Doc, should Ryan and I guard the entrance till everyone gets in?"

Doc yelled back, "Negative. Just get your ass inside and protect those in there already. Ryan, keep a count to make sure everyone is inside."

Doc hit his communicator one last time. "Open the doors … now!"

The doors began to open up as the group streamed in. Several assassins came crashing to the ground from above. Armed with steel, they began swinging at whoever was closest. They were relentless, but the goal was to dodge and not combat.

Doc was already in the command center, waving people in as he shouted, "Just get in!" Several shuriken were thrown at him, hitting the side of the wall; he barely dodged them.

Robert hesitated and drew his pole to the side. He cleared two of the attackers by sweeping their legs and then thrusting his pole into their faces. They instantly went down as he continued to fend off the other assassins. It was a mistake as they began to focus on the only static target that decided to fight.

Ken was about to pass him and enter when he turned back. He said, "Dammit, Robert!"

"Get in!" Doc bellowed.

Ryan shouted, "There's two missing!"

Doc said, "Yeah, I see them. Ken and Robert."

"No, besides them," Ryan said as he pointed behind them. "See? Reiko and Trevor."

Ken grabbed Robert from behind as they were just several feet from the entrance. He pulled Robert hard and tossed him into the command center. From the corner of his eye, he saw Ryan running back out and realized there must've been someone left behind. As Robert stumbled to safety, several shuriken's struck Ken in the back. His eyes popped open as he exhaled in pain, falling to one knee. Ken dug deep and reached for the pole that was on the floor. He hoisted himself up and struck a final pose. No matter what he would stand his ground.

Reiko was draped over Trevor's shoulder as one of her legs was immobile. Ryan came over to assist and notice a shuriken lodged in her calf.

Trevor said, "Hang in there, Reiko. We gotta move!"

Ken guarded the entrance and called out, "Ryan, hurry!"

Ryan looked at Trevor and said, "Go, I got her." He lifted Reiko, and Trevor made a dash toward the entrance as Doc yelled at them to get inside.

In front of the entrance, several shuriken connected to the front panel of the doors. Sparks flew, and the door slammed shut, sending Doc flying back. Just outside, Ryan was still carrying Reiko and stood all alone with Ken standing guard. The number of drones had dwindled to less than thirty.

Ken staggered to speak as he hit his communicator. "Sage, lay down a dozen drones in front of me ... now!"

Inside the command center, panic struck. Doc pounded the door and said, "Gwen, you gotta open this door!"

Gwen was working feverishly to reopen the main entrance.

Lance said, "Clear the entrance. If you can fight, prep for battle."

On the screen, Hunter was watching as Ken, Ryan, and Reiko were trapped outside.

Ken gave a final instruction. "Ryan, just protect her. I'll cover you."

"I can fight."

"Just do it!" shouted Ken. For the first time, there was no more Mr. Nice Guy.

About a dozen drones hovered right in front of Ken per his instruction, while the remaining formed a last shield around the trio. Ninjas began charging in from all corners. Ken ignored his pain and focused on the nearest target first, always. From the left to the right, all the way above, he was swinging the staff and connecting on target after target. He swore, "Die, motherfucker!"

Hefting his staff like a bat, he swung at one of the drones in front of him. "Come and get it, baby!" The drone shot forward, bowling several ninjas down. He took another swing to his side, toppling a few more ninjas at once and cracking the pole on the last one's skull. "I've got all day! Come on, you bastards!"

But, there were so many, too many for one man to deal with. Ken took several more shuriken during the battle, and he was losing a ton of blood. Driven to make a last stand, he continued to fight. In his hands, the pole was such an elegant weapon, cracking bones and swords with a flick of his wrist. Ken shouted, "You, too. You want some of this? Fuck you!" He held his pole in his guard position after the last swing, but suddenly a chain wrapped around it. The next thing he knew, it flew from his hands, engulfed in darkness.

Reiko was on the ground with Ryan hovering over her and shielding her the entire time. She looked at Ryan and asked, "What about you?"

"Don't worry about me…. I'll protect you." He glanced back to see how Ken was doing.

"Gwen!" shouted Doc.

At last, the door began to lift slowly. Ryan saw motion from below, but it stopped only a few feet from the ground. He began pushing Reiko through the small gap. "Ken, move … the door's opening."

Unarmed, Ken was delivering punches and kicks to whoever wanted a taste of them. His stance was losing form, but he was prepared to stand till the very end. He was exhausted and bleeding out, but he continued to fight as he shielded his friends. Ryan came back for him and slid him through the command center. He quickly followed him as well, rolling through the gap that remained.

Lance turned toward Gwen and shouted, "Shut the goddamn door!" The door immediately sealed as several more shuriken flew through, skipping through the narrow opening.

There was no time to catch their breath as everyone surrounded Ken to check his status. Robert came dashing through pushing the crowd aside. He yelled, "Clear some space! Clear some space!" Robert was stunned when he saw Ken on the ground with several projectiles lodged into him and cuts covering his body. He dropped to his knees and went to aid him.

Robert held Ken, "I'm sorry…. I'm sorry! I was just clearing the path. Why the hell do you always have to be the hero?" Tears were streaming down his face.

Ken smiled, "Because you're always the asshole." He struggled with his last words, "Always be you." He looked at Robert as he gripped his hand one last time and then closed his eyes forever.

As the drama unfolded at the entrance of the command center, Gwen could not celebrate even though she had cracked the second level. She turned away, realizing what had just happened. "I've broken into two of the barriers, but the third one is impossible."

#

Inside the server rooms, hidden from the chaos, the two janitors had taken advantage of the moment. Their well-disguised mop bucket actually contained several high-end laptops, and their mops attached to the sides functioned as a long-range antenna. Already hooked into the main server of the UFMF, they were monitoring the progress of both parties from the inside.

One janitor was busy typing away on his system. "Can you please not lean over me?"

The other janitor, Fawn, was standing above him draped in a large blanket that blended them into the background. He said, "You know this camouflage blanket isn't as light as you think. Besides, my job is to report back and make sure everything is done correctly, Wang."

Wang replied, "I told you to call me by my hacker tag, CMD64."

Fawn complained, "That's so hard to remember! And, I have no idea what that even means?"

"It's nostalgic to me … well my dad really. Besides it was his computer back in the days."

Fawn rolled his eyes, "You're boring me…."

Wang let out a deep breath and decided to ignore Fawn's comment. The paycheck at the end of this job, made even Fawn tolerable. He continued to monitor Gwen's progress on the screen, as he watched every step she was doing. "Man, this chick is brilliant. She's managed to bypass the two barriers set up by the UFMF in record time."

Fawn asked, "Will she be able to get though the third one?"

"No, it's totally impossible, even for her."

"But, you'll be able to help her punch through to the third one, yes?" He scooted from side to side, trying to look over Wang's shoulder.

Wang nodded, "Of course. I've just got to time it, so it seems like she actually broke through it herself."

Fawn stood up as he thought he heard a sound. "Shhh, you're talking too loud."

Annoyed by Fawn, Wang said, "You're the one talking to me. Just be quiet and let me do my work," as he continued typing away on his computer.

Fawn huffed, "Well, I'm the one pitching this tent."

Wang paused for a second with a concerned look on his face. He tilted slightly away from Fawn, who was standing directly behind him.

For the next ten minutes, they were quite involved in the game even though they appeared to be on the sidelines. Wang kept a close eye on Gwen's activities, but also informed Fawn of the happenings occurring with Watanabe and Kirin.

Fawn smiled, "You've also been manipulating the data to make sure all blame falls on Watanabe, yes?"

Wang replied, "From the very start, and my custom-made program will be done fully changing the data in about five more minutes."

Fawn asked, "What about the third code? Did you help her through it?"

Wang looked back and smiled, somewhat creeped out by Fawn hovering above him. "Yes," he said as he pointed on the feed. "My upload is almost complete. They'll be celebrating soon enough." He turned his focus back onto the screen as he adjusted his glasses.

Fawn smiled and said, "Wow, you really are good! So, you've pretty much completed your job?"

Wang nodded and continued to type. "Yeah, it's all on autopilot now. I'm just watching the show."

As the blanket continued to be draped over the two of them, hanging on Fawn's back, he slowly lowered his arms. Wang was busy watching the show as a knife lowered from the side of each of Fawn's hands.

Fawn said, "You've done an excellent job, Wang."

Wang replied, "Thanks. When will the payment—"

Fawn slashed across Wang's neck, making him choke on his own blood. His skill with the blades was evident as the cut was clean and the mess was minimal. He retracted his knives and caught the body before it fell onto the laptops. He lowered him to the ground as Wang quickly succumbed to his injuries. Fawn raised his hand as his index finger covered his mouth. "Shhh ... I'm sorry, Wang, but I can't have any loose ends."

He squatted down and reached over for the laptop. Without any remorse, he rested the laptop on top of Wang's body using it as a table. Fawn was pleased with his work and was ready to call it a day. He logged in and sent a message with the words 'job completed'. A few seconds later the user name MarOzawa appeared.

Fawn rolled his eyes again, "These stupid user names, couldn't Linda just use Linda." He clenched his fist, slightly perturbed for whatever reason and waited to see what she had to say on the screen.

MarOzawa: Activity at the top. Go up and investigate.
Ms.yumyum: You mean the very top?
MarOzawa: Yes.
Ms.yumyum: What about extraction?
MarOzawa: We can extract you from there if needed.
Ms.yumyum: Fine. Headed up there now. Toodles.

#

Doc looked at his team, who were all feeling the somber reality of Ken's death. Team 6.5 had lost their first member, but there was no time to mourn. The threat was still at large as the door to the command center was the only thing between them. It was up to him to lead the groups, so he mustered up everyone for what could be their final stand.

Doc yelled, "Everyone, pay attention!" He pointed to Gwen and asked, "Will the doors hold?"

Stationed by the main console, Gwen displayed the first hint of doubt. "I'm not sure. I still don't have full control of the command center."

"How much more time do you need?"

"As much as you can spare."

"Get on it."

Hunter turned to Doc.

"What is it?" asked Doc.

"Not good. Those red dots on the screen that were missing from the first floor. All of them … and I mean all of them are now out gathered in front."

Dock asked, "How many?"

"A rough guess, I'd say about seventy-plus, if not more." Silence fell over the group.

"Keep an eye on them and alert me of any changes," said Doc.

Gwen got back to work, with the third barrier being her last and most challenging. Lance sided with Doc and began gathering everyone around. Lance could see defeat in their faces. He had to challenge his team one last time. Injured and fatigued, still working mostly in the dark, they were drowning in doubt.

Danny was huddled up on the floor rocking himself, as Big T stood over him. Danny shook his head, his voice trembling. "We're screwed. How can we possibly…?"

Big T extended his hand to try to help encourage his best friend, but Danny ignored it and continued to talk to himself.

Danny mumbled, "There's too many of them. We may have the skill, but the numbers are overwhelming." He looked as if panic and fear had overtaken him.

Doc grabbed his shirt by the collar, pulling him back on his feet. He looked at Danny, who seemed to be lost, and slapped him hard on the face. It was uncharacteristic of Doc, but desperate times bring out one's true nature. His head snapped to the side along with his thoughts. Doc said, "You done?"

Danny wiped his tears and nodded.

Doc added, "Everyone, it's okay to be scared, but it's moments like this when we find out who we really are. Sifu always said you can either run or fight. Well, guess what? We're stuck right here, so there's only one option left."

Lance backed Doc up, "Remember what we all said before the start … no regrets." He took a moment to look at each and every one in the eyes. "No regrets!" he shouted at the top of his lungs.

"I can tell you that what we've uncovered in the short time here would make your skin crawl. The sacrifice that we're about to make is nothing compared to what will happen if we don't get back up and stop them. This is bigger than what we could ever imagine. But, if we quit now, our friends who have died would've died in vain. Their efforts will be for nothing if we don't take a stand and get that message out to the world. Can you live with that? Can you…? So, we either wait here and wallow in self-pity, or we decide here and now to fight till our last breath."

Doc stepped forward and clashed his pole to the ground several times. "Ryan, take Reiko to the back by Gwen, Sage, and April. Hunter and Lance, join them as well. It's up to you guys to protect them and be the last line of defense." He looked at Gwen who was working feverishly. Knowing morale was low, he added, "I know Gwen will find a way to crack it. Just make sure you give her the chance to. You got that?"

Ryan grunted.

Reiko stood up after tending to her wounds. "I can still fight!" She drew her sword from her sheath. "To the death."

Ryan turned toward her and muttered under his breath, "God, that's hot."

Doc nodded, "Good."

Trevor asked, "Where do you want my team to be positioned?"

"Listen up, everyone, if they get through and the doors open, we'll use the darkness as well. Stay clear of the direct path of the entrance, and let's draw them in."

"But, the computers and the lighting?" asked Sage.

"Yes, I know. They'll be drawn to those lights like bugs, so the moment they come in, we'll have to swarm them." Doc started pointing out positions for people to go to as everyone was scrambling to get in place. "Remember, one and done. Be quick with the deed."

Gwen shouted, "Doc, I've got a single drone hovering outside the front entrance."

"Perfect, we'll use what we can. The moment that door opens, beam a light right above the entrance."

"Got it."

Doc shouted, "Take a deep breath, everyone, and remember who the hell you are!"

The teams were all positioned, standing silent in the dark, with only a hint of light shed from the screens afar. Hearts were pounding, adrenaline was surging, and everyone in the command center knew this was the last stand. A sound echoed as the door lifted slowly. Eyes watched, but in the darkness, they could see nothing. They only felt the draft of the door opening. It finally stopped, leaving behind silence and a presence that could be felt outside the doorway. The single drone beamed its light downward, and the silhouette of their bodies formed long shadows that stretched from the main entrance. This time, there were no surprises. The remaining group charged in, prepared for one last showdown.

On the far end of the command center, Gwen looked at her screen and shouted, "I don't know exactly what happened, but we're in!"

Lance leaned over and looked at her screen. "You sure?"

"We're in," she nodded her head in excitement.

Lance asked, "What works?"

Gwen excitedly clamored, "You name it, we've got it."

The sounds of battle could be heard from a distance as the glow of their computers provided the only light source.

Gwen asked, "Should I flood us with lights now?"

"Not yet," Lance as he pointed to the far corner. "That thingamajig you showed me before?"

Hunter said, "The 3D printer."

"Who can operate it?"

April raised her hand and made her way to Lance, "Come with me."

Exhausted and embattled, the teams held together as best they could. They were clearly outnumbered and outgunned, and everyone had the battle scars to prove it.

Doc shouted, "Keep fighting!" as he took a slice to the arm and dropped his pole. He fell to the ground, fully exposed. An assassin came charging in, but Danny tackled him from the side. He grabbed a star that was on the floor and stabbed the assassin in the neck.

Doc got back up, but there was no time to celebrate. He quickly ducked down, avoiding several projectiles. As soon as one assassin was down, another would reappear, never giving a chance for them to even catch a breather.

Scott and Fergus fought back to back, their sticks covered in blood. They were surrounded by several assassins as they clashed sticks against steel. The chaos eventually caused them to separate. Fergus tripped over a body and dropped one of his sticks, which rolled away. He was exposed for that brief moment, and several assassins saw that he was vulnerable. Within a blink, an arrow flew through the air aimed right at Fergus, who covered himself and shut his eyes. The sound of the arrow penetrating flesh was all that he heard, but he felt no pain. He opened his eyes and saw his brother smiling at him.

Fergus looked at his brother, "Freddie?"

Freddie collapsed on top of him, but Fergus wasn't sure what had happened. He grabbed his brother and saw several arrows had penetrated his back. He had no time to cry as more assassins continued their onslaught. "Freddie!" He lowered his brother's head to the ground gently. Scott charged in and grabbed him from the ground, helping Fergus back up.

"Watch your distance," said Danny as he swung his pole, knocking over several of the assassins.

Big T looked to him, "I'm open to ideas. A little help?"

Two more from Team Bokken fell to the ground. The enemy's numbers were overwhelming. All hope seemed lost as the teams battled valiantly to the end. The option to run had long passed. Still battling in a haze of night, the blood blended in with the darkness. The sounds of weapons and screams continued to fill the air, as a silhouette of the battle was all that could be seen. Suddenly, the room was flooded with light, illuminating everything inside. Several of the ninjas with swords drawn hovering over Doc were knocked down in a blur.

"What the...?" Robert snapped back, to see what had just happened.

Now, even more ninjas were being knocked down one after another. All the teams turned around to see the source of their salvation.

Standing at a distance holding a high-tech gun was Lance. "Japanese steel meet American ingenuity … *sayonara*, bitches!" He fired several more shots, taking down a handful of assassins. The team found renewed hope with Lance as their backup, evening the odds.

Lance continued to fire, gunning down his targets from all directions. His level of damage made him the center of attention now. From behind, a ninja snuck up and drew his sword as Lance's back was fully exposed. Suddenly, a fist flashed across, sending the ninja flying through the room.

He turned slightly and saw April covering his back, posed in a Wing Chun punch. She was also armed with a set of double guns. He continued to fire and converse at the same time. "I didn't know you knew Wing Chun."

"Pffft, I was with Sifu for over a year. What do you think we did in Japan, eat sushi all day?" As another ninja came by his side, April spun around, delivering an inside diagonal hook across his face. The impact was solid as she tattooed him into the ground. She pulled out a set of guns. "Double tap."

Bang. Bang.

Lance turned to April, "You do know how to use that, right?"

April nodded and wailed, "Yeah, yeah … Southsiidddee!" As they stood next to each other, April was flicking her guns movie style and surprisingly hitting her targets. Her arms spread wide, she began spinning in a circle, picking each target off.

Gwen pressed the last button, and suddenly Kirin's message was everywhere, on every screen on every channel possible. "Yes!" She turned to Sage and Hunter, "Can you confirm?"

They both dashed toward their terminals and saw that Kirin's recorded message was being transmitted throughout the world.

Kirin had several cuts on her arms and thigh, fortunately wounds that only drew blood. Her adrenaline kept her going, but it was her determination and her will that kept the focus off the pain. Watanabe was skilled with the sword and made it extremely difficult for Kirin to close the gap. She calculated that, with Justice's association, he carried the knowledge of her fighting strategy. There was no way he would allow her to get within hand range. She knew the longer this fight lasted, the greater the chance that his steel would finally connect. Watanabe's plan to show a direct feed of what was happening to her friends kept her focus divided. Time was running out, and she needed to act fast.

Think, Kirin. Think.

Both of them were playing the distance game to perfection. Each knew just the right range that the other could strike. Watanabe's sword gave him the significant advantage, as he inched closer to Kirin. It was barely visible to the naked eye, thanks to the speed with which he slashed at Kirin. He was toying with her, and she knew it. She looked around the office, which had nothing she could use, but then she caught sight of her bag on the floor.

What's in the bag?

It was the only unknown. Maybe there was a reason Tobias had given it to her. Watanabe was blocking the path to the bag, but she had to risk it. She needed to make it seem like she had committed to a motion, using her body as bait so she could get to the bag. This time, she moved in hoping he would bite so she could reposition herself on the other side with the bag. He went for a cut, once again missing his mark by an inch. She was in close enough range for an attack, and she made the mistake of trying to dislodge the weapon from his hand instead of attacking his center. It was Watanabe who had baited her, as he countered her motion by ramming the *kashira*, the edge of the handle, into her gut. Kirin had managed to maneuver herself to the other side and lunged toward the bag. However, Watanabe caught flesh as his blade laid a mark across her back, cutting in deep.

"Nothing can save you or your friends now."

Kirin crawled toward the bag, gritting her teeth against the excruciating pain as blood dripped from her back. She hoped this was worth it; if not, it would only be matter of time before her defense fully crumbled. Instead of charging in, Watanabe watched from afar as he reveled her suffering. He performed a *chiburi*, a large flicking motion with his sword to rid his blade of Kirin's blood, which splattered on the ground as the shine of his sword returned.

Kirin grabbed hold of the bag and reached inside. She flashed a surprised smile. "Oh my god … Christmas came early!" She pulled out the *Bat Jam Do* that Sifu had made for her. She thought, *Thank you, Tobias*, as a glimmer of hope presented itself.

She stood up, re-energized and armed with her Wing Chun swords. A new confidence surrounded her as she faced Watanabe. "You were saying?" She pointed one of the swords directly at Watanabe, tracking his movement.

Watanabe flashed his sword and held it in front of him. He chuckled as he spoke. "This is a Shinzuki sword, forged from the ashes of the mountains in Japan. Its steel is unrivaled by any on earth. Do you believe your pitiful Wing Chun swords can clash with mine?"

Kirin said sharply, "Let's find out," as she held her swords to the side and began to approach Watanabe.

They drew within range as they circled each other. Watanabe held his sword casually to the side. Kirin inched just outside of his attack range as each fighter displayed their steel. Finally, both stopped at their current position, not moving a single muscle. Each drew a silent breath, staring into the other's eyes. The sound of the video playing was echoing throughout the room. Then Kirin heard Gwen shouting, giving her all the motivation to move forward.

Watanabe reacted, swinging at full force downward at Kirin, confident his blade would cut through. Kirin caught the blade by forming an X with her swords, stopping the steel in place. The clash rang through the air. His eyes bulged open in shock. His blades should've cut through her swords like butter. Kirin had neutralized the attack, and she used his moment of surprise to take a swipe at Watanabe's arm. He retreated backward. For the first time, Kirin had drawn blood.

Watanabe grasped his bloody arm before putting his sword up for guard again. "That's impossible. No blade can match the Shinzuki sword … no blade!"

Kirin held her swords up, making sure she had a guard before speaking. "You're right: the Shinzuki blade is unmatched. No blade on this earth can deal with it … unless these were forged by the great-great-grandson of Shinzuki himself."

Watanabe cursed in Japanese and said, "Shinzuki would never make a sword that wasn't Japanese!"

Kirin turned her blades and held them to the side. There, engraved on the very steel, was the Shinzuki family mark. There was no denying what Kirin had stated. These were, in fact, Shinzuki swords.

Angered by the betrayal that Shinzuki would make steel for a Chinese sword, Watanabe charged in. This time, Kirin had the advantage. The two swords allowed for simultaneous blocks and attacks. The blades sliced the air as the two warriors exchanged attacks, countering one another and waiting to feel when the other person would make a mistake. Kirin caught another angle toward Watanabe and drew a slash across his cheek. The two continued to battle as Watanabe found himself on the defensive for the first time.

Kirin pointed one of her swords at Watanabe, "Surrender now, and I might just spare your life."

Watanabe held his sword by his shoulder parallel to his body but did not answer her. They both kept their steel in front to make sure the other stayed honest. The momentum had suddenly swayed to Kirin, and both sides could feel it. From a distance, she heard the doors slide open and took a quick peek. Standing at the far end was Tobias.

Now she was more than confident as she spoke from a position of strength. Armed with her swords and Tobias by her side, she lowered her weapons, "Take my offer; because I'll say it only once."

When she felt Tobias nearing, she raised her voice and called out. "It took you long enough! What were you doing ... asking all three of them out on a date?"

Kirin kept her focus on Watanabe, relieved that backup was finally here. In the background, she could see and hear the video of what was happening to her friends. She couldn't wait much longer for an answer. She was about to speak when she found herself flying through the air and tumbling hard on the ground. She quickly recovered but was confused. As she looked up, she pieced together that it was Tobias who had bowled her over and was now standing side by side with Watanabe.

Why?

She was surprised by the attack and looked him straight in the eyes. She gasped. She had seen that look before when encountering Diesel and when fighting the thugs at the warehouse.

Noooo!

"It appears you are the one outnumbered, Kirin," Watanabe placed his hand on Tobias's shoulder.

She stood back up, clinging firmly to her swords. The weapons were her only hope. She now faced two foes, and her friends were struggling to survive in the Cube. Once again, the tides had turned.

Watanabe placed his sword back in the sheath and commanded Tobias, "Hurt her."

Immediately, Tobias charged in as Kirin took several steps back. His attacks were relentless, but she held her swords in a neutral position. His fist came flying in with deadly intent, handicapping her as she did her best to avoid him. Eventually, there was only so much she could dodge as she painfully ate a fist that connected to her face.

The impact left her shaken and gasping for breath. Tobias turned to Watanabe. Like a soulless beast, he was under his total control.

"Continue."

Kirin scrambled up.

Think. Think, dammit! It's over if I lose the swords.

Tobias nodded and then went on the offensive again. This time, she held both her swords with one hand, freeing up her right so she could at least attack. He came within range and attacked her center as Kirin used an angle to try to gain an advantage. Her line for attack was open, but she didn't take it. Instead, she caught his attack arm and went for a single lock. She almost had it in place, but he flowed with the force, spinning out of the technique and going for a sweep. She flipped in the air and landed hard on her back. Tobias hovered over her and waited for another command.

What can I do? I can't hurt him.

She crawled several feet backward from where Tobias stood. Time was running out for her as well as her friends. There wasn't a part of her body that wasn't in pain, and her thoughts were scrambled. She continued to lose breath, her heart racing as the inevitable end drew near. She had to let it all go. Nothing around her mattered. She closed her eyes briefly and focused on her breathing. The outcome wasn't important as a clear mind would be her best defense.

Watanabe was enjoying himself. A minion was doing his work for him, and everything appeared to be going as planned. Tobias looked at him, waiting for an order. Watanabe said, "It's time. Kill her now."

Tobias's head snapped back to Kirin, who was still on the ground with her eyes closed. He came charging in with one goal in mind. Armed with his skill and drugged with the power of no pain, he was the perfect super weapon.

Kirin's eyes finally popped open as she spun herself back on her feet with a kick up. Her breathing and her emotions were now under her control. Tobias was nearing, but she no longer saw him as an enemy. He was simply a flow of energy coming at her. In one hand, she held both swords while she kept her free hand out front as her guard. He threw a punch at lightning speed, but the touch could feel what the eyes couldn't see. Her hand quickly intercepted its path as her triangle had protected her. She felt his aggression as she continued to flow with the will of the force.

He countered her block and chained another attack to her center. This time, it didn't matter. She felt only for herself. Suddenly, at the point of contact, Kirin could feel the flow of the force run from her arm, through her body and eventually her leg. At that very moment, with the flow running throughout her entire body, she locked herself in place and stood still.

Watanabe watched but could not believe his own eyes.

There Kirin stood, a single hand touching Tobias on the arm, while he stood frozen. It was a skill level so high it had revealed itself to her when she needed it the most.

"Impossible!" he shouted.

Tobias tried to struggle from his position, but the harmony between the two structures was perfectly in place. Whether he gave more force or less, Kirin automatically countered his adjustment, leaving him locked and helpless to her will. When she released him from the hold, he launched another attack. Upon touching, she once again froze him on the spot.

"Enough!" An angered Watanabe was not amused. "Come here, Tobias."

Kirin released him from the spot, and he completely ignored her as he returned to Watanabe.

"You cannot win, Kirin Rise. Drop your swords and accept your fate."

Kirin placed her swords over her shoulder in a confident manner. She replied, "Oh, no … I think I can win."

Watanabe shook his head and chuckled. "So be it." His eyes glazed with darkness as he stood side by side next to Tobias. "Tobias, point to your enemy."

Tobias turned to Kirin and extended his right hand toward her. Kirin watched, confused by the strange command.

"Very good," said Watanabe. In a flash, he drew his sword and sliced Tobias's right hand off. The cut was clean as his hand fell to the ground.

The horror stunned Kirin. She gaped. Her heart racing, she shuddered in fear. Tobias stood there without a whimper, bleeding from his wrist as Watanabe smiled. "Are you going to let him bleed to death, Kirin?"

In an instant, she knew it was over. She dropped her swords, which clanked on the ground. She ran toward Tobias without any regard for her safety. All that mattered was him. She ripped off the scarf from her hoodie and made a tourniquet around his wrist. Kirin's face said it all. Hopefully this would be enough to keep him alive.

Watanabe stepped forward, knowing victory was at hand. "You see, Kirin? It's all about choices. Tobias, grab her now and hold her in place."

Tobias did as Watanabe commanded without hesitation. He lowered his severed arm, moved behind her, and held her firmly by the back of her neck. She tried to make eye contact, but he didn't react. She reached out to touch his face, but he slapped her hand away. She spoke in a tender voice, almost whimpering. "Please don't do this, Tobias. Please ... I...." Kirin struggled to finally say something she had never said before. "I, uh ... fight it.... I know you can do it."

Watanabe chuckled and admired the sentiment. "You underestimate the power of the drug. He cannot be turned. He is fully under my control, Kirin, just like everyone will be once you're eliminated along with your friends."

Tobias controlled Kirin from behind with a single hand around the back of her neck. He shifted her, so she was facing Watanabe. Kirin did not struggle, but she began to cry as she turned her head slightly to say, "No matter what happens, Tobias, I don't blame you. It's not your fault." His grip trembled as he squeezed her harder. Memories of the times they had spent together came flooding into her mind. She had feared the truth all this time and had run away from her true feelings.

Watanabe walked straight in front of her as he retracted his sword and held it to the side above his head. He looked at Kirin, who no longer stared him straight in the eyes. Her head was lowered, defeated, ready to accept whatever fate had in store. "Once you are done, I'll destroy your blades as well."

She thought, *No regrets.* With her last breath, Kirin whispered, "I love you, Tobias."

Watanabe screamed and with eyes closed thrusted his weapon straight toward Kirin's center. In a flash, the blade penetrated the flesh like butter, and the cut went clean through. Watanabe's eyes opened in surprise as his mouth dropped. He held his sword firmly in place, but all he saw was Tobias's back. Kirin had been tossed to the ground as he'd exchanged positions with her.

Kirin looked up at Tobias and the sword right through his center. Horrified, she screamed, "NO!"

Tobias grabbed the sword that penetrated his middle with his single hand. He pushed it against his innards, making it impossible for Watanabe to draw it back. He gave one last wink to Kirin before falling to the ground with the sword still inside him. Watanabe stood there unarmed and in shock.

Angered and in pain but now motivated by revenge, Kirin immediately switched gears and closed the gap on Watanabe. She sprang off the floor and rushed to destroy her target. He tried fending off the first attack, but she froze him upon the touch and delivered the first hit. She continued to rain blows down on him, and he could do nothing to stop her. Every move he made led to a hit by Kirin. Her will had made her unstoppable. Before Watanabe knew what was happening, she was on top of him. She began to hammer punches one after another onto his face as blood gushed onto her fist.

Tobias struggled to call out, "Don't! Kirin!"

She was breathing heavily, her hands covered in blood, and Watanabe lay on the floor helpless. She stopped with her last fist held right by her face, ready to finish Watanabe. Tobias's voice had the sound of kindness, causing her to pause. Kirin's mom's words suddenly echoed in her head. She thought of Justice and the emptiness she felt after taking his life. She'd felt the same after the two individuals at the warehouse and the Giant at the Battle Royale. It had become too easy for her to play judge and jury. But, he was only one more … and who would hold it against her after the atrocities he had planned?

Watanabe coughed blood, his face unrecognizable. "You can never win, Kirin. If you kill me, we all die."

Panting, Kirin was willing to pay the price for her action. Sweat and blood from her cuts continued to pour. He blonde hair was no longer pristine, as streaks of red ran through each strand.

Tobias coughed out more blood, "Don't…."

Kirin lowered her hand and saw the clear, circular pill that had rolled to Watanabe's side. She reached for it and stared at it for a moment. She said, "All for this … you invested everything in this." Kirin continued to look at it, "So, let this also be your fate."

She punched him in the gut, and his mouth opened, spitting out blood. She popped the pill into Watanabe's mouth and covered it. She pinched his nose and smothered his mouth until he was forced to swallow it. She remained on top of him, covered in her own blood as well as Watanabe's. She waited until his pupils changed and his demeanor was no longer the same. She leaned forward and whispered into his ear before finally standing and leaving Watanabe lying on the floor.

Kirin rushed over to Tobias, who was barely hanging on. Kirin wiped the blood from his mouth as he struggled to speak. She squinted and whispered, "This is going to hurt."

He grabbed her hands and stopped her action. "Leave it. Nothing can save me now."

"Tobias! You're so stupid. Why did you do that, huh? Why, Tobias? You're so stupid. Why'd you have to be the hero?"

Tobias smiled, which caused him to cringe as every part of him hurt. "If not me, then who?" he managed weakly as he coughed out more blood.

Their moment was interrupted as Watanabe stood up and looked at them both. He turned to face the window at the far end of the room and then began running at full speed. Tobias and Kirin watched as he crashed through the window and began his descent down one hundred floors from above.

Tobias struggled to lift his head as Kirin aided him. "What did you say to him?"

"Get away from me as quickly as possible."

He cracked a smile at the thought and began to speak. "I get it."

"You get what?" she whispered.

Tobias looked at Kirin's face, at the kindness he was able to see buried deep. "Sifu always laughed whenever one of us would say, 'I got it,' because that always meant we were the furthest from actually doing it or understanding it. But, honestly, I finally get what you've been saying."

"Stop talking so much and save your energy," Kirin scolded him as she tried to apply pressure to his wound. She was in a panic, trying to think of something she could do.

He pulled Kirin in closer as each word was now a struggle. "I finally understand what you meant … what you meant when you said that's not love."

Kirin cracked a hint of a smile as she was taken back by his words. She still could remember their argument in front of his apartment, that they had regarding love. "Shh," she murmured as she tried her best to comfort him. But, deep down, she knew he was on borrowed time, and there was nothing she could do.

Tobias stared beyond her eyes and into her soul. His words came directly from his heart. "When you love somebody, you just do it. Not for yourself, but for them, and in return you expect nothing back … because all that matters is how they feel, and hopefully that's happiness…." He gasped for air as more blood leaked from the side of his mouth.

Tobias touched Kirin's face, brushing his hand against her soft skin. "I get it."

She leaned forward and gave a tearful smile as she gently kissed his lips. For that moment, he felt no pain, and happiness surged through his entire body. She looked into his eyes as he said, "That's the first time we ever kissed."

Kirin struggled to smile, tearing uncontrollably. However, it was Tobias who suffered from seeing her in pain. He reached for the back of her head and pressed upon her lips once more.

Suddenly, the building began to alarm and then it spoke. "Warning. Warning. Ten minutes till self-destruct."

Kirin pulled away from his lips and looked around. "What's going on?"

The voice echoed again. "Warning. Warning. Please evacuate the building. The building will self-destruct. Nine minutes and forty-five seconds remaining."

Tobias said, "Watanabe, he said if he dies, we all die."

"Oh my gosh!"

Tobias looked at Kirin, "You have to get out of here!"

Kirin cried and tried pulling him up. "I'm not leaving you behind!"

"I'm done. Nothing can save me now. You have to leave me, Kirin."

"I'm not going to leave you. Never!"

Even as she protested, Kirin calculated their chances. There was no way she could move Tobias, and he was in so much pain. She went back down on her knees, rested her head on his shoulder, and just hugged him on the floor.

"What are you doing?" rasped Tobias.

"I'd rather be here with you," whimpered Kirin.

"Don't be stupid. There's still a chance. Leave me."

"You're in no position to give me an order," she argued as she hugged him and lay by his side.

A minute passed as Kirin accepted her fate. At least she would die with someone she loved. How many people could actually say that? She continued to try to comfort Tobias, who looked like he was about to fade. She felt eyes around her but ignored her feelings, it didn't matter. Regret was about to join her emotions as she wondered why she had waited so long to be truthful. But then she remembered the promise prior to the beginning of the mission. *No regrets.*

"Kirin!"

She ignored her name as the voice continued to repeat it.

"Kirin!!"

She looked up and saw Hunter running toward her.

Kirin shouted, "Get out of here! The place is going to blow!"

Hunter rushed to Kirin at Tobias's side. He stared down and saw what a mess Tobias was, but he did his best not to react. He realized how grave the situation was.

Tobias mustered the effort to open his eyes, but all he could make out was a blurred image. Only the voices in the room helped him recognize Hunter. The smallest of movements produced excruciating pain, but he found the strength to carry out his last plan. He waved for Hunter to draw nearer, and he struggled to hang on as he extended his hand. Hunter reached for it as Tobias gripped his hand firmly, pulling him within earshot.

Tobias whispered into his ear, "Do one last thing for me!"

"Anything."

"Get her out of here!"

Hunter promised, "I will."

As he was about to pull away, Tobias gave one last tug. "Take care of her." Hunter lowered him gently to the floor and released his hand. Tobias looked at Hunter and then slowly closed his eyes.

Kirin bawled hysterically and tried to cling to Tobias. Hunter yanked her from Tobias's side and yelled, "We have to go!" He didn't wait for an answer as he pulled her from the ground and forced her to run with him.

#

Kirin's voice was heard, and her message resonated around the world. Outside on the streets of New York, thousands had gathered, forming a human wall around the UFMF building. Traffic was halted for at least a mile in every direction, making it impossible for anyone to move closer to the UFMF building. Kirin's message had reached everyone, including the police and STDs, but they could not penetrate the spirit of the crowd who wanted to do their part in helping Kirin.

The alarm was ringing on all floors, and now Gwen had broadcasted the news that the building was about to collapse. It was important that everyone disperse as far away as possible. The police and STDs had switched their focus and were helping the crowd get away from the UFMF building.

#

Eight hours after the collapse, crews gathered to determine whether anyone had survived. The first responders had set up, and huge lights were beaming down on top of the rubble of the UFMF building. The dust still hadn't settled as an eerie cloud drifted through the ground. Crowds watched at a distance, drawn by curiosity rather than concern. Reporters were swarming everywhere but had little information as they did their best to keep the public informed.

On top of the rubble, crews were searching for any sign of life. Split into several groups, workers aided by a combination of modern technology and their four-legged friends sifted through specific sections that were marked. One of the first responders signaled to all the men and women who were working there to be silent. He grabbed his dog, which continued to bark as it circled around at a certain spot.

Machines were put on pause as Paul, the supervisor of all the first responders, leaned closer to the ground, listening carefully.

He waved the crew to remain perfectly still, and everyone froze in their place. Paul shouted, "I hear something!"

For the next fifteen minutes, a handful of first responders carefully moved pieces of the building. They were working together to make sure that anyone underneath wouldn't be in harm's way from further collapsing debris. As Paul removed a section, a small hand covered in dust extended forward, trembling in the rubble. He touched it just to assure the survivor that someone was there for them. He began excavating the survivor, who was covered with dirt, blood, and the ash of concrete.

Paul paused, wondering how this individual had survived, but then he took a second look. "Holy shit!" he exclaimed, and everyone stared as the first survivor came into view.

"Jesus … it's Kirin Rise," said someone from afar. Her name quickly spread. Within seconds, the reporters and the crowd caught wind of it.

Several first responders surrounded her as they quickly put a warming blanket over her. They began guiding her from the rubble while she looked around, still somewhat disoriented. Everyone began to clap, and the sound seemed to ring in her ears. She got to the edge of the makeshift rail and looked downward. Before her, she could see hundreds of people who were watching. Kirin glanced to the side and noticed a piece of garment buried slightly just below some concrete. She veered off course and went to grab it.

Her aide was caught off-guard as she tore away from his assistance. She got on one knee, grabbed the soft cloth, and realized it was a flag. It was covered in dirt, but it was still intact as Kirin carefully lifted it from the ground. She gently padded it several times with her hand as the dust flew off it. Somehow this symbol of America had survived through this destruction, just like her. She looked at it and teared, as she thought, *Bruised but not broken*. She took the flag and draped it over her shoulder, the weight of it felt comforting. Her attention once again turned toward the crowd ahead of her, as all eyes continued to watch her every movement. But for Kirin her eyes remained blurred, glazed with tears, as her body began to tremble. By some miracle she had survived, with a sacrifice that only she felt tearing deep into her soul. Her awareness of the moment grew, as thoughts began racing through her head: Gwen, Hunter, the gang, along with everyone involved in the mission. Did they survive? Then she recalled her last vision of Tobias and the realization of her loss drowned her in sorrow. She was overwhelmed. As she stood there, she began to feel dizzy and wobbled, losing grip of the flag as it fell to the ground. Her eyes grew heavy and the crowd faded from her vision.

Several Days Later

Kirin was already ten minutes into the interview, and the entire world was watching. Though she'd always shied away from being the center of attention, she constantly found her way back to what she hated the most. Even those at the studio working were glued to her every word. People had questions about what happened at the UFMF building.

Timothy Buckner was a local favorite amongst news reporters in Chicago. However, upon being selected by Kirin to do an exclusive interview with her, his name immediately catapulted to the top nationwide. He had scored the jackpot and was now seated across from her as they continued their conversation. "I believe for me, just like everyone else watching from the outside in … we can't quite comprehend what has transpired over the last several days," he said. "How would you fill in the blanks … in an abbreviated manner?"

Kirin stared into the camera as she replied, "It's a difficult time because I'm filled with so many mixed emotions. I've buried several of my closest friends." She began listing names from Teams Bokken and Eskrimadors before her voice became more choked as she added, "Kenneth Fischer and …Tobias Jackson." She paused and brushed away tears before continuing, "Along with others who sacrificed their lives to make a better world. My goal was to expose what the UFMF had been doing as well as their overall diabolical plan to control the entire world. In the end, I'm hoping that the people will see the light … the truth."

Timothy added, "Some say what you've done should be considered domestic terrorism."

Kirin replied, "Man defines laws, not for the basis of what's right or wrong, but for what's profitable. The largest corporation in the world decided they could play God and do whatever they want. Why, then, is that not considered global terrorism? Why are my actions labeled by the media in that manner?"

For the next hour, Kirin answered Timothy's questions as well as others that had been sent in by viewers. The ratings were astronomical as people worldwide were glued to their screens. It was Kirin's hope to sift through the disinformation that was floating around and to finally set the record straight.

As they were winding down, Timothy asked, "Any final words, Kirin?"

She nodded, pausing as she searched for the right words for her last statement. "At the end of all this, you now have the opportunity to forge your own destiny. You see the truth for what it is. Don't allow yourselves to be governed by those who have no interest in your own well-being. Take charge now and define who you are."

Three Years Later January 2037

The embattled UFMF corporation struggled for the next several years after the fallout. However, Thorne's maneuvers during Kirin's infamous coup attempt had left him unscathed, as the majority of the blame was brilliantly directed at Watanabe. Thorne continued to play the game, and he played it better than anyone. UFMF stock sank to record lows after the incident, and he bought a boatload of shares at the very bottom. The move allowed him to have majority control of the company at the time when no one wanted to touch it. Many experts felt it was a gutsy move since there was a significant chance the UFMF would become insolvent. But, this was Thorne. For him, it wasn't a gamble on the UFMF; it was merely an investment in himself. That was why he knew he would come out on top.

Thorne sat next to his faithful assistant, Fawn, in the hospital waiting room. They continued to converse as they had done for years, but all thoughts and concerns would be answered shortly.

Fawn snickered as he was always impressed by his boss. "You've been right about everything, boss."

"I try not to dwell on that, Fawn. A big head can lead to one's downfall."

"We're six months away from the brand-new opening of the UFMF fights. Do you think she'll have enough time to recover?" Fawn fidgeted like always as he awaited an answer.

"The doctors assured me that she will, and I believe our patient is more than motivated to make sure it happens. In the end, that's really all that matters."

"Boss, I can't believe you've pulled it off. You do it all the time, but for some odd reason, I'm always surprised."

"This is just the beginning, Fawn. Watanabe's passing left an opening for me to be in the biggest game ever. This is my ticket."

Fawn checked his watch and noted that they were behind schedule.

"Relax, will you, Fawn?"

"Yes, boss. Of course, boss," Fawn said. "I'm still in awe of your congressional hearing. They ate it up like candy."

Thorne nodded, "Motivation for those vultures is always the same. They just needed to be shown how they can make money. Human nature always fears new things, but if we can accept technology and advancement in one area, why not in another? Thus, the new age of the UFMF will embrace not only the new advancements we've made with the SSP761XT but also all those new technological enhancements."

Fawn asked, "And the next stage will be genetic modifications or enhancements?"

Thorne nodded. "In due time, Fawn. In due time."

A nurse came by and interrupted their conversation. "Mr. Thorne? My name is Katheryn. She's ready to see you."

Fawn clapped his hands in excitement, springing off his chair. Thorne got up and remained as cool as ever. He made sure his suit was buttoned and then gestured to the nurse he was ready to go. The nurse tried to make small talk as she guided them to the patient's room.

Nurse Katheryn said, "Here we are, room 204. She's awake and doing well. Actually, she's been awake for the last hour but didn't want any company until she was ready. I've brought her some food, but she's being a bit stubborn and not eating. If you could somehow persuade her, that would help me out greatly."

Thorne walked in and saw his star sitting up in her bed with all smiles.

Fawn leaped toward her and hugged her tightly. "How's our little princess? My, your hair is divine! Even in a hospital, you manage to keep it in perfect condition."

"So, how are you feeling, Ripley?" Thorne asked in a very calm and collected voice.

Ripley replied, "Like a million bucks."

Fawn shook his head as he scoffed at that statement. "A million? That's not going to buy you anything nowadays. That won't even get you business class." He cringed at the thought.

Thorne's gaze went directly to where her arm lay beneath the blanket, "Can I see it?"

Ripley grinned, "Of course, you did pay for it." From underneath the covers, she raised her right arm. Connected at the elbow, her mechanical arm ran all the way to her fingertips and looked like it was straight from *The Terminator*.

Thorne asked, "How does it feel?"

"I honestly can't tell that I don't have my arm anymore. It feels exactly the same. They said I'll have the skin graft put on this week."

Fawn sat next to her on the bed, "And the new SSP761XT? How do you feel?"

"I like the long-lasting effect of it. I can literally run off three hours of sleep and stay as sharp as ever. And, like you promised, I don't feel the need to throw myself off a building just 'cause someone says so."

Thorne smiled, "Beautiful," but he needed more than just words. "How about a demonstration?"

Suddenly a knock interrupted their conversation. All eyes turned toward the door. The door cracked open, and Linda came through, "I hope I'm not interrupting."

Thorne nodded, "Perfect timing … as always."

She closed the door and kept her distance, realizing immediately they were in the middle of something.

Ripley asked Fawn to hand her the tray where her food was lying. He did as requested and removed the food before giving her the metallic tray that lay underneath.

Ripley said, "Everyone, you might want to keep your distance."

Fawn and Thorne took several steps back, Linda inched closer and joined them. With her left hand, she held the tray and suddenly punched it with her right hand. The tray wrapped around her fist, preserving the shape perfectly. For the first time, even Thorne's expression changed to show that he was impressed.

Ripley added, "That's not the cool part. Watch this." She pulled her right arm out of the tray mold and gripped it with the same hand. She began crushing the metal tray until she finally shaped it into a little ball.

Fawn stared, "Oh my … you have a firm grip."

Thorne shared a devilish grin with Ripley. "And so it begins."

Ripley tossed the ball into the air and repeated, "And so it begins."

One Year Later 2038

Kirin was at the school she had opened several months ago. It was still closed, and classes were not for another couple of hours. Like always, she was practicing her Siu Lim Tao form alone. Time, more than anything else, helped ease the pain of the last several years, and it rewarded her with wisdom. She finally understood why Sifu had invested so much into this form. Like him, she did this religiously on a daily basis. She continued to breathe in and out, focusing on her single thought, which quickly disappeared into nothingness. Beads of sweat began to accumulate on her forehead while the emptiness and silence heightened her senses. She felt a presence nearby but continued to practice as her focus was steadfast.

A man with his child stood outside Kirin's school, double checking the address to make sure this was the right place. There was no sign to indicate it was open, so he took the initiative and knocked several times. Hunter peeked through the crack of the door, holding his four-year-old son by the hand as they waited by the entrance. "Knock, knock. Is it okay if we come in?"

Kirin's eyes lit up as she spun around, finally finding reason to break her form. A smile formed quickly, stretching from ear to ear. "Oh my gosh!" She didn't hesitate as she ran to Hunter, who took several steps to greet his longtime friend.

She jumped up and hugged him as he reciprocated the embrace, her feet dangling in the air. They held each other for a pinch as the separation of time had no meaning and the touch felt so familiar.

Hunter squeezed her tightly as memories flashed back from the moment they first met. "It's been so long," they both said.

"Jinx," Kirin giggled. She gazed at Hunter's face; he hadn't aged a bit.

Hunter asked, "How long?" although he already knew the answer to that question.

Too long, she thought before responding with a look of guilt written all over her face. "I know. I know. It's my fault."

Hunter looked at her with the kind eyes he'd always had. The sound of her voice touched his heart. "I know, my friend. Always busy saving the world. You never have to apologize."

Kirin shook her head as the words pained her. The last several years had been tough, and her scars were buried inside. Memories were still fresh as she let out a sigh that carried the weight of failure and frustration. "After all we did, everything we sacrificed, the friends we lost ... in the end, the people did nothing. They didn't care about the truth, in fact it scared them. It didn't seem to matter to them at all. All they cared about was a great story. Watanabe was right...." She hung her head and softly apologized again.

"Hey, he wasn't right. You just have to give people time. The truth is powerful, but the fear of change is even greater. It's all they've ever known." Hunter forced Kirin to look at him. "What you did was above and beyond, something people still don't understand. Kirin, you should never hang your head down ... because you'll always be my hero."

They stared at each other for a brief moment, enjoying each other's company.

The little boy, Aaron, boldly said, "Daddy, that's not Mommy."

At that little comment, Hunter released her from his hug and looked at his son. "I know it's not. This is Auntie Kirin, Aaron. You were just a newborn when she last visited you. Why don't you introduce yourself to her again?"

Aaron took a moment to look at Kirin, but the school had already captured his curiosity. "You told me not to talk to strangers." Something had caught his eye in the corner, and he began walking off to his goal, ignoring both his father and Kirin.

Hunter called, "Aaron...," as he reached out for him, feeling a familiar frustration.

Aaron, stubborn and determined, stormed off to the corner, ignoring his dad.

Kirin looked at Hunter, "Let me guess. He's why you're here."

Hunter scratched his head, embarrassed that she was right. "Well, Annie and I have tried sports and other activities, hoping we can tame the beast within, but he's a little stubborn guy. We were hoping that maybe some kind of martial art could put a little discipline in the boy. So, I thought … who better to seek out than a master of Wing Chun?"

"Well, unfortunately for you, I don't teach kids." She raised her shoulder in jest.

"What? Seriously, kids are big business. Why don't you teach kids?" Hunter sounded almost panicked as that comment threw a wrench into his plans.

Kirin didn't even bother to look as something clattered in the corner. The sound made her reasons obvious. She simply pointed toward the source of the ruckus, which directed Hunter's attention to the corner. He hesitated, not wanting to see what trouble his son had gotten into.

"Oh, right … Aaron, put that down now! Sorry…." Hunter dashed to the corner and picked up his son. This time, he held him as he struggled in his grasp. He talked to him, trying to reason with him and explain what was right and wrong. He looked to Kirin for some help, and she couldn't say no to one of her closest friends.

She thought, *A nice good pat to his butt should straighten him out.*

She quickly released a series of punches that snapped in the air. Hunter almost dropped his son, as the power caught him by surprise. Aaron, on the other hand, was finally captivated by Kirin's actions.

For the next several minutes, Kirin showed Hunter and his son around her studio. She pointed out the equipment and the wooden dummy, explained who was in the pictures hanging on the walls, and talked a bit about the art. Aaron pointed to a pair of swords hanging on the wall.

Hunter stared, "Is that … your swords from the…?"

"Yes, it is."

"Oh my god, I didn't know you were able to recover them."

Kirin didn't respond as the swords carried so much weight with the memory.

Hunter asked, "Did you ever bother naming them?"

Kirin shook her head. "They remain nameless."

Hunter snapped his fingers, "That's it. The swords have no name. Think about it. Things that are undefined usually create mystery and fear. Don't you think?"

Aaron repeated, "No name."

Kirin smiled, "I kinda like it." It appeared the more Kirin spoke the calmer Aaron became.

Hunter noticed Kirin's effect on his son. "He's never done that before," He looked at his son. "It's almost as if he's interested."

Kirin gave him a look, "You're still not selling me."

Hunter looked at Aaron, who was completely focused on Kirin. "So, what do you think of this place, Aaron? Do you think Wing Chun is pretty cool?"

Aaron didn't take his eyes off Kirin but remained silent. He gave his dad a kiss on the cheek, which melted his heart. He looked at Kirin and strangely, but confidently said, "Not bad, not bad."

The words jolted Kirin right away. She looked into the little boy's eyes and shed a tear. She continued to stare at him as the sight and feel of this little boy suddenly felt familiar. She almost lost control of herself but was able to snap back. "What did you say?"

He didn't respond and hugged his daddy tightly, looking away.

Hunter asked, "What's wrong?"

"It's nothing," Kirin said as she turned around and quickly wiped away her tear.

Aaron tugged at Hunter's collar, "Mommy, Daddy. Pick up Mommy ... remember?"

"What?" Hunter snapped from his trance, "Oh my God, you're right. I'm supposed to pick up Anne today from work. I totally forgot." He began heading toward the exit, where he turned around. "Sorry, Kirin. You know me and my timing. It's as bad as ever. I'll be in touch, okay?"

Kirin was hoping to spend more time with Hunter as she waved goodbye. Aaron continued to look at her as his father dashed out the of the school. His words rang in her head, and she fidgeted, walking back and forth in the same place until she was drawn toward the entrance of her school. She flew through the doors and was quickly outside, scanning for Hunter and his son. Finally, she spotted him from a distance, heading toward his car.

Kirin cased her hands together, leaned forward, and bellowed, "Hunter ... Hunter, I'll teach him!"

He spun around with his son still in his arms. "What did you say?"

She took several steps closer and shouted, "I said I'll teach your son."

Hunter smiled, "Really?"

She nodded her head in confirmation.

He shouted, "That's great! I really have to go. I promise I'll call you." He ran away as Aaron continued to look at Kirin. Kirin raised her right hand high and waved at him, and Aaron returned a thumbs up. Soon, his father placed him in the car out of Kirin's view. He spent a moment securing his son's seat and closed the door in haste. Hunter got into the driver's seat and then stepped back out, giving a final wave to Kirin.

From afar, a stranger was watching all of Kirin's interactions. Unnoticed by the parties involved, the stranger remained in the shadows.

Kirin stood outside her school and watched Hunter pull away. She felt a renewed vigor within her, as if her spirit had finally returned. A warm presence surrounded her as she wrapped her arms around herself, smiling.

Not bad, not bad.

The End

"The greatest lie ever told is that people want the truth." — Kirin

www.ingramcontent.com/pod-product-compliance
Lightning Source LLC
Chambersburg PA
CBHW052341020726
47503CB00001B/55